RAINSTORMS

-BOOK 1-
THE ANNA STONE

B. A. MEIER

RAINSTORMS

ISBN: Softcover - 978-1-64318-115-8

Imperium Publishing
1097 N. 400th Rd
Baldwin City, KS, 66006

www.imperiumpublishing.com

RAINSTORMS

-BOOK 1-
THE ANNA STONE

IMPERIUM PUBLISHING
CREATE YOUR STORY

COVER ART BY JUDITH WHITE

B. A. MEIER

DEDICATED TO HEIDI, TRACY, CHRIS,

NIKKI, AUTUMN, AND ADAM

THIS ENTIRE SERIES IS FOR ALL OF YOU IN AN ATTEMPT
TO FIND ENOUGH WORDS TO TELL YOU HOW MUCH I
LOVE YOU.

IN LOVING MEMORY OF ANNA

AND TO FRANK, THANK YOU.

INTRODUCTION

He held his nerves when the alarms sounded through the palace. The bells were ringing from every direction, and he could feel his heartbeat speed up along with his steps. It wouldn't be long before the dead guards to the hidden vault in the treasure room were found. He killed them quickly. They never knew a moment of fear or pain before he stuck the needles in their temples. It was the one mercy he was able to give; they had always been kind to him.

He hid when he heard footsteps and put an ear to the palace walls. It was the king himself.

"What did they take?" The monarch's tone was steady, but he could hear the underlying fear.

The thief smiled.

"My Lord, they took the stone."

There was silence for a split second.

"Stars above."

"Sire, they left this."

He knew that the retainer was handing the king the brooch he was instructed to leave behind. He could almost hear the color drain from the king's face.

"Toler." he breathed, "This isn't good. Have my ten fastest messengers meet me in my study immediately."

The thief held in his laughter and waited for them to walk away before he calmly walked out of the palace and used his two-way mirror to contact his employer.

"Do you have it?"

"I do. I left the brooch, as requested."

"Excellent. Meet me at the Water Caves in the Green Forest. If, for some reason, I'm not there on the date I've given you, continue to Thoron and take it to him. He'll know to expect you, and you'll have safe passage in and out."

The thief could see the amber eyes of his employer blazing with excitement, "Anything else?" The thief asked.

"Did anyone suspect you?"

The thief laughed, "The group that I travel and work with doesn't even suspect me, and they won't. Nobody will."

"Good work. You'll receive your payment when you deliver the goods."

The man nodded and closed the mirror. The thief composed himself and headed back into town, down a street lined with taverns to look for the rest of his group.

"Truman!"

Truman turned, seeing his brother, and rushed in to join him.

"There you are. We were looking for you. Kevin wants us to leave in the morning. We're headed back."

"That's fine."

"Where were you?" His brother walked by his side like he always did.

Truman smiled, though he neglected an answer.

His brother leaned in. "Who was she?"

Truman let out a loud laugh and put his brother in a headlock. "Anna."

CHAPTER 1

The sun had started to set as a young man made his way along the ancient streets. They had been cobblestone, but time, along with footsteps, horses, and carriages, had worn them down to dirt. He kept his horse following the street toward the older section of this city, and he admired the architecture around him. The style was more elegant and refined, like buildings from over two centuries ago. Miork was the second oldest city in the kingdom of Larindana, and the beautiful buildings at the center of it were part of its charm.

The young man looked through his glasses with his piercing blue eyes, taking in his surroundings. He sighed with relief when he saw his destination, even if it wasn't as impressive as the surrounding stone buildings.

The tavern doubled as an inn and was in great condition, even though it didn't look like it from outside. The roof, even with a few rough patches here and there, was solid. While the exterior paint had weathered away, it had withstood the elements and time better than most buildings in the city. The awning slouched something terrible, but it was just as steady as the rest of the building. The whole building was charming, all the regulars knew, and even most traveling through knew that this was one of the best establishments in town. They made fantastic home-brewed beer that had been a family secret for years. The food was second to none with its aroma reaching the streets.

He unloaded his traveling pack and saddlebags, slinging them over his shoulders, before handing the reins of his black mare to the stable hand, giving the young boy a tip. He had also made sure to hide his weapons well, not wanting to frighten anyone. He went inside while putting his cigarette out before he did.

Just as he suspected, the place was not packed, but comfortably crowded. Men were smoking their pipes with their friends, an elderly pair of men played backgammon, and another group of men was throwing darts. At the bar, a man flirted with a pretty lady, and a couple of other women sat with their spouses or boyfriends. Even the bartender, as busy as he was, held a conversation with a couple of patrons while playing a game of chess with another man at the bar. A small stage sat at the rear of the room where a man lazily strummed a guitar while chatting with some of the patrons. And a steady stream of waitresses bustled to and from the kitchen and from behind the bar.

The walls and support beams in the room were all made from finely-polished wood, so the room had a warm, cozy feel emphasized by the large stone fireplace adjacent to the bar. The smell of the cedar was enough to make him want to take in a deep breath, even through the thin haze of pipe smoke. The tables, chairs, bar stools, and the bar itself were made from oak, carved with fine details of trees and animals on them.

"Can I help you find a seat, sir?" a waitress asked. He found her adorable. She was tiny with short curly red hair and had a sunny smile. He looked between her and the bartender and realized she had to be the man's daughter. She looked just like him.

"Actually, I have a letter about a meeting here in one of the rooms upstairs," he told her with a smile as he showed her the letter.

She glanced at it for a moment. "Stairs are right over there. Once up them, you'll want the last one on the very left of the hall, and the washroom is across from your room. There are bunks with fresh blankets and sheets, and if you want a bath, ring the bell in the washroom, and we'll send someone up with hot water." She stopped when she glanced over her shoulder and saw about five different hands go up to signal her over. "If you'll excuse me."

He walked up the stairs and made his way to the last door on the left. He took a deep breath and went in.

He found himself in a large room. It was barely lit from the sun that was still descending. He lit a candle in the simple wall sconce and examined the space.

There were four sets of bunk beds in the room with a large table and several chairs in the middle. Next to the fireplace sat a couple of comfortable-looking easy chairs. They looked very inviting after his long ride from the capital. A changing screen stood at the farthest corner of the room, along with a couple of vanity tables with mirrors. Next to the open window sat a table with a chess set and two chairs.

He appeared to be alone as he walked to light the candle on the end table and then lit the fireplace. Maybe it was the uncertainty of why he was there, but he felt as if he was being watched. He glanced over his shoulder. There was nobody in the room. As he worked on the fire, he smelled pipe smoke. He turned again. Nobody. Since the window was open, he figured that it must have been from someone outside.

He sat his bags down and then took off his black traveling cloak with the dark green lining and hung it on one of the pegs along the wall. He then looked into one of the mirrors and checked himself over. His black hair was a bit of a mess, and he tried to fix it, annoyed that he already had a few silver hairs starting to show. He smoothed out his beard that was black with hints of red. The two loops pierced in either ear made him unique among his colleagues, but he liked them. His black shirt and pants were clean, even after the ride in. He was tall, and he knew his weapons could easily intimidate others, but when he *did* travel, he knew the roads could be dangerous. The large double-bladed axe and his sword were two things he wouldn't travel without. He knew how to fight and fight well, but he was also a man of knowledge and a pacifist by nature with a calm temperament. He unhooked the weapons, laid them beside him, and sat down with an audible sigh of relief in one of the easy chairs by the fire.

He hadn't been sitting for more than a minute before he heard footsteps. He looked over when the door opened, and another man with a letter in his hand walked into the room.

The man was short with a tuft of hair on his chin. He had dark, shaggy, brown hair and brown eyes to match, and looked to be the same age as the other. The man of knowledge could tell just by the way the newcomer carried himself that he was extremely powerful despite not looking like much. He carried an intricate staff in his hands and was, in fact, a wizard.

"Hey."

"You get a letter too?" asked the wizard, peering through his glasses. He took a moment to clean them on his black robes, though they still seemed dirty. "Did it say the same thing as mine? By request of the crown, your assistance is needed at T.J.'s Tavern in Miork. Go to the Elk Room. Be there by six?"

"Yeah, it's almost six, so hopefully whoever they are, they'll show up here soon. Would've been nice if there had been a little more reason behind it, but what do you do?"

"No explanation, no signature. Just the royal seal." The wizard checked his pocket watch. "It's about a quarter 'til, so we're early. Mind if I have a seat?"

"Go ahead," the man told the wizard, standing up for a moment to shake hands before sitting back down.

"I'm Onyx, and you?"

"Twarence Herion of Fern. I'm guessing you're a wizard?" Twarence motioned to another chair by the fire.

"Was it my commanding presence that gave me away, or the staff?" Onyx joked when he sat down. "I'm from the Hitum Mountain Order. You're armed, but I don't take you for a fighter."

Twarence laughed. "Eh, these are only for self-defense. I'm a professor at the University of Fern. Do you know if anyone else is going to show, or are we it?"

Onyx shrugged.

In the next moment, both turned their heads when they heard the door open.

This time, a beautiful young woman stood in front of them. She looked charming in her dark green dress with an intricate pattern embroidered in lighter green along both the hem and the collar. Her mahogany hair fell against her fair-skinned face and to her shoulders. She sat her bow and quiver down by the door and hung up her brown cloak. When she turned to them, her brown eyes looked with curiosity while her small nose ring glistened from the light of the fire.

"Hello," she said, surprised. She walk over while glancing at her letter. Uncomfortable in a new place with people she had never met before—especially when she didn't know why she was there—she still gave them a polite smile.

"Here for the meeting in the Elk Room?" Twarence asked her kindly, feeling her unease.

"Did you send this letter to me?" she inquired, keeping her voice even.

"No, we both got letters too," Onyx said, "and whoever sent them is taking their sweet time." He stood up along with Twarence. "I'm Onyx, and this is Twarence."

Twarence brought over another chair from the table for her to use.

"Thanks," she said, appreciating the gesture. "I'm Aria Morena of Cirus."

"Cirus?" Twarence eyed her green dress again. "Are you a healer?"

She nodded. "Sure am."

The men were impressed. A healer could heal a person with only the touch of their hands. The strength of their talent was dictated by a mixture of natural ability and how hard they studied. Some could heal only minor injuries, some serious. Some could save a person even as they took their last breath.

Cirus was a town famous as a home to powerful healers—a training ground for many of them. They wondered how good she was. They also realized something big was going on if they had a healer.

"What do you two do?" she asked.

"I'm a scholar and professor over in Fern at the University, and he's a wizard." Twarence found himself already drawn toward Onyx, as if he were a friend.

Aria nervously smoothed her hands over her dress and then turned her attention to the elf just walking through the door.

He looked young, like them, but he was well over one hundred years old. His light, nearly-white hair fell along his ears and in front of his pale blue eyes before cascading to his shoulders. He was dressed semi-elegantly in a white silk shirt with gold-trimmed hem, black leather pants, and a leaf green traveling cloak. He left his sword and cloak at the door and, before he said a word, pulled up a chair next to them. He seemed apparently indifferent until he broke a big smile when he sat down.

"Hi, I'm Arkon of the Spirit Elves. A pleasure to meet you," he said. Even while he smiled, there was a formality to his greeting that was customary with all elves. One arm stayed at his side while he placed his other hand over his heart with a small bow of his head. It was the custom required when not knowing the company.

"This is Aria, Onyx, and I'm Twarence. Did you get a letter, or did you send it?"

"Nah, I got a letter too, and whoever sent it is going to be running late at this point." Arkon smirked. "I could've run a couple more errands before I showed up." He was trying to keep the situation light.

At that moment, another man walked through the opened door and closed it behind him. He looked the same age as Twarence, but a little taller and with a slender build. This man appeared simple and calm. Even his clean-cut beard gave him a look of serenity. Trying to smooth over his brown hair—which didn't do much good—he adjusted his glasses and looked through them with his brown eyes. On his left hand, he wore a curious bracelet with a chain that connected to a ring worn on his middle finger.

He dressed simply, but his eyes were alert, even while taking a casual moment to brush some of the dirt from his brown pants and dark orange shirt. He was smoking a cigarette, and though he didn't remove his sword from his side, he didn't appear strong or threatening. But so far, everyone in this group was more than they appeared. The man's eyes were kind and gentle, yet, they searched for any movement that would cause him to grab hold of his weapon.

"Hello," he said cheerfully like he was greeting an old friend. He walked up to them with a smile and offered a handshake. "And I'm guessing you are not the ones who sent for me, based on the looks I'm getting right now."

"So you didn't send for *us*?" Arkon asked.

"Nope, I didn't even know more people would be here. Anyway, I'm Jaras Luca of Tremlar. It's nice to meet you." He flicked the ash from his cigarette into the ashtray.

Making their introductions, they told Jaras their names and professions. When it was his turn to tell his occupation, they noticed that, although he heard them, his attention was elsewhere. He stood in silence, focused.

Jaras looked out the window, curious about a puff of smoke that drifted toward the window from inside. He followed the smoke back to its source on top of the bunk beds next to the dark window. The only light came from the fireplace and the single candle that Twarence had lit earlier. There, Jaras saw the dwindling sunlight illuminate a stray lock of blonde hair that had been caught in the wind. Someone was back there. He raised an eyebrow.

"What is it that you do?" Arkon asked.

Jaras didn't respond.

"Jaras?" Aria chimed in, turning her head to see what he was looking at. She saw nothing.

He smiled a little, only because he could feel the person in hiding also had a smile on their face. Whoever it was looked right at them. He could feel it.

"Hey." Arkon walked over and waved a hand in front of him.

"Sorry, I was waiting for them to say something. I didn't want to be rude." He motioned to the top bunk bed on the side of the room not caught by any light. Jaras winked at whoever was back there.

They all turned their heads and looked. They saw nobody.

"What?" Onyx looked suspicious. "I cast a charm when I got here to see if anyone else was in the room."

"I did the same," Arkon told him, looking at the wizard. "There wasn't anyone here."

"You're good," said a cheery female voice.

The travelers were stunned.

In the next moment, a young woman hopped off the top bunk and walk into the light, adjusting her gray cloak. "You found me, so that makes you a warrior," she said, grinning. The tone of her voice was kind and playful, and she seemed impressed that he was able to spot her. "To be fair, though, I wasn't trying that hard to hide." She gave him a friendly punch on the shoulder and winked.

None of the others had any idea what she could have been called there for. No one except for Jaras. Her appearance gave them hardly any clues. Shorter than all of them—standing at five feet four inches—she was unassuming. She seemed around the same age as them, carrying herself with casual confidence. She wore a sleeveless dark blue blouse that rested right above her brown pants, unusual for a woman. They fit well enough around the waist but were almost too long for her, as they fell just above the soles of her brown boots.

From the upper cartilage of her left ear dangled a large earring. Her light blonde hair stopped a couple of inches short of her elbows while her blue eyes with just a touch of gray smiled happily at them.

They noticed, as well, that she carried a dagger—a beautiful one tied to her belt, made to stay in place at her leg with a black sash. On her other side was a small pouch attached to her belt. A fighter, maybe, but a female fighter?

Her eyes were playful as she extended a handshake to Jaras. "Barina Raine of Miork. I'm right, aren't I?"

Jaras scoffed and nodded while the two of them sat down at the table, conversing as if they were old friends. The others could only watch, still shocked that this woman had been in the room the entire time. Barina herself, while she seemed friendly, was a person they were unsure about. Her appearance as a fighter and the fact that she had kept herself hidden from them threw them off.

"Nice to meet you, girlie," Jaras said with a smug smile, showing how proud of himself he was for winning her little game.

"What gave me away? How did you spot me?" Her eyes were curious, and she swung her feet playfully.

"I smelled the pipe smoke, then I saw the smoke was going out the window instead of coming in. And the wind blew your hair into the light."

"I knew I should've tied my hair back." She tilted her head just a bit as she eyed his chest and then poked at him as if noticing something. She pulled the collar of his shirt aside just a bit to reveal chainmail over his undershirt. "Sinclair's work, I take it?"

"He's the best. Do you use any armor?" Jaras asked her, impressed she recognized the maker of his chainmail.

"Nah, it's uncomfortable, and it slows me down."

"But it can save your life."

Barina shrugged. "Still kickin'."

Twarence threw his hands overhead in exasperation. "How long were you back there?" he asked, amazed he hadn't noticed her.

Jaras and Barina looked over, snickering. She thought about it for a second. "About ten minutes before you got here," she replied, putting her pipe away.

"Why didn't you say anything?" Twarence's eyes began to soften, amused at this woman.

"I wanted to see who I'd be meeting to decide if I wanted to stick around or not. Just can't be too careful these days." She then bumped fists with Jaras. "But then this guy spotted me as I figured he might. No point in staying hidden."

"How did you get past both of our detection spells?" Arkon asked. He was studying her, still not sure about her.

She put a finger to her lips. "Trade secret."

"Speaking of trades, what do you do, Barina?" Aria asked.

"I, uh, I obtain objects of a rare and sensitive nature." It was obvious that Barina was trying to figure out the best way to word her job description.

"What does that mean?" Arkon was oblivious.

"So, you're a thief then," Twarence guessed, patting Barina's back.

"Well, it's not like I go out of my way to take things. No wait, I do for work. But everything I own I've paid for. It's just my trade for this gig."

Aria's face paled. "Thief?"

Barina tried to put on her most innocent face. "When called, I am. It's not a hobby or anything, and it's literally just me recovering things that have already been taken, for the most part."

"A thief." Aria said again.

Barina nodded. Her smile, for the first time, vanished when she saw the panic on both Aria and Arkon's faces. "Don't worry. I only take what I've been asked to take, I give you my word. I know that doesn't seem like much. You know nothing of me, but if I don't think it's necessary for an object to be obtained or recovered, I won't do it."

Choosing not to worry about Barina for the time being, Arkon brought his attention back to the situation at hand. "So still, this doesn't clear up why we were all asked here, and on royal business." He shot another glance at Barina.

Arkon watched everyone carefully. He could tell that Aria felt the same about the thief. He didn't understand how the others could remain so calm knowing about Barina and her trade. It was as if they actually took her at her word.

Barina's face darkened ever so slightly. "We're here for something very big and something very dangerous."

"How can you say for sure?" Arkon asked.

Barina saw him averting her eyes. "Only a handful of people know that I'm a thief or even how to get ahold of me. Like I said, I only steal if I think the reason is valid, important, and for the better cause. The only time I'm ever called in for a job is when something of great value has been taken and they need me to get it back. Nobody else has the experience that I do. Jobs that I take are difficult, and the places that I break into are heavily guarded. We're going to have to get something back, and it's going to be dangerous. That's why I know I'm here."

They stared at her in silence. No one had any idea what they would be doing for this job, but it sounded as if they were going to have their work cut out for them.

"She's right, you know," Onyx added. "Think about it. Why else would they need a wizard, and why else would they need a healer? I was trained by one of the highest orders in the world of wizards. If it wasn't something big, they would've called someone from one of the other orders."

Without warning, the hearth exploded into red and purple fire. Everyone jumped back—Jaras and Twarence standing at the front, their weapons at the ready. Onyx had a sphere of pure red energy in his hands, ready to fire. Arkon's whole body was crackling as lightning surrounded him. Aria stayed back, her bow drawn. Barina stood by calmly, not moving but watching what would happen, her fingers close to her dagger if she should need it.

When the fire faded, a man stood in front of them. He was middle-aged with dark gray hair, light blue eyes, and a petite frame. He was dressed in a simple white silk shirt and a gray pants. He brushed some of the ashes off of himself and then looked at all of them.

"You can put those weapons away. I hired you, and I'm here on behalf of the court."

Everyone lowered their weapons and breathed a collective sigh of relief. Jaras glanced over at Barina. He had seen, just out of the corner of his eye, that she hadn't drawn her weapon like the rest of them? He wondered why and would have to ask her about that later.

The group sat down quietly at the table while the man took the chair at the head.

"Thank you all for being here on such short notice, but this couldn't wait. And what I ask of you isn't easy. I gathered you here because I need a group of people who have been the most renowned in their trades while staying discreet over the years." He took a moment to light his pipe. "Let's cut to the chase."

"I will assume that all of you have heard of the Sacred Anna Stone. It's an important relic of our kingdom. If its powers are discovered and placed in the wrong hands, that person could be more dangerous than any of our worst nightmares." He took a deep breath and continued. "One of our own men went behind our backs and stole it, taking it to King Toler in the kingdom Thoron. If he can use the stone, then not a soul alive will be able to stop him and the hell he will unleash. His army isn't alone either. He has the loyalty of the dragon Uraki."

Jaras glanced over when he heard Barina hiss under her breath.

"Been around him before?" he asked her quietly.

She nodded.

"What's he like?" Jaras asked, amazed that someone had come face to face with this beast and lived to tell the tale. "Pretty terrifying, I would imagine."

"That's putting it mildly," she told him. They turned their attention back to the conversation.

"So, what does…what does this have to do with us?" Arkon asked the question that he already knew the answer to.

"Think about it," Onyx said. His eyes had gone dark at the mention of Toler. "He wants us to bring it back."

The man nodded. "Exactly. You've been chosen from the best for your skills, trades, and secrets to bring it back. You are essential to recovering the stone, all of you are. And you'll have to work together. Toler doesn't have the stone yet. It'll be a while before it gets to him, since it was only taken two days ago. If you leave in the morning, by the time you get to Thoron, he'll maybe only have had it for a day or two. Hopefully by then, he won't be able to do much damage even if he is able to use it."

"Explain some more," Arkon demanded, "everyone's skills and how they apply." He was giving Barina a cold stare. He knew they would need a thief to ultimately get the stone back, but it didn't mean he had to like her being there.

"We have the scholar, Twarence, of course. One of the most prominent professors at the university in Fern, he has knowledge of the places you'll be traveling. Most importantly," he said, turning to the professor, "you are the only one who knows the true powers behind the Anna Stone—powers that must only be revealed when the time is right. You will know when to tell and who to tell. You are also a pretty decent fighter when need be and can hold your own."

"Aria, with your healing powers, that should go without saying. With all the dangers you will be facing, having someone of your talents is essential. The rest of you must protect her so she can save you if needed."

He then turned his attention to Onyx.

"Our wizard is, hands-down, one of the most powerful in the world. You are strong enough that even Toler, who is a pretty impressive man of magic himself, would be hard pressed to duel you. Few people are stronger in magic. You can use that magic when human strength alone won't work.

"Arkon, your elfin family is trusted above all others in your kingdom. You have powers that Onyx doesn't, and you're so in tune with nature that you will be a vital asset. There are some things on this journey only an elf can do—an elf of the Spirit Clan. I'm hoping you'll be strong enough to help tame Uraki if you have to." He set his pipe down before he continued.

"Jaras, you are the guardian of this party. You are one of the most highly-trained fighters in the area. Everyone here can fight and defend themselves, but you are the sole protector of the group.

"Then, there's Barina. You are the one who will retrieve the stone. You can hide in the shadows, only revealing yourself if you choose to be seen. You are also an amazing fighter, probably one of the best. Barina can face danger head on or as a last line of defense."

Barina's eyes blinked, not expecting him to know about her fighting skills. She tilted her head a bit. Jaras caught the look on her face.

"Despite your appearances," the man continued, "there are few who can match your abilities. You are knowledgeable about the creatures ahead since you've traveled these roads. Twarence, while you know the map and some of what lies ahead, you don't know all of it. There are some beings that hardly anyone has lived to tell about, and Barina is someone who has lived. If something happens to her, Twarence, you need to guide the rest and figure out how to get the stone back without her."

"How long of a trip is it to Thoron?" Aria asked, becoming nervous.

"I've never traveled there by foot, but I know it's a long and very dangerous journey," he replied with honesty.

"About three months or so," Barina said, her eyes still locked on the man speaking to them. "And it's very dangerous, even if you do know what you're doing. It'll kill you if you don't."

"Such a long time. I don't know," Arkon groaned, rubbing the back of his head.

Onyx glanced at Barina, Twarence, and Jaras. He was on high alert, and he could see that the other three were as well.

"If you wish, you may decline. If not, you start tomorrow morning. I know it's a lot to ask without time to think about it, but it must be decided now. Time is of utmost importance." The man looked at them. "So what will it be?"

"Well, I don't know," Aria said out loud. "I've never traveled this far from home, but…"

"I've got my family and friends, my clan to consider." Arkon was trying to buy himself time to think. "I know I need to, but is this a mission I want to take?" he mumbled to himself.

"There's also Uraki," Aria mentioned. "Just thinking of him scares me." She knew perfectly well about that dragon and his temper.

"I'm in." Barina said as she relit her pipe. From the tone of her voice, it sounded like she had made up her mind before the man had even finished asking.

"How can you decide so soon?" Arkon was shocked by her quick answer.

Barina flicked the fire of the match out and puffed the smoke in her pipe, shrugging her shoulders. "I just can."

"This is so dangerous, though." Arkon had an air of warning in his tone. "Shouldn't you think it through a little more?"

"This is kinda what I do for a living. Besides, I have plenty of friends to help along the way. I even have contacts in Thoron." She yawned. "He's right, you know. There are creatures that nobody has ever seen, and there are some that you can't see. I know them."

"Won't your friends and family worry?" Aria asked her kindly.

"Nope. I also know of Toler. I rarely fight when requested, only when the need is great, and this need is great. Part of my reason is to destroy the wicked. They don't get worse than this guy." Barina's voice was firm and stubborn. "I'm going."

The man looked over at the rest of them. "Well, anyone else?"

"I'll go," Onyx said, seeming eager. "I have personal reasons for confronting Toler. It'll give me a chance to use my powers to do some real good in the world."

Jaras and Twarence nodded together. They didn't even explain.

Aria took a deep breath, then nodded as well. She knew it was going to be dangerous, but this is what she had trained for her entire life. It's why she learned to develop her powers to the level they were—to save lives. She had to go.

After much deliberation, Arkon agreed as well.

The man pointed. "There are supplies in the bags by the window and money for your traveling expenses. Are there any questions?"

"Who are you?" Aria asked, as it was the one thing about this guy she really wanted to know.

The man gave them a little smile but kept quiet.

"You're not going to tell us?" Aria asked, her face falling.

"But you have to tell us," Twarence pleaded.

"It's not important right now, just worry about the stone," he told them. "Anything else?"

Barina spoke up. "How did you find out about me?"

"That's for me to know and you to find out later. But you're like everyone else here—good at what you do while keeping a low profile. The reward for this journey, if you succeed, will be great."

"No, seriously." Barina didn't stop pressing. "How did you learn about my fighting ability? How did you find me?"

"I learned all I needed to know when I found out who trained you," the man said with a grin. "I spoke with him not long ago."

Barina pouted before her mouth twisted into a smirk. "Making a mental note to stop by my place in case he's there so I can kick his butt."

"He's at your place?" the man asked, surprised.

"Was this morning. When he's in town, he crashes with me. I never really know when he's coming or going, so maybe."

She looked at the others and then back at the man. "So Vic, you're really not gonna tell them *who you are*?" She had a smug smile on her face.

The man's jaw dropped a bit. "How do you know?"

She crossed her arms. "I'll tell you if you tell me."

The man laughed. "You're good. He warned me of that." He bowed to the others and said, "Good luck everyone." With the clap of his hands, he was gone in a cloud of smoke.

"You figured out who he was?" Twarence asked, looking over at Barina.

She stood up and nodded. "Little bit."

Twarence sighed, then looked at the others for a minute. "This is going to be a lot more interesting than sitting around the university all day, not that I mind the classes. But still. I finally get to see some of the world. I'm going to grab something to eat from downstairs. Does anyone else want anything?" he asked, opening the door.

Jaras sat at the chess board with Onyx. "We'll be down later, thanks."

"Barina, did you…" Twarence then saw that she had slipped past him and was half-way down the hallway. "Wait up."

"That girl is kind of odd, isn't she?" Arkon asked quietly after the door closed.

Onyx peered up from his glasses. "I wouldn't be too quick to judge."

"I'm with Onyx," Jaras agreed, moving a pawn.

"But she's a thief," Arkon argued. "How much can we set in store with what she says?"

"Until we see otherwise, we have to believe what she says," Jaras said. "I think she's a thief when she really needs to be, like now. She was probably a fighter first." He yawned and scratched his chin while Onyx made his move.

"I wasn't trying to be an ass, but honestly, a person who makes a living by doing something dishonest…"

"She said she only takes things that were already taken." Onyx interrupted.

"Aria, come on," Arkon grumbled. "You're nervous about this too."

Aria blinked and thought about it. "I am, but I need to give her a chance. It's hard to trust, yes, but we need to be fair to her."

"You guys just don't care about this, do you. A thief. There is nothing to trust in a thief." Arkon couldn't believe everyone was so easygoing about it.

"Just 'cause I'm a wizard doesn't mean I'm going to incinerate everyone either. Give her a chance, she might surprise you."

Arkon stormed over to the fireplace and buried his nose in a book from his traveling bag.

Onyx looked up at Jaras and quietly asked, "Have you met anyone here before today?"

"Not that I know of, you?" Jaras studied the chess board before moving a piece.

"No." Onyx did not hesitate to move his next piece.

Jaras moved a rook. "Why do you ask?"

Onyx moved another piece. "Just, you seemed very chummy with Barina."

"Maybe, but you and Twarence were the same with each other."

"True, but I think, well…we just have a meeting of the minds. Whereas you and Barina seemed like old friends."

"Oh, that." Jaras waved it off. "Warriors and fighters. How do I put this?" He scratched his beard. "Most of us who have been in the game for a long time have an unspoken kinship. We understand that someday it might come to blows, but till then, we might as well make friends and help each other out when needed."

"When did you figure she was a fighter?" Onyx watched Jaras move another piece before he moved another without a second thought to it.

"She picked up on my trade right away. That was a clue. But the big kicker was she identified my armor under my shirt and who made it. Not many can do that unless they're in this trade," Jaras told him, lighting up a cigarette.

Onyx smiled. "Wonder how long she's been in the business, you know, both fighting and her side career."

"Not sure, but I'm guessing for a long time." Jaras put his hands between his legs, still studying the board.

"How's your guess on that?"

"She doesn't seem to want to talk about it. And from what this Vic guy was saying, she was also formally trained. By who, I don't know, but I'm going to have to do some digging."

"Good luck with that," Onyx offered.

"Thanks. Oh, and checkmate," Jaras said with a big smile.

"Son of a bitch!" Onyx couldn't believe he'd lost. "Want a rematch?"

Aria had been reading but, after about twenty minutes, she tired of the silence and left the room.

CHAPTER 2

Twarence and Barina were finishing up a chicken pot pie they had split as they sat at a table going over a map. Barina had been to Thoron, but Twarence was to be the guide, so they wanted to make sure they had this planned out.

"I don't like the path Vic circled for us," Barina was saying. "Once we get past this first valley in the Black Mountains, it's not safe." She stuck a fork into the pie, then decided to let him have the last couple bits.

"It's the most direct path though," he said. "Where else would we go? We can't go lower, and going through the summit would take extra time."

"Not too much time to go through the summit. Just a couple days. I would rather take a bit longer to be a little safer. I mean, we sure as hell can't go around the mountains. That would take another two weeks."

Twarence looked up over a forkful of veggies. "A *little safer?*"

"Well, the summit is always cold—blizzards and such—but there aren't as many things that could kick our asses. I can pass through the lower areas without much trouble anymore, but not everything there is okay for newcomers," she said, meeting his eyes.

"What are we talking about if we take this path? I read there are trolls, goblins, and bears. What else?"

"The Throwers. That's what they call themselves. They're dangerous, so very dangerous. They're a colony of creatures that look like they were carved out of the sides of the mountains. They lay on the ground, blending right in with it. You may not notice till you're literally on top of them, and if they're hungry, they just say *aahh* and you're lunch. If you're not lunch, you'll find yourself flung into the mountainsides, so very dead. They're huge, about the size of this building we're in. There are about twenty or so in a colony. Oh, and they breathe fire too. The only way to kill them is by getting to their heart through their throats. It's not easy, and they don't like strangers," she told him quietly. "If we take the summit, all we have are maybe trolls, and that's only the really stupid ones, and the snow cats."

Twarence was writing all of this down in a journal he took out of his pocket. "I've never heard of either the Throwers or the snow cats."

Barina's eyes looked up from the map. There was a hint of regret in her piercing gaze. "There's a reason for that. I lived, others haven't."

"Could you get us past the Throwers?" he asked. "I mean, since you know them?"

"They let me by, but there's a reason for that too." She was debating if she wanted to tell him. Finally, she gave in with a huff. "I avoided them as much as I could, but once, I didn't have a choice. I had to fight one and damn near killed him. I spared his life, and with that, I showed that I could overpower them. That's literally the only thing that keeps me alive when around them. That proved me to them. As long as I'm just passing through, I'm okay. I can't do more than that. I'm hardly allowed to even say more than my name to tell them I'm there. I could get us through but, Twarence, I don't like to have to fight if I don't have to. These guys just want to live in peace, they know that I mean no harm, but they aren't so quick to let others by."

She scratched the top of her head. "There are a lot of other creatures there, but these are the most dangerous."

Twarence studied her for a moment. "Okay, we can go through the summit, but you and I have to sit down, and you have to tell me about all of these creatures."

Barina lightly punched his arm. "It's a deal, I'll sit down with you every night on these. Aside from that, the route he drew for us is okay. It's the same one I would take if I were going the long way."

"Long way, so you have a shortcut? Where, how?"

Barina twitched an eyebrow. "I'll explain another time, but I can only go that way if I travel solo. I'll get some extra furs and such for you guys in the morning, so you don't freeze at the summits."

Aria came walking down the stairs with a very frustrated face.

"Be right back," Twarence told her, lighting up a cigarette while standing up.

Barina nodded and turned to watch the people in the room. She leaned back so the waitress could take their empty dishes, but kept her short glass and sipped on her drink while she glanced over the map some more.

Twarence met Aria at the bottom of the stairs. "How's everything going up there?"

"Arkon isn't too willing to give Barina a chance due to her trade." She sighed a bit. "I get a little nervous about it too, but I need to give her a chance. She deserves that much. She knows just as little about me as I do her."

"Don't worry about it, kiddo. Arkon will get over it. And if not, I don't think she cares. Have a drink with us. She's good for conversation."

Aria smiled and joined them at the table.

Barina ducked just in time as the waitress brought Aria a glass of wine. "You okay?" she asked their new companion. "You seem a little upset."

"I'm fine, thanks." Aria gave her a thin smile before glancing at Barina's empty glass. "Drinking a little fast there?" she said, lightening the mood.

Barina yawned a little. "Nah, that glass was already empty. I've just been sipping on my whiskey. Probably my only drink tonight."

"Really?" Aria had always pictured thieves as party animals.

"Yeah, it dulls the senses too much. Plus, hell, too much more, and I'll be up all night. I don't sleep much when I'm working anyway."

"Seriously, keeps you awake?" Twarence looked at her from over the top of his glass while taking a pull of the hard cider in it.

"And coffee calms me down more often than not."

"You're weird, B," Twarence teased. "But you're not the only one I've ever heard of that happening to."

Barina leaned in. "The biggest reason that I really only drink a couple here and there is that I will almost always get one hell of a hangover. The ride up is great, but the ride down…no, thank you. I drink, just normally not enough to get drunk."

Aria and Twarence laughed together.

"Lightweight," Aria commented, taking a sip of her wine.

"Don't I know it?" Barina agreed. "How did you get into healing?"

"Well…" Aria had to think about it. "I was about ten years old. A friend of mine had died, and that trauma was what triggered my abilities. Later that week, my older brother had broken his leg. He was in so much pain, but when I touched his leg, it started glowing. By the time I let go, his leg was healed.

"We told my parents, and they had me study with my aunt back home in Cirus. She showed me how to develop and control my healing, and I'm really kind of excited. I'm glad I'll be able to if needed. I've never done any serious traveling for my trade, so this will be good for me."

Barina lit her pipe, her smile still thoughtful. "Wish I could do stuff like that."

"Don't you like what you do?" Twarence had completely forgotten about his drink, becoming more involved with the conversation.

"I'd think you'd have a lot of fun, at least with traveling," Aria added.

"It has its ups and downs," Barina admitted. "Just like anything. I travel a lot, and I've met some very interesting people and creatures. I've made a lot of good friends over the years. I've also made some enemies, which is unfortunate. I like to help people, but in this line of work, enemies will be made.

"But this isn't easy, you know. It's a lot of hard work with my training, which I don't mind. I do stay busy, it's just very, well, you've gotta commit. I can only hope to help as much as I can." She held her pipe in her mouth, thinking on her last words some more.

"How did you get into your line of work, Twarence?" Aria then asked. She could tell that Barina really didn't feel like talking about her line of work too much.

The professor took up the conversation. "I started talking when I was really young, in complete sentences, and was reading by the time I was two. My parents sent me to school when I was four, but I was so bored with the teachers and finished all the lessons by the time I was nine. A man from the university was notified and took me to the university in Fern. My parents we're from Fern anyway. Hell, we can see the palace from our house. I've spent a lot of time studying, and I give lectures too, when needed."

"Fern? Who was your primary teacher?" Barina asked curiously. "I know some people at the university."

"Julius."

Barina looked surprised hearing that name. The fact that Twarence and Julius should be associated with each other sparked something very familiar about Twarence in her head. "Julius, he's brilliant," she blurted that out before she could stop herself.

"Know him?" Twarence wasn't sure about that look.

"Yes." She went quiet again, the wheels in her mind turning.

Twarence couldn't help but feel that she knew something he didn't, knew about him.

She was piecing things together, not just about him, but with everyone there. Something was important about this group of people that was going on this errand, something more than Vic was letting in on.

"What I'm curious to know is when you learned to swing those bad boys around?" Barina nodded at his weapons. "Hell, they're almost as big as me. Those are two-handed weapons, and you only need one hand for each? That's impressive."

Twarence smiled. "Why do you ask?"

"I'm a warrior first. I learned to fight before I ever thought about my other work. Stealing was just another way for me to learn the shadows and study their game, and I've gotta pay the bills somehow. I'm curious." She leaned further onto the table, taking another sip of her drink.

"Picked them up when I was fifteen. Just liked the way they handled. The guys at school laughed, saying that a scholar should keep to the books. Too much brawn is bad for the brain, and I shouldn't sacrifice my intelligence for it. I didn't see why I couldn't do both. Julius agreed with me. I'm nothing like Jaras, but I know how to take care of myself if I need to." Twarence shrugged his shoulders while taking another drink, as if he was justifying to himself why he did what he did.

"Smart man," Aria agreed, nodding her head a little. "Everyone should know at least how to defend themselves."

"By the same token," Barina said, "I do agree that there are too many fighters who don't use their brains, at least not the right one. But you should always know how to fight to defend yourself or your loved ones."

"Is that why you learned to fight, to protect people?" Twarence asked.

She nodded while sipping her drink. "Let's talk about something else please. I don't like discussing my fighting."

Twarence and Aria's eyes met for a moment, both intrigued by what she said. Both had crossed their fair share of fighters. Plenty had no problem talking about their abilities and how good they were, but they also were the ones who had something to prove. The seasoned warriors, the ones who really knew what they were about and were the real threat, they didn't talk much. Twarence and Aria would have to do some digging because keeping her silence said something about Barina.

"May I ask why you don't like to talk about it?" Twarence leaned in. It was his nature, he had to know.

"Being a fighter of my size, silence is my best weapon." She then turned red and grinned. "Funny that silence would be a weapon since I talk a lot… too much sometimes. I'll just ramble on and on if I don't watch myself. But I will never ramble about my fighting." She took a sip of her drink. "I'm sure Jaras doesn't like to talk much about what he's able to do either. It's smart."

"Why not for someone your size though? I would think it would give you an advantage." Aria took another long drink from her glass.

Barina's face was blank. "If you don't hype yourself up and you have to run to save your skin, then your opponent will see you as wise for knowing when you can't win. If a person was to brag about such a deadly trade, and someone does challenge, then that person better be able to live up to what they say they can do. If they can't and they have to run, then they will be seen as a coward and probably struck down. By not talking about it, I have only myself to challenge and only have to fight as hard as I must for who I'm dealing with." She was feeling very uncomfortable with their questions.

Aria knew she shouldn't pry, but she couldn't help it. "Have you ever had to run from a fight?"

Barina took a deep breath. She didn't answer.

"May I ask how good you are?" Aria finished off her wine in one large swig.

"Nope." Barina stretched, standing up for a second.

"Why?"

Barina turned her chair around so she hung her arms freely and rested her chin on the back rest. "This is really good whiskey." She wasn't saying anything else on the matter of fighting.

Her eyes traveled to another side of the room, and her two traveling companions followed her gaze. They could hear a man at the bar talking louder and louder in hopes of trying to impress a young lady. He used big words and mocked almost everyone else around him, blowing them off as pointless and unintelligent. The man ogled the girl with his dark eyes that were glazed over from one glass too many.

Twarence's eyes narrowed. "Back to our previous conversation, there are also too many people who think that they have a lot of knowledge. They might in an academic sense, but not common sense. It doesn't do a damn bit of good if all a person does is know how to use large words but not actions."

Barina scoffed a little laugh. "Yeah, that guy is an ass. I can't believe he manages to attract as many girls as he does." She wasn't moving her head from its comfortable position. "Nels is one of the few people out there who can really piss me off."

"How do you know him?" Aria asked. She looked a little sad that there wasn't anything left in her glass.

"We used to be friends a long time ago. Then he got the idea that, just because my buddies and I could never afford to sit in a classroom, we were stupid. I was trained. I know how to read and write, in more languages than one. Our teacher was better than all of his put together but, since we never set foot in a classroom, that made us stupid. He broke off the friendship, even after we had saved his life once. For the most part, he ignores me, which I prefer. But sometimes, sometimes he'll see me and try to find the best way to push my buttons. I usually ignore it." The whole time they spoke, she was more focused on getting an eyelash out of her eye than paying him any bother.

Aria looked up at the clock. "It's getting late. I should get some sleep," she said with a yawn. She and Twarence both stood up.

The professor gave a little nod. "I'm gonna head up and read for a while. I want to try and familiarize myself with where we're going a little more before tomorrow."

"Goodnight kids," Barina said. "I see Onyx and Jaras, so I'm going to hang out with them for a while."

Twarence and Aria said goodnight to them all.

Jaras and Onyx stopped by the bar to get some drinks and then came to join Barina.

"Hey," Jaras said, standing by his chair with a small glass of wine in hand.

"Either of you up for some darts?" Barina saw that the board was free, and she stood up slowly from her comfortable spot.

"Why not?" Jaras shrugged.

"I'll just watch," Onyx said, sitting with his tea. "I'm not very good."

"Neither am I," Barina told him, "but I still like to play." She handed Jaras his set of darts.

"And Vic thinks you can fight?" Jaras teased, nudging her arm.

Barina laughed. "Playing darts didn't need to be in my resume. You'll see what I mean."

Onyx grabbed a piece of bread from the loaf on the table. "About what? That you can fight or that you can't throw darts to save your life."

"Both." Her first dart missed the board completely by an inch. "So, what did you boys do before you came here for this job?"

"You do realize that you're supposed to aim for the dart board, right?" Jaras tapped her on top of the head with his darts.

For the entire game, Barina didn't hit a single dart to the board. "It's either a bullseye or nothing, there is no middle ground with me." She sighed, rolling her eyes. "Anyway, Onyx, talk."

"I've been studying at the Hitum Mountain in the north beyond the forest. I've been there since I was five. Rutherford said he sensed my ability when I was born. When I was fourteen, he was killed in a battle." Onyx paused. "After that, I learned all that I could and more from his books and journals. He taught me a lot when he was alive, but I kept going after he passed. I've laid low since then, but I use my powers when needed and practice them every day. Something as great as what we're going to work for, I take it. And since we're going after Toler, I couldn't resist."

Barina nodded, very impressed. "Rutherford? He was the best, if I remember correctly."

"He was. You knew of Rutherford?" Onyx's voice lingered, very curious about that.

"I did. I understand your reasons for wanting to go on this job. Vengeance is a powerful force, my new friend." Her voice was sympathetic. She understood something of Onyx, of his past, and something of hers too.

"How did you know of him? He was powerful, but there weren't many who knew him outside of the world of magic."

Barina looked away, as if she'd said something she shouldn't have. "I travel a lot, I hear things." She wasn't lying, but there was more to her story than she was telling him. Wanting to change the subject, she asked, "Jaras, what about you?"

Jaras exchanged glances with the wizard.

"Well, I'm from Treklea and began my training about eleven years ago. Within about six years, my teacher said I was finished. I became a bit of a freelance fighter, and I also helped my teacher train other students. I'll only take work like this if it's something really important." Jaras adjusted his glasses.

Barina blinked. "Who was your teacher?"

"Darien Bell of Treklea."

Barina looked impressed but kept a big smile at bay. "Not many who would dare go up against him even in a sparring match."

"Heard of a lot of people, haven't you?" Jaras' tone was very suspicious.

She lit up her pipe again. "Part of my business to know."

"Well, your turn Barina," Jaras said with a sigh. He knew it wouldn't be easy getting information from her.

"I'm from here in Miork. I've been training to be a fighter since I was about six, as soon as I could pick up a weapon. Went to study abroad when I was thirteen for about four years and started working to obtain objects when I was seventeen. I don't feel bad about stealing things that were already taken, and I can avoid hurting people unless I have to. Sometimes I take things when paid to do so, sometimes I catch wind of something, and I'll go pro bono."

"Ha, I told you that's how she was." Jaras smiled looking at Onyx.

"I never said I didn't believe you. But you did nail it." Onyx rolled his eyes.

"Wha?" Barina looked confused.

"He said that's how you ran your business. But I don't think that Arkon is going to be as easy to convince."

"Give him some time," she told them, throwing another dart. "He'll either come around or he won't. As long as it stays civil, I'm happy." She did a little dance. "Bullseye!"

"So, either of you have a special someone in your life?" Onyx asked. He pointed at his cup with a finger, and it filled again with tea.

"That was incredible!" Barina blurted out, pulling his hand closer to look into the cup.

"Hook me up," Jaras insisted, holding out his wine glass.

Onyx grinned and refilled Jaras' glass for him.

"Cheers! You are coming to the next party we go to."

"Sweet. I'm guessing since neither of you were distracted from my little magic there that you aren't in any relationships." Onyx moved aside as the waitress brought him a bowl of stew. He dug in with a smile.

The two both shook their heads.

"What about you?" Barina asked. "Any girl, or do you just conjure one up when you feel the mood strike you?"

"No," Onyx said, almost choking on his stew. "And holy shit you're a twisted woman. I spend so much time in the mountains, I just don't really focus on it. Someday I'll meet someone I'm sure, but right now, not worried about it." He then shifted a little uncomfortably. "Plus, well, it's always been hard for me to meet people. I'm a little shy."

Barina tilted her head and gazed thoughtfully at the wizard. "You have a lot to offer."

"Thanks. How come the two of you are still single? Just never met anyone?"

"Something like that," Jaras told him honestly. "I've had a few relationships and what not, but they've just never worked out. I'm more focused on work right now too. B, what about you?"

"I travel a lot and, well, if you haven't noticed yet, I'm not your average girl. I'm never in one place for long, and I dress in men's clothing, a lot for work. And I refuse to live the life of a housewife. Nothing wrong with it if that's what a girl wants for herself, but it's not for me. I have no dowry, and it would take a very special man to want to be with me."

"You'll find your prince charming," Jaras said, lighting a cigarette, "and have your happy ending someday."

Barina laughed a little. "I'm not looking for a prince charming, and I don't believe in happy endings, but I do believe in happy moments and in love." Her smile was just as bright as always. She took out her pocket watch and took a moment to think. "I'm gonna head back to my place. I need to pack. Hey Twarence," she said when he rejoined them.

"What? Where are you going?" His blue eyes seemed restless.

"She was heading back to her place." Onyx finished his drink and looked at the thief. "Mind some company? It's a nice night, and I kinda wouldn't mind walking around the city a little. I've never been here."

The other two men looked at her with as much interest as the wizard did. She blinked.

"Well, okay."

Jaras gave her a questioning look. "You didn't seem too sure about that."

She shrugged. "I'm sure. Just had to double check my instincts on you three. You're good."

Twarence lit up a smoke and asked, "What do you mean by 'checking your instincts'?"

"I have maybe a dozen people who know how to find my home. It means I trust you." She gave him a kind smile. "Let's go."

They followed their thief out of the tavern and into the streets of Miork. The traffic from horses, carriages, and people was starting to dwindle as the evening wore on. As she led them through town, the men were interested to see how it was laid out. They passed by restaurants, bars, and taverns all lined up giving out aromas, bakeries that were closed for the day, candy shops, trades where you could buy clothing, and cobblers for shoes. Some were still open, many of the owners getting ready to head home for the night. Barina answered any questions they had about what was what. The government buildings where the high lords of the region would meet, and the streets that would take them to more homes and fewer shops, they passed by all of them.

It was a pretty night, and the residential streets were becoming quiet as families turned in or simply sat outside enjoying the quiet summer night. Barina walked very content, occasionally waving at one of the people.

They followed her toward the edge of town, no houses in sight. When they came to a bridge, she led them down the hill to the bottom where a river, while not very deep but very wide, rushed by them. She moved along the wall to what looked like nothing more than the rocky side of the hill they were on. The only thing different were some wild rose bushes growing in one spot.

"B? What is this?" Twarence asked.

Barina grinned as she walked in between the rose bushes and put her hand on what looked like a rock. The others heard a doorknob turn, and then she pushed a door open. It was painted to look exactly like the rock that surrounded it. No one would know it was there unless they knew how to look.

"Come on in, and please close the door behind you." She lit a lantern on the wall while the guys filed in. They stood in a small room about six feet long with a door leading to another room. She slipped her boots off. "Oh, if you guys wouldn't mind taking your shoes off, I'd appreciate it."

As soon as their shoes were off, they hung their cloaks and jackets on hooks along the wall, and she had them follow her past the next door in cave. They weren't sure what to expect, but it wasn't this.

Twarence cried, "Holy shit!" Like the others, he was in awe. "Barina, what in the world?"

"Tadaima!" she called out and set the lantern on a table before going to light another.

The men would never guess they were underground. The main room was small and cozy, but it felt spacious. Strange, light yellow flooring covered the ground, mainly around the center of the room and anywhere that was obviously seen as a walking path. The areas beyond had items like a chest, dresser, bookcases, and a few other storage items sitting on the stone floor. The walls had what looked like white paper and a light wood lattice over them. The room felt bigger than it really was.

In the center of the room was a large fire pit in the ground. Above the pit there was a metal hood covered in soot that made its way to somewhere outside. The ventilation was good enough that there was no smell of smoke. There were cushions around the fire pit, and they could see where she had left a book. There was a low table at the side of the room with cushions around it, but no chairs.

She let them walk around and check things out while she lit a fire and grabbed a tea kettle—filling it with water—to hang on a hook above the flames.

They walked to another room separated by a curtain. The men were pretty sure they were in a kitchen. Three tiers of clay and stone were molded to each house something different. One held a deep pot, one a grill, and another had a flat surface. They saw another hood over them with pipes for more ventilation. There was a prep table to the side, and on a shelf dug out of the walls sat plates, bowls, and cups.

Part of the floor in the last room was raised a little bit. They saw a bucket, a small stool, and a washcloth. Then there was a large covered tub resting over a stone fire pit meant to heat the water.

"B, where did you come up with an idea for this place?" Jaras asked when they walked back into the main room.

She had just finished packing a few items into a large traveling bag and was now checking the water above the small fire. She looked over, grabbing a canister that held some tea and put some in an infuser.

"Oh, um, my teacher took my two best friends and I to study abroad, and I lived overseas for four years. I liked a lot of the design elements, right down to how they take their baths, and I've incorporated a lot of that style to my home here."

"What did you say when we walked inside?" Onyx asked, still walking around.

Barina blushed a little. "Oh sorry. I said *I'm home.* We got so used to saying it over there that it kinda stuck. Plus, I wasn't sure if my teacher would've been here or not."

Twarence was looking around. "This cave does keep nice and cool in the summer. I like that. But there's no bed or bedroom."

She pointed. "That large thing on the far side of the mat, that unfolds to my bed. Saves space on days I decide to actually fold it up. I have a couple of them for when my teacher or some of my friends from overseas come to visit." Her eyes went to the table where she saw a folded piece of paper addressed to her with a pencil next to it. She opened the letter and read it.

"From your teacher?" Twarence asked.

Barina nodded. "Yeah, Berk left while I was out meeting with you guys. Said he'd probably be over in Estella in a couple months then back here after. My friend Josh lives there, and my friend Jason and his girlfriend Tyra are moving there right now. Those two boys and myself all studied with him. Must mean he's gonna help Jason and Tyra get set up when they get there."

"From what you say, it sounds like he travels a lot," Jaras added.

"Yeah, he really does. But to be fair, so do I." She took a minute to write on the other side of the paper. *Dear Berk, I'm traveling to Thoron. Should be gone for about three months. Maybe I'll run into you when we pass through Estella on the way there. Travel safely. With love, Barina.* She folded it up and put it back on the table.

"How did you find this cave?" Twarence was still checking out the room.

"Jason, Josh and I found this when we were kids. Hung out here all the time. It was our little getaway. High up enough from the river to not worry about flooding, and close to a water source. When we came home, they helped me hook up the system with the chimneys so that I don't have to worry about smoke in here. It made sense for me to live here when we returned from studying." She stretched. "It's safe, and I can leave my things here without worrying that anyone is gonna find it."

They were nodding.

"This is really neat," Jaras said, applauding her efforts. "I like it. I mean, even with it being a cave, you'd never guess that it was a cave. Way to make the most of a small space."

"Thanks. It's not much, but it's home." She gave each of them a cup of tea. "I'll have to have everyone over after all of this is done, and I'll make dinner for you. Too bad Aria and Arkon had gone to sleep already. Wouldn't have minded having them here too. But now that you know where I live, you have a standing invitation to visit."

"Thanks. This tea is really good too." Onyx smiled.

The group sat for a while enjoying their drinks before Barina got a bottle of something out of a cupboard and took out four tiny cups.

"I want to share something with you guys that I've been holding onto for a special occasion." She took the stopper off the bottle, then filled each cup. "I have the feeling that this is the beginning of a great friendship, and I want to share a glass with you."

"What is this?" Jaras held up the small cup containing a white liquid. "Smells good."

"I brought a few bottles of this back with me last time I visited overseas. It's a wine made from a grain from there. Tasty." She lifted her glass.

The men each grabbed their cups and lifted them.

"To new friends," she said, and she started sipping on her drink.

Each of them took a little taste, surprised at how much they enjoyed it. They took time to finish their drinks, and then made conversation while Barina finished packing her bags.

"Okay, are you guys ready?" She smiled, putting the wine into her bag.

Jaras grabbed a bucket of water to put the fire out.

"Not staying home tonight then?" Onyx asked. "I figured you'd want to sleep at your place one more night."

"I do," she agreed, "but I'm gonna have to get up early to grab us some extra supplies tomorrow, and it'll just be so much easier if I'm already in town."

The fire was out, and she held the lantern in front of them as they headed for the door.

"So, you said it's gonna take us three months to get there," Onyx said when they started walking back to the tavern.

She nodded. "Yeah, long trip. Vic's right about it, though. There are things that only an elf of the Spirit Clan can do, providing we run into a couple situations that I hope we don't. And there are things that only a wizard is powerful enough to take care of."

"What I don't get is why I'm here." Twarence breathed out his cigarette smoke as they turned another corner. "I mean, what's the point if you already know the way there. You don't need me as a guide."

Jaras shrugged. "Perhaps that just means there's an angle that we're not seeing with you."

"We need your logic and reason," Barina mused out loud. "There are going to be things about all of this, hell, there are already things about all of this that haven't added up—things that I think only you will have any insight about as they reveal themselves. I mean, there are things I don't get, I don't understand. You might be the piece that is able to help us understand more of this puzzle."

Twarence looked humble. "I don't know, I hope you're right. Right now I feel like I'm useless."

"Don't ever say that about yourself," she said, nudging his arm. "I'm sure everything will become clear as we go along."

The four of them made their way through the streets and back to the tavern. It was quiet out, and even outside the tavern, the air was still. They headed inside and ordered another round of drinks just to top off the evening before heading to bed.

"So, you've never been to Treklea?" Jaras couldn't believe the two men with him had never gone. "I'll have to take you to visit sometime. It's beautiful there. You've been to visit, right B?"

She nodded, doing her best to hide the fact that she had just realized she had met all of these men when they were younger. She would wait until they said something first, but the fact that Jaras didn't remember was a surprise. Barina had been in Treklea for three weeks.

Jaras sensed amusement in her eyes but made nothing of it. "It's beautiful," he said. "The capital looks just like something out of a storybook."

"I've been beyond the edge of the Isles," Twarence said, sipping his wine, "but not much further than that. It was mainly to do some work at other universities as a visiting professor. How far have you guys all traveled?"

"Pretty far," Jaras said, "though Miork is about as far as I've gotten. I've done some travel, but mostly I stay in Treklea and help my teacher training his students."

Onyx took a breath. "I've just passed the Great Desert in my travels. Wizard stuff."

That got Barina's attention. "Geez," she let out in a whisper. "You really are good."

For the first time since he had met the thief, Onyx knew he had someone with him who could fully appreciate what it meant to travel to the Great Desert, and what it meant getting there in the first place. He could see in her eyes, she knew. "You too?" he asked.

She nodded.

Onyx leaned in closer. "Likewise, with you."

Twarence leaned in a little more, slightly annoyed by the fact that these two were speaking almost in code. "We're still here."

"Sorry, we'll talk to you about all that later." Onyx gave a sheepish grin, trying to apologize for being so cryptic. "Let's just say, going there was part of my training to become a wizard, and she understands that."

Twarence gave in to the fact that they weren't going to talk about it. "What are you guys planning on doing after this is over?"

"I don't know," Jaras said. "I was kinda thinking of buying some land and opening up my own school of defense. I mean, I think we'll make enough from this job where I could make that happen. I've been saving up for a while anyway. How about you guys?"

"Haven't thought about it much honestly," Onyx said. "I mean, I guess there are some artifacts I wouldn't mind getting. Maybe do repairs at home. Twarence?"

"I'm thinking on the lines of Jaras. I love teaching at the university, but I wouldn't mind opening a school for those who can't afford it otherwise. You B?"

"I don't know. Been thinking for a while about restarting the family business. My father had been a smith, and I learned everything he did. This would be enough for me to buy everything I'd need." She decided to grab a handful of darts and tossed one at the board.

"What, not gonna settle down and have a bunch of babies?" Twarence teased. They all started laughing.

"Fuck right off with that. I think I'll be good for a while."

Just then, Nels snickered as he passed by while walking back to his date at the bar. He had requested a song from the bard who was playing a soft tune now. He flipped his shoulder-length hair and turned to look at her.

"Barina really," Nels yelled from the bar, his brown eyes narrowing. "You know you'll never be married because you're a stupid, ignorant, little bitch."

Barina threw another dart, a perfect bull's-eye, and said calmly with her pipe still in the side of her mouth, "Ignorant and stupid no. A bitch yes. The bitchiness, you bring that on yourself."

Her companions shot a dark look at this man who was insulting their new friend. They didn't know him, but they didn't like him. They had a feeling, too, that she wasn't going to let him get the better of her.

Before he could get out another word, Barina said, "So Nels, who is this girl with you tonight? What happened to the red head you were seeing last night, or that pretty girl with the dark hair last Monday? Do you really have her believing that you're the kind of guy who will give a damn after you get her in bed?" Barina met eyes with the lady next to him. "Trust me honey, you can do much better than this. There are men out there who will love you and be true, you just have to look more carefully at their hearts than their looks."

Barina's eyes connected with the girl who knew she was speaking the truth. Yes, Barina wanted to humiliate Nels, but at the same time she didn't want the girl to get hurt.

People in the tavern started to look over, waiting to see what would happen, hoping to be entertained. The bard even stopped playing.

Nels, on the other hand, turned red in the face. He didn't want Barina to ruin his chance at getting this pretty girl in bed.

His date turned and looked at him. "You bastard!" she snarled, standing up. "You told me you hadn't been with anyone in over a month."

Nels's lips moved but no words escaped.

Barina wasn't finished. "Honey, I wish you could find out easier, but women to him are just the flavor of the week, day, or whatever he wants.

Find yourself a real man, cause that guy, he ain't one." She snuffed out her pipe and put it back into her pouch.

Convinced, the pretty girl left without another word.

Nels stood and, with all of his strength, threw his empty mug at Barina. She batted it down as if she was lightly swatting away a fly and let it fall to the ground.

"You goddamn bitch!" he yelled.

She rolled her eyes. "What have we learned from this, Nels? Next time keep your mouth shut and mind your business, you fucking tool." She kept her tone light and free of anger.

As the tension between these two heated up, nobody would have been surprised if it came to blows. People in the room started to back away.

"Who the hell are you to talk about finding a man? At least people can tell that I *am a man*. They don't even know what you are! You dress, talk, and act like a man!"

Barina dressed in pants, yes, but there was no denying that she was a woman. In a dry tone, she simply said, "Oh ouch, burn. I'm more of a man than you are. Anyone could be a better man than you. It's not that hard to do." She turned her interest to a moth that flew past her.

Nels's smile turned cold. He knew how to push her as his voice went dark. "Any girl except for your mom and your sister. Let's see them be more than, oh wait, that's right, they…" He didn't get to finish his thought.

In the blink of an eye, Barina jumped over two tables and pinned him to the floor, her left forearm pressing on his neck so hard he couldn't breathe. Her dagger was unsheathed, pointing between his legs, the tip touching the fabric of his pants.

She spoke just above a whisper. "You ever talk about them again, and you'll lose more than your date." A fire burned in her dark eyes.

"Barina, let him go," Onyx said quietly. "He's not worth it."

Twarence and Jaras reached for her, but they didn't need to pull her away. She stood up, but not before she saw the anger in Nels's eyes turn to fear.

"He's not worth the air I breathe," she said, making a point to step on his chest as she walked to the stairs.

Everyone in the room stared, frozen.

Nels stood up after a minute. He grabbed his neck as he held onto the bar trying to catch his breath. He stared after her with more hatred than ever.

The traveling companions started up the stairs, but before they got too far, Barina whirled around and threw her last dart. It pinned on the support beam right next to Nels' head, not more than a quarter inch from his ear. "Have a nice evening."

"I want you out of here for good, Nels," the bartender told him. "Don't ever come back. Her little sister used to play with my daughter, and her mother was good friends with my wife. How dare you insult their memory like that." The bartender looked ready to punch Nels himself.

Under his breath, Nels said, "Next time we meet Barina, I'll kill you." He glared at the bartender. "Go to hell, Terry." He grabbed his cloak and left the tavern.

Jaras was fuming, his fist rolled into a ball. "I'm half tempted to go find that guy and give him a piece of my mind. And my fist."

Onyx kept an eye on Barina as they walked into the room. Aria and Arkon were already asleep. The thief took a deep breath while she folded her cloak and tossed it on the top bunk above Aria's and took off her boots. She looked like she did before that little scuffle—like nothing bothered her. But Onyx worried. Something terrible had to have happened to the girl that would cause her to lash out.

Barina moved to the fireplace to look through her traveling bag. She grabbed her hairbrush and started to brush out her hair.

Onyx walked over, speaking quietly. "Barina?"

She looked up at him.

"What was he talking about back there?"

Jaras and Twarence shared a glance and then looked back to Barina.

She took a second to finish brushing her hair before she motioned for them to follow. She led the three men out of the room and to the doors at the end of the hallway. They went out and sat on the balcony.

She lit her pipe as they took a seat. "Might as well tell you guys. It's not a secret in this town what happened to my family or who my family was. But a lot of people forgot about me after I left Miork when I was thirteen. I try to keep a low profile whenever I'm back. Folks like Terry, the bartender, remember me, but he's known me since I was a kid. And he knew my family well, too.

"My family was murdered. Killed and our house looted. Stuff like that didn't happen in this city too often. And nobody expected anything like

51

that with my family. They never did anything to anyone. They were good people." She took a moment. "My father was an honest man, my mother about as good as you got. My big brother and my little sister, they didn't deserve what happened to them. Those two, their bodies were thrown into the fireplace. Nothing left to bury even, but I buried their ashes next to my parents.

"My teacher, Berk, had planned on taking my friends and I overseas to further our training, but when that happened, it accelerated the process. We left the next day."

Barina's eyes clouded over for a moment. "I killed the men who killed my family. The only time I killed out of vengeance and as close to flat out murder I've ever committed. I don't like to kill unless I have to. Thankfully, I like to think I'm good enough to know when it's absolutely necessary."

The tension in her face eased. "I've made a lot of peace with what happened. Not completely, but a lot. I have no problem talking about my family and what happened to them, but I can apparently get pissed off when someone insults their memory. Nels knew my family, what they meant to me, and he was so close to getting my foot up his ass tonight," she grumbled.

"Wow, kid, that's insane," Twarence said to her while squeezing her shoulder.

"Sorry you had to hear all of that. I fight to protect and defend those I care for—the innocent, the causes I see just—and to destroy the wicked. You guys made my list of those I will protect." She let out a big yawn.

"I believe that's our cue to hit the hay," Twarence said, yawning himself. "I set the alarm for seven. It's going to be a long day tomorrow."

They shuffled back to their room and got ready for bed.

Barina had changed into a green, knee length nightgown before she climbed up onto her bunk and let out a sigh.

"Something wrong?" Onyx asked, looking over.

"I always have trouble sleeping when I'm not at home or outside. Home is home. Outside the stars are comforting. They tell me stories, help me sleep."

Onyx was propped up on his elbow, looking at her. He made a twirling motion with his fingers, whispering *Cosmo* under his breath. A little section just above Barina's bed now looked like the night sky with twinkling stars.

She sat up and looked over at him, beaming. "You are the best wizard ever!" she squeaked out.

"Of all the things that you're probably truly capable of doing, this is what makes you the best wizard ever." Twarence laughed, laying on his bed.

"It's the little things in life you know," the wizard said, grinning and fluffing his pillow.

"Hey, this is really sweet," Barina said staring at the stars. "And it's what you do with your powers that makes you the best wizard ever." Her voice was sleepy. "Goodnight guys."

"Goodnight," they all whispered at the same time.

CHAPTER 3

At least four people groaned when a bell above the door rang at seven in the morning. Jaras opened his eyes and threw his pillow at the door, letting the maid know they were awake.

Aria sat up with a stretch and smiled. "Good morning," she chimed in a happy voice, running her fingers in her dark hair. She took a long look out the window, smiling and seeing the rising sun paint colors in the sky. "It looks so pretty out there."

"A morning person?" Twarence said in a gruff tone. "Disgusting."

"Oh whatever. You guys are pathetic." Aria then punched the top bunk trying to poke the thief awake. "Barina, wake up." There was no response.

Arkon looked over from his top bunk. "She's not there. Bed is made and everything."

"What, seriously?" Twarence stood up, taking a look. "I'll be damned."

"She didn't leave, did she?" Arkon asked while climbing down from his bunk.

The door to the room opened, and Barina walked in holding a cup of coffee and had a toothpick in her mouth. She was fully dressed in her brown pants, dagger at her side, and a clean dark blue sleeveless blouse, brown boots and her hair in a low braid. Her gray cloak flowed behind her as she walked in humming a little tune and sipping her coffee. She held a book in front of her, reading through glasses that they hadn't seen on her before.

"Morning. I told the maid to bring up some water to the bathing rooms for you guys. Should be ready by now. The stable hands will have your horses ready in the next hour, and breakfast will be downstairs ready to go after you get cleaned and dressed. I also picked up extra furs for when we go to the summit. You'll need them. They're in the packs already." She went over to sit in front of the fireplace, but there was no fire. "Hey magic men, can I get a fire over here?"

Arkon pointed a finger at the fireplace, and a warm fire burst into flame. Everyone looked at Barina, stunned.

"You've had a busy morning," Arkon said. "When did you wake up?"

"Couple hours ago." She turned a page in her book.

"See, I'm not the only morning person," Aria told them, grabbing her traveling bag as she got out of bed.

"I'm not a morning person," Barina countered, keeping her eyes on the book. "I just don't sleep much when I'm working. There were also a lot of things to gather before we left."

The group got themselves moving, enjoying their baths and then a nice large breakfast. Barina was still by the fireplace reading when they came back to their room. She placed her book into her pack and checked to make sure she had everything. Her reading glasses went into the little pouch on her side.

Vic had left them extra things for traveling, but it was mainly money. It seems as if the thief had done some shopping for all of them early that morning. She liked to travel light, and wanted everyone's horse to carry only one extra saddle bag apiece.

They did one last sweep for their things before Barina followed them out of the room.

She waited outside the stables, enjoying the sunshine and making small talk, while the others got their horses. Jaras sat outside with her, smoking a cigarette.

"You don't have a horse either?" she asked him.

"No, it's one more thing to worry about."

"I know," she agreed, "and I'm faster on my feet too."

Twarence and Onyx both felt bad about her having to walk, both offering her rides if she got tired.

"Your horses will tire out before I do," she smirked, standing up.

"I'll believe that when I see it," Arkon said. "I can make it so my horse doesn't need sleep for a couple days."

"Slick. I approve of that," Jaras told him.

"I think he does win on that one." Barina winked up at him while they passed through town. "Okay, so *you* will tire out before I do."

"I can do that for myself, too," Arkon joked. He had decided that he really did need to give her a chance.

Barina nodded thoughtfully. "Neat."

Twarence rode up next to her. "Well, I'm glad that you don't want to borrow my horse. I was just offering to be nice. Not like I really wanted to walk."

"Nice to know that there are still some quasi-gentlemen left in the world." Barina laughed at him. "Ass." Her face lit up. "Oh, excuse me for a minute. I need to run into this bakery really quick. I'll catch up," she said as she rushed ahead of them.

By the time they were another block away, she was back and carrying something in cheesecloth. It smelled good.

"What was that about?" Twarence asked.

"It's my aunt and uncle's bakery. I spent all of yesterday with them before I met up with you guys, and had to tell them goodbye before I left town." She opened up the cloth and handed them each a sweet roll.

"These are so good," Twarence mumbled with his mouth full. "Do you have any more?" he asked, not caring that the buns were almost too hot to eat.

She handed him another one.

"Wow, they know how to bake." Arkon was enjoying his rolls too.

"So where are we heading first?" Onyx asked as they turned down another street.

"Through the Black Mountains," the professor said, checking his map. "We should get there in a couple hours."

Aria put on another cloak. "It is chilly," she said, shivering. "I just can't stay warm." She looked over at Barina. "Are you warm enough wearing that cloak? It doesn't look that warm at all."

Barina's cloak didn't have any lining, and she didn't have a blanket with her even in her traveling bag. "Uhh, it's early summer," she said. "How can you be cold?"

"I'm always cold," Aria told her with a sigh.

They shrugged their shoulders and kept walking until they crossed a bridge and saw the incline of the path to the Black Mountains. After a couple of hours, they came to the foot of the mountains and headed up the steep incline. The path led far back behind jagged points, hiding its twists and turns. Nobody but the thief had been this close to the mountains, and their looming presence was a little unnerving.

"I've heard tales of these mountains," Aria said. "They're crawling with all sorts of creatures." She felt a cool breeze go by.

"I've been here a lot," Barina told them while she walked from the back of the group to the front. "Teaming with life, and it can be dangerous. It's mainly 'cause stupid people came through and destroyed all the safe ways, and now all that's left are the not-so safe ways." She grumbled a bit. "Stupid people abusing the laws of the mountains. There went my idea of building a summer home out here."

"Summer home. Cute." Arkon smiled, enjoying her sense of humor.

Aria was carefully watching where her horse stepped. "What rules of the mountains?"

"Same as any place you go," Arkon told her, grabbing a snack from his pack. "Respect your surroundings. Don't think that you own the place."

Jaras then looked over to Barina. "What's the most dangerous place you've ever been through?" He hoped that asking questions like this would help him find out more about the type of fighter she was.

She glanced at Onyx knowing he had the same experience. "The Sheruna," she said.

"What?" Everyone but Onyx gasped. He didn't blink.

The Sheruna was by far the most dangerous place anyone knew of. It could take days to go through. Half of it was a frozen wasteland so cold that any skin that was left exposed for more than a minute or two would freeze. The creatures that lived there killed anything they could get ahold of. So little was known about them, and that lack of knowledge made it even more dangerous.

The other half of the Sheruna—once past the Heart—was such a dry and barren desert, and so hot that people had been known to rip the flesh from their bodies. If one lived through a trip there, it was nothing short of a miracle.

"Why on earth would you go into the Sheruna?" Aria could barely get the words out.

"It wasn't for fun," the thief replied. "I did it cause I had to. Some friends were in trouble and, at the time, it was the only way for me to get to them."

They were still in awe and knew that it must have been important if she had to travel through there.

Arkon whistled through his teeth. "I've never even had a glance at it, but from what I've heard, I don't ever want to."

"Consider yourselves lucky," Onyx said. "I've had to go a couple times—magic things—and it was the longest four days of my life." He swallowed hard and then looked to Jaras and Twarence. "This is what she and I were talking about last night when I mentioned that I had been to the Great Desert. The Sheruna is on the other side. She realized I had been through the Sheruna to get to the Desert."

Looking nervous, Barina carefully met his eyes. "Did you duke it out with those at the Heart?"

Onyx nodded. "I had to. It was part of my training. Did you?"

She nodded as well. "You lived. That means you're really good."

"What are you two talking about?" Twarence was trying to learn more about a part of the world he had only heard about in horror stories.

"I'd rather not talk about it," Onyx said, trying to shake that memory away.

"Barina, why…" Arkon was cut off.

"It really is a beautiful day," Barina said. "Don't you think, Onyx?" The two of them walked ahead in silence, their attention back to the situation at hand.

That seemed easy enough for their wizard and thief not to talk about the Sheruna, but the others were hard pressed to take their minds off of it for a while. They decided to respect the silence and brought their attention back to the trail through the mountains.

The Black Mountains were beautiful, even if they were barren in many parts. From the first incline, they could see the entire city of Miork and even the palace all the way in the capital city of Fern. They also could see that this mountain chain would take them weeks to get through.

After a period of quiet, Arkon piped up. "Is there any kind of vegetation around here? It's been pretty bare."

"There is a little," Twarence said, "but not much of anything anymore."

"Little vegetation?" Barina sounded exasperated as she stopped in her steps. "You call the forests little? Plants trying to bite your legs off, flowers that set off deadly gasses, giant bugs the size of houses, and spiders bigger than the damn bugs."

Twarence crossed his arms and grinned. "Okay, let me rephrase that. The vegetation isn't little, there's just not much of it around. Is that better, Miss Picky?"

"Yes. Accuracy is important."

"And don't talk about spiders. Yuck." Twarence shivered at the thought.

"Afraid of spiders?" Jaras asked, a little amused.

Twarence was not ashamed of his phobia in the slightest. "Hate them."

"I'm with him on that," Aria said. "They are disgusting things who..."

Barina spoke up. "Who will take care of bugs like flies, locusts and, in the case of the spiders here, the really, really big bugs that are more harmful? Trust me, if you see a giant grasshopper, you'll be wanting that spider."

"I think I'll take my chances with the grasshopper." Aria was still grossed out by spiders.

"Suit yourself," Jaras told her. "I'm going with the girl that's been here before."

Aria then noticed something else about the mountain sides—little deep pockets obviously carved right out of the mountain rock. "Why are these called the Black Mountains anyway?" she asked. "That's something I've never understood."

Twarence finished lighting his cigarette and handed the match to Jaras before he answered. "Diamonds. They used to hold black diamonds. Veins ran everywhere and easy to find, and there were sides of the mountains that would glitter from them. It's probably been about twenty-five years since the last ones were taken, that I know of, but the name for the mountains stuck. Too bad they're gone. I would've liked to have seen them."

"I bet they were beautiful," Aria told them.

"I've seen a few" Arkon said. "The king of the elves has some on his scepter, given to his predecessor as a gift from the gnomes who live here. They're amazing. Hard to describe how beautiful they really are. I'm going to have to take all of you to the Forest sometime, and you can meet my clan."

They looked over—all of them beaming—except Barina who had wandered ahead quite a ways.

"That would be fantastic," Jaras told him. "You'd really want to do that with us?"

"Sure."

"Even, well, you know?" Onyx shifted his head to indicate Barina who was now taking a moment to re-braid her hair.

Arkon nodded. "I'm giving her the chance she deserves." He pulled out a tiny pipe from his pack and lit it. After a couple puffs, he added, "She seems nice."

The first few hours in the mountains went smoothly until they had no choice but to stop.

"That's a hell of a road-block," Twarence grumbled.

"What the hell?" Arkon stared at what lay ahead of them.

"Oh, hey look, it's a dragon," Barina told them with a bright smile.

"Thank you Captain Obvious." Twarence peered from around the boulders he hid behind.

Barina gave him a playful glare. "You're welcome." She studied the dragon briefly. "I'll be back," she said, and she started to approach the beast.

Aria tried to hold her back. "I don't want to wake her up."

"Most dragons are nice," Barina said calmly. "And we have to ask if she will allow us to pass by. She's guarding…well, if she lets us by, you'll see." She kept walking toward the dragon, away from the group.

"I think the girl is nuts," Aria said as she went to hide.

"Yup," Barina called looking over her shoulder.

Aria's eyes widened. "She heard me?"

"Seems so," Arkon said, staying back with Aria.

"I have very good hearing," Barina said a little louder. "I just don't always pay attention."

Jaras looked over at Twarence. "Care to join me? I'm gonna go with her."

Twarence nodded, and they joined Barina as she approached the dragon.

The dragon was huge—forty feet in length with beautiful black scales on its body. The beast had dark red wings, and the spikes that curled around its face and along its back were a brilliant orange. The eyes were the same color as well. The dragon was as beautiful as it was terrifying. And it was sound asleep.

Barina adjusted her cloak and made sure to brush off any dirt as best she could. She noticed the boys following her. "Stay back about ten feet. Trust me." She walked right up to the dragon and placed her hand on its snout.

"Excuse me," she said calmly. The dragon opened its eyes slowly and looked at the girl. "Forgive me for disturbing you, but I must ask something of you."

The dragon lifted its head and looked at the girl and the two young men with her. They seemed nervous, but still they stood with her. A wizard sat farther back idly leaning on his horse, not nervous at all. He was more distracted by the clouds passing. There was also a healer and an elf, keeping their distance. The dragon smiled at the blonde girl in front of her. This young lady held no fear for the dragon in her eyes. In fact, she smiled.

"I am Na'imah," the creature said in a deep voice. "What do you need?"

"I've come to ask that you allow my friends and me safe passage. I know what you guard, and I give you my word that we will bring you no harm."

"You know what is beyond me here, do you? Who are you?"

Barina then gave a small bow to the dragon and did something that left the men who stood by her in awe.

"Ta coo Barina Raine o Miork. Ta coo mota no Usami shem Yamona." She stood upright with her hands folded in front of her and a poker face that still hinted of a smile.

Thoroughly amused, Na'imah's laughter shook the ground. "Graln sepkti shrekt suke. I smell no lie on you my child, and I know of you. I have heard of you from Usami. I am the leader here, and I will escort you and those with you to the other side. You know the rules when you come here, I gather, so please explain to them what they must know as well." The dragon then raised its head in the air, and a chirping noise came from its throat.

Barina bowed her head slightly again. "Thank you." She silently led the men back to the group.

"We have safe passage," she told them. "But there are some things that I need to tell you before we go with Na'imah." They could see her eyes blink for a moment while figuring out which words to use.

"Wait a second," Twarence finally said, puzzled. He turned Barina to face him. "You speak dragon? Why didn't you say anything?" The rest of the group shot a wide-eyed look at Barina.

She nodded. "Dragonie to be accurate. I told you I can speak in multiple languages. And you never did ask if Dragonie was one, did you?"

Onyx chuckled. "We never did ask."

Twarence was making a sour face. "By other languages, I thought you meant something human, like that of the Northern Regions."

"I can speak that, too." She delighted in surprising the scholar.

"What did you two say to each other?" Jaras then asked.

"I am Barina Raine of Miork, an ally of Usami the Great. She laughed and said it's been over three hundred years since she's spoken to any but a dragon in her tongue."

"She? What was that chirping noise she was making?" Arkon asked.

Barina looked at him in shock. "What are they teaching elves and wizards these days? You should know this. I thought it was mandatory for you to learn the speech of all the magical beings in the world?"

Arkon turned red. "Hey, there's a lot to cover. I don't start with Dragonie till next year. That's the last language for me to learn, thank you."

"Fine." Barina turned to the wizard as if she was teaching a class of students. "Onyx, do you know what she was doing?" She looked like she could sucker punch Arkon and might do the same to Onyx if he didn't answer correctly.

"I wasn't paying attention. But I think she was calling another dragon," Onyx said while watching Na'imah from where he sat.

"Thank you, yes. She was calling another dragon to keep guard while she escorts us."

"I thought she said she was the leader in this area," Jaras said as he checked all the horses' hooves.

"She is, but that doesn't mean leaders don't work." Barina checked her pocket watch.

"Who is Usami?" Aria asked, slipping gloves onto her hands. "It sounds like just being chummy with him was enough to get us in."

Arkon confirmed with a nod. "It would be if you know him. He's the leader of all dragons—the oldest, wisest, and most powerful in the world."

Barina grinned. "It's not the only thing that's getting us in, but it helps."

Aria's jaw dropped. "And you're his friend? How, and wow."

Barina waved her hands to stop the questions. "It's not important. Well it is, but not right now. I've gotta explain to you about where we are."

They all hushed and looked at their thief.

"We're about to go through one of their lairs. It's a homestead of dragons, and probably about one hundred or so live there. I can't believe

Vic would have us take a path like this, but I didn't realize there was a lair in these mountains. Dragons are very good about keeping their lairs private, and if we were able to stumble on it so easily, then all the safe roads really are gone." She sighed to herself and then got back to the subject. "We have to follow Na'imah and not stray from her. If she stops to talk to others, we wait. If she gets tired or hungry, we wait. Don't go near the eggs unless we are asked by Na'imah and her only.

"Each egg takes five years to mature, and each one is precious. If you even touch one without Na'imah's permission, you WILL BE KILLED, and there is nothing I can do to stop it. I like all of you, but I will not defend someone who brings them harm when they are being so kind to us. If danger comes to the lair while we pass through, we have an obligation to fight and defend the lair.

"Dragons are strong and very powerful, but any who ask to go through the lair is expected to fight and defend them, and to the death if need be. That's the price we pay for being allowed passage. If they were to ask us to go in, then they would defend us. But since it's us who have made the request, it's the other way around. And in all honesty, since it was me who did the asking, I can do the fighting if it comes to that. Well, Jaras, Twarence, the two of you were standing with me, so you'd have to fight too.

"All magic is neutralized in the lairs, so Onyx and Arkon, you guys won't be able to use your powers. Aria, it's different with you. You can still heal if needed. And if a dragon is sick or hurt, expect to help them."

Barina then gave them all a very serious look. "I need you guys to understand something. I have built up very good relations with the dragons over the years. They are kind and wise creatures, but they won't, and I won't, tolerate any rudeness while in their home." Her face relaxed. "Feel free to ask her all the questions you want, though. Dragons love to bestow their knowledge on others. They love to teach. You won't have many other teachers as good as them."

Everyone looked apprehensive, but they all nodded. They were about to enter a dragon lair—an area of the world that few ever got to see.

Barina turned around. "Follow me."

As they approached Na'imah, another dragon who was small in comparison—maybe only thirty feet long—walked up beside her.

The new dragon was, for lack of a better word, adorable. She had sunny yellow scales on most of her body and a petal pink underbelly. Her eyes were a soft green, and they looked up to her leader.

"Yes mother?"

Na'imah looked lovingly at her daughter. "Arana, keep guard for me. I am going to take visitors through."

As Arana looked at the traveling party, her eyes lit up. "Oh?" She was interested in the people there. "Who are they?"

"The little one with the light hair is Barina Raine of Miork," Na'imah told her.

Arana lowered her head to Barina and sniffed her. "Usami's told us about you. I thought you'd be taller."

Barina started laughing along with Na'imah and Arana.

"Umm…" Twarence began. "What's going on?"

"Sorry," Na'imah said. "It's just that every time Usami talks about Barina, he has a tendency to exaggerate how tall she is. I think last time he her to about twelve feet. Anyway, come along everyone. Arana, call if there is trouble."

"I will, Mother."

Na'imah started walking through the canyon. Arana stepped aside, and Barina and the traveling party stepped forward. They walked through the barren canyon for a few minutes before they came around a bend and saw something unbelievable.

An enormous valley spread for miles before them. It was lush and green. Giant sunflowers, roses and daisies grew ten feet tall. There were pools of water where a few dragons sat lounging for a drink and talking with each other—some laughing at their own jokes. By another pool, a couple of young male dragons were having a contest to see who could create the largest stream of fire. A few dragons slept comfortably on large mounds of earth, while smoke billowed from caves in the sides of the mountain. When the group looked carefully, they could see eggs about the size of an eagle egg resting on beds of hot rocks. Every ten minutes or so, a dragon would blow fire onto the rocks to keep them warm.

"Five years of that?" Aria breathed.

"Five years of keeping an egg warm and turning them once a day to make sure they develop," Na'imah told them. "If one day is missed, one dragon is lost." She walked slowly so they could keep up.

"This is the most amazing place I have ever been in my life," Aria said, watching the birds fly overhead.

Twarence marveled at the view. "You would never guess a place like this was in the mountains. It's incredible."

"Thank you," Na'imah said, nodding slightly. "We love it here. This has been one of our homes for the last two hundred years." She then gave a thoughtful look. "Ask any questions you wish, scholar. I can answer all of them. I know you're eager to ask."

He rode closer to her. "Is it okay if I write this down?"

"Please do."

The rest of the traveling party listened carefully while Barina straggled behind. She had pulled her pipe out of her pack and lit it. After taking a second to get a good light on it, she joined them. Jaras grabbed his pipe too, but kept a sharp ear on what Na'imah spoke of.

"Okay," Twarence began, "so how old do dragons live to be?"

"On average about thirteen hundred years. But most of us will live to be about sixteen hundred. Usami is the oldest of us at one thousand, six hundred and ninety-eight years."

"Seriously, that's wow." Jaras smiled up at her. "So, how many eggs do you lay in a lifetime?"

"Two. We will lay two eggs in our lifetime."

Everyone grew quiet.

"Now you understand why we guard our eggs and our children so fiercely. We only get a couple of chances, and our children, for the first ten years of their lives, are very vulnerable. We all care for them together." She turned her head toward the mountainside. "Walk, we can go closer if you wish to see them. Don't touch the eggs, but don't mind if some of the babies approach you. They're curious and love to play."

They followed Na'imah to the line of caves, and they could feel the heat from the fires keeping the eggs warm. As they kept walking, they came to a field where dragons the size of large dogs romped with each other next to ones the size of three-week-old kittens still learning how to walk and hold their heads up.

"They are so cute!" Aria's face was shining at seeing the tiny dragons.

"Their colors, they're so pale," Arkon added, looking down at the little dragons. "Not very vibrant."

"They won't gain all their coloring until they're older. They don't even have their scales yet. Just flesh." Na'imah's nose dipped down, and she blew a little breath onto a couple of the baby dragons. They flopped over on their backs, making little chirping noises, and it looked like they were being tickled.

Onyx scratched one on the head while Jaras tried to stop another one from chewing on his cloak. Arkon and Aria cautiously stood by one and petted its wings.

One flew, jumped and flapped its wings, and almost fell on the ground. Barina caught him before he hit. He was no bigger than a fully-grown cat. When his eyes met hers, he made a sound like the sob of a baby crying. She gave him a kind smile as she placed a finger under his chin. "Do toe, do toe. Yot tiye chiram."

The little dragon stopped his sobbing and licked his tongue to her cheek. He then put his head on her shoulder and purred. She rubbed his back, and he was asleep in seconds.

"You have a way with the little ones," Aria said looking over at her.

"A little encouragement goes a long way for them," Barina told her quietly.

"Come." Na'imah smiled at them. "We still have a distance to go."

Barina set the baby dragon on a sunny spot in the grass. He was still purring when a couple of other dragons snuggled up next to him, and they fell asleep too.

"Which one is his twin?" Barina asked Na'imah. "So hard to tell while they're still so young."

"Oh, the one closest to his face there, she's his sister."

"Twin?" Aria asked.

"We only lay two eggs ever, two at the same time. Every dragon has a twin. We have a boy and a girl each. My son is with my brother attending to Usami's twin sister who is a little under the weather."

"Ima's sick?" Barina asked, looking up at the dragon.

The dragon rolled her eyes. "She has a fractured wing. She knew better than to race the young dragons, but can't turn down a challenge. She hit her wing on the side of a boulder and..." Na'imah sighed while they continued through the valley.

Barina smirked. "How old were the younger ones, what like, one hundred and fifty years old or something?"

"If only. They were seventy-five."

Barina scoffed. "Teenagers. But did she win?"

Na'imah laughed. "She's still the fastest flier."

They walked on through the valley. Na'imah enjoyed talking about her home and about dragons in general. It was rare, especially for those not associated with magic, to learn this much. Even Onyx and Arkon were learning things that they had never known before.

They discovered that the younger dragons weren't shy about making jokes to anyone or showing off cool tricks they could do while breathing fire. The older dragons were more subdued, sitting quietly in their conversations, some reading and drawing on the ground, others looking to the sky in deep thought.

"Are you hungry?" Na'imah asked them at one point. "Do you need to rest at all?"

"Well..." Barina looked over her shoulder at the group. They did look a little worn. "I think that would be nice, yes. It's almost noon anyway. Thank you Na'imah."

The travelers slid off their horses and sat enjoying a nice lunch, making small talk with each other. Barina sat with their escort making quiet conversation while she ate a bar of sorts for her lunch. They couldn't take too long if they wanted to make good time so, after a half hour, they were packed and ready to go on their way.

As they walked, they noticed their thief slowing down. Jaras saw her eyes change focus and her head tilt back toward the entrance to the valley. Na'imah stopped too, hearing something in the distance.

The dragon's eyes were wide with worry for only a split second, then they went fierce, and she let out a roar that shook the ground.

"Twarence! Jaras! Come on. The rest of you catch up," Barina ordered. She dropped her backpack and left it, taking off in a sprint, backtracking from where they came.

Barina and Jaras ran next to Twarence on his horse. The others were going to have to ride quickly to catch up. Na'imah had taken to the skies, flying fast back to the entrance of the lair.

"What is it?" Twarence called.

"Danger," Barina told him. "I don't know what, but something got past Arana and into the lair." She jumped over a small creek, Jaras right next to her.

"What kinds of things would go after the dragons?" he asked.

"Human dragon hunters will try. Poachers. Wyrms sometimes but…" Her voice trailed when she saw what was happening ahead. "Giants? Why the hell would giants be here? It's not their style at all. They're peaceful, on good terms with dragons, unless…" She was thinking out loud, piecing things together. "We have to hurry."

They stopped when they heard a horrible cry. Two giants hurried away with two sacks full of a dozen dragon eggs. The giants stood about fifteen feet tall, all seasoned warriors. They rode on their large warhorses through the valley, avoiding any dragon that came after them, even maiming a few on their way.

Barina cried, "Like hell!" then looked at her companions. "Do you think you can handle flying?"

Twarence and Jaras nodded.

She looked back at Arkon who was quickly catching up. "Arkon, we'll need your help. Onyx, you stay with Aria and help her with the wounded. Get to the gates as soon as you can. Arana must be injured!" Barina looked to the sky. "Gromala do tam!"

A couple of young dragons landed near. "Need a lift?" one asked.

"Yup," she said. "Take us to the giants please." She turned to her friends. "Your horses will be okay, don't worry."

The men looked at her, astonished.

"Seriously, fly with a dragon?" Arkon asked. "Let's go."

Twarence and Barina mounted one of the dragons while Jaras and Arkon climbed onto the other. The young dragons started to fly quickly toward the danger.

"Had to be giants, didn't it?" Twarence grumbled to Barina. "Like you said, though, I thought that giants were on peaceful terms with the dragons of the world."

"Yes, they are. But I've been hearing rumors—and just rumors—of a giant in exile who has been trying to recruit an army. From what I understand, he wants to carve out a kingdom for himself."

"I've been hearing those rumors, too," Arkon called over to them, watching the commotion below. "Our generals have been keeping an eye on him, but up till now, he hasn't done anything. Why would he, or anyone, mess with the dragons? This just doesn't make any sense."

She shook her head. "If he's doing his own thing, then the alliance between giants and dragons won't matter. He'll go after any allies of his old home. That or, maybe he thinks he can raise a small army of dragons to work with him when they get older. I don't know. I don't care. All I know is, we have to get those eggs back where they belong or they'll die in the next few hours. If the giants got into the valley, Arana must be injured too."

They could hear the worry in her voice, but as soon as they closed in on the giants, her face went blank and her eyes darkened.

"Drop us just in front of the giants please," she told the young dragon as they descended. When they landed, the four slid to the ground.

Jaras looked to the two dragons. "The other woman we are with, Aria, she's a healer. She can help with your wounded."

The two nodded and flew off leaving the traveling party to join the battlefield of giants.

"Be careful," Jaras told them as he pulled his sword.

He and Arkon ran at the closest giants—a group of five who were carrying stolen dragon eggs. They had precious little time to return the eggs to the caves. Arkon jumped, soaring high off the ground, and delivered a powerful kick to the nearest giant, knocking him off his horse. The giant recovered quickly and jumped to his feet just in time to duck a swipe of Arkon's sword. The elf spun to block another giant who had jumped off his horse to help his companion.

The average height of one of these deadly warriors was thirteen to sixteen feet, and they were strong and fierce. Normally a peaceful race, the warrior class was no easy prey.

All elves have the ability to wield all of the elements, but Arkon's strength was as a Spirit Elf—manipulating the spirit. He could've literally stopped the giants in their tracks if they were anywhere else. But in the dragon lair, his powers were neutralized. He only had his physical strength to rely on at that moment, but he was fast and still very strong even without the use of his magic. His light blue eyes went almost white as he spun his blade over and under, slicing the kneecaps of one giant before running him through. The second was an excellent swordsman, clashing and paring with two blades. In minutes, Arkon had run this giant through as well.

Barina called to him. "Arkon! The eggs!" She was ready to fend off the other giants to give him time to run.

"I'm on it!" Arkon grabbed a bag and rushed back to the nests in the caves.

Jaras was taking on three giants at once. He struck down the first two without problem, but with the third, things got personal between them.

"Pretty good for a human," the giant snarled through his long black beard. "You and the other two humans you travel with."

"Giants are peaceful," Jaras said as he drove his sword toward his foe. "Why are you doing this?"

"Orders," he replied, his tone bitter.

"Bullshit! What's the real reason?"

"I have purpose again," the giant said. "I have a reason to fight. It's what I do." He swung again at Jaras. "Our commander, he is powerful. He will reward us with our own estates, and we will have our own kingdom someday."

Jaras packed enough strength in his strike that, even though he missed the giant, the impact that hit the ground knocked the giant to his knees.

"At what price?" Jaras asked. "And why dragons? Why the young? Giants are not ones to hurt others needlessly? That's why you've always been respected."

"Silence!" the giant snarled at him. "We have nothing else to fight for. You of all people should understand. A warrior must be given a purpose!" He slashed at Jaras's arm.

Jaras dodged, jumped, and drove his blade home into the giant's heart.

"But to hurt the innocent? Giants have always been protectors."

The giant's breath came short. "Casualties happen."

"The young? Dragons?" Jaras knelt over the dying behemoth. It wasn't like them to harm the innocent or to take what was not theirs.

"We were going to build an army, take back what was ours." He closed his eyes. "I'm not proud of it, but we wanted a home. That's all. I should've found another way, though. Something else. I didn't realize we'd be taking dragons till now. None of us did. But it was too late. Perhaps, if I had found a reason to fight again outside of Saran…" He shook his head, understanding his fate, and looked as if he remembered something.

The giant struggled to breathe, his sword falling out of his hand. He smiled at the human as he pulled a pendant from around his neck. It was a simple green stone wrapped in gold wire. He placed it into Jaras's hand. "I was given this by a giant I defeated and he, the one before him. I am to give it to the one who defeated me. Carry it. It's a sign of strength."

Jaras's face dropped, though he knew the outcome of this fight would have been the same.

The giant laughed. "Don't look at me like that. No pity. I knew this would happen someday. Take care and…" His eyes strained to look in the distance.

Jaras followed his gaze. There, they saw Barina and Twarence take down two giants apiece.

"Is that…her?" His eyes began to glaze over.

"It is her," the giant assured him. His body went limp, and he was gone.

Jaras said a silent prayer and stood looking in the direction of his traveling companions. He watched Barina, studying her carefully. She hadn't used more than two strokes of her dagger to take any giant down. Her eyes stayed intent and focused, hardly any emotion touched her face. She was smooth, knew exactly how to strike and where, and none of her enemies could get close to her. If he hadn't been trained to the level he was, he wouldn't have known how impressive this was. She made it look easy.

Just who the hell are you? he thought. And he knew he wouldn't have an easy time getting information out of her. For now, he had bigger things to worry about. They had to keep more giants from interfering with Arkon as the elf returned eggs to the caves.

Farther up the valley, Twarence had pulled a giant off his horse while impaling him on his sword. The scholar climbed on the large warhorse and went charging after three other giants who had a bag of eggs with them. He took down another giant without a second thought, but then found himself on the ground with a sharp pain in his arm.

One of three had thrown a long, thin wire with a three-pronged hook that stuck into the scholar's arm. It yanked him off the horse and painfully dragged him on the ground toward the three. Even grunting in pain, as soon as he was close enough, Twarence flung his axe into the legs of one of the attackers. The giant fell, and Twarence managed to regain his footing and use his sword to barely block the next attack. His arm still had the hook in it, and it hurt badly.

He felt weak, sure there was now poison in his arm, but it could've been a simple loss of blood. Either way, he didn't have much time before he would need help, and he didn't fancy a dirt nap anytime soon.

Twarence hadn't seen that the last giant he fought was not the only giant standing. The one who held the bag of eggs had run away, but there were seven more to replaced him as they fought the scholar. Twarence held his arm, trying to refocus, but his vision was getting blurry.

The giants laughed as they towered in front of him. Twarence stood his ground even though he knew how this was going to go down. But damn it if he wasn't going to take a couple with him.

He propped himself up against a large boulder, preparing for one last fight. He coughed and felt the sweat dripping down his forehead as chills ran through his body.

"Stupid humans," one of them laughed. "Weak and u…"

In a single heartbeat, Twarence had been pulled back, and Barina pulled the giant's head down by the beard. She buried her dagger into the soft tissue under his chin until the point came out just under the base of his skull. She pulled the dagger from his head and, with the other hand, physically pinned him to the ground.

Her eyes were unlike anything Twarence had ever seen. They were so cold, so fierce. No emotion touched her face. She glanced at Twarence and the hook in his arm. Pulling it out, she started checking the dead giant's pockets. The other giants began to advance until she looked up with those fierce eyes. She found what she wanted—a small vial which she handed to Twarence.

"Drink this or you'll be dead," she said, her voice kind and friendly.

With her back turned, the giants started to lunge at them. She didn't blink as she turned and, in one swipe, gutted the two closest to her. Then she sliced the necks of the next two. She threw her dagger at the fifth and, with the sixth, jumped high and broke his neck with her bare hands. The seventh…Barina gave him a glare so unnerving that he shook. Retrieving her dagger, she walked up to him and flipped the blade in her hand a couple times.

Barina's voice was low and menacing. "Lord Nortel and Lady Marita wouldn't be happy about this."

The giant gasped, completely surprised. Sweat began to bead on the giant's face that had gone pale white. "You…" he began, and then turned tail, jumping on the nearest warhorse to run after his fellow giants.

Twarence could hear the giant yelling—*RUN! RUN!*—as loud as he could.

Barina watched until she knew he wasn't coming back, then turned to Twarence who still hadn't swallowed what was in the vial. "Seriously, drink that," she said.

He fell face first onto the ground, trying to prop himself up.

She turned him to his back and pulled the stopper off the vial with her teeth. Worried she wouldn't get the antidote to him in time, she pressed her fingers to his cheeks to open his mouth. "Twarence," she said firmly, putting an arm around his back and tipping his head back.

He felt the wooden vial touch his teeth and liquid slowly pour into his mouth. He swallowed, noting the horrible taste. The antidote worked almost instantly. Twarence's breathing went back to normal, and he could see straight again.

"Wow, that's some good stuff." He smiled up at her.

She nodded. "You'll be okay," she said, relief in her voice. She set her gaze in the direction that the giant had run. "Jaras will be here in a moment. I have to run." She disappeared into the large forest of grass.

Jaras arrived within a minute. Onyx and Aria were close behind on his horse, and Arkon was still caring for the eggs he had recovered.

"Twarence!" Aria jumped off her horse, and her hands were on his arm in a second. Moving fast, her hands glowed green and, within seconds, his injury was gone. It was as if he had never been hurt in the first place.

"Where's Barina?" Onyx asked, looking up.

Twarence stood and pointed forward. "After she whooped up on these guys," he said, indicating the dead giants around them, "she headed that way."

Arkon rode up. "Those eggs I had are safe," he said, out of breath. He took a moment to let the relief wash over him. "Which way did the rest of them go?"

Onyx looked at the others before he took off to find their thief and the rest of the eggs. Jaras and Twarence climbed onto the warhorse again, while Aria and Arkon followed only steps behind Onyx.

"There is more to her than we know," Jaras said to Twarence. "A lot more. She knows giants. Like really *knows them*."

"I know," Twarence said. "She spoke of Lord Nortel and Lady Marita."

"Who?" Jaras asked.

"Rulers in the Valley of Giants. They rule all giants everywhere." Twarence took a moment to clear his mind. "She told the last giant standing that the lord and lady wouldn't be happy if they knew of this. The giant seemed to realize who Barina was. Either way, he ran, screaming for the other giants to follow. She is a scary fighter. I wouldn't want to fight her if she looked at me like she did them."

Jaras grinned. "I'll have to see this."

Suddenly, two giants jumped from the tall grass, ready to pounce on Onyx. He pulled his staff into two pieces—each half concealing a spear—and pierced the hearts of both giants. He flung the blood off the spears and put the staff back together.

"That was pretty impressive," Twarence said. "Apparently the wizard has a couple tricks up his sleeve too."

They rode as fast as they could until they came to the rocky passage that would take them to the entrance of the lair. Every dragon in the passage—nine including Na'imah and her daughter—were injured and unable to move. Their wings had been pierced and their backs broken. All they could do was lie on the ground and watch in horror at what was happening. They cried in pain and for the lives of their young.

A small army of giants, around thirty, carried the eggs and the baby dragons who were trying to escape. One giant stood taller than all the others. He wore armor that was leafed in gold and a battle helmet that was the same with horns that curled above his head coming off of both sides. He carried a massive sword over his shoulder and a spiked club. He was waving to his men to follow him casually as they had what they came for.

One giant hurried to the crowd, jumped off his horse and ran. "Saran!" he called. "Saran!" He was practically screaming as he rushed through.

The leader turned and looked, angered to see one of his men yelling as if he were scared.

"She's here! She's here!" The giant's face was pale and scared.

Saran and the other giants looked up, confused.

"Who?" Saran asked.

The frightened giant fell dead, as did the five who had been next to him in the crowd. No one could see what had killed them. Another four fell dead.

As the traveling party moved into a small clearing, what they saw next left them speechless. The humans and the elf tended to the wounded dragons, ready to jump in and help if Barina gave the word. But from what they could see, she had this situation under control.

She would appear only for a moment—blade flashing as it would be embedded into an enemy—and then she would disappear. Any giant that had a young dragon would find his arms missing the second before he died. She would take the young ones to Na'imah. She moved so fast, hardly anyone saw her until there were only twelve giants left.

Barina ran right through the crowd of giants, dodging and shifting out of their way. She ran till she found the giant with the sack of eggs. She didn't bother killing him, but grabbed the eggs from his hands and disappeared again before the giant realized what had happened.

"She has the eggs!" he yelled.

The invaders parted, circling Barina. Only the leader, Saran, and two others—who seemed to be his second in command—stood apart from them. They sat on their horses to watch this woman, curious as to who she was.

Barina stood still, holding the precious cargo in her arms, her eyes still very fierce.

"Do you think you can run from us?" Saran called to her.

Barina knelt down for a moment, setting the bag on the ground. She took off her cloak, placing it on top of the eggs. When she looked over her shoulder, her tone was neutral. "Yes."

She sheathed her dagger as her fingers took hold of two heavy chains on the ground—weapons belonging to two of the dead giants. She wrapped them around her hands several times. One chain had a large metal ball on the end, the other a half moon blade. The length of each was about forty feet. She stood up, her eyes dark as she stared at Saran, the ends of the chains dangling just an inch off the ground.

"Whoa, that's one hell of a battle aura!" Jaras breathed through his teeth.

Saran and his companions laughed. The half-moon blade was about three feet long, and the metal weight was close to forty pounds. "Those are made for creatures of our caliber. Do you really think you can play with the big boys?"

The other giants' laughter was quickly silenced. They hadn't see her move as the blade met the neck of the giant on Saran's left, and the metal ball smashed in the face of the one on his right. Both giants fell from their horses, dead. Saran couldn't speak. The remaining giants in the circle froze.

Barina yanked the chains back, wrapping the links around her hands again as they flew in the air. Then she whirled the chains, one forward, one backward, on either of her sides.

"Yes, I do." Her voice was ice.

Arkon grumbled, "Apparently they didn't notice all their dead friends."

Saran could barely whisper, "Kill…," then shouted, "Kill her!"

Two attacked—one from behind, the other from the front. They made it about three steps before the chains launched out of her hands. She let them go completely—the half-moon blade taking down the one in front of her, the metal ball missing the one behind her. She pulled her dagger and held it above her head as the giant lowered his sword to her.

"You would never guess these guys were almost ten feet taller than her," Aria said as her powers focused on healing Na'imah. "I mean, wow. She's remarkable."

Barina held her attacker's sword at bay with her left hand. She slid down to guide his blade to the ground and sent a blow from her right arm to his side before landing a kick and slicing his neck open at the same time.

He fell to the ground. Barina flicked the blood off her dagger as she put it back in the sheath. The other giants didn't move.

"Who are you?" Saran's voice was shaky.

She looked up as she put her cloak back on, triggering recognition in the giants. Saran and his soldiers went pale. "You have ten seconds to leave, or I'll kill you," she hissed at them.

Saran and his foot soldiers ran from the lair as fast as they could.

Barina kept her stance until they were out of sight, her eyes still searching while they ran.

Aria quickly worked to heal the dragons whose injuries were horrible. It just took a tremendous amount of time and energy. The second that her hands touched a dragon, not only did her hands glow a deep dark green, but the dragon would too. When she finished, she was exhausted.

Jaras and Arkon each placed an arm around her to help her to her horse. Twarence rode with her as she leaned against him until she had her strength back.

While the others were distracted, Barina nodded for Onyx to come with her and headed back to the nesting grounds to return the eggs.

"You know they're going to have questions about all of this, right?" Onyx said, sharing his horse.

Barina nodded and then smirked at the wizard. "You're not asking them?"

"Nope."

"Were you planning on telling anyone that your wizard's staff was more than that? Or that you can fight hand to hand combat?"

Onyx was surprised that she knew. She hadn't seen him unsheathe his staff earlier. "No, but I had a feeling you would've figured it out anyway. And I can't do much as far as fighting without magic, but enough to save my skin. I don't find it necessary to tell all that there is about me, much like you and your trades."

She nodded and adjusted her cloak. "Thank you for understanding."

"Thank you for the same thing." He smiled.

Barina and Onyx hurried through to the nesting grounds and took the eggs back to the coals. They knew the proper procedures for resting the eggs.

A huge dragon with copper scales and sapphire blue eyes approached when he saw then near the nests.

"Don't worry," Barina assure him. "They're still warm." She opened the bag of eggs, using her cloak to touch them. Inside, the eggs were still too hot to touch with her bare hands.

The dragon started to bare his fangs to her.

"Ta coo Barina Raine o Miork. Ta coo mota no Usami shem Yamona," she said calmly, still working with the eggs.

He blinked. "Che do?" The dragon looked to the wizard.

Onyx stood his ground and looked up. "Onyx o Hitum Mountain. Su mota."

The dragon nodded his head. "Any other humans, and I would've killed you already."

"We know," Onyx said. "Na'imah and the others are being treated for their injuries, but we had to get the eggs back. I'm guessing Arkon brought the other batch of eggs to you. What's your name?"

"Lynxs, and yes, the young Spirit Elf returned the other eggs."

The wizard and the dragon watched as Barina worked carefully to set each egg at an exact thirty-five degree angle on the coals before Lynxs blew a warm fire over them. When all were where they needed to be, she gave a sigh of relief and smiled.

The humans quietly left the cave and sat down to wait for the rest of their group. They saw Na'imah walking and figured their companions were with her, but it was impossible to see them in the forest of grass.

Barina puffed on her pipe and dug an apple out of her pack, cutting it in half to share with Onyx. He grabbed a canteen to share the water between the two of them. They waited in a comfortable silence, a calm and a peace that these two could appreciate between them.

The others came into view—Jaras at the front with Twarence just behind him. Arkon was guiding Aria on her horse and keeping close watch on her till her strength came back. They were still out of earshot for the moment.

"Those two and their questions," Barina groaned quietly to Onyx. "It's just a matter of before they ask," Barina groaned quietly to Onyx.

He glanced up and saw Twarence and Jaras staring at Barina as they came through the thick grass. "Jaras on your fighting, and Twarence will grill you about how you know of the leaders of giants."

"I don't just know of, I know them, personally. We're friends."

"I figured as much."

"I had a feeling you figured." Her eyes twinkled.

"I am a wizard. Are you surprised?" he asked, chuckling and nudging her arm.

"No. Are you surprised with me?"

He thought about it for a second. "No, I'm not. You knew who my teacher was. That means you know more than you let on. I figure that, when and if you want to talk, you will."

"Wow, a rational wizard. Few and far between." She was laughing to herself.

Onyx rolled his eyes. "You're hilarious. Who all do you know in my world? Which orders?"

"Tell you a big secret? You promise not to tell the others unless it's necessary?" She was debating telling him.

He nodded.

"Including you. I've now met the leaders of each order except for that of the Bask."

"Seriously?"

"Yeah, and geez, just last year. Salt needed me to sneek into the Shrine of Silence to find some artifacts for him. Safest place to keep something from other wizards is a place where wizards can't go," she whispered, seeing that the others were getting closer.

"That's impressive," he said, still looking forward. "How did you know that I'm the leader of my order?"

"Because Rutherford only taught you, you are the only member of your order. He had a cousin who was in the order with him, but Jamel was killed three years ago."

"Done your homework really well or did..." Onyx began, wanting to know how much more she knew.

She interrupted. "Maybe later."

Onyx found this new friend interesting. She knew her stuff in the world of magic, and that was somewhat comforting to him. She also knew how to keep her head down and keep matters of wizards close. He was pretty sure that what they had just discussed wouldn't be told to another living soul unless she found it necessary.

"Hey guys." Barina yawned as the others came out of the clearing. "Aria, you did great. Thank you guys for helping." She stood up and looked to Na'imah. "Are you going to be okay? How is your daughter?"

Na'imah had a gleam in her orange eyes. "Arana is fine thanks to you and your friends. I can never repay you for what you have done today. You have all saved an entire generation of my race. Thank you so much."

"We were happy to do it," Twarence told her.

"If you will follow me," she said, "I will lead you to the other side of the lair. Aria dear, do you need to rest for a while?"

Aria shook her head, even though her eyes were drooping. "I'll be fine, thank you."

"Follow me then."

"Na'imah, may I speak with you in private?" Barina asked, her eyes looking to the others.

Na'imah extended one large hand for the human to step into, then lifted her onto her shoulder while they walked on ahead.

"Are you guys really okay?" Onyx asked as he grabbed some cheese out of his bag. "Aria, eat this, it'll help."

She gratefully took the food. "Thanks."

"We're okay, thanks," Jaras said while glancing at the thief. "Did she say anything to you about her fighting while you waited for us?"

"Or her relations to the giants?" Twarence added, exchanging the warhorse for his own.

"No, we just helped the dragons, then talked about my work," he replied while stretching and patting his horse on the neck. He was going to respect the thief and the information she kept to herself.

"I'm just glad we were able to help." Arkon considered contacting the head of his clan. "This is so weird. Why would giants be going after dragons? It makes no sense. And what was the name of that giant, Saran?"

The others nodded.

Arkon rubbed his chin, very deep in thought. "I really don't like this at all. Giants—most of them anyway—are very peaceful."

Twarence agreed. "It's something to be concerned about. The generals. You'll have to speak to the generals and then to the king himself, right?"

The elf nodded again. "Only if the generals think it's worthy of the king knowing, but someone in the court will know. Done your research on elves, haven't you?"

"Study everything. It's an interesting culture. I don't know the name of the king, hell not many do, but there are so many clans." Twarence had pulled out the map and was studying where they were headed next. He then looked out of the corner of his eye. "You're awfully quiet Jaras."

"Just thinking," Jaras said, his hand on the hilt of his sword. "Something about her fighting, something is familiar. But at the same time, I've never seen anything like that before in my life. I mean, those stances...it's...I haven't seen it before. At least I don't think I have. I'll wait till we get out of here to talk to her about it, but this is gonna bug me."

CHAPTER 4

With her arms and legs crossed, Barina sat casually on Na'imah's shoulder as they spoke privately. They came to the other end of the dragon lair where another dragon, just as young as Arana but with dark blue scales, waited for them.

"Here you are my friends," Na'imah said. "Good luck in your journey." She turned to Barina and waved her claw. A tiny flute appeared smaller than Barina's hand. "Barina, I have a gift for you. Take this flute. Play a tune, any tune on it, and I will come when called."

Barina looked surprised and very humbled. "Are you sure? You can only give this gift to one being."

Na'imah's face went soft. "Because of you and your friends, we are safe. My daughter lives, and our babies have a chance. Even I can tell that this is a group you will be near to for a long time. So, if they need me too, they can reach me through you. Take it, Barina."

The thief gave a low bow and put the flute in her side pouch. "Thank you, thank you so much."

Na'imah returned the bow to Barina and her friends. "Thank you. Safe travels."

"Valata," Barina said, smiling at her.

"Valata." Na'imah and the young dragon beside her watched the travelers walk away.

Once they were about a mile from the lair, Aria finally showed signs of regaining her strength. She glanced at Jaras. "What's that around your neck?" she asked, noticing the pendant.

Jaras touched the pendant and then looked briefly at Barina. The light in her eyes gave away her surprise, and she was a little impressed.

"One of the giants I defeated gave it to me. Said it was handed down from warrior to warrior." His smile was bittersweet.

"I've heard of stones like the one you wear," Twarence said. "You are lucky. Any gift from a giant is very special—a lot more than it seems. They hold special abilities, but it only works if it was a gift." He leaned over to take a closer look. "Can't remember what that type of gift is called. Begins with an H, I think. Halu…Hala…" Twarence was scratching his brain.

"Haluex," Barina chimed in while she checked her pocket watch and looked up. "You must've impressed the hell out of him."

Just as curious as everyone but the wizard, Arkon asked, "How did you know? How do you know so much about giants and about their gifts?"

"I make it my business," Barina said. Nobody but the wizard saw her hand glide against her cloak. "But those that know anything about giants know that any gift from them is going to do more than just simply lie around your neck or in your pocket. That there, buddy, is a special stone. It will give you more speed, strength, and endurance than you would have normally when you need it the most."

"And how, by the way, do you know Lord Nortel and Lady Marita in the Valley of Giants?" Twarence asked.

She shrugged. "We're friends."

Jaras wanted to pry further. "That was some pretty impressive fighting back there, too, young lady. I tried to pick up those chains after you finished off those giants. I had to use both arms just to swing one. How are you able to do things like that, so smoothly and fast?"

"It's going to be a nice night I think," Barina said, changing the subject completely. "Probably won't even need to pitch the tents when we decide to camp."

Jaras snorted. "I'll let you win this one, but I'm not done prying."

Barina rolled her eyes, but she was still smiling. "Thanks. Oh man, we lost a lot of daylight back there, but it was worth it. We should still be able to cover some decent ground before we have to call it a night."

Twarence was writing things down in his journal while smoking a cigarette. "So, what routes did you normally take to get through the mountains? I know you said you had been here before but not through this lair."

Barina lit her pipe. "I would take the old paths before they had been destroyed, or the mountain gnomes normally let me pass through here.

I've done them some favors, so they let me through most of the time. But since I have newbies with me, I'm pretty sure it wouldn't have worked."

"Friends with gnomes, too?" Arkon asked with a little grin.

She shrugged her shoulders. "Yes, I am, and they have really good wine."

That first night, everyone slept like a log except for their thief. She was asleep after them and awake before them. They would've taken shifts their first few evenings, to keep watch, but Barina assured them that they were in no danger on this route for now.

Though they had only been in the mountains for three days, they could see the change in terrain as they ascended the summit path. There was not much vegetation, but little flowers and green grasses lined the path as birds chirped nearby. A barren tree marked the change in the path. Beyond that, there was nothing—no trees, no flowers. Nothing. It was like a clear thick curtain separated them from where they stood now.

"Stop here," Barina said while she took down the extra packs she had set on Twarence and Onyx's horses. She started to remove furs. Lots of them.

"Jaras get rid of that chain mail. You don't want to be wearing that once we start on this trail. The second we get past that tree, it'll suck all the warmth out of your body." She was taking off her own necklace and piercing. "All of you, any metal on your body, get rid of it."

"What if I have to fight?" Jaras asked, looking appalled at the idea of removing his chain mail.

"We have a healer with us. Put the chain mail in the pack," Barina said. "I'm not exaggerating when I say we're about to go to one of the coldest places I know of. Everyone off your horses. I have to put these blankets on them too. You ride bareback till we're over of the summit. No bits, nothing. Anything metal will freeze to them and can kill them. Thank goodness that their horseshoes aren't affected by the cold." [Wondering why the cold won't affect the horseshoes, and do we even need to mention that they are wearing them?]

"But I never tried to control a horse without…" Aria began.

"Arkon?" was all Barina said.

He understood and started to walk to each beast. With his eyes closed, he held his hand just above the horses' eyes. The others could see his lips moving but heard no words.

Barina handed pants made of fur to the men and a set for Aria. "Put them on under your dress," she told her. Then she gave the men fleece undershirts and long-sleeved fur tunics. Aria had to layer a fur top over her dress.

"I hate wearing fur," she sighed. "Those poor animals that had to die."

"Yes, I'm not much of a fan either," Barina agreed, "but don't neglect the leather shoes you're wearing. An animal died for those too. The man I got these furs from is very good about using every part of the animal. He doesn't just take them for their skins. Plus, these are the warmest things that will get us there. We'll need them."

She handed everyone hats and thick wool gloves, and tied furs around their boots. Arkon fixed himself up when he finished with the horses. Barina then tied large fur blankets around the horses' bodies, and loosely tied furs to their legs and tight around their heads.

She removed her belt and dagger to fix a pair of fur pants over her own before she put her belt and dagger back on. She layered a fur vest over a long-sleeved fur shirt. Her cloak was curious. There were slits at the shoulders which she unbuttoned from the inside. Large arm-covering drapes unfurled, and she buttoned up the front of her cloak. Once she put on a fur hat, she nodded for the others to get back on their horses.

"You guys ready?" she asked, and motioned them to follow.

The moment they passed the dead tree, they understood why she had them dress the way they did. The wind howled something fierce, and it was freezing. Never had any of them felt a cold like this. The wind almost knocked them off their horses. They ate when they felt the need and refilled their water bottles when they could. At night, Barina had them camp by the wall of the mountain, hanging up several oiled wool blankets to keep the wind out so they could sleep.

After four days of traveling on the cold mountain pass, they were as close to the summit as they would get. A handful of miles from the top of the mountain chain, the weather had reached its worst.

The snow was deep—up to Jaras' knees—and freezing rain and driving snow pounding the group. There was no shelter anywhere near them. The exposed parts of their faces were red, chapped and hurting, and they didn't know how much more they could take. Arkon used his powers to keep the horses warm. The cold would've been too much for them otherwise. Aria had to use her powers twice a day on everyone but their thief to fend off frostbite. The rugged and white terrain seemed unbearable by their fourth day on the path. They hoped that Barina was taking them on this road in their best interest and not to get them killed.

"This road sucks!" Aria shouted over the loud winds.

"You've mentioned that a few times," Onyx grumbled, shaking the ice from his staff.

"Isn't there a better road we can take?" Aria then yelled.

Barina, at the front of the group, looked over her shoulder. "No!"

"Damn it!" Arkon growled. "I'm freezing my ass off, this is…"

"This is the safest way! The warmer the climate on the mountains, the bigger and stronger the creatures get." Barina had taken her hood off briefly to tuck her hair back under her hat before putting it back on. "Don't worry. We should reach the steam caves by nightfall. We'll be able to stay warm there and regroup."

"We never made you our leader," Arkon stated.

Barina tilted her head, confused for a moment. "I never said I was."

Twarence looked at Arkon. "But she's right, this is a safer way than the one that was originally mapped out. She knows the beings on the lower parts of the mountains, and doesn't want to fight them if she doesn't have to."

"Thief, if you can fight them, then why are we here?" Arkon was very unhappy.

"Unnecessary battles."

"But we wouldn't be near hypothermia," he spat. "We'd be warmer, right?"

Barina glared at Arkon. "With all the fires of hell that the creatures would use if they thought you were a threat, yes, it would be warmer. I am a friend to many here, but for some, I'm only able to travel through their turf without confrontation. I don't know how they would be to newcomers, and if they thought you were to bring them harm, they would follow you with teeth bared and claws aimed at your neck till you were gone. I don't wish you any harm, but I don't want to fight if I don't have to, so I will guide you as best I can."

Onyx decided to intervene and ask Barina questions about her trade. "How have you become friends with so many beings?" When it came to the magic of giants and dragons, it was part of his trade too.

"I've never given them a reason to see me as a threat, and I've helped them a lot. Some see me as barely a friend or just something to ignore as I pass through. Many of them don't trust humans at all."

"So, we have to freeze to death since you don't want to fight," Aria grumbled.

"Oh, stop your whining!" Barina scoffed. "Do *you* want to fight these guys? No, probably not, so shut it and keep going." She lingered at the back of the group. "Freaking crybabies can't handle a little cold. 'Why won't you fight them?' It's only our lives and those of the creatures I'd face. I'm not going to kill beings who are simply trying to live their lives like everyone else and are *defending* their homes. They don't trust humans, and they have plenty of reasons not to. They barely trust me, and I know that I'd have to fight them to convince them to let all of you by. It is not worth possibly hurting or killing one of them because you are fucking *cold*." Her grumbles became less audible.

"I can't feel my legs!" Twarence cried with a laugh. He had apparently had enough of the previous discussion.

Onyx chuckled. "Really," he sighed.

Twarence was still laughing. "Couldn't help myself."

Onyx rolled his eyes and shot a small burst of energy at Twarence. Not enough to hurt him, only to push him. The scholar turned around and shot a playful glare at the wizard.

"Wasn't me," Onyx said and started laughing with him. The two had definitely changed the mood for the better.

Jaras though, felt something was close by, something dangerous. He looked around and saw paw prints—huge cat prints—lining the snow-covered ground. He looked back at Barina who had already drawn her dagger. Jaras walked to the back of the group next to her.

"What kind of things do we have to worry about up here?" The snow was blowing so hard, he could barely see to the front of their group.

"At this altitude, well, I call them snow cats. They're pure white with bright blue eyes, big teeth, and large claws. They travel in packs, are very fast, strong and hard as hell to fight. Look almost like a mountain lion, but they're all white and much bigger—as high as my shoulders on all fours—and are about twelve feet long. Much more dangerous." Her voice had gone quiet.

"Wow."

"I can't blame these guys for being so vicious," she explained. "At this altitude, food is hard to come by. They can go for a month without a meal, so they feed when they can."

"How will we see them? Are they pretty easy to pick out?" Jaras started looking around.

"Nope. The blues of their eyes stand out brilliantly, but the rest of them blend in perfectly with all this snow. And in a blizzard, it's going to be tricky. They always attack from behind, trying to pick off those who walk farthest away." Wanting a full range of motion, she pulled the hood of her cloak away from her head. "Don't worry Jaras, I've got your back." Barina walked even slower and said, "When they show, act quick, stay low. I know I can fight them and so can you but…" She looked to the others.

"Not even Onyx and Arkon?"

She shook her head, rolling her eyes at their luck. "Funny thing about the mountains is that so many beings here have an immunity to magic. The magic men are out. Elves can't even pick them up with their sight, Twarence and Aria, no."

Jaras understood what she was getting at, so he ran to Twarence at the front of the group.

"Twarence, stay close to the others, and when we tell you to run, you run. There are some creatures that we're most likely going to have to fight off soon."

"Snow cats? Barina told me about them." Twarence rubbed his fingers along his beard. "But we can't leave you."

"My job is to protect you, and that's what I'm going to do, so when it comes to your safety, you listen. She said that Onyx and Arkon are out. These things are immune to magic. You need to get the others to the steam caves. You're the only other one besides her who knows how to get to Thoron. If we tell you to ride, you ride. Keep the others close to you," Jaras ordered and went to rejoin Barina at the back of the group.

Twarence did as he was told. None of the group liked the idea of leaving Jaras and Barina behind—not because they wanted their fighters with them, but they didn't want their friends hurt or killed.

Jaras had known he was taking a risk when he accepted this job. So did Barina, but she wasn't to be the lead fighter. Still, Jaras knew she wasn't about to leave him alone with these things lurking around. She was to fight if needed, and she was needed.

The others stayed on their guard, moving ahead, while Jaras and Barina kept an eye on the footprints. As the two walked, they let themselves fall farther and farther behind until they stopped altogether, noticing that the tracks had also stopped.

"They're here," Barina whispered, keeping her face forward, her breath condensing in the cold air. "At the bottom of the walls on either side of us."

Jaras looked toward the mountain walls. Sure enough, he saw, only barely, a set of brilliant blue dots pinned on them. Soon, he could see almost a dozen pairs of eyes.

He glanced at Barina. She was still looking directly in front of them, not at them. But her dagger was level with the closest set, ready to lunge if needed. Jaras could almost see her ears working to hear the cats and her nose sniffing the air for their scent. She didn't see them, but she knew where to look. *Not many warriors I know can do that,* he thought. *Sense them before you see them. What kind of warrior have you trained to be?*

Jaras had been waiting for something like this, any kind of action that would highlight her abilities. He wanted to see what she was capable of. When she fought against the giants, he hadn't been next to her. These fine-tuned senses—there were only a handful of people in the world he knew who had those abilities. He realized that he was probably, right now, about to fight alongside someone very special in their trade.

"I can see their eyes," he whispered.

"Don't look directly at them, and stay right next to me." She took hold of his arm. "If we can avoid a fight, we should try. I really hate to hurt creatures that are just going on instinct. They're not evil men or beings that live for the purpose of killing. But I will fight to stay alive."

They walked slowly, barely able to see the last of the horses now. They weren't walking long when Barina let out a little groan. "Damn it."

Jaras was suddenly yanked to the ground as Barina stepped over him and thrust her dagger forward. She felt the metal find resistance as it dug into tissue. She then punched a flash of yellow bone—claws reaching for her. The momentum pushed the paw away and to the ground. She put her weight into the beast as it let out a loud roar, her shoulder pressed into the chest of the cat as she laid him on the ground and stabbed at his neck.

Jaras didn't miss a beat. He looked to his right, and his sword instantly came out of its sheath. Using the blue eyes as a guide, he made an arched motion that cut right into the neck of the creature.

The rest of the group turned, horrified, when they heard the loud thunderous roar of a lion behind them. They could see, barely through the blizzard, Jaras and Barina engaging something, but they weren't sure what. Not even Arkon—the being of nature—could see what they were fighting. The only thing they could see was the ground turning scarlet.

Barina fell to the ground, pushed by something. Once on her feet again, she turned and stabbed forward. Unable to see the beast, she still knew right where to attack with her weapon—jabbing her dagger into its heart. She still received a small bite on her arm, but not enough to keep her down. She pushed the cat off and was going after another one.

"Twarence, go!" Jaras shouted to them.

Twarence didn't move. He couldn't, not when every fiber in his being said help. It didn't feel right leaving them behind, even though he knew he should.

Something in Arkon snapped. "I...I can't. I'm not leaving them!" He jumped off his horse and headed for the two fighters who were battling it out with something he couldn't see. But he had to fight if he could.

Barina side tackled Arkon and shoved him to the ground. He saw something take a nick out of her arm, but couldn't see what. It wasn't until he saw the blue eyes and then the pale pink and black on the inside of its mouth as it let out a snarl that he knew what they were fighting. Before he could respond, Barina's dagger sliced into its neck and it fell.

"Go back to the group!" Barina snapped.

He met her eyes. "No, I'm going to fight!" He didn't see her roll a fist.

"Sorry!" She sent a punch to Arkon's gut powerful enough to immobilize him. "But I don't have time to save your ass." She picked him up with both arms and threw him back toward the group.

"Twarence, get him and get the hell out of here!" Barina rushed back to Jaras who had just taken down two more.

Twarence and Onyx dragged a nearly unconscious Arkon back to his horse, but they were taking too long.

"Son of a bitch!" Jaras grumbled.

"Snowball fight?" Barina packed a snowball and hurled it at the nearest horse, which startled it and sent it running. She then turned back to the cats, pulling Jaras away from another that was ready to slice him.

Jaras turned and threw another snowball while Barina worked with the cats. The horses took off running. Between the growls and roars and being pelted, they weren't stopping for anything, not until they felt they were far from danger.

Aria looked back one last time as Jaras fell to the ground. She felt the tears well up in her brown eyes. Barina and Jaras were losing the battle, and she wanted to be there. She wanted to heal them, but she knew that if she got anywhere near the fight taking place, she wouldn't last a minute. No matter, the horses wouldn't stop. They ran through the cold mountains till night covered the snowscape and they reached the mouth of a large cave.

They led the horses inside and couldn't help but let out a sigh of relief. For the first time in days, they felt warmth, but they wouldn't rest until they knew the fate of the other two.

In the blizzard, Barina and Jaras kept fighting back to back. They made a good team, but it was five minutes after the others had gone before they could truly let their guard down and assess their situation at hand.

Jaras glanced at a gash on his leg. "Oh that is going to sting in the morning," he said. "You okay, B?"

She put her dagger back into its sheath and pulled her hood back over her head. "I'm okay. A little stiff, but good. You?" She then looked at his leg. "Oye, that's going to be nasty till it heals. Come on, we should be able to make it to the steam caves in the next hour or so."

"Mmmm, a warm place to sleep tonight," he said, pulling the furs tighter.

"I know. I'm excited about hitting up one of the springs to soak in. It'll be nice." She leaned over and picked up one of the dead snow cats. It was bigger than Barina, and she had to wrap its front paws around her shoulders, its head hanging limp. "You poor beasts," she said, sadness in her eyes. "I wish it wouldn't have come to this. Hopefully your deaths will feed others of your kind. Speaking of which…" She held an uneasy smile.

Jaras raised an eyebrow. He was learning that every one of her smiles meant something slightly different.

"Dinner," was the only word she uttered.

***

The steam caves were dark but warm. Onyx created enough light to illuminate the cavern. The springs of the steam caves were back far enough that the moisture didn't affect them. The group stayed dry and comfortable.

They built a fire with the wood they had brought along for the trip. There was also an ample supply in the caves themselves. It seemed that it was custom for those traveling through to bring a small stock to leave if someone else needed it.

The group was upset. None of them knew what to do about those they had been forced to leave behind. But what could they have done to help?

"I wonder if they'll make it," Onyx said, throwing a couple of twigs into the fire. He kept his head down.

"We'll wait till morning," Twarence replied. "If they don't show, then we keep going. It's what we have to do." He hoped they were alive, but he wasn't sure how well he would do as the one to guide this group to safety. He was also worried because Barina had become his friend.

He was worried about Jaras, too. They had spent a lot of time in the evenings playing chess and talking about the world. Jaras had studied with the best in the world of fighting and would explain to Twarence aspects of the warriors he didn't already know.

Twarence smoked a cigarette, thinking on what he would do if they didn't make it. It was a lot to take in. But he also had spoken at length with the thief about the best routes to take, and she had given him the names of her contacts in the towns and cities along the way.

Aria sat quietly with her thoughts, her eyes looking over at Arkon. He seemed to be more bothered than the others about something. "What's wrong?" she asked, breaking the silence. "I know you're worried, but what else is it?"

"She saved my life," he finally said in a quiet whisper. "I haven't been exactly the nicest guy and still, she saved my life."

Aria smiled to herself. She could see he had gone from being completely unsure about the thief to having a crush on the girl. He was worried about the woman he was smitten for.

"She did what any of us would've done," Aria said kindly.

"No, I wouldn't have done that for her. I don't think. Not until now. She knew that too, I'm sure, but she saved me anyway. Saved me from, well, whatever it was." Those last three words were bitter for him. He hadn't seen what was there, and he should have been able—before anyone—to see beings of nature.

Onyx started laughing. "I just want to know how she managed to pick you up and throw you."

"If she had punched you, man…" Arkon said, smiling. "The girl has a nasty right hook, and I don't think she hit me as hard as she could." His face turned red.

They talked for a while, making light conversation while they rested. But after some time, they went silent and sat with their own thoughts. They were deeply worried about their friends, and also a little paranoid. There were things out there that could hurt them—things that they couldn't see. They hoped that whatever their fighters were up against didn't come after them in the caves.

After a while, the silence unnerved them. Every sound from outside—the wind, the snow, the ice, every breath—gave them reason to worry.

Aria kept herself busy by poking at the fire while reading a book. Not knowing if Jaras and Barina were alive, not knowing what might come to attack them, was getting to her. She was also thinking about how there was something extremely familiar about Barina. Aria was sure she had met her when they were young and, perhaps, helped heal some her wounds. Aria remembered a man, a large warrior—the best fighter in the land was what she was told by her aunt later—bringing an unconscious girl in his arms to her Aunt Lily to be healed. The little girl's father, along with another warrior, her sister, and her two friends, were also there. The unconscious girl was suffering from hypothermia and had a broken leg and arm. The girl had jumped into a frozen river to save her sister. Aria healed the leg. She remembered speaking to the boys, but never spoke to the girl since she was asleep.

Twarence spent his time trying to count how often in a half hour the geyser in the back of the cave would give off steam. It was something to distract him, but he always lost count. He was tired, both mentally and physically, after a week on the road, and this journey was already taking a toll on him. What really got to him were all the places that they were going and the creatures they would encounter that they knew nothing about. He was called on because of his knowledge, but there were a lot of things in these mountains where his knowledge fell short. At times, he wondered why he was even here, but he was the only one who knew the true powers behind the stone. That brought his mind to something else.

Growing up, he lived in the capital city of Larindana, in Fern. Most of his days, since the age of nine, were spent living at the university. He never had people his own age to play with—no real friends aside from his teacher, Julius, and a few of the younger servants.

One day, a man—a huge warrior with black skin—came with his three students to visit Julius at the university. He spent time with the three youngsters in a massive snowball fight and then at one of the hot springs at the ground level of the university. There were two boys and a girl, all three of them special—blessed with a marking on their backs. He couldn't remember the significance of the markings or what they looked like, but he remembered Julius telling him that there was something very unique about the girl, and it involved her fighting. He was beginning to question if Barina was that girl. He had been friends with her and the boys for only one day, and never knew what happened after they left or why they didn't come back. He always hoped to find them again.

Onyx was trying to stay in a meditation while drifting in and out, thinking over spells in his head that would help if they encountered creatures none of the others could deal with. He was also thinking the same thing as Twarence. Onyx didn't have many friends. He had lived in seclusion for most of his life in the Hitum Mountain. He would go home to see his family—other wizards and magical beings—when there was a council meeting, but normally kept to himself for weeks at a time. He was finding Twarence, Barina, Jaras, Arkon, and Aria easy to talk to and, for him, it was a connection he didn't realize he had needed. They could make him laugh and give him confidence in himself. Barina seemed to know as much about magic as he did. While she wasn't a woman who could wield magic, she knew a lot about it. Though she hadn't said much, she knew of his teacher and of the other orders. Those facts alone were enough to make him realize she knew more than she was giving away.

It also made him wonder if he had met her before when he was young. He had a memory in the back of his head of three children with their teacher coming to the mountain one afternoon. Back when his mentor Rutherford was still alive. He remembered two boys and a girl. They had been a lot of fun, but he couldn't remember their names. He did remember the girl's light blonde hair. If Barina was one of those three, then how great for him to be reunited with a friend of the past.

Arkon finished scrying into his mirror. He had been talking with the head of his clan, and now he was trying to clear his mind, though he was doing a poor job of it. Since the beginning of this trip, he hadn't been very nice to Jaras or Barina, but now he found that they were willing to lay down their lives for all of them. He had to admit that he wouldn't have done the same—not until what happened earlier that day.

Jaras was genuinely a good person, and he had proved that time and again this last week. He was as honest and true as people got. That was hard to find in the world. Arkon hoped for his safe return.

Barina was just as true and honest—even as a thief. Arkon had yet to hear a lie escape her lips. Still, he had been cold toward her. He vowed that, if he were to see them again, things would change. He would be better. He would treat them with the kindness and respect they deserved, and the honor of friends.

Arkon wondered, just as his fellow travelers in the cave that evening, if he had met Barina when he was younger. Once, in the Forest of Elves which isn't far from Miork, he spoke with three children—two boys and a girl. They spoke his language, and they were so happy to get the translations right. They only talked briefly before Arkon and the other elves had to return to their clan.

None of the four in the cave spoke of this to each other. Each recalled a fond memory of their thief when they were youngsters themselves. Even Aria, who hadn't spoken with the girl she remembered, thought them as good.

Suddenly, the four looked up, weapons bared when they heard something outside.

"What is that?" Aria drew her bow back, her arrow ready to fire on whatever came into the cave.

"I can't see anything." Twarence had both his axe and his sword drawn, ready to fight.

It was dark, and the blizzard made it impossible to see anything beyond the entrance. They heard footsteps crunching in the snow, and whatever was there was moving slowly.

After two long, nerve-racking minutes, two figures entered. Their cloaks were pure white, covered with snow. The shorter of the two carried a large white beast of a cat and dropped it in front of them. Jaras and Barina took off their hoods and looked at the group with cold and tired faces.

"Well, you'll be happy to know that the blizzard is still going on," Jaras sighed. "Damn, it's cold."

"Can't handle a little weather, you big baby?" Barina nudged his arm.

He winked. "You're freezing too."

She scoffed. "Am not. My cloak is great. My face is only cold cause the hood fell off for a little bit."

They looked at the others with a smile.

"Glad you guys made it here okay," Jaras said.

The group hurried to offer their companions warm hugs as soon as their snow-covered cloaks were off.

"So glad you're alive," Arkon said to Barina. "Thank you for earlier."

"You bet."

"You had us worried sick," Aria complained, holding them both. "I'm so glad you're okay."

"Is that one of them?" Twarence asked, looking down at the cat.

Onyx poked it carefully. "It's huge."

"This is a snow cat. We were fighting this and about eleven of its friends," Jaras told him in a somber voice. "Beautiful creatures. Shame."

Barina agreed, then yawned. "That's also our dinner." She started removing her boots.

"Do these things taste okay?" Twarence asked.

"Like chicken," Barina winked.

Everyone chuckled but Aria who turned away from the dead animal. "Gross."

"Someone else should cook it," Jaras suggested. "I think we've earned a break." He turned to Barina. "You said hot springs?"

She nodded, grabbing her pack. "Back of the cave."

The two warriors gingerly made their way deeper into the cave. The others blushed when Barina and Jaras began stripping off their clothes as they walked. Barina unlaced her top and peeled it off her body, dropping it on the ground before unbuttoning her pants. She stripped to her undies and bra. Jaras took off his shirt and was undoing his belt, eventually stripping to his small clothes. It was so dark, they could barely see their way to the springs until Onyx made his way back with the others, lighting the way with the orb on his staff.

The rest of the group followed, watching the two warriors stand half naked, staring at the steam rising and looking like their deepest desires were about to come true. Barina stepped in on one side, Jaras on the other, and they carefully sank into the hot water.

"Oh, my stars," Barina purred, a look of bliss on her face. "This is the best thing ever." She crouched deeper into the spring until the water was at her waist. "I could cry, I'm so happy."

Jaras just let out a groan—part pleasure, part pain. "Oh it stings, but it feels good." He looked up. "Nice ink work by the way." He pointed at Barina's tattoos.

"Thanks." She glanced down and saw the gash on her arm and then the one on her right side. "Hmm, this is tender." She sounded surprised that it bothered her.

Jaras poked at a gash on his chest with half a wince.

"It's all good pain, Jaras," Barina said, looking at herself.

They were now becoming fully aware of their injuries.

The others watched in silence, as if the fighters were crazy. Their injuries looked bad.

Distracted by how little Barina was wearing, Arkon stood. "I'm going to go back and get dinner started."

Aria knelt next to Barina and touched her shoulder.

"Your hands are freezing!" Barina complained and jerk away as goosebumps formed on her arms.

"Barina, you need to let me fix your side," Aria pleaded. "And Jaras, really, your leg. Let me help."

The thief nodded. "Aria, I will. Just, give me a few minutes. I need to warm up."

Jaras agreed. "With the weather as cold as it is, I don't think I'm in trouble. I'm fine, really."

Aria crossed her arms then looked up at Onyx. He knew what she wanted him to do.

Jaras snorted a laugh. "I don't think we're going to have a choice in this matter, B."

"At least warm up your hands," Barina told Aria.

Onyx pointed his staff, and suddenly, neither of the two could move. "Aria, they're all yours," he said, grinning. "I love my job."

"Thank you, Onyx." Aria looked pleased.

Jaras let out a small sigh while she rested her hands on his shoulder. "Sorry, Aria. It's just after doing this so often, rarely do you even think about an injury or having someone tend to it. I mean, you fight as much as I have, and probably as much as her, and you have to keep yourself from noticing the injuries in the fight. Eventually you stop noticing altogether."

Barina nodded. "We both normally tend to ourselves, and we were going to after we soaked. I guess, we also feel bad about bothering someone else."

"Shut up," Aria commanded. "That's stupid, and it's why I'm here. I've seen too many people become septic and close to death or even die because they were hurt and didn't get help. All they needed was to get looked over to avoid infection, and they didn't."

"Thanks," Barina said, looking humbled.

Aria held her hand on Jaras for just a little while. It was just as hard for her as the others to see the injuries that he and Barina had sustained and lived.

The gashes and rips in Jaras's flesh cut all the way to the bone. He really had learned to move past the pain. There was also a large cut on his upper leg that went deep into the meat. Aria was glad she was tending to these so they wouldn't get infected or become another scar.

Barina's injuries were just as bad. On her right side, there was a set of claw marks about four inches long. On her left, there was a large tattoo of a sea turtle swimming through grasses.

Aria thought *I've read books and seen drawings of these animals. She must've seen some in her travels.*

There was a large tattoo of a pirate flag on the thief's lower back. A skull with two cross cutlass blades dripping with blood decorated the flag, and a patch covered one of the eyes on the skull. Aria had seen the tattoos on Barina's arms, but not these.

"What's so funny?" Barina asked, though she already had an idea.

"A pirate flag, really?" Aria asked while the wound on the thief's arm healed.

"Well yeah. This Jolly Roger is identical to the one on the ship I sailed with for a while." Barina made it sound perfectly normal.

"Sailed the seven seas and all that?" Twarence asked as he sat on a rock with a cigarette.

"Just a few of the seas. I was only with them for about a year. They wanted someone who knew how to steal and fight, so there I was. It was also a way for me to take care of some other matters. I need to go see them again when I get a chance," she mused to herself.

"What was the name of the ship?" Onyx asked.

Barina glanced up and winked. "Really wanna know?"

"Oh, come on," Twarence urged along with Onyx.

Barina shifted a little bit in her seat. "Fine."

Onyx's jaw dropped. "How did you move? You can't be immune to this spell."

"I can't move my legs without it feeling like there's a weight on them, but I've trained for years to overcome things like this. No offense Onyx, but it has to be one hell of a powerful spell for it to immobilize me completely." She smiled at him kindly.

"What the hell, B?" Jaras hissed. "I can't even look over with my eyes. I'm lucky I can blink." He tried turning his head, but nothing moved.

Barina turned her head and looked seriously at Jaras while placing a finger on her lips. "Shhh."

"Back to the original topic. Name of the ship." Twarence was just as stumped as anyone that Barina could move, but a female sailing on a pirate ship was much more fascinating.

"I'm a member of the Black Iris under Captain James."

Jaras's eyes went wide, and Twarence breathed through his teeth.

"Whoa. Really, I'm surprised there's not a bounty on your head," Twarence said quietly, as if someone might overhear.

Barina tried to look innocent, but the corners of her mouth twitched.

"What?" Arkon said, hearing the last part of the conversation as he walked back from cooking. "Who put a bounty on your head? Which kingdom?" He sounded ready to track down whoever it was.

"No monarch has a bounty on me," Barina assured them. "No, I take that back. Queen Jillian of Meiakan had one, but that was before I was a pirate. Totally unrelated."

"Had?" Jaras asked, able to raise an eyebrow. "With you, I've learned to pay attention to little words like that when you speak."

Barina pressed her lips together, her eyes avoiding them. "She died. It lifted."

Onyx had heard of this monarch—mad and cruel all at once. "Why?" he asked. "Did she die from natural causes?"

"I'm not a natural cause," Barina said, unapologetic. "To be fair, she had kidnapped Clara and was holding her to be executed unless Clara's father married her. William asked me to get her back. It came to blows and, let me tell you, Jillian was no lightweight. She hits hard."

"How high of a bounty?" Aria then asked. She was still trying to fix a couple of stubborn wounds.

Barina thought about it again. "Four hundred thousand pieces of gold." Then added, "Dead or alive, preferably dead, I believe the notice said. She really did not like me. I know that was the last major one I had, except for the pirate thing. Don't think there are any others."

"Wait, William, as in King William of Treklea?" Jaras asked, this was his home kingdom, and he knew the king and his children.

"Yeah, we go way back." Barina looked as if she was waiting for Jaras to pick up on something.

"I know them well too. I used to go see them about once a month for dinner." Jaras was still oblivious.

"You guys sailed in the southern seas, right?" Twarence asked.

"There and a bit beyond the isles."

"Isn't there a Weird Beard and Trench Mouth on that ship too? Those are two names I've heard." Twarence was searching his mind.

"Huh? You mean Nate and Alex."

"Are those their real names?" Twarence's eyes grew big. "Holy crap! I've heard they tried to kill people for using their real names."

"I won the right to know Trench's name in a bet. And Alex *did* try to kill me when I called him by his real name. Became friends after that. Pretty nice guy actually."

Twarence flicked his cigarette ash to the ground. "Wow, what's James like?"

"You don't want to piss him off. I've seen it. Not pretty, but he's good to me." She thought of the pirates fondly. "I miss them. Need to check in on them after I finish this. I know Nate's angry cause he hasn't had a decent musician on the ship except for Alex since I left. Alex and I also have a chess game to finish. He and I have played over thirty games and always have a stalemate. We have a wager on it."

"What's the wager?" Arkon asked, enjoying hearing about Barina's travels.

"I get to call him Alex without complaint. If he wins, I was supposed to tell him the name of my teacher, but since he learned that already, I have to tell him my biggest secret."

"What do you play?" Jaras asked. "Did you bring an instrument with you?"

"Ocarina and lute, and no, I haven't brought anything with me."

"Damn," Arkon said, "some music would've been nice. How long ago did you leave the ship?" He headed back to check on dinner.

"Couple years ago."

Twarence was writing this down. He was learning things about the world of pirates he didn't already know. "Did you ever meet Black Blood?" he then asked.

"Eli." Her face shifted to an odd expression.

Even Jaras knew the name of this pirate. "Old as the sea itself and has claimed countless lives."

Aria looked at Barina's face. She was hiding something, but the healer was still trying to work on the wounds. Some were very deep, but she wouldn't stop till they were healed.

"He was only a couple years older than me," Barina said, "and hadn't killed that many people. It was more the way he went about killing them. That's how he got the reputation." She shrugged in her seat and looked away.

"You had a fling with Black Blood the pirate, didn't you?" Aria blurted out.

Barina's face went crimson. "The fuck did you pick up on that?"

"You still smitten for him, even a little?" The healer wiggled her eyebrows.

"That double-crossing son of a bitch? No." Barina was disgusted by the thought of him.

"Is he dead?"

Nervously, Arkon asked, "Do you kill all your ex-boyfriends?"

"I didn't kill him. My pirates did. I mean, he was trying to kill me. He held a knife up to my neck, literally. You could say it was a mutual break up."

"Maybe this is why you can't get a boyfriend," Onyx suggested with a laugh.

"Okay, did you ever meet Molly, the Mistress of Shadows?" Twarence was enjoying questioning her about her time on the ship and who she may have met. "Oh, and did you know Artemis, Slayer Under the Moon?" he asked, scribbling in his notebook.

Jaras was stifling a laugh. "How do pirates come up with these names for themselves?"

Barina's lip twitched. "Yes to all of the names above. Molly, he's a blast and can wear a dress better than I can. Mistress, well, yup, we've met." She glanced at her reflection in the water, hiding her smirk before clearing her throat. "And as for Artemis, who do you think gave me some of my tattoos? And Jaras, pirates are given their names by other pirates, they don't pick them for themselves." Barina stretched her legs in the water. "You almost done there, Aria? My fingers are starting to wrinkle."

"Yeah, just finished." Aria was disappointed in herself. There were injuries that she still couldn't heal. "Onyx, we can let them go," she said.

Onyx snapped his fingers, and it was done.

"Thanks Aria, before we forget to say anything." Jaras' eyes were grateful. Barina nodded in agreement.

"You're welcome."

Jaras called to Arkon. "How's the food coming?"

"Almost done!"

The fighters climbed out of the spring. When they did, Jaras noticed something on Barina's back that he hadn't expected. It was a small marking, a tattoo, just between her right shoulder blade and spine. A beautiful silver dragon that had the characteristics of a turtle caught the light and glimmered—it's blue eyes piercing orbs. The mark was only a few inches, not big at all, but it gave him pause. He was sure she knew of its significance—that marking and in that exact spot. It was a pretty ballsy move on her part, and it surprised him. He decided to ask about that at another time.

Jaras headed back to the front of the cave to dress himself, and the boys followed so Barina could have some privacy to change as well. She grabbed a set of dry clothes while humming quietly to herself. Aria stayed back with her.

"I'm sorry I was taking so long," Aria told her, lowering her eyes. "There's an injury on your right shoulder blade and one on your lower right hip that my powers won't work on."

Barina removed some bandages from her bag and placed them on her shoulder and hip. Her smile faded. "Those probably just ripped back open. They do that every now and then," she said in a soft voice while putting on a clean blouse.

Aria looked up, confused. "How…I mean, I don't understand. I've never seen anything like this."

"I don't like talking about how I got them. Sorry, it's a painful topic." Barina quickly put on a pair of dry pants and went to join the others at the fire. "I'll save you a seat."

Aria knew that she was one of the best at her trade and could heal damn near anything. She didn't know what could cause an injury to occasionally reopen and not completely heal. She stood, straightening her dress, and walked to join the others.

Barina sat smoking her pipe while talking quietly with Twarence. Jaras, Onyx, and Arkon were checking the bit of meat cooking on a spit. Since eating meat affected her powers too much, Aria grabbed the food she had brought.

After dinner, they set up shifts for night watch. Twarence, Arkon and Onyx went to soak in one of the springs before bed while Aria opted not to get half naked in front of them. As the men were dressing, they noticed something out of the ordinary—some writings on the wall in the back of the cave. Between Onyx and Arkon, it was hard to tell who noticed it first, but there was magic afoot in the cave.

"What is this?" Twarence asked, leaning in closer to inspect the writing. "It looks like a seal of sorts."

"Not sure," Arkon said. "It's of another race of magic though. Crap, maybe I have two languages left to learn." He examined it closer. "I think it might be gnome. Damn it, I *do* have a lot more to learn."

Onyx called to the others. "Hey, the rest of you, come here!"

It wasn't long before Jaras and Aria were walking back. "What's up?" Jaras asked.

Onyx pointed to the markings.

"Hmm, interesting. Never seen anything like this," Jaras told him while examining it.

"Neither have I," Aria admitted, brushing her fingers along the engravings. "This is weird." She turned to the two magic men. "And you two don't know what it means?"

"I'm still learning how to read everything out there," Arkon sighed. "Takes a long time to become fluent in all the magical languages."

"Where's Barina?" Onyx asked, then turned to look.

Wearing glasses and reading a book, she came straggling behind and almost tripped as she stumbled over a rock. She tried to play it off like nobody had noticed, but then realized they were all snickering at her. "Damn, so what's...up?" Her eyes moved toward the far wall. "Ohhhhh."

"Picked up on that pretty fast, didn't you?" Aria was impressed.

"Umm, well, ummm." She was at a loss for words.

"How often do you wear glasses?" Arkon seemed surprised when he noticed.

"Just for reading, but almost to a point when I'll need them all the time." She walked up to the wall and read the writing. "That's ohh, yeah, umm, this is gnome stuff. We really don't wanna mess with it."

"What does it say?" Jaras asked, leaning in even though he couldn't read it.

"I'm not going to recite it word for word, but basically, if you try to get beyond this door without permission, you're going to be lucky if you die a quick death."

"There's a door there?" Aria was still brushing her fingers along the walls.

Barina took her wrist and gently pulled it away. Her face was one of caution to the healer. "Yes, now please don't mess with it. The gnomes see more than you realize, and if they think you're trying to get in, they'll let you know what they think about it. I've read you the warning. Chances are they know it. Try to find the door and there could be trouble. They are peaceful beings but don't appreciate their kindness being taken for granted." Barina put herself in between the wall and the others. "Now if you would, let this be. I'm tired, so I'm going to rest, but only after you guys walk away from here."

That didn't sit well with the elf. "Don't you trust us?"

"This has nothing to do with trust. I just don't want any mistakes, not with this." She took her glasses off and crossed her arms. She wasn't budging.

"How do you know so much about all this stuff?" Twarence asked. Like the others, he wondered how she had so much insight into so many random things.

"It's part of my business," was all she said.

"What's behind there?" Onyx asked in a quiet voice. "There's energy. A lot of it."

Barina gave him a cautious look. If it was just her and Onyx, she would tell him more. Since it wasn't, she considered her words. "A storehouse. I don't have permission to tell you more. Please, go back to the fire."

They slowly made their way back, Barina lingering till they were out of sight. She turned her head to the wall of the cave.

"I would take it as a favor if you wouldn't hold their curiosity against them," she said quietly.

A small spot on the wall, not even as large as her fist, shifted. A very tiny door opened, and a small creature popped his head out. His skin was tan, his black beard long, and his glittering black eyes looked up at her. He wore colors that matched the rock on which he stood and, if she didn't know where to look, she could've missed him.

"Think nothing of it. You can tell them what is here if you wish, just don't let them inside."

"Thanks, Bata. Tell the king I said hello," she told him with a small bow.

"Will do Barina. Take care." And he closed the door.

She walked back to her companions and saw Arkon staring at her. His face was blank, but his crystal blue eyes fixed on her.

"Who were you talking to just then?" he asked. "I heard someone else speaking with you."

"A gnome. The guardian of the storehouse. His name is Bata," she told him while grabbing a book from her bag.

"I just remembered something," Onyx said. "Isn't it true that the mountains still stand because not all of the black diamonds are gone?"

She nodded and put a finger on her nose.

Amazed, Twarence asked, "You mean there's gems back there? Black diamonds?"

Barina nodded again. "Magic still exists in these mountains because these gnomes protect them. If there's still one black diamond, then the magic of the mountains will be fine. If gone, then…well, the magic will be gone as well. And we'd lose so many species."

"Wow, do you think, maybe some time after this is all done, you could introduce me to a gnome?" Twarence asked. "I've learned a lot from the books I've read, but it's not the same as getting to speak with them."

"I'll see what I can do," Barina said. "I'm going to go read for a while. Come get me when it's time for my shift. Goodnight kids."

Barina walked back to the spring while the others talked quietly only for a little while before they went to sleep.

CHAPTER 5

Twarence and Onyx sat in front of the fire while the others were slept soundly farther away.

"I'm gonna go ahead and say it," Twarence joked quietly as he munched on an apple. "What a week."

"We met a dragon, battled some giants. Barina and Jaras almost got killed, and this is just the beginning." Onyx was counting the events on his fingers.

"I'm curious, and I've wanted to ask you for a while now. How much magic can you do?"

Onyx pushed up his glasses. "That's a pretty vague question. How do you mean?"

Twarence searched for his words. "Let me see, um, what kind of stuff are you able to do? What's your area of specialty?"

Onyx leaned in. "I've studied my whole life to be well versed and mastered in the areas of combat, nature, learning about other magical beings and the magical places around the world, and well, there's a lot more, but there you go. I use my magic to do good, and to help people when I can."

"Good to know," Twarence said. "I've been noticing that you do use your magic to help. Between you, Aria, and Arkon, I know all three of you are the reason we haven't frozen to death here."

"That's been a group effort. We've all been doing our parts to keep warm. Still can't believe that B convinced us to go this way." Onyx shrugged his shoulders. "I understand her reasons though, completely. I don't like to duel unless I must, either. I mean, we'd have to fight simply because we wanted to get from point A to point B, and it's not worth the possible loss of life."

"I know. Still, this path has been brutal even without things to fight."

"But still safer." Onyx yawned. "So what's your specialty at the university?"

"Well, I teach mathematics and philosophy, and I do a lot of study into politics, geography, world cultures and, well, pretty much anything I can get my hands on. I have literally read all but about one hundred books that we have at the university, and that includes all the rare ones we have in the vaults and archives. Thankfully, I soak everything up like a sponge. Once I read it, I don't forget."

"So, have you decided to tell everyone how the Anna Stone is so powerful?" Onyx asked. "I know the story behind it, but I doubt the others know."

"No, not yet. Eventually, but I just don't know if they're ready."

"I think you should, and soon. They should know why this thing is so important."

Twarence took a deep breath. "I will. It's just, well, this thing holds a lot of power."

Onyx sat back and thought about it for a moment. "And if they let it slip to the wrong person along the way, yeah, it could put everything in jeopardy."

"And now that we agree on this, I want to double check our notes on it. Created by none other than the great witch Tazel."

"Check." Onyx nodded. "Given to the founding king of Larindana, King Theodore, over four hundred years ago. Named after his wife."

"Check. And is Tazel still alive?"

"Yeah, she's scarce as all hell, but alive and still doing her thing. I saw her at the council meeting last year."

"Damn, that woman is ancient," Twarence breathed through his teeth. "So the stone can give the owner powers beyond anything they could imagine. They could literally do anything. But only one person every thirty-five years, selected by the stone when they're born, is able to use it."

"Check. Tazel designed it that way. The first was King Theadore, but he lost control of his power when he became enraged and lost his temper with a prisoner. It killed more than two dozen people, his wife Anna included. He took the stone off, never to be used again, ever."

"That was smart of him, too. Who knows if the next person to have it would be someone corrupt or good. I mean, there are only a couple ways to tell if anyone can use it. One is obviously holding the damn thing and the emblem, a star, will appear on their foreheads. The other is when we cross Rose Lake, there's a spot at the center of the lake where, if one drinks the water there, the emblem can appear. I don't know if that bit is true or not. It might just be hearsay, but there's that. And then I think there's a potion or spell or something, I don't know." Twarence was scratching his brain for that.

"Well, the lake thing is theory," Onyx said, he was cleaning his glasses on his robes while his mind was turning, "and I don't know a spell to make that happen. But that gives us two people alive who can use the stone and, from what I know, it would put one at twenty-three and another at the same age as King Toler, who is fifty-eight. It could be anyone, unless Toler found a way to figure out that he was one of the people who can use it. I've done a lot of research on the stone and the lore behind it, so I know the numbers."

Twarence nodded. "That's the dangerous part, him being a real possibility to be able to use it. I have some theories on who the other might be. Just ideas of a few people, and I'll let you know if I'm able to confirm them. It's just, if…god damn, if Toler is able to use that stone, Onyx then…" Twarence shifted uncomfortably. "I also think that Toler *can* use it."

Onyx closed his eyes, pondering that possibility without much effort. "He wouldn't have had it taken if he hadn't found out somehow that he was able to use it." the wizard sighed. "If he gets it, we're all screwed."

"That's putting it mildly. And why did she go with every thirty-five years for the stone and such?"

Onyx threw his hands up. "Pssh, how the hell is anyone supposed to know how Tazel's mind works? She's brilliant and all, but she's always been so random."

Twarence laughed a little bit. "So I've heard. I think our shift is about up. You want to get Jaras, and I'll find Barina? I think she's still back there reading."

Onyx nodded and stood up.

Twarence walked to the back of the cave and found Barina curled up in her cloak and asleep. When he was about ten feet from her, she opened her eyes and looked up at him.

"Is it time for my shift?" Her voice was small and quiet.

"Yeah, how come you slept back here?" He knelt down in front of her as she sat up.

She put a finger to her lips then pointed up. There he could see, and just barely, a faint gleam.

"Is that a black diamond?" he whispered.

She nodded. "I told the gnome who guards the storehouse and figured I'd watch it till either it was my shift, or they got it."

Twarence patted the top of her head, and she gave a smile. "You fell asleep on the job."

She yawned while giving him a side-eye smile. "Not a very deep sleep."

"How much would something like that bring to the right buyer?"

"Given how incredibly rare they are, one is worth over one million pieces of gold, and that's just for a half carat at a cheap price."

"Wow, a couple of those and you could buy your own kingdom."

"True, but I wouldn't take them if asked. They need to stay here. Even if it weren't for the fact that I wouldn't want to do it, knowing it'd destroy my friendship with the gnomes and that they'd do everything in their powers, which is a lot, to destroy me, is also a good motivator."

Twarence scoffed a small laugh. "Also a good reason. Hey, what's that around your neck?"

Barina lifted a chain from under her shirt to reveal a small, round, pewter pendant that had a single diagonal line engraved on it.

"What's the story behind that?" he asked. "Never seen anything like it."

Barina yawned again. "I trained to fight alongside my two best friends Jason and Josh, but even before we began our formal training, we were teaching ourselves. When we had our first real fight together, and I mean life or death fight against some bad guys, we realized that, not only would we always be friends, but that the three of us were unstoppable in battle when together, and that we need each other.

"We took a vow. 'We learn together, we fight together, and forever we'll be together.'" She held the pendant. "Since this is my work, and not strictly fighting, that's the only reason they're not here.

"Josh made us these pendants. We each have a third and, when together, it forms a triangle. Each of us is strong on our own, but when together, well, yeah. I've never taken it off."

Twarence smiled at the warmth she carried for these men she spoke of. "I hope I get to meet them someday. They sound like they're really great people."

"They're the best. Come on, let's get back and you can go get some rest."

They headed back to the fire where Onyx was saying goodnight to Jaras. Twarence waved to them, and Barina sat back a few feet from Jaras by the fire.

Barina and Jaras were quiet for a little bit. They let their actions talk while Barina put a kettle over the fire and added the tea to it. Jaras rummaged for some dried fruits and cheese to snack on. She poured each of them a cup, setting the kettle in front of them, before sitting next to him herself. He set a cloth with the fruits and cheese in between them. They sipped their tea and enjoyed munching on the snacks, savoring the quiet that surrounded them. It was when she poured them each their second cup that they finally started talking again.

"I'm curious, when did you start training under Darien?" Barina asked him as she pulled out her pipe.

"God, I was nine years old, I hardly remember what my life was like before. It started just with my parents wanting me to have some lessons to be able to hold my own. My younger brother was learning too, but it turned into something I really had a gift for. It was enough that King William also had me learn how to help with the military and study that too."

Barina looked at him curiously. "Then what brought you into this line of work? I mean, King William of Treklea is a good man to follow. I like him. Why not take that?"

Jaras shrugged his shoulders. "Ah well, the paycheck was nice, but I just don't like the idea of not being able to make my own choices. Doing something just because it's on orders doesn't appeal to me. I talked it over with Darien, and he said that taking up jobs to help others, like what I'm doing now, would be good. Just for me to be careful what I pick. I occasionally hear about work like this, otherwise I stay back and help Darien with teaching his classes."

"That's fair. What about your family?"

"My parents live in Treklea along with my brother. My brother did join the military under King William, and he does well for himself. My parents are cobblers though, and they love what they do." He smiled.

Barina shared his grin. "That's good."

"What was your family like?" He wasn't shy asking the question.

"They were pretty great. My father was a weaponsmith. Swords were his specialty. I mean, he made other weapons too, but swords were the trademark. My brother was a couple years older than me and so smart, he was doing really well in school. My mother worked around the house and taught my sister at home. My brother helped teach my sister too. My sister was a couple years younger than me and a pistol—red headed with the temper to boot sometimes—but she understood me and accepted me for being the odd duck that I've always been."

"What were their names?"

"My older brother was Tobi, my sister was Anya. Mom's name was Madeline, and Dad's name was Adrian. Dad really didn't want to pass the trade to me, but since Tobi was given the chance to continue his education, and mom didn't have any more kids after my sister was born, I got to learn. I really wanted to learn anyway.

"My little sister, Anya, was such a charmer. She had such a big heart and was wonderful. We all picked on each other but, when push came to shove, we had each other's backs. She loved to dance and was really sharp, too. I think she would've become such a beautiful woman by now, both inside and out.

"My mom Madeline, she was great. Amazing mom, hard worker, and not a bad cook. She could be a little crazy at times, but I'm sure my siblings and I did that to her. She was amazing though," she mused about them.

"What about your dad?"

"My dad and I had an interesting relationship." She sighed. "I loved my father and had, still have, an amazing amount of respect for him, even if we didn't always see eye to eye. My dad was glad that I was learning the trade and loved me dearly, but he never hid the fact that he would've liked me to do something else besides becoming a weaponsmith. 'It's not a girl's place, but someone has to do it,' he would tell me. He really hated that I learned to fight, but eventually it came to be that, if I was going to learn, it might as well be from the best.

"We did get along everywhere else though. We'd go see musicians and plays together. He just had no idea how it was that I came to be so different in my thinking than everyone else. I want people to be true to themselves and to hell with social norms. He always knew that I wouldn't be able to follow the life of a normal girl."

"What do you think he'd think now?"

"I don't know. I think in one aspect that he would hate me fighting because he would worry, but be happy that I'm using my abilities to help people. Which is why I wanted to learn to fight, to help people. He would hate my tattoos." She gave a little smirk at that last bit. "But he knew that, as much as it hurt me to go against his words, I couldn't pretend to be someone that I'm not."

"I think he'd be proud of you," Jaras told her. He blinked as he was connecting the dots on who her father was. "What was his name again?"

Barina already knew the reaction she would get when she said her father's full name. "Adrian Raine of Miork."

Jaras sat up straight and let out a gasp.

"Here we go," she said to herself.

"*The Adrian Raine of Miork*? The sword smith, Adrian Raine of Miork?"

Her father's name and reputation had been well known—even years after his death—among the world of warriors.

Barina nodded. "Yes."

Jaras took his sword and showed it to her. It wasn't the first time she had really taken a good look at it. She knew this blade.

Jaras' face was beaming, "You recognize the work."

She gave a little smirk. "DayLily."

"You remember it?" That surprised him.

She leaned in. "That's the first one I ever made without any help from my dad."

"Get out of here." Jaras was all smiles and trying not to laugh.

"Look under the hilt. My mark is there, two wavy lines. I named it DayLily. It's the flower I got my design from," she explained. "Coiled hilt that is leafed in white gold that blooms like a lily at the top to cover the hand and protect it. In the center, I embedded citrines in the middle and garnets blossoming from the citrines. At the bottom, the hilt is horizontal and balanced perfectly. The blade itself is four feet long and two inches wide. Made of a steel mixture that only my father and I have ever known. It's as strong a sword as it gets. I hope you've liked it."

Jaras looked under the hilt and found her mark and grinned. "My father gave me this as a gift when I started my training. I have never found one that's better, so I've always used this one. I can't believe that you were, well, that this…wow, you did this."

"Darien told me one of his students had my first sword." She winked and sipped her tea.

Jaras choked on his cigarette smoke when he let out a chortle. "So you have met Darien before?"

"Made his sword, too. The Desert Rose. Rubies and bloodstones on it. He originally wanted Dad to make it, but it would've taken forever for Dad to get to him, so he went with me. Love that guy."

"I knew that his sword came from your dad's workshop and that Adrian's daughter of all people made it. Wow, small world. Darien has always been very happy with that sword."

He knew that his sword and that of his teacher was from the workshop Adrian Raine of Miork. Barina's father had been considered one of the best there was, and there were few that were equal to what he created, unless he outdid himself. And now Jaras knew that Adrian's daughter was just as gifted as her father.

The rest of the evening, till their shift was up, they enjoyed each other's company. They had become good friends, and they had a kinship as warriors with a great amount of respect for each other.

They were both glad to see Aria and Arkon come for the next shift. Neither one of them realized how tired they had been. Barina curled up again to sleep back in the caves where she was earlier, and Jaras went to join the others.

Thankfully, the rest of the night passed without problems, and they were able to get a decent start in the morning. After a warm breakfast, they brace themselves before they headed back outside into the snow and ice of the summit of the Black Mountains.

The rest of the week took them through the snow-covered tops of the mountains. Thankfully, the blizzard had passed, and there were clear skies, but it was still bitterly cold. At night, they were able to find decent shelter in caves, not warm like the steam caves, but they were at least out of the cold. They had no more problems with snow cats, and when they came down the side of the summit and saw Barina with a big grin on her face that developed on its own, they knew they were about to get to warmer weather.

"Almost there. You see that big tree there, with all the giant leaves?" she pointed out. It was easy to see even a mile away. "Once we get past that tree, we won't need the furs."

They picked up their steps and, sure enough, as soon as they passed by the huge tree, they felt the warm summer breeze and the sun beating down on them. They took time to change out of the furs and fix the horses up with their saddles.

"This is so much better," Aria purred. "I think it's going to take me a week to defrost from up there." She took a deep breath of the warm air and basked in the rays of the sun. She was so glad to be out of the cold.

Onyx was rolling up his cloak and putting it in his pack. "I am not much of a hot weather person but damn, this feels so good right now."

"Hey, is that one of the forests that you've told us about, Twarence?" Aria asked. "These trees and the flowers are huge."

Twarence nodded. "There are plants that can swallow you whole. The flowers can be deadly, and some of the trees can come to life and eat you."

"And don't forget the spiders," Jaras snickered.

"Stop that." Twarence glared at him right as a tree right next to Jaras swung a branch and grabbed him by the foot. In the next second, Twarence grabbed his axe and, with one swipe, was able to cut his friend free.

In the next moment, the large flowers began to uproot themselves, their razor-sharp petals whirling in the air as they ran at the group. Aria grabbed her bow and shot a few of them down.

Arkon's body turned a deep shade of blue as he called on the spirits to stop the attacks. He was able to freeze the plants until they were well away from them.

"Let's hurry, I don't want them to pick up on where we've gone." Aria was brushing some leaves off of her.

They headed only about a couple miles more before they turned a corner and came to an immediate stop.

"Holy shit," Aria breathed.

"Yup, agreed," Jaras said as he began to pout.

They were face to face with three creatures that looked like giant ladybugs, each one standing ten feet tall. Saliva dripped from the pincers on their mouths.

"I'm on it." Arkon raised his hands.

Onyx added, "I got your back," and held up his staff.

"No!" Barina tried to run and stop them from using magic, but it was too late.

They both shot a beam of energy at the bugs, but the bugs absorbed their powers.

Arkon had never seen anything like this. "What the...our magic."

"Are you kidding me?" Onyx blurted out.

The bugs all reared on their feet and gave a low roar. Barina grabbed both the elf and wizard by their shirts and pulled them back. They barely were able to dodge when the bugs shot the energy right back at them.

Barina rolled her eyes. "You just made them angry. Hurry and hide," she told them.

"Where the hell do we hide?" Aria spat at her. "What were you thinking, bringing us here?"

"Are you high?" Barina was exasperated. "You get pissed because I take you on a colder but safer path because I don't want to have to fight the big guys in the warmer climates. And now we're at the warmer climates, dealing with the big guys I was trying to avoid, and you're pissed? You've got to be kidding me! We are also on a dangerous mission. Dangerous!"

"Why doesn't our magic work on them, Barina?" Arkon drew his sword.

"I told you that there are certain beings that live in the mountains that have an ability to not be harmed by magic and can even repel it. These are some of them," she told them as they ran behind some large boulders. "I can fight them even though my blade was made by those with magic, so wait here and..." Her voice trailed off as she looked down to the ground. "Just kidding. I don't need to." And she sat down on a large rock.

"Are you insane? This is not the time to take a break!" Arkon spat at her.

"Show some manners. We have company," Barina said, pointing to the ground.

"What are you talki..." Twarence's words were cut off and his face went pale. So did Aria's.

Hundreds of spiders, if not thousands, were scrambling around them and down from the mountain walls. They were easily the size of a man's fist, and they were very fast.

"They won't hurt us. They're going after them," Barina explained, pointing to the ladybugs. "Try not to step on the babies, okay. And you might want to stay back when the big ones pounce."

Twarence's face got even paler. "Big...ones..."

In the next breath, three enormous, black and blue spiders, larger than the ladybugs, leaped from the side of the canyon walls and landed on the bugs. They bit into them, injecting them with venom. Within a matter of seconds, the bugs were wrapped in their silky graves.

The largest of the spiders looked over and approached the party.

"Barina, is that you?" the spider asked. Her voice was deep, and she sucked in her spit when she spoke, almost making it sound like she had a lisp.

Barina stood up with a smile and gave a little bow. "Hi Orba, how have you been? Are all these little ones your babies?"

Arkon held out his hands, weighing them back and forth. "Giants spiders talk. Barina is friends with them. Hard to say which is more surprising."

Twarence and Aria stood frozen, still terrified.

"Most of them," Orba said. "Mara had a bunch of her eggs hatch too. Hentzi is too young still to have any."

Barina looked a little shocked. "Mara, you look good, honey. And Hentzi, really, you're almost all grown up. Last time I saw you, you barely came up past my knees." One of the larger of the young spiders sat next to Barina who was petting her back gently while she addressed Orba, Mara, and Hentzi. "Good to see you too, Arna," she said to the spider who's back she had a hand on.

"I had a growth spurt," Hentzi said, twirling around a bit.

"And thank you, Barina. My babies seem to be taken with you and your friends. Don't worry, I can tell there are two who are not too fond of our kind. My children know not to climb on them." Orba leaned her head down to Barina.

"I take that as a lovely courtesy to them. How are things here, any more trouble from the...you know?" Barina asked her, looking up.

"No problems since you helped us, for that we will always be in your debt. Would you and your friends care to stay with us for the evening? They can rest if they'd like a night to relax," Orba said kindly.

"There's never any debt to be repaid for my help. I wish we could join you, but we really need to keep on our way. I'll stop back in the next few months though, and we'll get caught up. Thank you for your help with those bugs."

"Think nothing of it. We have to eat and, while I know you can handle them, one less problem for you, right?" Orba grabbed one of the silk-covered bugs. "Till next time, take care. Come on, kids!"

Orba and the other spiders, within only a minute, were gone without a trace.

Barina looked back at Aria and Twarence. "Are you two alright?" Her tone was gentle.

They nodded.

"Very nice of them to recognize that we're kinda terrified of spiders." Twarence took a drink of his water to calm down.

"They're very considerate." Barina nodded, patting his back.

Aria climbed onto her horse and took a deep breath. "We need to keep going." Her voice was still shaky.

Twarence stood up, nodding his head. "Let's go."

Arkon stayed back with Jaras and Onyx for a moment. Barina had already started to move ahead of them.

"Giant spiders. And they're friendly." Arkon shook his head with a smile. "I'm starting to really like that we have that thief with us."

CHAPTER 6

A month of hard traveling through the mountains, and the group was feeling the trip. They were tired, sore, but they were keeping their spirits up. They were giving themselves a day to make camp early, recognizing that they needed the extra rest. Jaras, Twarence, Onyx, and Barina were sitting around the campfire talking and joking, Arkon was taking a nap, and Aria had gone outside to take some time for herself.

"You told the bounty hunter what?" Barina's jaw dropped, looking at Jaras.

The guys started laughing.

"The fact that I was able to get that expression from you is saying something." Jaras lit a smoke. He was laughing hard enough that he was choking on his smoke.

"Well shit man, I've said and done some things, but that…damn." Barina was trying to hold in her laugh and failing miserably.

"Hey, it's not one of my prouder moments, but what do you do?" He kept smirking.

"Jaras wins this round." Twarence smiled, and his eyes went to Barina. "So B, where did you move to when you left Miork? You know, after your family passed?" he asked, changing the subject.

Barina glanced up as she was packing her pipe. "The natives call it Nippon. My teacher was already planning on taking me and my buddies there to continue our training,but my family dying sped up the process. We went to train under his master as well as under him."

"What kind of weapons did you specialize in?" Onyx was curious now too.

"Anything I could get my hands on." Barina took a long drag of her pipe.

"Really, so you can fight with a sword just as well as you can with your dagger there?" Jaras hid his smile. He was determined to get some information about her fighting style. He was curious. He couldn't help it. As a warrior, he wanted to know how others were able to fight and what they could do. He explained to the others that their suspicions about a warrior's willingness to talk about what they do, or lack thereof, would speak volumes about what they were able to do. Barina didn't talk about it, so that told him that she was probably pretty good.

"I can fight with either," Barina said. "Berk gave me my dagger the day we met. I can hold my own with a sword, but my dagger comes in handy as a thief."

"Can you show us an example?" Jaras tried to keep his voice casual.

Barina hesitated. "I don't know about that."

"Please? I'd like to see something." Twarence pleaded with a smile.

Barina turned to grab some more wood for the fire and scratched her back. "I really don't think that'd be a good idea, guys."

"Please, it doesn't have to be anything fancy," Jaras asked her again.

Barina shook her head.

"Why are you so against it, even with us?" Twarence wasn't trying to pry too much, but he couldn't help it. He wondered if she didn't trust them.

"I guess it's a force of habit. It can only help keep people safe if I don't talk about it or reveal more than I need to," she explained.

"Even I'm curious, Barina, but it's up to you," the wizard told her, his facial expression gave way to the fact he was okay with her deciding either way.

Barina was silent for a few moments. She really didn't want to demonstrate anything. She had made it a rule in life never to display more than what she needed, but she was with them. Maybe there wouldn't be any harm in a little demonstration. Nothing too much, but enough so they would stop asking questions.

She looked up and nodded. "Okay, but just something small."

The guys stood up and were eager to see what she was going to do.

Barina reached into her pocket and took out a coin and held it up. "Would one of you take this back into the cave till I ask you to stop."

Onyx took the coin and started walking, the only light from the staff he held. Twarence was walking with him.

Barina stood up and watched. "May I borrow your sword?" she asked Jaras. "Keep going!" she called.

Jaras had left his sword by the fire and went to get it.

"Okay, put the coin down!"

Onyx put the coin on a rock, and he and Twarence stood back.

"Here you go." Jaras gave her his sword.

Barina nodded in thanks. She held the weapon for only a second before she tossed it up in the air, caught it by the blade, and then hurled it to the coin.

"Holy shit!" was a unison chorus from Onyx and Twarence.

Jaras ran back and saw that from over twenty feet away, with very dim lighting, the coin was cut in half. Perfectly.

"Not done!"

The next second, they saw a dagger pierce one of the halves of the coin.

"That…what the fuck was that?!" Jaras' voice was high pitched. He was walking back and trying to piece together what the hell just happened. "That was not something small."

"The coin was small I guess." Twarence was laughing with Onyx. "Where the hell did you learn something like that?"

"Also, what gives? You can do that but not play darts?" Onyx couldn't help but make the joke. He had grabbed her dagger and handed it back.

"I can show you how to *not* play darts." She was grinning. "And my teacher showed me how to do that."

Twarence then had a rough question, but he didn't think she'd mind answering too much. "B, how many…how many people have you killed? How old were you when you had your first? I'm not trying to make you uncomfortable, so you don't have to answer if you don't want to. I'm just curious."

Barina blinked, her face serious. "Too many, but they were all beyond saving. As for the other question, it was my twelfth birthday. That was the day I met my teacher, got my dagger, had my first kill. And," she held out her right forearm to reveal a scar, "I received this in return. A reminder to me of the day my life changed forever."

On the inside of her right forearm, from just above her wrist to just below her elbow, was a scar that, while it had faded, it was still there.

"Why did you kill that person?" Jaras asked.

"He had a knife to my sister's throat. I gave him the option to let her go, but he refused. So I took his hand and his life." Her tone was neutral.

"He was going to kill her. I try not to kill, I hate it, and if I can avoid it at all costs, I will. By the same token, I understand that there are times that it can't be avoided."

Jaras then questioned Barina calling her teacher Berk, like it wasn't his full name. "What was your teacher's name?"

"Berklion."

Jaras was speechless, absolutely speechless. At the same time, he almost felt as if he had known this all along. *Did we meet when we were younger?*

Hearing that name for Onyx and Twarence brought up memories of this man and his students. Barina was the girl both of them had remembered from their youth. Onyx, it made him happy to have an old friend back in his life. For Twarence, there was more. It clicked that he knew her from his past. But now he knew why he and Barina were both on this mission.

Both the men looked at each other, and they realized their memories had come back, but they would need to discuss it later.

"Is this Berklion the same, Berklion of Halk?" Twarence asked, his voice shaky.

She nodded with a smile, thinking of her teacher. "Yeah, those of us who know him best call him Berk." Barina's eyes showed a deep love and respect for the man. "He adopted me after my parents died, took me in without a second thought to it. He's my bonus dad. He's a good man. One of the best."

Twarence was laughing. "Well that just told us a hell of a lot more about how you can fight. The most feared warrior in the land is your freaking teacher. Nobody else can hold a candle to the man. The only one who can fight close to his level is Darien Bell of Treklea, right Jaras?"

Jaras was laughing too. The scholar was right, there wasn't anyone else who was considered better than her teacher.

"I was trained by who is considered the second greatest fighter in the land," Jaras said. "Darien. You, though, you were trained by *the greatest.*" He couldn't stop laughing.

Barina blinked and looked away. Jaras still hadn't figured out how the two of them had met when they were younger, even though they'd spent weeks around each other. Twarence and Onyx were remembering, she could tell by the looks in their eyes. She had to turn away to roll her eyes. *How does he not remember that Berklion and Darien are best friends?*

"I forgot that he had students till now. Not many people knew that he had taken on teaching anyone," Twarence mused. "I know he was very strict about not wanting to teach people. Did he ever have any other students?"

"Just my two friends Jason and Josh."

"Why didn't he tell anyone about you guys? Why didn't you ever tell me about who taught you?" Jaras then asked. "I would love to tell people that's who trained me."

"I'm guessing he wanted to let them keep a low profile. If other warriors learned that they were trained by Berklion, they might want to pick fights to see if they're really that good. Plus, there's the element of surprise too," Twarence told him.

"Cool. I'll be curious to see what else you can do." Onyx patted her back.

"Guys, stop," Barina mumbled. She didn't like people glorifying her abilities just as much as she didn't like talking about them.

They all looked at each other, startled, when they felt the ground begin to rumble and then heard an enormous roar from outside the cave.

"Never a break," Onyx sighed.

Arkon sprinted toward the front of the cave. "Holy crap! I didn't know if we'd see this while we were here or not."

The others rushed up behind him and saw what he was looking at.

It was a huge beast, the size of a building, standing on his hind legs. It looked like a giant bear crossed with a warthog. With brown fur, razor sharp claws, and fangs, this creature could breathe fire and jump from the large boulders like a frog on lily pads.

"What on earth…," Jaras blurted out ducking back into the cave.

"Comuhing, I've heard about them, but I've never seen one. How amazing. He's beautiful." Arkon smiled. "Dangerous as all hell and damn near immortal. But they're very rare, and I wouldn't kill it if you asked me to. We'll have to wait here till it falls asleep or leaves."

"They are pretty incredible, aren't they?" Barina had to agree with him.

Just then Twarence said something that made their stomach's drop. "Where's Aria?"

They all looked to each other, their eyes wide, and then turned to look outside. Then they saw her running back toward the cave, trying to stay out of sight of the Comuhing. The beast saw her.

Onyx looked to the elf. "Arkon?"

The elf had already rushed out of the cave. There was a blur, and Arkon was now standing in front of the Comuhing. The beast saw him and let out a low growl. Arkon held his hand in front of him, moving closer to it.

"Easy friend," he said calmly. Arkon's body began to glow, and his eyes were shining a brighter blue. His magic was working. He closed his eyes as a very soothing blue light went from his hand to the beast.

Within moments the beast sat on his haunches and chirped, lowering his head so that Arkon could move closer and scratch its mane. The elf smiled at him and nodded. After a few seconds, the beast wandered off and left them alone.

"Are you okay?" Arkon looked to the healer who was now coming out of her hiding spot.

Aria was catching her breath and her nerves. "Thank you! That, wow, that was impressive."

Arkon gave a little nod. "Thanks, that's one of my gifts, being able to calm animals and speak with them to some extent. Come on back in. We should all get some rest."

The two headed back into the cave and to the fire, curling up in their blankets.

They decided that Onyx's protection spell on the cave would be enough, and their thief assured them that they would be fine, so they all slept that night. Arkon woke up at one point when he heard movement in the cave. It was just Barina who had gone off to a far spot to relieve herself and was on her way back.

She glanced over when she saw him, but didn't say anything as she went back to her bedroll.

"Barina, did you know about the Comuhing being up here?" he asked quietly.

Barina's look said it all. "Yes, but I also knew we had you."

Arkon blinked. "That's fair." He gave her a soft look when he registered what she had said. "You knew we wouldn't have to hurt it, that I could talk to it."

"I don't like to hurt anything if I can help it," she told him with a yawn. "I'm gonna get back to sleep. Goodnight."

Arkon went to sleep that night warmed by the heart that she held within her. She was kind, and he liked that. Maybe there was hope for them after all.

CHAPTER 7

The next couple of days were peaceful and without any incidents. They were finally, after a long month of traveling, out of the Black Mountains. They could see the little village just before the large lake that they would sail over to get to their next point.

They made their way through the town.

"This village is so cute. The people here are really nice, too." Aria smiled as they rode through. "It's great to be out of those mountains."

"Speaking of the mountains, how did you get to know all of those things about the mountains, Barina?" Twarence was walking alongside his horse for a while.

Barina looked over at him as she took her hair down from its braid and left it free. "Some of it's from experience, and then some of it is from the gnomes that live there. Anytime I've helped them, I'd stick around with them, and they'd teach me a thing or twenty."

"It's too bad we didn't get to meet any of them. Maybe next time." Aria grinned looking up to the sunny skies, she was loving the warm weather.

The village consisted of maybe three dozen homes and a couple of businesses, one of which was at the docks, renting out boats of every size to those who would pass through. Barina squinted her eyes a little as they came closer to the jetty, smiling at seeing the man sitting outside the building. He was relaxing in a rocking chair with a cup of tea next to him on the table and was knitting something out of white yarn.

"Hi Lee!" Barina called when they were within earshot.

The man was in his late sixties with a long white beard and a bald head. He was short and a little pudgy, and his big heart matched his smile when he saw who shouted his name.

"Barina?" He stood up and set his knitting down. "How are you?" He walked over as she was rushing up, and they greeted each other with a warm hug.

"I'm good, how are you? What are you making there?" she asked, looking at his knitting.

"I'm great. This is going to be a blanket. I have a new granddaughter, and I'm making one for her." His face was beaming with pride.

"Awe, congrats! That makes four grandkids now?"

"Yup. I love getting to spoil them." He saw the rest of her group and realized she was traveling. "I see you're passing through, aren't you? Well, Jason and Tyra, you literally missed them by a couple hours, but with the way you sail, I imagine you'll catch up to them."

"I steer a ship just fine, thank you."

Lee was laughing at her a bit. "You do know how to go through a storm decently and fight off the Microlos." His eyes twinkled at her with a grandfatherly affection. "Come on, I'll get you to a ship."

They followed him to the end of the docks to where a large sailboat was sitting in the calm waters. The yacht had a nice sized cabin, and there was a special room that had been built just for the horses. It wasn't anything too fancy, but it was in good shape and would get the job done.

"I'm glad it's you here too. You don't need someone to guide you over Rose Lake or to sail for you. You have that covered," Lee mused while he helped them get onto the ship.

"What do you mean when you say 'How she sails a ship'?" Twarence asked while he brought his horse onto the deck.

"First two boats came back to me in splinters." Lee raised his eyebrows to see her reaction.

Barina put her hands on her hips. "That was not my fault and you know it." She was laughing. "And I paid for the damage."

"Barina?" Onyx was a little weary even.

"The storms that form out there are crazy. I had to abandon ship. And considering one of my former professions, I'd better be good at sailing."

"She's actually quite good, it was just the two ships." Lee couldn't stop laughing.

Barina rolled her eyes with a smile and helped her traveling companions get settled onboard. Lee was helping as well.

"The Microlos, they've been getting restless out there this week, from what people have told me. So be on your guard. The winds have been favorable though, so I expect you should be in Fortania by first light tomorrow."

Barina's gaze had turned to Rose Lake. "Micorolos I can handle. The storms, well, I think we should be okay. I think we're all set here Lee. I'll write to you soon, and we'll get together for dinner after I get done with this job." She gave him a warm hug.

Lee hugged her back and walked down the ramp—Arkon pulling the ramp onto the ship after he was clear. Lee used a long pole to push the ship away from the docks. "Bye Barina, safe travels."

Barina waved. She pulled the cord to release the sails so they could catch the winds, and they made their way to the open waters of Rose Lake.

They had a good breeze to push them along, and Barina was right, she knew her way around the ship. She had Twarence take the helm while she worked for a minute to secure the sails. After a good twenty minutes, they were all sitting with Twarence while he steered. Barina had just finished looking over everything to make sure they were set.

"You've been through this area a couple times, haven't you?" Arkon sat next to her on the deck.

"Yeah. Lee is a sweetheart, isn't he? I never have enough time to visit with him for more than a couple days though."

"So, what are the Microlos?" Aria had grabbed some bread out of her pack and was glad for the snack.

"If I remember correctly," Twarence relied quietly, "and this is just what I've heard from people cause I've never seen it written down anywhere, they're kind of an eel that are about twelve feet long and about three feet in diameter, right? They spit sludge and are known to jump into boats to eat people."

Barina put a finger to her nose. "Hard little bastards to kill. They mainly live in the middle of the lake, but there are ways to tell when they're around. You'll smell roses in the air. It's the scent they emit when they're near."

"Is that why it's called Rose Lake?" Aria hadn't hesitated to make herself comfortable and was lounging back on a bench.

"I would say that's a safe bet." Barina leaned back, sitting on the floor. "Man, it's a nice day."

"Safe bet? You have no idea, do you?" Onyx poked her with the end of the staff.

Barina smirked before she closed her eyes, her hands behind her head. "Nope."

The rest of them laughed a little at that.

"Let's hope for a calm ride. It'd be nice." Arkon sighed lightly.

"Famous last words." Jaras lightly punched the elf's shoulder and sat back as well.

"You did totally jinx this entire voyage over the lake." Twarence was smiling.

Arkon laughed a little bit, looking over at the thief as she closed her eyes, trying to be comfortable. "Sorry, my bad."

"Microlos are fine. Well, they're not, but I can fight them. The storms come out of nowhere, and those are the real danger." Barina opened an eye. "Have…have any of you traveled past the Black Mountains?"

"Not on foot, I always traveled by portal with magic," Onyx told her. "I can only do that from the Hitum Mountain though, so I can't just magic us to Thoron."

"I've done all of my fighting east of Larindana, so that's a no from me." Jaras rubbed the back of his neck before he lit a smoke.

"You smoke that thing by the railing. I don't want any of those embers floating on in here." Barina shot him a look. She had a smile, but she was dead serious.

Jaras stood up with a sigh and went to the edge of the ship.

"I've studied the areas we're going to, so I have a good idea what to expect, but obviously it's not the same as experience," Twarence said with a little yawn.

"And I'm like Onyx, but I traveled on Elvin roads if I had to go anywhere. Unfortunately I can't bring humans on those roads."

"And it's a solid no from me whether I've been this far from home." Aria wasn't even messing around with her answer.

"Well then…" Barina closed her eyes again.

Aria, like the others, wasn't sure what Barina was thinking. "What?"

"Mind you, I do a lot of work on my own, every now and then working with others. But they all knew the roads. It's all good though. We'll be okay."

For the first couple of hours, things were very peaceful and they were enjoying the trip. There was nothing but the pristine waters of the lake as far as the eyes could see. It was a beautiful afternoon and the temperature in the air couldn't have been more perfect.

Barina was taking a little nap on the deck, Aria sitting next to Jaras reading a book while he read a book of his own. Onyx and Arkon were sitting together exchanging magic tips and knowledge with each other, and Twarence was at the helm. Barina had told him to keep heading west, so that's what he was doing.

In the distance, dark clouds vanished not far ahead of them. It must've been one of these storms that Barina was talking about. Twarence could make out a ship there, and it didn't look like it was in good shape.

"Hey Barina?" he said quietly. She stirred and opened her eyes. "Guys!" he called to the others. They looked at him as he pointed in front of them.

They saw a flag waving back and forth. The people on the ship were in trouble.

"Twarence, may I?" Barina stepped up to take the helm. "I'm gonna bring her alongside their ship, and I'll need you guys to get the buoys starboard side and toss them a line when we're close enough."

The group jumped into action, working to get their ship ready to help the others.

"Ahoy!" came the call of the man on the ship when they got close enough.

Barina smirked when she heard the voice of the man calling to them. She brought the ship around, and they tied off to it. The sails were busted, and the ship itself was starting to bring on water.

"Thanks," the man said, grabbing the rope so he and the woman he was with could tie theirs to them. "One of those stupid storms got us and now, well, we're sinking."

"I see that. We don't mind giving you a lift at all." Arkon climbed over their ship. "We can help you carry your things to ours."

"Did you call for a knight in shining armor?" Barina's smile grew even more when the man saw her.

The man rolled his eyes, and the woman with him started laughing.

"Goddamn it." He was shaking his head with laughter.

"She's not ever going to let you live this one down Jason," the woman said.

"You know it, Tyra." Barina gave her a thumbs up.

"I had to get saved by you," he grumbled and tossed a bag at her, which she caught and set down.

"Surprise!" and in a second Barina jumped onto their ship and tackled both Jason and Tyra in a big bear hug.

The man was the same age as Barina and stood five feet eleven inches with brown hair and green eyes. He had stubble on his face since he hadn't shaved in a couple days. He wore a pair of black pants and a green shirt, and was laughing when he gave her a hug. The woman with him was a couple of years younger, with brown hair, blue eyes, and was fairly tall herself. She wore a simple tan skirt and a purple blouse.

"Lee said that you had just passed through a couple hours before we did, I was hoping we'd catch up to you." Barina was helping them get their things. "See a storm got to you."

"Yeah, it was only there for a couple of minutes, but enough to do the damage and kill the ship. I'm not bad at the helm but damn, nobody could've stopped that," Jason sighed to her.

"I'm glad you're here," Tyra said. "Kinda worried about sinking. Is this the group you were meeting with for that job you were taking?" Tyra asked her.

"Oh, where are my manners?" Barina couldn't believe she was being so rude.

"Didn't think you had any." Jason snorted a laugh and was quickly punched on the arm. "Ow!"

"This is Twarence, Jaras, Arkon, Aria, and Onyx. Guys, this is Jason and Tyra. They were moving from Miork to go live in Estella where our friend Josh is. Jason is a blacksmith, and Tyra has been studying medicine and is heading there to finish her training," Barina told them. "Josh has been excited, and I talked to Mason not long ago. He's been getting all giddy about it too."

"Nice to meet all of you." Jason was giving each one in the group a long look, as if they were familiar to him. "Yeah, we got Mason's letter right before we left town. It'll be nice to finally get there."

They all greeted each other and then quickly went to get the rest of their things and the horse onto the unscathed ship. They had to abandon the broken ship as it sank to the bottom of the lake.

"I am so glad that Josh took a bunch of our things with him when he came to visit," Tyra breathed through her teeth.

"Hi Lucy, how are you girl?" Barina gave their horse a little pat on her nose and a scratch behind her ear. "Come on, I'll take you to the other horses." The horse nuzzled Barina's shoulder as she led her away.

"She won't own one, but she for sure likes them." Tyra yawned.

"Does she just not know how to ride a horse?" Arkon asked. "What's her deal with that?"

Jason held a smile. "She can ride a horse, she's an expert at it, honestly. It's just, with her job, having a horse isn't practical."

Jaras glanced over. "She's an expert?"

Tyra nodded. "I've seen her do some impressive riding. Her and Jason both are pretty talented."

"So, are you her friend that's known her forever? The one she's talked about? You learned to fight from Berklion?" Twarence asked as they headed to the helm again.

Jason looked at Barina as she walked back over to them. "Barina?"

"They got it out of me, okay?" She knew she had been caught breaking a rule of theirs. "Took them almost a month. I didn't talk about my fighting, but eventually the question of who trained me came up. Don't worry, they're legit," she reassured him.

"That's a yes." Jaras liked watching this interaction with them. "So you've known her forever then, haven't you?"

"Pretty much. We grew up together." Jason made a spot for Tyra to sit next to him.

"He's been one of my best friends for as long as I can remember." Barina smiled happily.

Tyra's smile had the joke. "She has a horrible memory," she teased her.

Barina stuck her tongue out at Tyra, but her smile never left her face. "I wish I didn't remember, but ya know."

"And she kind of just walked up and decided she was going to be my friend. I didn't have anything else going on, so figured, why not." Jason was laughing with the others now. Barina was a good sport about it. Her eyes were locked on him with both mischief and annoyance in her stare. Jason saw her arms move, but he knew he couldn't move fast enough to stop her, so he did the next best thing. Her intention was to push him into the water and make him climb back onto the ship.

Barina let out a gasp. "Sonofabitch!"

Jason had grabbed her arms and pulled her with him. He gave a victory laugh even as they both went falling off the ship and into the blue waters below. Jason and Barina swam to the surface and exchanged looks for a second before they started laughing and climbing back onto the ship. The others would've helped but they were laughing too hard.

"Well, that backfired a bit." Barina was still laughing as she jumped back onto the deck.

Jason was shaking with laughter and held two fingers an inch apart. "Just a little."

"Tyra, is this normal with these two?" Aria was still laughing.

"Yeah, they do stuff like this all the time. You get used to it after a while." Tyra was watching Barina and Jason as if they were a couple of toddlers.

"Barina, stunts like that, you have to be careful. What if the Microlos were there?" Arkon put a hand on her shoulder.

"Please, I knew the risks. We weren't in any danger, they're not near right now." Some of her laughter subsided a bit.

"I just don't want to see you get hurt." His face was concerned.

"Only thing that could've hurt her there was me." Jason smiled nudging her shoulder. "Would it be okay if Tyra and I rested for a bit? We're pretty tired from riding out that storm."

"Sure, come on." Barina smiled and took her friends below deck to get them situated.

"Those two will be a nice addition for a while. Estella is on our way, so having a second person trained by Berklion and someone who can help if there are injuries will only help." Jaras was smiling as he leaned against the railing. "I haven't seen B light up like that."

"She's really in her element now with them. Maybe some of us will see some of our friends while we're out here." Aria was glad for the extra company on the trip.

Arkon was smiling thinking of Barina and then looked fondly when he saw a blur with blonde hair rush past him. She came back up onto the deck wearing a dry set of clothes—a tan pair of pants and a white blouse—but she was walking barefoot so her boots could dry. She had also let her hair down for it to dry. He watched her rush up to quickly sit next to Aria and put her head on her shoulder to look at the book their healer was reading. Aria started laughing and leaned her head against Barina's, patting her on the shoulder. Aria laughed. "You're a nut, Barina."

Arkon went up to join them and saw that Barina was writing in a journal while she still leaned against Aria. Jaras closed his eyes to take a nap, and Onyx and Twarence sat watching the horizon in silence while Onyx was still at the helm.

"So, who's making dinner?" Aria asked after they sat in silence for an hour. "I'm starting to get hungry."

"Is there a kitchen on this ship? I didn't think there was." Arkon looked over at them.

"There's a tiny galley down below toward the back of the ship. It's nothing fancy, but it'll get the job done," Barina told him while still writing in her journal.

They then all turned to the former pirate. Barina looked up, her face saying *what?* when she felt everyone staring. "God damn it," she said, but she smiled as she stood back up. "Thankfully for us, the ships normally have a stock of at least potatoes, carrots, and onions. Lee's always been particular about that. I'm gonna go fishing and see if I can catch anything."

Barina headed to the back of the ship and dug in some of the storage compartments till she found a net that was tied to a rope. She cast it over and waited.

"Guess we should've discussed that a little sooner huh?" Aria grinned. "Might take a while for her to catch something."

"We're gonna have dinner made for us by a real pirate." Onyx had a smirk on his face.

"Are you able to eat fish? Does that interfere with your powers like other meats do?" Twarence was curious about that.

"Strangely enough, no it doesn't," Aria told him. "And I freaking love fish." Aria's eyes grew big thinking about it. "God I hope she gets something good."

The guys laughed. "Well, we found a weakness for her." Jaras was smiling.

"Who doesn't like food?" Aria asked in her defense. "And I'm not gonna pretend like I'm not eager to see how a pirate can fix a meal for us. Girl has to know her way around seafood, right?"

"Let's hope, and dang, she does not mess around, does she?" Jaras looked impressed seeing Barina coming toward them.

She had four fish caught, deboned, and filleted. She was whistling happily and disappeared below deck to the galley. The last thing they heard from her as she went down the steps was her singing, "Yo ho yo ho, a pirate's life for me!"

That got a laugh out of them.

"Dinner with a pirate, but on a lake and not the sea. I wonder if she has any rum on her." Aria then jumped up to rush down the steps to find out.

"Well, she wants to get hammered apparently." Onyx smiled. "Wouldn't be terrible to have a few drinks."

The next moment, they heard Aria bursting with laughter as she came back up to the deck holding a flask that she had gotten from the thief.

"No rum. She has a little bit of brandy though. Told her she was a disgrace to pirates, and she started using pirate talk on me, throwing in an accent and everything." Aria was still laughing as she took a drink from the flask and then passed it around. "There's not a lot, but it's something."

They each took a drink from it—only one drink, before it was gone.

It wasn't even an hour before Barina called everyone to dinner. The food was delicious even though they hadn't asked if she was able to cook. They all ate below deck, getting to know her friends better, while Barina wanted to be outside and took the helm.

"So how long have you known Barina?" Twarence asked. He noticed that Jason wore a pendant that looked just like hers, sharing in one line of the triangle that was completed by their friend Josh. Jason was another who had learned under Berklion. "She seems like an interesting character."

"We were pretty young. Her father had come to mine to get some new hammers made for his smithy, and Barina was there with him. While our dads were going over their order, she saw me cleaning and came over to say hi. I wasn't exactly the most talkative person, and I was kinda shy. I wasn't expecting her to come over and just start up a conversation with me." Jason started laughing thinking about it. "She always said that she decided in the first couple minutes that she was gonna make me her friend, and I still haven't been able to shake her. She introduced me to our friend Josh and made each of us swords. I still carry mine and, after her family died, Josh and I went to Nippon with her and Berklion. After we got back, she took to living under a bridge on the outskirts of town in Miork in a cave."

"She took Onyx, Jaras, and me to her home the first night we met," Twarence said. "It was a neat place, and we drank, well, she had us drink some kind of wine." Twarence smiled while taking a drink.

Aria looked over at them. "I didn't know you went to her place that night? Why didn't you come get us?" She was as surprised as Arkon to hear this.

Onyx answered with a mouthful of food. "You guys were already asleep, otherwise she said she would've brought you."

Jason's smile grew. "Must mean she really likes all of you, that she trusts you. Yeah, I've always been a little jealous of how she's fixed up the place over the years. It suits her needs. Safe, secure, and hidden. She's not home a lot anyway, so knowing her stuff will be safe while she's out is good.

"Barina refuses to let Josh or me join her when she's called to do what she's doing now. Which is understandable, but if she's just fighting, then we go with her."

"Why won't she let you? And why the hell didn't she take up her father's trade?" Arkon then asked.

"Money is her big reason she doesn't continue her father's trade. Josh and I both were able to build off of our dad's businesses, save up to start our own. Barina would've taken over the business when she was older but, after her dad died, I mean, she was thirteen. She had no money to keep the business going, and this is one that had been handed down for three generations. Most of the equipment had been destroyed. I think her aunt kept a few things that she could find, but it's really expensive to be able to set up an operation like that. This, the work she does, this is so she can make a living," Jason told them, finishing his dinner. "As for Tyra, a few years ago she came into the picture."

Tyra finished her wine and poured another glass. "I met Barina one day when I was walking home from work and a couple of guys started to harass me. She saw it and managed to get them to leave me alone. I don't know what she did to them, and I don't think I want to, but it worked. Anyway, she walked me home and then invited me to dinner with her and her friends. I met Jason that night, and we started dating not long after.

We're planning on getting married next summer. Figure, get set up in Estella, and then have the wedding. Josh moved there a few years ago, and we've always been really drawn there. It's a great town, and they're really needing doctors, so we're going there."

"What about Barina? She'll be in Miork by herself?" Aria was kind of surprised that Barina wouldn't have her friends there.

Tyra shrugged her shoulders. "Like we said, she's not home much. She'll be home for a few days every couple of weeks, but she travels a lot. She's not exactly attached to the city. I think she only lives there because of us and her aunt and uncle. She has friends all over the place, so it's not like she's by herself."

Jason smiled as he piled a bunch of food onto a plate. "She's a big girl, and she can handle herself." He stood up with the plate in his hand. "Speaking of that klutz, I'm gonna take her a plate and chill with her for a bit."

"Klutz, she's a klutz?" Arkon didn't even try to hide a smile. "I have seen her stumble a couple times."

"Oh, my yes. I'm surprised she can walk sometimes." Tyra winked while taking a bite of her potatoes.

Jason waved at them and headed above deck. The wind was still calm—just a slight enough breeze to move the ship—and a fog had settled over the water. The moonlight would reflect patches where the water was visible. It was very peaceful. He found his best friend steering the ship while smoking her pipe. She smiled seeing him walking up the steps.

Jason handed the plate to her, taking over at the helm.

"Thanks. Did you spit in it?" she asked, taking a bite of her dinner.

"Always."

"Poisoned too, right?"

Jason smirked. "Wouldn't taste right without it."

This was an old joke with both of them.

"Food was pretty good. Thanks for cooking," Jason then told her. Leaning against the wheel, he lit up a cigarette.

Barina shot him a look.

"Don't worry," he said. "I have a glass of water with me right here. I'm keeping the smoke there when not taking a drag." He then lunged forward at her with the lit cigarette and tried to get close enough to her arm to singe her a bit.

She dodged it. "Mahh, stob dhab!" she scolded him with a mouth full of food. She danced away from him, holding her plate, and gave him a scowl.

"Not even a little burn?" he teased.

Her eyes went darker, but he still saw the smile in them. "Ass."

Jason started laughing. "I knew you missed me."

"We'll go with that." She was laughing too, and then held up her hand with his matches in it.

Jason's eyes went wide. "You sneaky little...I'd call you a thief, but that's too obvious."

"You'll get them back when you start behaving." She put them in her pocket.

Jason stuck his bottom lip out. "Please, can I have them back?"

Barina took another bite. "That face doesn't work on me."

"I bring you dinner and this is the thanks that I get."

"I made the damn food."

"And it's delicious." Jason gave her a cheesy but sincere smile.

Barina leaned back against the railing, tossing his matches back to him. "Arigato."

"You're welcome."

Barina and Jason sat quietly while she finished eating her food. She set the plate down and took her pipe back out. "Nani?" She could tell there was something eating at him.

Jason finally blurted out what had been on his mind. "You do realize that we've met all of them before, right?"

Her mouth turned up a little. "Yup, well, except I don't remember meeting Aria."

Jason nodded. "You wouldn't, you were out cold, literally, but you realized who she was. Do they realize it?"

"Onyx and Twarence both have picked up on the fact that we all met when we were younger, but the rest of them, I'm not sure. Jaras is still clueless." She was in as much disbelief as her friend was.

Jason couldn't believe what he heard. "But we spent almost a month hanging out with him when we were visiting Darien in Treklea. How?

You even kicked his ass in a sparring match, twice. We were all at Darien's wedding. How does he not remember that?"

Barina shrugged her shoulders. "Search me, but I'm waiting for it to click before I give him hell for it." She had to laugh some more.

They were both quiet for a moment. Barina had something she wanted to tell him but wasn't sure how to phrase it.

"Spit it out already," Jason said, grinning a little, but his eyes were serious.

"I think Arkon's been hitting on me," she said quietly and then shifted uncomfortably.

Jason met her look for a moment, letting that process. "The elf, right?" She nodded.

"Hmm, I thought I saw him looking at you a lot earlier."

Jason's eyes seemed to be looking inside himself for something. Barina knew he was searching his intuition, trying to get a feel for someone.

"I just don't know if I want to deal with this kind of thing right now, especially while working. I mean, for the right person yeah, but I don't know. He wasn't too welcoming of me at first, and I'm happy that we're buddies now, but I don't know if I'm really interested in him."

Jason snorted a laugh. "That would be a 'no' then. Man, you've just never really had any good luck in the relationship department. I really didn't like Nick or Eli. It's a good thing your pirates took care of Eli first or he would've had to answer to me. And Nick, he was a freaking ass."

Barina's smile was warm. "Aren't you just a sweetheart?"

"Can't help it." Jason put his smoke out. "Why the hell were they such bastards?"

"Just their nature, I guess. Course Nick really wanted me to settle down and be a little housewife for him. There's nothing wrong if that's what a woman wants for herself, but that's not what I'm looking to do."

"Fair enough." Jason then started to laugh to himself. "Still surprised that David asked you to marry him. Well, no I'm not. He was interested in you when he met us before we headed to Nippon. I knew he'd probably fall for you again if he saw you when we got back."

Barina shook her head and rolled her eyes. "I hope he finds himself a girl better suited for him. I'm not royal material."

Jason thought about it. "I don't know. Queen Barina doesn't sound too bad." He gave an elaborate bow at that. "And Darien would've had a hay day if you became future queen of his kingdom."

Barina raised her eyebrows. "Do I look like royalty to you?"

Jason thought about it for a moment. "Yes and no. I think you'd make a good leader. You have a good head on your shoulders and you're fair. But I really didn't want David as your husband. He wasn't right for you."

"He's attractive and all, but not for me."

Jason then let something out that he had been holding back for a while. "And I'm sorry—prince or no prince, if I heard him tell you one more time that you could be so beautiful if you wanted to be or to put down your blade or to start wearing make-up, I was gonna punch him. Could be so beautiful if you wanted to be, that's not a compliment. If he couldn't see who you really are, then he never would, and he didn't deserve you. He kept trying to change you to some docile wall-flower, and I wasn't okay with that." Jason was visibly irritated. "I know I say I'll support you with whoever you decide to be with, but that was one I was gonna put my foot down on, B. I know you only went on a couple of dates, but seriously, ugh. What an ass. I'm glad you never let him once, not ever, convince you to be someone other than who you are."

Barina's face turned red, her smile was warm. "Thank you," was all she could say. She hadn't realized how much that had bothered Jason. Barina wasn't about to let anyone turn her into someone she wasn't, prince or no, and it was good to know that Jason would've personally gotten in the middle of this one if it had come to it. It was sweet.

Jason took it as a personal insult to himself when someone would hurt her. "Too bad things with you and Kinnoskuke didn't work out. I liked him," Jason mused, thinking back on one of their old friends.

Barina smiled a little. "He was a good guy. We ended on good terms, and there was no bad blood there. I heard that he's engaged to Kotoko."

"Good for them." Jason glanced at her. "And thank goodness she finally decided against Naoki. He was a dick. He treated that girl like shit."

Barina raised her arms in the air. "Right? She did so much to be kind and good to him, and he was always insulting her and bullying her. She couldn't control that she loved him, but finally she wised up, I guess."

Jason was laughing. "I like how he tried to treat you the same, only to find out it was because he liked you, thinking it would make you want him more and you were like…"

Barina finished the sentence. "Baka. I would rather be alone than be with someone who treated me like garbage."

Jason was still laughing at her reaction. "Do you think Arkon would treat you badly?"

"No. I just don't think I'm attracted to him in that way," she said with a yawn.

"Then it's a no. Trust your instincts. If he's not for you, he's not for you. I mean, my gut tells me no with him for you. If you decided on it, I would support you, but I just don't think he's right."

"You do have one hell of an intuition about people."

Jason nudged her arm. "I know."

"So how have you been? Getting excited to get to Estella?"

Jason nodded, but not by much. "Eh," was all he said, which honestly meant that he was pumped about it, since the word, eh, could mean so much with him.

"Barina." Jason's tone was quiet. She could tell he had something heavy on his mind. "Are you ever going to stop traveling all the time? Since we got back from Nippon, you're never around for more than a couple weeks at a time. And sometimes you're gone for a few days, sometimes weeks and, hell, months or even a year. I miss you when you're gone for so long. Are you ever going to stop?"

"I've really been thinking about it."

The blacksmith wasn't expecting that, and he focused on her. His eyes, for once, were excited and smiling. "Seriously? Do you think you have enough saved up yet?"

"With this job, I just might have enough to do it. I want to open my own shop. I mean, I'm not going to pretend that I don't enjoy what I do right now. The last few years since we've been back from Nippon have been amazing. So many great stories and adventures. I've made some great friends, and I've done a hell of a lot of good, but I miss out on too much. I really do want to start making swords again." She took a long puff on her pipe.

Jason's green eyes perked up, and the smile in his eyes matched the one on his face. "So you, you really think you're going to be able to after this?"

"I started to learn to fight to be able to protect the people I care about and to help those who need it the most. I think I've been doing a good job of that over the years, and I can still go and help when needed. If I open my own shop, I set my own hours. I can travel when I want, and I'd still be on call to help when needed. But I miss the forge, and I'd like to have a real place to hang my hat at the end of the day. I mean, my best skills are fighting, stealing, and sword making."

Jason interrupted her. "You've always been damn good with a lute or an ocarina too. Too bad girls aren't seen much as bards."

"I know. It's getting a little better for us females with that, but there's a long way to go."

Jason was smiling more. "I'm excited to see what you'll be able to make. And thanks again for my sword. It's never failed me."

"It better not. I put too much work into that." She grinned with a little wink. "If you and Josh were gonna fight beside me, you were going to have the best."

"These were the best to ever come out of the shop. The only ones that were even close to these were the one your dad made for Berklion and, well, there was another one…" His voice trailed off.

Barina nodded. "I know which one you're talking about. It was one of the last ones he was making, but I have no idea what happened to it after he died. That one *was* the best sword to ever come out of that shop. I never found out who it was for, either. That one, along with a bunch of other swords, were freaking stolen the night they died. Still makes me mad."

Jason's face went sour. "That still pisses me off." Jason's gaze set to his sword that was hooked to his belt. "Why did you name my sword Poison Ivy and Josh's Poison Oak? You never did tell me that."

Barina didn't skip a beat. "Cause you're both like a bad rash that won't go away."

Jason's eyes went level. "Should just toss this damn thing."

"Next one is gonna cost ya." She gave him a sassy smile.

"Just cause I couldn't afford another one." He was still smiling at her though before he shook his head. "Do you have your ocarina with you by chance? I wouldn't mind hearing some good music."

"No. Broke the last trip I took." That wiped the smile right off her face.

143

He saw the light change in her eye and the pout. "In a fight?" He knew it wasn't that but wanted to hear her admit something else.

The thief finally groaned out, "No, literally the last trip. I was walking up the stairs, tripped, landed on it. I just haven't gotten another one since then."

Jason busted out laughing. "Freaking klutz!"

Barina huffed out a sigh. She could be so graceful when she was fighting, but any other time, not so much.

"Ass," she breathed.

Both Jason and Barina turned their heads upwards at a sudden flash of lightning and a crash of thunder. Clouds began to swirl overhead and, in seconds, rain and pea-sized hail started to fall onto the ship.

"Shit!" Barina looked to Jason and began to give orders. "Get the others up here, then I need you to get those storm sails up." She took over at the helm.

"Guys, get up here now!" Jason yelled. "We have a storm!"

Within seconds, the rest of the group was above deck and ready to help.

"What do you need from us?" Twarence called over the wind.

"Get that mainsail down, then get the jib and try sails up!" Barina was yelling over her shoulder.

"What are those?" Jaras called back.

"Those small sails attached to the railing there and the other small one by the mast!" She then grumbled while looking at the waters. "Bubbles, come on, let up."

The group did as they were told and, working together, they were able to get the sails switched out and then ran back to her.

"What now!" Aria asked.

"Hold onto your butts!" Barina was going to have to use all her concentration to get them through this storm. The lake was a strange place, the storms came and went quickly—no warning, rhyme or reason. That was just the way it was. Well, she knew the reasons, but at the moment, she had other things to worry about.

Barina's eyes went wide, and then she looked rather annoyed when she saw what was ahead of them. "Fuck."

Aria groaned. "I just know I don't want to see what it is you see."

They all heard her swear when she looked in front of them, and they turned to see an enormous waterspout raging in front of them. Barina grabbed the wheel to bring them around and steer them away when she rolled her eyes. "Of course I smell roses! Brace yourselves!"

Jason unsheathed his sword, staying close to Barina, trying to give her less to worry about so she could control the ship. He saw Tyra, who was next to Jaras. He knew she'd be okay with Jaras. Tyra looked to Jason and nodded, knowing and understanding what he was doing.

Arkon ran to the front of the ship and raised his hands. His whole body began to glow and, within moments, the light from his body began to expand.

Barina put a hand on Jason's shoulder. "Protect him, I can handle myself." She had to shout over the storm.

The two friends met eyes, and he nodded before he hurried over to the elf. Everyone seemed to think the same thing. They all rushed to guard Arkon. He wouldn't be able to fight for himself. Even Tyra took out the hatchet that she carried with her and was on the ready.

Twarence was the only one who stayed with Barina, his blades out.

A large wave splashed up on to the ship. Twarence found himself on the ground, not from the wave, but because he was pushed there by the thief. He looked up as lightning crashed above his head and Barina, with one hand still on the helm, took her dagger and sliced an enormous eel-like creature in half. It let out a loud screech as it wriggled.

It wasn't the Microlo that made him freeze. It wasn't even seeing a creature that he had never known existed in front of him that made him catch his breath. The fifteen-foot-long beast now lay in two pieces as its long fangs still lashed out, its gills moving as it tried to take one last breath while its milky-white eyes still searched for prey.

There was something else, something so monumental that he saw, that it could change the course of everything. Twarence couldn't move. He couldn't take his eyes off what he was seeing.

It was when he saw Barina punt either half of the Microlo off the ship and hold out a hand, "Are you hurt?" that he was brought back to the situation at hand.

Twarence took her hand as she helped him up. "Thank you. You saved my life."

Barina gave him a slight nod. "Stay sharp, it has friends."

He looked and saw another half dozen of the Microlos slither onto the ship, making their way toward the group.

The Microlos raised their bodies up, their mouths opening as they let out their low hisses. In a flash, they lunged, their long bodies moving like a whip that crossed the ship.

Jason and Jaras moved first. The creatures hardly saw the fighters strike. They were that fast, and the Microlos were without their heads.

Another one was racing for the helm. Twarence, this time, was ready for it. It was fast, faster than he could've imagined, and it dodged his attacks. Twarence finally started following its movements and was able to get a solid strike on it before he threw it overboard.

Aria took one down with her bow as it closed in on her, but another one leaped on her before she could stop it. She had a hand on either side of her bow, pressing it up into the jaws, trying to keep the Microlo's fangs from closing in on her. She didn't see Tyra pounce and slam her hatchet into its skull. The two women pushed the monster off and back into the water. Both women smiled at the other with a nod.

They then turned, both in awe at the magic men.

There was a huge school of Microlos trying to get on from the bow of the ship. Onyx wasn't having it. He aimed his staff, sending shock waves of energy at the creatures. One of them got close, and Onyx took his staff apart and sliced at the creature while sending shock waves with the other half of the staff. He was trying to give Arkon more time to do what he had to do.

Arkon drew in the energies around him. This was a storm unlike anything he had ever felt in his life. It was powerful, wild, and there was no sense to it. Most storms that he knew, they followed patterns. There was pressure, temperatures, air flow, factors that played into what made the storm what it was.

This storm was alive. It was a literal deity that was controlling the weather on the lake. Not just that, the lake, the deity was the lake. Her domain was only this area, but hers, nonetheless.

He shifted his focus, and he could see her completely. She was beautiful. Her white hair cascaded down with the rain, and her deep blue face was smooth while the strong winds blew from her mouth. Her hands moved the waters back and forth. She was one of the most beautiful beings he had ever laid eyes on.

"Spirit Elf, you can see me?" She seemed surprised.

"I can, Your Grace. Please, can you halt the storm? People I care for are on this ship, and this can hurt them."

Her eyes narrowed. "Humans have done nothing but bring harm to my waters. They throw their waste, their filth, their dead, and they care nothing for what their actions do." She looked at the Microlos in disgust.

"We don't care for the Microlos either."

"They are horrible beasts who are not native to my waters. A man, a magician, created them, and he decided to drop them in my waters to see what would happen. Since then they have been destroying any life they can claim."

"I think..." Arkon had to focus more. "I think I can eliminate them. I think I can destroy them. You're right. They're an abomination. They were never meant to be created. They live to kill, not even to feed when they do. This magician...he's dark. He was very dark. Will you calm the waters so that I can focus my energies on them?"

The deity looked at him. "You can do that? Are you really powerful enough to do this?"

"I think so. The humans with me, they're good."

The deity leaned in closer. "The woman with you at the helm. I've seen her pass through here many times. She is good. I've seen her kill Microlos by the dozen. More than that. She's never thrown waste into my waters, no filth, and she never takes a fish she doesn't eat. She is good."

"She really does seem to make an impression, doesn't she?"

The deity smiled a little. "Yes, she's always been a kind soul." She turned her attention back to the elf. "I will calm the storm if you give me your word you will do your best to eliminate the Microlos completely."

"On my honor of the Spirit, you have my word." He gave a bow of his head. "Thank you."

Within moments, the waters settled, the skies cleared, and there was calm on the water again.

"Oh, thank goodness," Aria sighed in relief.

Arkon turned to them. "My work isn't done. I made a deal with the Lake."

Twarence tilted his head. "The Lake?"

"The Lake is also a Deity. She's been angry with how humans have treated her over the years, dumping their waste, their filth, killing for sport and not food. The Microlos are not natural beings. They were the creation of a magician who left them in this lake and since then, they kill for killing's sake and not for just food. She doesn't like them here," he sighed. "It's the way humans have treated her which has caused the storms over the years." Arkon then gave a warm smile to Barina. "She had good things to say about you though."

Barina blinked. "Huh?"

Arkon laughed a bit. "Says that every time you've been through here you don't waste in her waters, you don't catch fish you don't eat, and you kill a lot of Microlos."

Barina smiled. "Would explain why I never had a storm when I traveled alone. If people were with me then yeah, but never when I was alone." She looked at the water and waved. "Thanks!"

The others were laughing.

"Dork." Tyra breathed with a laugh.

"What deal did you make?" Onyx then asked.

"To eliminate as many Microlos as I could," he told him simply. "I think I can do it. I think I can get rid of a whole lot of them, if not all."

"Oh." Onyx sat up with a smile. "I like this deal."

"We can keep an eye out here for any that try to attack while you do your thing," Aria agreed. She knocked an arrow to her bow.

Arkon gave a slight nod and knelt down, going into a deep trance. His body not only glowed but became almost completely transparent.

"It's not in my nature to go after any creatures of the world, but these things are not natural. They were never supposed to be created and, considering that all they do is cause destruction in their wake with no benefit to the surrounding area, I can safely say, they can be wiped out." Arkon normally used his powers with animals to sway them to do no harm, but this was an exception to the rule.

He reached into the lake with all of his powers and sensed every single one of the Microlos. He was at his limit, reaching for so many creatures in this large space. It was taxing on him. Arkon had to search over every rock, under every weed, everywhere to find all of the Microlos. He sensed that they stayed away from the docks and the shore, but if a person were to go out more than twenty feet into the water, they were fair game.

He linked his energies to all of them and, once he had them, ZAP! He fried each one of them.

Arkon sat down, his body back to normal, and he took a deep breath. "It's done. They're all gone. It was quick, and they didn't feel a thing."

"That's a nicer mercy than most would've given them," Jaras scoffed.

Arkon gave him a look. "I didn't want them to suffer."

Barina smiled, understanding. "Just because they were an abomination and weren't meant to be, they weren't asked to be brought into existence. It's not their fault they were the way they were. I get it."

Arkon slumped over, smiling at Barina. "It's nice to know you understand." He reached up toward her, his eyes beginning to close. He was out of energy.

Jaras got a hand behind the elf. "Hang on there, bud." Jaras caught Arkon as he fell back. "Jason, help me get him below deck so he can rest."

Jason helped Jaras as they both got an arm under Arkon and helped him to his feet, guiding him down the steps. The rest of the group looked to the waters as they started to see dead Microlos float to the surface.

"I think this is my cue to do the clean-up," Onyx said to himself.

He raised his staff and was able to lift all the creatures into the air and then burn them to a crisp. They were nothing more than ashes now.

"That's one problem solved for good," Tyra said with a yawn.

"Let's start setting up shifts and letting people rest." Twarence was patting Tyra on the back.

"Twarence, how about the two of us taking the first shift?" Onyx leaned against the railing. He finally saw the stars peaking through the clouds.

The group waved everyone goodnight while Twarence and Onyx started to clean the deck from the mess made during the storm.

"This has been a pretty interesting trip so far. Who would've thought that the lake was also a deity?" Onyx couldn't help but laugh to himself while he pushed a broom across the wooden deck. "I mean, I've seen some magic in my days, but nothing like this. Arkon did really well and…" the wizard trailed off when he looked back to see Twarence at the helm of the ship.

Twarence hadn't heard a word that was spoken to him. He had even taken a flask out of his pack and had taken a couple of drinks.

"Twarence." Onyx approached him slowly and took a good look at him.

Twarence was deep in thought, and he had sweat running down his brow. Onyx looked even closer and could see that the scholar was shaking and trying to steady his breathing.

"What is it?" Onyx asked carefully.

Twarence wanted to tell him something but he couldn't form the words.

"Talk to me." Onyx said sitting next to him.

"Onyx, I will tell you what this is about, but I don't know if…it's big," Twarence told him. He was still trying to catch his breath.

Onyx's mind was moving quickly, trying to piece together the who, what, where, when, and how. It didn't take him long to come to a conclusion.

"What happened in the storm? What happened?"

Twarence was debating with himself if he should tell what he knew or not.

"What did you see?" The small wizard came closer.

Twarence finally pulled him near and whispered what had him so rattled. When he did, Onyx's face went pale, and he was at a loss for words.

"Great spirits," Onyx finally breathed out. He grabbed the flask from Twarence's hand and took a long pull. As powerful as he was, Onyx wasn't prepared for news like that. He sat down and put his face between his hands.

"You understand what I'm dealing with here?" Twarence took another swig.

Onyx nodded. "This is…this is. We knew there was the possibility of people being out there who could. But, here? Do you think that old man knew?"

"I think so. I think he did. I think he knows more about all of this than he told anyone. I think he knew, and he did it this way as a safeguard." Twarence took out a cigarette and lit it.

Onyx offered up his opinion. "To make sure in case the wrong person was able to use it, that there was someone to counter them."

"Or in the event that they're corrupt. Put them down, or at the very least keep them away from it, too," Twarence countered. "We tell nobody about this. Not until we know more."

"Agreed. And until we know more, we act as though we know nothing," Onyx told him. "Honestly, I don't think that they would be corrupt. I've seen too much good to think they'd be bad."

150

"Let's hope you're right," Twarence said. "Oh, and on your original topic, I never would've guessed the lake was a deity."

Onyx started laughing a bit. "Subtle."

"I'm the king of subtlety."

The two of them sat talking for a while when Twarence noticed Arkon walk onto the deck. The elf seemed rested but worn down at the same time. Eyes alert, but he was still pale in the face and moving slowly. Even while traveling through the mountains, he was normally semi put together. At that moment, his hair was hanging limp, his shirt untucked and unbuttoned.

"Take the helm. I'm gonna check on him," Twarence said.

Onyx took over, putting a spell on the helm so that he could sit back and enjoy the scenery.

"Hey, how are you feeling?" Twarence was glad to speak with Arkon. "What you did earlier was the most impressive thing I've ever seen. Thanks, for saving all of us."

Arkon nodded. He was only half listening. He gave Twarence a half smile too.

"What's going on?"

"I hated having to kill all those creatures. It's weighing down on me some." He sighed before he met eyes with the scholar and felt a wave of comfort come over him. There was a sense of peace he felt while looking in Twarence's eyes—a peace everyone there felt when they were with him.

"I'd imagine for someone like you, who works and is able to speak with animals, it would be hard. You understand that coming to blows might happen, but having to wipe out an entire species, it's probably not something that you're conditioned to do."

Arkon nodded slightly. "Most animals, I can speak with them, or at least sway their thoughts to leave us alone. I wasn't able to use my powers on the snow cats at all. They were immune to even that aspect of my abilities. These things though, they had a heart, but there was no talking with them. They were made to be the way they were. They should never have been brought into creation, but it wasn't their fault that they were made. I really hope to find the magician someday who did this and just... What that magician did is wrong." The elf was furious about this, still. "Those creatures needed to go. They served no purpose aside from killing, and they had no natural predator. They had to go."

Twarence placed a hand on Arkon's shoulder. "I'm sorry you were put in this position, but you've probably saved a lot of lives, and you've saved all the animals that do call this lake home."

"I know. That's the only reason I was able to do it." The elf then let out a loud groan and put his face in his hands. "And then there's her! Too much crap on my mind!" For a minute, Arkon hesitated to go on. He was trying to find the words, and finally he said, "I can't seem to get her to take an interest in me. I've been nice and all that, even tried to have some time with her, but it's like, none of that matters."

Twarence was completely thrown off. "Huh, who?"

"Barina."

Twarence felt his eyes pop. He hadn't even realized that Arkon was interested. "Well, honestly, she may not realize that you're interested, and even if she does, she might not be looking for anyone either."

Arkon seemed as if that wasn't an option. "I really like her though. I know at first, I didn't, but that changed, obviously. I mean she's funny and strong, and I'd like to give her a chance to be with me."

"A chance to be with you?" Twarence tilted his head. "You're talking as if it should be an honor."

Arkon shrugged. "Elves, we can be picky. I'm not easily attracted to humans. I mean, Aria is a real looker too, like really pretty. I wouldn't say no to her at all, but I think she's even out of my league."

Twarence was taken aback. "Let me get this straight, you want to go after Barina because you think she's easier to…"

Arkon stopped him. "I'm not saying this to insult her. She's more open to relationships than Aria. Aria isn't interested in being with anyone. Barina is a strong and intelligent woman. She would be an acceptable match for me."

Twarence clapped a hand on Arkon's back and let out a big sigh. "Can I give you some solid advice?"

"Please."

"I've studied so many things about this world. So much, and I'm far from being an expert on women. But this, I don't think it's a good idea. You're going for the girl because, in your eyes, she's obtainable in your book. She's nice and smart and all that you said, but you're speaking of her as if she's a second choice, as if she's something you're picking out from a shop. That's not fair to you and especially not fair to her.

"I mean, you can take your chances if you want, but don't get upset if she turns you down. And if you give it a go, and she finds out that she was a second option and kicks your butt to the curb, don't get angry."

Arkon's eyes rolled in disgust. "That's your advice? Nothing supportive?"

Twarence didn't have much of a temper, and not much got him bothered, but the way Arkon was speaking touched a nerve. "If you weren't making it sound as if Barina should be lucky that you're even thinking about her, and that Aria was nothing more than a trophy instead of the incredibly talented woman she is, maybe I could be. I like you. We're friends. But how you're speaking of these two remarkable women, I'm not okay with it. You need to rethink how you see them and make sure that this is what you really want."

"I know what I want, but I'll think it over like you said." His crystal blue eyes set while looking at the scholar. "Are you going to tell either girl what we talked about?"

Twarence put his smoke out by pouring water on it with his canteen and put the butt in his pocket. "I want to, but I won't," he said and walked away.

Arkon went back to looking over the waters. He did care about Barina, and he was hoping that she'd want to be together. He didn't see why she wouldn't want to be with him. He was attractive, strong, graceful, and he was sure these were things that she'd be interested in. From what he understood, many human women did. He really did think she was a lot of fun and a strong woman, which were things he enjoyed.

Barina wasn't the beauty he was used to seeing with elfin women or found himself wanting from a human woman, but she had confidence, and that was attractive to him as well.

He looked over his shoulder when he saw Barina come onto the deck. She had changed clothes at some point, again. Which made sense since hers had been drenched in the storm. She was wearing another pair of tan pants and a blue blouse, still walking barefoot. Her cheeks were turning pink from the cool air, and her smile was calm when she smelled the fresh air.

She sauntered over slowly to sit next to Onyx and nudged his shoulder. She said something that made him start cracking up. She gave him a cheesy smile and then, while Onyx and Twarence turned their attention back to the helm, she set to doing a workout.

Arkon had noted that she was a goofball who liked to have fun, and she could be completely random when she was talking. She could be talking about one thing, then go to another topic before circling back to a conversation from hours if not days ago, all without any warning. That spirit made him smile.

Barina did a round of sit-ups, push-ups, and a few practice forms before she sat back down with the guys. She didn't do anything with her workouts that looked impressive, he figured it was just enough to stretch her legs. Then she sat writing in a journal.

After a bit, the guys waved goodnight, and she smiled—putting a foot on the wheel—and went back to her journal. Arkon walked over and took the wheel from her.

"Thanks." She smiled, not looking up. "I'm just about done here."

"Your friends seem nice." He gave her a sweet smile.

Barina nodded. "They're the best." She still hadn't looked up at him.

Arkon kept the huff he was about to breathe out to himself. He waited patiently until she put her journal down.

"All done?" he asked, glancing behind his shoulder.

"Yeah. I have so many things that go on that I have to write it down. Today, thanks to that cool thing you did with the Lake Goddess, I had a lot to write about."

"Glad I could bring something interesting to the table."

"True." She looked up to the sky, enjoying the stars. "So, what really brought Vic's attention to you?"

Arkon wasn't expecting that question. "What?"

"I've done a lot of work. Plenty with an elf along for the ride. It must mean you're powerful, and you're either looking for adventure, or that you are needing to prove yourself to your clan for the next step up. Are you training to move up in the ranks?"

Arkon's jaw dropped. He had not expected to hear that. "How the hell do you know stuff like that?"

Barina's face looked at him as though this were a perfectly normal conversation. "Like I said, I've done a lot of work with elves. I learn things." She was casually grabbing a match to light her pipe.

"I, uh, yeah. If I succeed in this, I'll become the highest ranking general in my clan." He saw her slow in her movements while she registered what he just said. It was only for a second before she went back to working on her pipe. He wondered.

He continued. "I have to take on a quest in the human world to build my relations with them. It's good for us to have contacts. Thankfully, since I've been on this job, I've been making very good friends, not just contacts," he told her. Arkon saw her stare at him for a second before he continued. "Twarence, he's going to go places, and Aria is a very powerful healer. Onyx is one of the most powerful wizards I've been in contact with, and we haven't even seen him use a quarter of his power. Jaras, he's very strong and just a good guy." Arkon turned to her. "And you, I still haven't figured you out. But you sure are showing, little by little, that you are way more than anyone knows."

Barina shrugged her shoulders. "I'm just a girl that's really good at getting a hold of things that nobody else can, and I pay attention."

He could see she was studying him, and her mind was going through the files of information. Arkon leaned back a bit. "I'd imagine, in your trade, that knowing every little detail about what you're doing comes in handy."

"It can be a matter of life and death. I don't go into any job without doing my homework about what I'm taking on or knowing who I'm working for."

"Smart. I mean, that's really smart. How far have you traveled?" He took out his own pipe and lit it. "I mean, it sounds like you've really been everywhere."

"I've seen some places. Places that nobody from our part of the world has seen yet, and honestly, I hope don't see for a long time. Lands so beautiful, creatures so amazing, I couldn't have dreamed of them."

"How long did you live on the other side of the world?"

"Four years. Studied there and loved it. I go back to visit from time to time. My sensei Yuhii and my adopted brother Stephen are there, and it's home." She was thinking fondly of the land she had lived in.

"Got back and been traveling ever since, right?"

Barina tilted her head, curious. "Been doing some research of your own?"

He finally had to ask. "I saw the way you reacted, and barely, when I said I was going to become the highest ranking general in my clan. Do you know something about that?"

Her face was neutral, but she replied. "I know that the king of all the elves is selected from the generals of all the clans. That the generals will have to each compete in four tasks. Magic, might, mind, and soul. Whoever is the winner, is the one who becomes the next king." She took a long pull on her pipe. "I didn't realize how powerful you are. Are you related to the current king?"

Arkon was left speechless for a moment. Not many understood this about the world he came from. The crown wasn't passed on through blood, it was earned. Children of the king were royalty, yes, but it didn't automatically earn them the right to rule. Normally, they would stay on as advisors after a new king would take the place of the former.

"No. He and my mother had been childhood friends and still are, but no relation."

Barina nodded and went back to looking over the waters. All he could do was stand, impressed for a moment, before he started laughing. She gave a little smile to her friend.

"I'm glad we're getting a chance to talk like this." Arkon stood closer to her, and his tone and energy changed.

Barina froze again. "Hmm," she agreed.

"It's really a beautiful night. Glad that I have some nice company to enjoy it with."

She didn't say a word.

"You're a mystery Barina." He stood and paced in front of her. "You wear your heart on your sleeve, and your emotions are genuine, but you have secrets that nobody but your absolute closest friends know. I'm sure they don't even know them all. You know how to keep secrets, even those that don't belong to you. I have a feeling that you're a friend to those in the magical community."

Barina was eyeing him now. She wasn't sure what he was getting at. His stance and movements were more formal and elegant than normal. It was as if he were trying to impress her. *Oh, please no.*

Arkon turned and gave her his most charming smile. "It's one of those things I like best about you. You can be trusted, and you know with my race how incredibly important being able to trust someone outside of our people is. You're smart, funny, and you have a good heart." He gave a warm smile. "I think traveling with you, with just us, would be fun. We'd probably have a lot of great adventures."

Barina kept her face blank but, in her mind, she was letting out the loudest groan she had ever had to suppress. She really hoped he didn't see her eyes struggle not to roll. She was really hoping that he wasn't interested and that this talk would never have happened. *And seriously, these are the worst pick-up lines I've heard in a long time.*

"Hey, I might go and grab a drink. Did you want anything?" Barina was trying to change the subject to keep Arkon from asking her what he was about to ask her. She had jumped to her feet and was heading below deck. She stopped when she felt a soft but strong hand take hold of hers.

"Barina wait." He pulled her back to him.

She turned and tried to avoid looking in his eyes, but she knew she couldn't.

"Barina." He stepped closer to her, touching a hand to her hair. She pulled back a bit. "I can't pretend that I haven't developed feelings for you since we've met. I was hoping that you would be interested in being with me?" He sounded so sure of himself, that he knew what he would say. He put an arm around her and was trying to pull her close.

"Arkon, please." She held a hand up and backed away from him.

The elf looked confused and almost taken aback.

"I appreciate the interest, but I'm afraid that I don't share the same feelings for you."

Arkon scratched the back of his head. "I, but, I don't understand. Why?"

Barina blinked. She found no reason to not be honest. "Oh boy. Well, I'm not attracted to you. I see you as a friend and a co-worker, but I'm just not attracted to you in that way. Yes, you are attractive, but I'm not attracted to you, and our personalities just don't meet up enough to be more than friends."

He was staring at her as if she were speaking another language. He still wasn't convinced. "I just, I thought human women were attracted to elves. Wha...I...I guess I just wasn't expecting a no." He took a deep breath. "Okay then. I can respect your position, Barina. Still friends?"

Barina gave him a very warm smile. "Of course we're still friends."

Arkon yawned. "Do you think that you'd be okay if I went and rested? I didn't realize how tired I still was from earlier."

Barina nodded. "Get some rest."

Arkon gave her a last glance before he headed below deck. He couldn't believe what happened.

"Arkon, you alright?" Twarence whispered when he saw him walk past. All of them were sound asleep on the floor but Twarence who was closest to the door.

"You were right about her. She wasn't interested," Arkon told him. "I need to get some rest. I'm still beat from earlier."

Twarence nodded and gave it a few minutes before he headed above deck to check on Barina. As he got closer, he could hear her talking with someone in hushed tones.

"He did not say that?" came the voice of a woman.

"Oh, don't pretend for one second like you weren't listening." Barina was trying to hold in her laugh.

"He's damn powerful, that's no joke. I'll forever be grateful for him eliminating the Microlos, but that guy needs to work on his game," the woman said in a matter-of-fact voice. "Plus, even I know it's going to take more than just somebody's pretty looks to get your attention."

"Right? He is just not my type. I've never even shown any kind of interest, so I don't know where he got the idea that this would work. I'm not really sure why he would've been interested in me in the first place."

"Have you seen yourself? You're one of a kind."

"Thank you, Bubbles."

The other woman was laughing. "You know you're the only one who knows of me that I let call me something other than my actual name? But it's cute, so I let it slide."

Twarence moved to where he could see them. Barina was steering the ship while having a conversation with—Twarence wasn't sure how to describe it—a woman made of water. She had the right shape, but she was pure water.

The two women turned when they saw him, and then looked at each other and laughed.

"Come on over scholar." The water woman smiled at him.

"Twarence, this is Her Grace, Beli, the Goddess of the Lake. Beli, this is Twarence."

Twarence started to laugh. "So you *do know each other?*"

"I never said I didn't know the lake was a deity, and nobody asked. Bubbles here, she didn't touch on that either. She didn't have to, but Bubbles, well…"

The deity spoke up. "I don't tell people who Barina knows. That's her business, not mine."

Twarence smiled at them. "I won't say anything, it's just funny. Barina sitting up here just hanging out, talking with a deity like old friends."

"Well, she and I are old friends." Beli smiled. "Well, in human time we're old friends. I've been around for centuries. But the first time she came through here, we became friends."

"Did you realize that the lake was Beli and a goddess the first time you crossed here," Twarence asked.

"Oh no. That was a big surprise, and I just happened to find out." Barina was trying to hide her laugh.

Beli giggled a little bit, and actual bubbles floated off her body.

"Now you see why I call you Bubbles! Ahh you're so cute!" Barina popped one of the bubbles. "I'll have to fill you in on how she and I met someday, but for now, mum's the word."

Beli let out a yawn. "I'm going to go and rest. You'll be safe the rest of the way to Fortania. Take care."

"Bye Bubbles. Sweet dreams." Barina waved to her.

"It was nice to meet you." Twarence laughed, waving to the goddess as she evaporated into the air.

The scholar then turned his attention to the thief. A laugh erupted from him. Barina smiled big and tried to play innocent. He put a hand on her shoulder. "You, I can't even handle you sometimes kid."

She stuck her tongue out. "I needed to talk to someone, so I called her."

Twarence made himself comfortable on the ground, sitting down and looking up at her. He was tired, but he had so many questions.

"I take it you needed to talk after Arkon asked you out?" He lit up a smoke.

She nodded. "You knew about that?"

"He talked to me about it earlier."

Barina simply nodded. "I'm just not interested."

"Didn't think you would be. He wasn't too happy when he came below deck."

"I know, but I have to be honest. I love elves. I'm friends with many, but those who haven't worked with humans, have very interesting views about humans, especially about human women. The men are generally very shocked to find that they can't persuade human females as easily as they have been told." She was looking down. "I feel bad, and I don't get angry about it. They've learned these things about us growing up, and it's not till they get out into the real world that they're able to see that we're a lot more complex than they were made to believe."

"Really?" Twarence took a long drag of his smoke. "You'd think that those who have been out here would teach the younger ones."

"That's not exactly how things work there. Once an elf starts taking on work in the outside world it means they're trying to build up contacts and train to learn more outside of the land of elves. They're working to become the new leaders within their race and have very little time to teach the young about what they learn. Once they start working outside of the world of magic and with mortals, they get real busy."

"You learned all of this just working with the elves?" Twarence knew that he wasn't going to get a full answer, but he had to ask anyway.

She gave him a look that said it all. He wasn't going to get a reply.

"You should head back down and get some rest. I'll be okay till the next shift comes up."

Twarence huffed out a breath as he stood up with a groan. "Oh, standing up on a boat can suck sometimes."

The thief watched her friend as he headed below deck. He was grumbling something to himself.

Twarence went back to his bedroll and fell asleep. He had so many questions about so many things. He knew that he wasn't going to get any answers, and that was beyond frustrating. But Twarnece also had a secret of his own, one that only Onyx and he knew. It was probably the most important bit of information that he had ever known. It could change the world and, hopefully, for the better.

CHAPTER 8

The next morning, after a quick breakfast, Jason and Tyra helped Twarence get the horses ready to ride. Jaras and Onyx were cleaning the deck. Aria was in the crow's nest keeping an eye on how close they were getting to land. Arkon was gently guiding the sails toward Fortania, and Barina was at the helm.

Aria smiled when she saw the town coming closer to view. It was a large town with shops, homes, and most everything else that they could want. The buildings were painted in pretty colors that made them pop against the massive forest beyond the town.

Climbing down from her perch, she set out to help Jason lower the sails while Tyra and Twarence threw the bumpers over the sides. Within a half hour, they were dropping anchor.

One of the men at the docks helped them tie up the ship and started to help Jaras lead the horses off the docks.

"Well, there's three people I haven't seen in forever!" The dock hand's eyes lit up when he saw Jason, Tyra, and Barina.

"Robin!" Jason rushed over and gave the man a hug. Robin then wrapped his arms around all three of the friends at once.

He was a very large man—at least six foot six with curly brown hair, brown eyes, a goatee, and a couple years older than Barina. He beamed at seeing the lot of them pull up.

"It's good to see you guys. Are you passing through, or are you here for a visit?" He put an arm around Barina. "Meow, meow."

Barina gave him a warm smile as she snuggled up to her friend. "Meow, meow." It was obviously a little joke between them. "We're just passing through. We'll be here the rest of the day and leave in the morning."

"Where are you heading?"

"We're moving to Estella," Tyra said, "and Barina is passing through on business with this lot." She pointed a thumb at the group of people behind her.

"Where are you going, B?"

Barina shook her head. He knew that she couldn't always talk about what she was doing with her work.

"Understood. Who are your friends?" he then asked, looking at the others.

Barina turned red. "Where are my manners?"

"Didn't think you had any to start with," Robin teased her while ruffling her hair.

She gave him a level look before she turned away. "Hmph. I was gonna buy you a beer later. Now though… Anyway, this is Twarence, Aria, Arkon, Onyx, and Jaras. Guys, this is our friend Robin. He lived in Miork for years but moved here to study. Course, don't know what he studies aside from putting his foot in his mouth or how to get a swift kick to the ass, but he's studying something."

The two exchanged mischievous grins.

"My main area of study was ways to piss off little blonde girls who make a better arm rest than they do, well, anything." Robin placed an arm on top of Barina's head. "Now though, I've moved on to finding ways to completely destroy one in particular."

"You need to wash your armpit, Stinky," she grumbled, pouting.

Robin puffed his shirt to send his odor toward her.

Barina glanced over. "I hate you."

"Nice to meet all of you. I'm really here studying under the best beer masters around. I'm hoping after I'm done to open up my brewery somewhere and make a name for myself." He was all smiles to the group. Barina tried to slip away but Robin put one large arm around her waist and picked her up to carry her like luggage.

They were all laughing. Even Barina had a little grin. "You do realize this means war, right?"

He was laughing and gave her a bit of a wink. "It's always been war."

"Is that how you pick up women?" Onyx had to make the joke.

The thief narrowed her eyes at the wizard. "I can get out of this, just so you know."

They all scoffed at that.

Barina started grumbling as she worked her way free of her friend's hold. "Always been like this since the day we became friends. Putting my shoes somewhere I couldn't reach them. Just cause you're over a freaking foot taller than me and have over two hundred extra pounds, doesn't mean..." She slipped out of his arm and was back on the ground.

"This is an old game with you two, isn't it?" Arkon was laughing at the two of them.

Barina leaned up against Robin. "Yup."

"We're old friends, and it's all good fun," Robin mused. "Do you guys have all of your things? Which inn are you taking them to?"

"I was thinking of Charlie's. He's pretty reasonable, and the place is pretty clean." Barina lit her pipe and watched the others climb onto their horses.

"Alright, I'm done here at four. I'll swing home to clean up, and then I'll find you and we can grab dinner and drinks. You guys up for that?" Robin smiled.

"Getting drinks with the man who is studying to be a brewmaster, I think that's acceptable." Jaras had a smirk as he lit a cigarette and stood next to Barina.

"I do know some good places. You guys head out. I need to get my work done, but I'll see you soon." Robin was getting ready to climb on their ship so he could clean it and have it ready for the next set of travelers.

The group started through town and toward the inn they would be staying at for the evening.

"It'll be nice to be able to rest for the day, catch our breath." Aria let out a breath while enjoying the sights of the pretty town.

"I'm just glad you guys don't mind us joining you on our way to Estella," Tyra chimed. "Jason is pretty handy in a fight, and I can always help Aria if people get hurt, or hell, if she gets hurt."

"Well, it is on the way, and you're right. A couple of extra good hands to help is welcomed." Aria was really growing very fond of Tyra. "Tyra, do you want to head over to that shop later?"

Tyra's jaw dropped. "Oh my yes, I think I want everything in there."

"I knew I liked you."

"Speaking of being liked, Barina, do you come to this town often?" Jaras asked, nudging her arm.

Barina was waving to a couple that was sitting at a café. "Why do you ask? Hi Tom."

Jaras looked at her like she was crazy. "Cause like, I've counted at least two dozen people saying hi to you, and a couple giving you a pat on the back." He saw another man tip his hat and shake her hand. "I mean, how many people do you know?"

Barina turned red. "Quite a few."

"I thought people didn't know who she was," Aria blurted out.

"Lots of people know who she is," Jason said. "They just don't know what she does for a living. She'd like to keep it that way too. Most people think she's just a wanderer who goes from town to town, occasionally picking up a little work at a shop or something, maybe gamble a little bit, stopping fights, and every now and then do some serious ass kicking when needed." Jason grinned while he lit up a cigarette. "Miork is the only city where she needs to be more careful than normal. A few people there do know about her specialty in obtaining objects."

"Gambling?" Onyx wasn't expecting to hear that.

Barina was giving a couple of little kids a hug. "It's good to see you two! You've both gotten so big. Hurry to school!" She looked over her shoulder. "Huh, oh, yeah, I don't often, but it's fun if someone wants to play."

"Don't play her in cards." Tyra's eyes were shining. "Ask Robin about how badly she's beaten him."

"And you really seem to know people almost everywhere we've been so far," Twarence added, looking at another couple of people that waved to the girl.

Jason caught on to what was happening and started laughing. He hopped down from the cart as Tyra took over steering, and he put an arm on Barina's shoulder. "Didn't she ever tell you about all of her connections?" Jason asked.

"What do you mean? We know she has people here and there, but connections?" Onyx was now curious.

"Barina knows people and creatures from everywhere. She's friends with all of them. We're not only talking about your average Joe either, but nobility and very powerful beings from everywhere."

Barina's face was speaking volumes. She clearly didn't want Jason to say all this. "Jason!" She raised her hands.

Jason gave her a smile and was about to reveal one of her biggest secrets. "Relax, I wouldn't say it if I thought it would hurt." He then looked over at them again. "She knows Lord Nortel and Lady Marita, rulers in the Valley of Giants, King Harl'arl of the Gemstone Cave gnomes, Captain James from her ship, which is a given. We both know the royal family in Nippon, as well as their shogun and most of the warlords in general. She's really good friends with the king of the gnomes in the Black Mountains. Over in the Cloudburst Mountains she's friends with all the magical creatures there, good friends with King William of Treklea, hell his son wanted to marry her, but she turned him down. We've even befriended your king, Arkon. And that's just the tip of the iceberg with who she knows."

Arkon stopped in his steps. That, out of everything else, got his attention. "How do you know my king? What's his name if you know?"

"King Trekto and I go way back." Barina then elbowed Jason hard. "You know how touchy elves get about their king. Why would you say that?" she hissed.

"Oh please. He'll learn eventually anyway," Jason said in a hushed voice that was not that hushed. "Yeah, but it's better if they learn from their king about this, sorry."

Everyone, except for Tyra, stopped for a moment while these two were arguing. Not many other than elves ever knew the name of the king of the elves. Fewer had met him, for he lived in obscurity. Not even Twarence the scholar knew who the Elvin king was. Barina and Jason did.

"How come you haven't ever told us about these connections?" Twarence asked, shocked.

"Wasn't important, and you never did ask. Plus, if the wrong people find out, they can use those friendships as leverage," Barina sputtered. "These contacts are not merely contacts, they're dear friends, and I won't betray that trust. It's one of the reasons I don't reveal who I know till later."

"And if I'm accurate, and I know I am, she's probably made some more friends on the way here."

Barina was still glaring at Jason as he spoke.

"Na'imah," Aria whispered.

"See, told you." Jason leaned over to whisper to Barina. "Who?"

"Dragon."

Jason was impressed. "She'll be a big help someday, and I mean big." He was laughing at his own joke. Barina laughed too.

Arkon was still thinking very hard on this. He had met with his king hundreds of times and spent a lot of time at the palace. He had heard of all Trekto's human contacts, all of them, except for this one. Then something dawned on him.

"Barina, in the throne room of King Trekto's palace there's a painting. The king and his family along with a woman who looks very similar to you, holding the Diamond of the Great Desert. That wouldn't happen to be you, would it?" Arkon stopped her and demanded that she tell him.

Jason looked surprised. He didn't know anything about that.

Barina's face lost all emotion, and she nodded.

"Why? Why were you holding the Diamond of the Great Desert?" the elf demanded.

"Ask your king?" she said without hesitating.

"Barina, tell me." He demanded again.

She stayed silent. Her look was set. She wasn't going to say a word.

Jason gave them all a look to calm down. Even though he had spilled her secrets first, he was going to protect Barina from having to talk about this.

Arkon's eyes narrowed, and he was trying to keep his calm, but this wasn't easy. She had blown off his request to be his partner. That was bad enough, but the fact that she refused to talk of how she knew his king, that damn near put her into the danger zone with him. Why was she in a portrait with the king and his family while holding a very valuable relic? Was she a true friend or foe?

They were quiet the rest of the way to the inn. As soon as they arrived, Barina went all sunny with the innkeeper. He gave them half of the top floor which was more like an apartment, with beds enough for everyone and a gathering space for them to relax in. Charlie normally reserved it for people who were going to be staying for at least a week, but Barina was able to sweet talk him into letting them rent it just for the night.

The group opted to explore the town a bit, but Barina and Jason wanted to stay behind. She wanted to get some rest as she hadn't slept much the night before, and Jason had a book he was itching to keep reading while he had a chance.

Barina rested on one of the beds, and Jason sat on the one next to her.

"Thanks for getting Arkon to calm down earlier," she said with a yawn, curling up under the blankets.

"I remember us meeting Trekto, back when Berk took us through the Great Desert for the first time. The whole bit about the Diamond though, I don't know about that. Curious too, but I know that you don't always want to talk about your fights, and from what I can tell, you might've done something dishonest."

She held two fingers up about an inch apart. "Just a bit."

"Do you mind if I ask what happened?"

"Not at all." Her eyes smiled, but she stayed quiet.

He rolled his eyes at her silence then threw a pillow at her. "What happened?"

She pulled the pillow off her face, giving him a smirk as she closed her eyes. "I was traveling through the Great Desert on my way back to Miork. It was just after I had left the pirate ship and the Desert is on the other side of town the ship was docked in. I wanted to say hi to some of the elves there anyway, so no biggie to go that way. One night when I was there, I came over a sand dune and saw a campfire and...they...*they* were there, Jason."

Jason sat up. He knew who she meant.

"I knew something was going on with them, that they had done something terrible. I waited till they were asleep and went to investigate. They had taken the Diamond and they were planning to destroy it. Jason, that Diamond, it would strip the elves of the Desert of their powers if something happened to it."

"Yeah, I know, but still, they had it?"

"I took the Diamond and ran like freaking hell. Thankfully those things were still asleep at the time. As soon as I got to the entrance, I called the Desert elves. And remind me to thank Berk again for teaching us elfin. I got to the Desert elves and, thankfully, Trekto was there. Told him what was happening and who was after me. By that time, I knew that they would know the Diamond had been taken back."

"Is this when you pull a dirty trick?"

"It would only be dirty if it weren't against them. I hid, and the second they came into the elfin homes, I stabbed them in the back. I mean, I did have to take a couple head on, but that meant it was only three, not ten."

Jason shook his head. "I still remember when you were thirteen and you killed two of them, on your own. How does that happen? I mean it takes groups of people to kill just one of them."

"You can fight them on your own, too. We've fought them together before." She said with another yawn.

Jason snorted. "Not to the level you can. When you were in the Cloudburst Mountains, when, well when everything happened, what was that like?" He glanced over. "I still feel awful that I wasn't there, that I wasn't there to help. You've never spoken about it, at least not much."

Barina was quiet, trying to gather her thoughts. "It's still hard to talk about. But Jason, there were forty-something of those bastards. I can still see those white, glowing eyes." Her voice was steady. "I wasn't afraid, I was angry."

Jason knew what she was talking about. It was an event in her life that had caused her so much pain and grief that she hadn't spoken about it since it happened years ago. It was as painful as when she lost her family.

"B?" He jumped off the bed and sat next to her, placing a hand on her shoulder.

"Fighting them wasn't the hard part. It was...Jason they took him right from my hands. I couldn't protect him, and they took him. I couldn't even sense that they were there till it was too late. They had a cloak on that even I couldn't feel. I can now, but damn it. I wonder about him every single day." He could see her lip start to quiver a bit.

"Hey, B." He looked down. "I am so sorry that I wasn't there when it all happened. If I were, maybe I could've..."

His friend cut him off. "Don't. I know if you were there then you would've helped. I followed those bastards for weeks, but they disappeared without a trace." She sat up, shaking her head.

Jason saw that her right shoulder had blood soaking through her shirt. "When did..." It clicked pretty quickly. "Is this an old wound from them? Your side is bleeding too. Did they do this?"

Her look gave him the answer, and he went for his bag to grab bandages.

"The one on my shoulder was from when everything in the Mountains happened. The one on my side from a couple years ago. They opened up again when I was up in the Black Mountains and again just a little bit ago. They still hurt."

"Too bad Aria can't fix them. Only one thing can, and we don't happen to have a unicorn handy." He took the bandages, and Barina pulled her shirt down enough for him to dress the wound. "Why haven't you had O'rien look at these?"

"Haven't been back to the Cloudburst Mountains more than a couple times since everything happened. Been busy." She had come up with her answer pretty quickly.

"Really, busy?" He didn't believe it. He tied the bandage off, and she lifted her shirt a little bit so he could start working on her hip. "O'rien is your friend, he'd help you."

"I know he would."

"Matrikal will turn up. I don't know how or when, but he will. I get this feeling that he's still somewhere."

"I hope so."

"All tied up. Go change your shirt and get some sleep. I'll be here." He closed his eyes and turned his head away so she could change.

Barina put on a clean shirt and climbed back into bed.

"Wake me when they get back." She yawned.

Jason had drawn the curtains and only had the lamp on a low setting. He looked to Barina, glad she had fallen asleep. She had had a hard time sleeping well, for years unless Josh, Berklion, or himself were close by. He was hoping that she'd have a decent nap.

* * *

The others were having a lot of fun walking around the unique town of Fortania. There were shops that couldn't be found anywhere else. Fortania was known for some of the best beer, candies, chocolates, and the best cooks anywhere in the kingdom of Larindana. The smells were intoxicating.

"This place is amazing, and I didn't realize how hungry I was till we started walking." Onyx took a deep inhale of the food. His eyes were being drawn toward a candy shop.

"Here."

Onyx jumped almost a foot in the air. He hadn't seen Tyra sneak up behind him, or notice that she had gone into a chocolate shop and come back with a box of treats. She held them out, her mouth already full of chocolate. Her eyes twinkled knowing that she had startled him. She hadn't meant to, but she took that as an unexpected bonus. "I guess I've learned more about stealth from Jason than I realized." She held the box out again. "Have some."

Onyx shook his head, trying to stifle a laugh. "Thank you, Tyra."

"Oh, sweet spirits, what on earth is that?" Aria rushed over to a window and was looking at the treats on display.

Tyra followed. "Let's go."

They headed inside the bakery and, for most of the morning, everyone wandered in and out of shops, eventually stopping at a café to grab some lunch.

"I'll need to visit here again." Twarence smiled while enjoying a cigarette after his lunch.

Jaras eyed the match, and Twarence passed it so he could light his smoke. "I'm ready to go have a beer with Robin when he gets off work. And can I just say that I'm so glad that we're taking the evening to rest. We really need this. It's been over a month of hard traveling."

"I know, I'm beat. And I'm glad that the weather is so nice today too," Aria mused. She sipped her tea and enjoyed the breeze.

"It's almost enough to make you forget that we're working." Onyx gave a couple of his scraps to a dog that passed by, patting it on the head.

"You guys have made great time, too," Tyra said. "Barina must've pushed you hard, though. She can do that. Jason and I left about a week before you guys did, and we even took a shortcut through the mountains thanks to the gnomes. In all reality, you guys shouldn't have made it to this point for another two weeks. But you're traveling at her speed, and if she felt she could push you faster, you'd be farther than this." Tyra was enjoying her coffee while she and Aria were now looking at some of the trinkets they bought.

"Wait, what?" Twarence had to know more of what she meant.

"Girl knows how to move. When she's with a group, you'll feel like you've been running for hours by the time you stop for the day, but still wake up feeling energized. When she's flying solo, well, let's just say she can get from point A to point B faster than people in point B can get to point B. She's really good at what she does."

Everyone realized Tyra was right. Barina really had been moving them quickly.

"Remember, she does this for a living." Tyra looked over her table and saw Arkon who was sitting silently with his tea. He had been quiet the whole time they were out. Deep in thought, his face would either sour or be emotionless. His eyes looked to Tyra off and on.

"Do you have something to ask me, Arkon?" Tyra's tone was level. She just couldn't take him staring her down anymore.

"How does Barina know my king? How deep does she go with the elves?"

Annoyed more than anything, Tyra tried to contain her eye roll. "You need to talk with her about that."

"Why?" Arkon stood up, crushing the tea cup in his hand. "What are you protecting her for?"

The group wasn't expecting this hostility from the elf, and they watched, frozen.

Jaras moved first. "Calm down, man."

"I will not calm down." Arkon did at least keep his voice quiet. "That thief knows the secrets of my world, and she won't talk. How do I know she doesn't know something that could kill my king, or my kind, or take us over?"

This time Tyra didn't hide her disdain. "Paranoid much? Barina probably learned what she did from simply talking to elves. You don't understand, do you? People trust her. Without ever meeting her before or only talking to her for a few minutes, they trust her. And she has never betrayed that trust to anyone. Maybe that's why she knows your king. Do you really think there would be a painting of her with your king and his family in the throne room if there wasn't a good reason? Would he let her near his family if there wasn't a good reason?"

Twarence raised a finger and quietly whispered, "Point for Tyra."

"You'd better be telling me the truth. If I find out that she's a threat to my people, I'll…" He was cut off as Tyra stood up and came within an inch of him.

"You'll do what?" Tyra hissed. They locked eyes for almost a full minute.

Arkon took a breath and calmed himself. "I'll have to take your word. You know her better than almost anyone. I'm sorry I lost my temper. I just got over protective, I guess." He looked rather embarrassed by his outburst. "Can we move past this?"

Tyra crossed her arms, thinking for a moment. "Yeah, we can. Just, if you have a problem with her, you need to talk to her. And don't threaten her. this time you just had me to deal with. If it had been Jason," Tyra said, smiling, "you haven't seen over protective till you've seen how he gets about her."

Arkon's face expressed a genuine apology, and the others let out a sigh of relief. Thankfully, the elf bent and apologized. "I'd almost be afraid as to what Jason would do." He held out a hand, which Tyra took. "Thank you."

Tyra nodded. "Want to split a turnover?"

Arkon laughed. "Yeah. Remind me to stop in Estella after we leave Thoron, and I'll buy you guys some drinks."

"We'd appreciate that. You can meet our friend Josh and our friend Mason. Mason has a tea and spice shop there. Josh is the third of the trio with B and Jason." Tyra smiled thinking about them.

Arkon knew he shouldn't take his frustrations out on the people around him. Tyra was right. "I just have to trust that my king has a good reason for trusting her."

They ordered their treats and started back to the inn after they ate. Everyone was exhausted and wanted to rest for themselves.

They didn't get far when a man bumped into Twarence. He didn't think anything of it on a busy street where people frequently ran into each other. Then another man ran past them, pointing. "He just stole your money!"

A tall man, slender yet strong of frame, ran past and slammed into the cutpurse, knocking him to the ground.

"What's wrong with you? You're scum!" The man grabbed the thief by the collar. The thief looked confused, but only until the man pinned him down and launched several punches to his face.

"Hey!" Jaras pulled the man off the thief. "That's enough." Jaras needed Arkon's help to hold him. "That's enough, I said. He's had enough!"

The man stood over the thief, who was now unconscious, and spit at him. "Here, he took your money. I just couldn't stand back. It makes me so mad when people steal from others."

"But there's a limit," Twarence breathed. He hated seeing the man on the ground barely breathing.

Aria knelt down and began to heal his wounds.

"You're healing him? But he's a…"

Before the man could stop, Aria replied, her eyes set on what she was doing. "He's hurt. Stealing is wrong, yes, but maybe he had a good reason. Maybe he desperately needed that money. He certainly doesn't need to be beaten within an inch of his life."

When she had healed the thief, he sat up and looked at her. "Do you need some money to help you get by for a while?" she asked kindly.

Confused, the thief looked around, his eyes darting from them to the man who had hit him. He scrambled to his feet and ran as fast as he could.

"Well, you tried." Onyx extended a hand to help Aria to her feet.

"Little hard on the guy, don't you think?" Onyx's voice didn't hide his exasperation.

"It just makes me angry when people try to steal. And I still can't believe you healed…" his voice trailed off again as he took a good look at Aria. He gave her a little smile. "I suppose though, that your heart won the day. Maybe I should take a page out of your book, Miss." He held out a hand. "I'm Ken."

Aria extended her hand. "Aria."

"Charmed."

Aria was trying to hide her smile. He was an attractive man with long dark hair that he had tied back at the moment. His captivating amber eyes were shining at her. His shirt was unbuttoned a bit to show a toned chest, and he was giving Aria a charming smile.

"Thank you."

Jaras intervened. He decided he should play wing man. "Ken, would you like to follow us back to where we're staying? We were gonna get our friends and grab some drinks."

Ken nodded. "Sure, thanks. So, you guys are just passing through?" He lit a cigarette while he walked with them.

Aria walked closer to him. "Yeah, just passing through on business."

Ken was trying to hide his laugh, "Business, really? Not vague at all."

The rest of them were laughing at that. "Well, it's nothing special. We're heading just past Estella to do some work at a school," Twarence said, creating a cover story.

"Except for Tyra. She and her fiancé, Jason, are moving to Estella. They're friends of Barina, our other companion, and we happened to run into them on the way here." Arkon's grin grew while speaking with Ken. He really liked this guy. "We're taking them as far as Estella, and then we'll keep on our way."

"Oh, nice. I'm heading back home, which is just in that direction."

"Really?" Aria didn't hesitate to make the next suggestion. "Well, we can talk about it, but maybe you can come with us for part of the way?" She gave a little sheepish grin to the others.

They were trying to hide their snickers except for Tyra who gave out a loud, "HA!" and they headed to the inn. They could tell Aria had already developed a crush on this man. His eyes gave way that he was very okay with joining them.

Once back and in the apartment, they found Jason sitting on a sofa, reading still. Barina was sitting next to him, her hair wet from washing, and writing in her journal.

"Hey guys." Jaras waved after hanging his cloak on the peg.

"Hey, uh…" Jason hesitated seeing Ken walk in the door. He nudged Barina's arm. She glanced over, not giving away any emotion at seeing the new person. They both sat analyzing him, trying to figure him out.

Barina leaned closer to Jason. "Nanka…Usankusai," she whispered quietly in Nihongo.

He nodded. "Un, yukinohana wa dokoda?"

She then said quietly, looking down, "Kaban ni."

"Woe, what language were the two of you just speaking?" Jaras hadn't heard this one before.

Tyra sat down on the armrest of the sofa and handed a box of treats to Jason and Barina. "Nihongo. I don't understand it, but I recognize it when I hear it."

"It's nice to meet you. I'm Ken. Sounds like I might be traveling with you and your group for a while, since I'm heading that way." He held out a hand to each of them.

They both shook his hand, to get a sense of him.

"Hello," Jason said while forcing a smile.

"Hi," Barina said quietly. She was trying to get a good look at him.

Ken must've taken her extended look for admiration of his good looks. He gave her a wink, and she could see the interest in his eyes. He took his hand away slowly and went back to the others.

"Baka," Barina breathed to herself.

Jason heard what she said and held in his laugh.

She gave Jason a little wink before she stood up, slipping her journal back in her pack. "I'm not wrong." She put her boots on, looking up at the others. "I'm gonna go run some errands before Robin shows up. I'll be back in a bit." She took off without a second thought.

Jason went to sit closer to the rest of the group. He wanted to figure out more about this man who was now joining them. "So where are you heading to, Ken?" Jason asked while he lit up a smoke.

Ken lit up a pipe, eyeing Jason. "To a spot just before Estella. I have work to do there, and then I'm headed home after that."

"Yeah, where?"

"The Water Caves, if you know those markers. I'm heading there. They're a few days into the forest not far from here. I'm a buyer of gemstones, and they're getting me some rare items." Ken kept his tone steady, but locked eyes with Jason. He could tell that the blacksmith didn't trust him. "I heard you and Tyra are moving to Estella. What takes you there?"

"We have close friends there, and it's a nice town. Tyra is going to be working under a good doctor till she can take over for him, and I'm opening up a forge. Miork didn't have a lot to offer us anymore, so we're moving. Where are you from?"

"Just beyond Larindana." Ken was looking at the others. "I'm just trying to figure out what a scholar, wizard, elf, healer, warrior, and whatever Barina is, are doing traveling together."

Jaras slid his eyes to him. "We were asked by the school to bring our skills to give lectures on our abilities and how to apply them in certain scenarios."

Tyra met Jason's eyes, reading him. She knew that he didn't trust Ken.

"Nothing else?" Ken asked.

Onyx saw a glint in Ken's eyes. "No, that's really it." Onyx kept his tone casual. "Why do you ask?"

Ken shook his head. "I'm just trying to get to know the people I'll be traveling with. Speaking of which, Barina, what's her job?"

"She's extra muscle." Twarence wasn't going to relay all of her info to this guy, but a little couldn't hurt.

"Been one hell of a guide too," Aria added. "Knows her stuff."

Ken queried an eyebrow. "Muscle, really? She can fight?"

Jason nodded. "Better than me, and better than the man who trained us too." Jason felt that wave of protection seer through his body, he couldn't help it. He had been like that when it came to her since they were kids. He was just as protective over her as he was over Tyra, his friends, anyone who meant anything to him.

Jaras shot a look at Jason, using all of his restraint to not drop his jaw. He was hoping nobody else saw it, though he saw Jason smirk when Jaras set his gaze on him.

Ken was laughing. "That little thing? That's impressive, good for her. Why would you be taking an extra fighter with you to this school? That's what I don't get."

Jaras exhaled his smoke. "Dangerous roads. She's good help, plus, she'll be able to give extra training when we get there."

"Who taught her to fight?" Ken looked at Aria. He was enjoying the view, and she returned a little smile.

"That's not important," Aria answered this time. "Not trying to be rude Ken, but a lot of what you're asking doesn't concern you. She doesn't like people prying into her life, and we've learned to respect that. She talks about herself when she wants to. Sweet girl, but she believes that silence is one of her best weapons." Aria was respecting Barina's request to keep her fighting skills quiet.

Ken thought about it, nodding. "I can understand that. Course, it makes you wonder how good she is."

"You have no idea. We've all been wondering how good she really is, but like Aria said, we've learned to respect her wishes." Arkon sighed a little.

Jason stood up. "I'm gonna go grab some air for a bit. I'll be back before Robin shows up."

Jaras nodded to Jason who motioned for him to follow. The two men stepped out of the room and headed downstairs. Jason wanted a drink and ordered a couple of beers for both of them. They sat outside, quiet for a few minutes before Jaras spoke up.

"Can I ask you something?"

Jason glanced over. "Sure. I know it's about B and, with you, I don't mind answering what I can."

"Is it true what you said up there? You said you think she's better than your teacher. Do you really think she's better than Berklion?" He kept his voice lower than a whisper.

Jason gave a single nod. "I know she is."

"Spirits above." Jaras took a pull from his drink. "It's just, I've seen her in action a little bit, but she doesn't seem like she's doing anything."

Jason snorted a laugh. "You won't see her do a whole lot unless she has to."

Jaras was confused. "What do you mean? I mean, all of us do that, only use the energy that we need to."

"Not like this. You'll eventually see what I mean."

"I'll take your word for it." Jaras went quiet.

Jason hesitated before he said something else. "She's overpowered Berklion."

Jaras just about dropped his glass. "What? But he's your teacher. Why...?"

"It was when her family was killed," Jason said. "I'm telling you this in the strictest of confidence. Do I have your word that you won't say anything about what I'm going to tell you? At least, not until the others get to know her better."

"On my honor."

"When we came back to her house and found her family, Jaras, it's something that still haunts me to this day. Something happened to her. She, I had never seen her like this, and I haven't seen it since. I've never seen *anyone* like this. She was the most terrifying thing I had ever been around." He took a deep breath again. "We were surveying the damage, trying to decide if we could save her mother. Madaline had still been breathing when we walked in, but it was too late. She took her last breath. Barina's mother had been murdered, her father decapitated with one of his own damn swords, and her siblings," Jason shook his head. "We found bloody weapons next to the fireplace where...we found hair, clothes, and there were two bodies burning in it. Couldn't even recognize them, their skin was black and gone." Jason's lip started to quiver. "She was kneeling on the ground. The shock kept her from crying. It did something to her.

"The air in the room changed, and her breathing got heavy. Goddamn, I've only spoken about this once since it happened, and that was to our sensei in Nippon. She grabbed the fire poker that had her sister's red hair on it, and the hatchet that had a sliver of Tobi's shirt still on it and stood up. Josh and I tried to approach her, but she looked up, and we couldn't move.

"Her eyes, they, her eyes alone could've killed. We knew we couldn't stop her. She was going after the men, and Berklion tried to stop her. She picked up—little thirteen-year-old, five foot four Barina—picked up six foot five Berklion of Halk with one hand, a man who is nothing but pure muscle and strength, and threw him. He hit the wall, leaving an imprint, and fell to the ground. She took off running. Josh and I followed her. We didn't know if we could stop her, but we couldn't risk innocent people getting hurt if she had to get through them, get to the men who murdered her family. If anyone got in her way, we were the only ones who stood a chance of stopping her.

"Jaras, she didn't leave any prints in the snow. That's how fast and light she made herself."

Jaras could hardly breathe while listening.

"When she got to those men, she still didn't show a tenth of what she was capable of, but I believe, in that moment, she could've taken out an army." Jason finished his mug and then refilled it.

"What happened that day, her fighting, it wasn't by any means the most impressive or the craziest thing I've ever seen her do. But she was at her most dangerous, and if pushed to the brink, she, well like anyone really, can do things that are out of character. She cried after she took out those men. Berklion forgave her easily, picked her up and held her while she cried, and he took us to Nippon the next day."

Jaras lit up another smoke. "Damn, that poor girl. I feel bad for her, but she always seems to have a smile on her face."

"And she means it too. She's a happy person. She's learned to live with her past and push beyond it. That's the upside with her."

Jaras gave a little smile. "I'm glad she's happy." Then he shook his head. "And to think she does all of her fighting with a dagger. I'd be curious to see what would happen if she carried a sword. She gave us a small demo using my sword, but never saw anything more than that."

Jason grinned. "She has a sword with her. It's in her bag. I asked her to make sure, you know, when we were speaking another language up there."

Jaras threw his hands in the air, exasperated. "I give up with her? Why the hell doesn't she carry it on herself instead of in her bag?"

Jason was laughing, enjoying this more than he probably should. It took him a minute before he could answer. "There's a couple of reasons." He filled Jaras' glass for him before he continued. "First, her sword is from Nippon, and it doesn't look like any sword you've ever seen. The only other swords I've seen of the quality that's made by the best smithies there are what her father and she produced. It's excellent quality. Josh and I both have swords from Nippon as well, but we've been so used to the ones she made us that we prefer them. I'll have to show you when we get a chance, see if she won't show you her sword.

"The second reason is…" Jason scrunched his face to find the right words, "what have you seen her do with a dagger so far?"

"Defeat giants, fight snow cats, and Microlos. When she fought giants, she even used some of their weapons against them. She left the giants terrified when they realized, well, I don't know what, something about her."

"Barina is regarded very highly in the world of giants. She saved them, literally. She saved their race single-handed. Everyone in their world knows of her, and she has a reputation with them as a protector."

Jaras took a long pull on his cigarette. Jason did the same. Jaras was quiet as he listened.

"What did you think when you saw her fight the giants?"

Jaras put his words together carefully. "She didn't move a lot. She didn't need to, but the stances, the movements, all of it, I had never seen anything like it. I *do* know that I didn't even see a fraction of what she's really able to do, and that was before I learned who taught her."

"Jaras, she's great with all weapons, more so with a dagger over almost any other weapon. The exception is with a sword." Jason's voice lowered and was very quiet. "If she holds a sword, well, she becomes something else, on another level. Not you, not me, not Berklion, not Arkon or even Onyx. Not all of us together could stop her if she really decided to cut loose. If she takes hold of a sword, it means shit has gotten very real.

"I can fight pretty damn good, I know what I'm about. You were trained by Darien, so I know what you're about. We both learned how to overcome magic, myself to an extent, her, almost completely."

Jaras took a breath. "The caves?"

"What?"

"We were in the steam caves and Onyx put a spell on her and me to keep us from moving so Aria could heal our wounds. I couldn't move at all, she was barely phased."

"She has to be that way. Think about Berklion. Hell, think about someone like Darien. What would happen if they could be stopped by magic, or worse, compelled by someone who is powerful enough to make that happen?"

That thought made both of them shudder.

"We had to learn to be more. I think that you can learn this too. You know how to block magic from your mind, right?"

Jaras nodded.

"Good, you can't be compelled. With the physical magic, I might see if Barina and I could work with you on overcoming those spells. From what she says, you could." Jason was getting off topic. "Yeah, we could help you with that."

Jaras nodded in approval. "I'd be okay with that." He held his drink a little closer.

"Has she been too much of a klutz yet with you guys?"

Jaras gave out a belly laugh. "Absolutely! It's been great. I don't know how she's able to walk some days. It doesn't happen often, but when it does, it's classic." Jaras kept laughing. "I like it almost as much as when she drops little or even big surprises on people."

The two men sat chatting for a while. Jason was glad that, on this journey she had undertaken, these people were those Barina could call friends. He liked them and felt he could call them friends too. Most of her jobs were just that—work. She'd work with people every now and then and, while there was a level of respect that sometimes grew into friendships, most of the people she worked with she never saw again. It was just the nature of the job. Jason even knew that these were good people, and he was a great judge of character. He knew he could trust Jaras.

"My favorite so far," Jaras said, remembering fondly, "was when everyone saw her tattoos in the steam caves. Well, and the fact that everyone was a little surprised that she and I just kinda stripped down to just our underwear."

Jason was laughing. "She's not shy at all. And those steam caves are so nice that it almost makes it worth going along the summit." He then lowered his voice to a whisper. "Speaking of not being shy and all that, I can't…" He was laughing even harder now.

Jaras interjected, knowing what he was talking about. He was trying not to laugh. "I cannot believe Arkon asked her…oh my god? What was that man thinking?"

"Barina is single. He's a good-looking guy, but I mean, she never gave any indication that she'd be interested, did she?" Jason didn't even try to hold back his laughter.

"Nope. I mean, when they first met, he was so skeptical of her. He came around fast enough, but I just, it doesn't make sense." Jaras let out a sigh while having another drink. "I just hope her rejection doesn't come back to bite her in the butt."

"Right? Young elves can be petty sometimes. It's one of the reasons why they're required to go out into the world. Experiences like this—learning what people go through, learning about humans—it's important. It helps them put things into perspective. They're required to take on a quest if they want to move up in the chain of command."

Jason scratched the back of his neck, reaching his hand down the back of his shirt to get his itch. Jaras thought he caught a glimpse of a marking on his back. It was a gold outline of a dragon with characteristics of a turtle almost. It wasn't a large marking, and the gold wasn't overly bright and the eyes of the beast were green. He noted it looked just like the one he had seen on Barina back in the steam caves. He'd have to ask Jason about those later.

"That's what I've been learning about since we've been doing this," Jaras said. "I'll help keep an eye on him. I'm glad you and Tyra are with us on this trip, at least till Estella."

Jason stood up with a little stretch. "Thanks, glad you guys managed to get to us too. I'm gonna go get some supplies before we meet up with Robin. I'll see you in a bit."

Jaras gave a little wave.

Jason went on his way. He took time to pick up more supplies that he and Tyra would need as they traveled. He saw a shop and popped in, just to see if they had what he wanted. He smiled as he picked something up and walked back to the inn.

"Jason!"

He turned when he heard Barina calling his name. She was running up the street to catch up to him. Her hair was different. She had gotten it trimmed it seemed, and she carried a small package in her hands.

He stopped to wait for her. "What did you get?"

"I found a book for Twarence and a neat ointment that Aria might be able to apply with her healing powers. I was almost out of pipe tobacco too, so." She smiled as they continued on their way back to the inn.

"Did you get your haircut?"

"Just a little trim. It was getting pretty scraggly." They were quiet for a little while as they walked. "I've been thinking some more. When you get to Estella, will you see about finding an apartment for me? Or even a house? I'm gonna do it, I'm gonna live in Estella after we're done. I think that's where I want to set up shop."

Jason's eyes got really big and hopeful as he stopped in his tracks. "You're going to move to Estella?"

She had a bright smile on her face. "I've been thinking about it a lot actually, and I think, well, yeah. I mean, I can go visit my aunt and uncle anytime, but other than them, I don't have many people Miork. I'd rather be close to you, Tyra, Mason, and Josh."

"I never thought I'd hear you say that. I think that's a great idea. What are you going to do with the cave in Miork?"

She smirked. "I'm still keeping the cave. It's still good for a safehouse or if I happen to be out traveling."

Jason understood to an extent. "You think you'd really need a safehouse?"

She shrugged her shoulders and sighed. "I've made some enemies over the years. I can't overlook the possibility that they might someday decide to come after me or people I care for. The cave is as safe a place as I can think of to lay low if need be."

"And it is a pretty neat pad."

"That too." She was laughing.

The conversation turned serious.

"I don't like Ken," Jason told her.

"Haii, I don't like him either. There's something very off about him. I guess though, since we have the two of you traveling with us now, it would be unfair of me if I didn't allow them to bring on a traveler."

"Yeah, but on the other hand, you know us. Nobody knows him. If one of them knew Ken and could vouch for him, it'd be okay, but they just met him."

"I know. I'll just have to keep my eye on him." She was scratching her head. "There's just, there's something about him that's familiar, something that I just can't put my finger on."

"We'll both keep an eye on him. It's not that the group isn't well protected, even if I weren't here." His smile was smug. "They have Jaras."

Barina gently slugged his shoulder. "Ass."

"Oh, here." He tossed up a small pouch in the air at her, she caught it, barely. "Geez, would you be careful? If you break this one too, you're on your own."

She looked in the pouch. "Seriously, this is awesome!" It was a new ocarina—simple, no decorations, but that was her style. "Thank you, but what's the occasion?"

"Just wanted to hear some good music and, knowing you, you'll think about buying one then get distracted and forget for like, a year."

Barina gave him a little hug. "Thank you." She started to test it out, and Jason smiled contentedly when he heard her play even a couple of scales.

They headed back to the inn, Barina playing the whole way.

The group went to hang out with Robin once he showed up. The banter that he, Tyra, Jason, and Barina had with each other was hilarious. They enjoyed drinks and a great meal, and probably stayed up later than they should have. The whole night was full of good times and light hearts, knowing that they needed to enjoy this time while they could.

Ken hadn't joined them that evening. He agreed to be back in the morning, saying he had things to take care of.

CHAPTER 9

In the morning, everyone felt refreshed and ready to continue on their journey. Ken showed up at the inn right when he promised he would. He sat on his horse, ready to ride.

"We're heading through the Green Forest, right?" Aria asked. "I've heard it's really pretty here. Aren't there some really unique caverns, not just the Water Caves?"

"Yeah, they're really beautiful. Jason and I went exploring a few of them last time we came this way." Tyra nodded while sipping on her canteen. "Man, you guys really got some nice weather for traveling, especially in the middle of summer." She was smiling, feeling the breeze blow her hair.

"It's still warm, but it's been really nice," Twarence had to agree.

Aria's cheeks blushed. "I wouldn't mind it being just a little warmer."

Ken was trying to hold in his laugh, his gaze on the healer. "You're the only one I've ever met who could be chilly on a warm summer day. Do you need my cloak?"

Aria raised an eyebrow. "Maybe later."

His smile grew hearing that. "So Barina, I didn't really get a chance to talk with you yesterday. They were saying something about you being a fighter, did you have any formal training?"

She nodded, "Yes."

"You don't hear of that very often, a woman learning to fight. That's pretty impressive. How long have you been fighting?"

"Quite a while. What about you?" She looked at the sword on his belt. "You're training?"

"I've been learning since I was ten. My father felt it was important. We do a lot of trade in our family, and if I'm going to take over the family business someday, I need to be prepared for whatever comes my way."

"I'm surprised that, given what you're going to be trading, you know, gemstones, that you're traveling alone. I figured you'd have bodyguards or something. It's dangerous to go alone." Barina was picking her words very carefully, trying to learn more about the man who had now joined their group.

"Ah, well, yeah, but this one is pretty special. The fewer people working on it the better. Hence, I need to know how to hold my own. Sometimes, if it's a very rare piece, it's better to travel alone or with just a couple people."

Barina was nodding, thinking hard on what he was saying. "Where are they bringing your goods from?"

"Oh, I think they were coming from just outside of Fern."

His amber eyes met with Barina's blues, and Ken understood from that simple look that she was giving him a chance, but she didn't trust him.

Barina nodded, her mind racing. "So ka na."

"What are you speaking? Seriously, what language is that?" Ken asked, fascinated.

"Nihongo. I lived there for a few years." She was trying to give him the benefit of the doubt, so she would make small talk.

"Really, wow. I've seen watercolor paintings that have been traded from there, and they're beautiful. Makes me wonder how amazing it would be to see it in person."

The two shared a smile.

At least he's not a complete idiot...I think. "It's one of the most beautiful places in the world. I loved it there."

"I've seen some of the weapons that come from there too. Katanas, naganakas. Those were my favorites. You don't happen to own any of those do you?"

She nodded. "I have a sword from Nippon with me." She could talk about weapons.

"Do you have it with you? Could I see it?" He seemed really excited about it.

Her companions looked over at her, each of them stopping, their jaws dropped.

"What?" Barina wasn't sure what they were looking at. She glanced over her shoulders.

"You have a freaking sword with you?" Twarence blurted out. "What? Where?"

She nodded. "I keep it in my bag."

Aria was laughing a little. "What the hell? Why didn't you ever tell us or show us?"

She shrugged her shoulders. "Nobody asked. Plus, since it's a different style than most people are used to seeing, it can bring more attention than I want."

Jason was laughing hard again at their reactions. Tyra was trying not to break into giggles, but she couldn't help it.

"Good lord girl, you could've been fighting with a sword this whole time." Arkon was laughing, he couldn't help it. "Well, let's see it."

Barina pulled a cord on the bottom left side of her bag. She put her right hand up to the now open pocket. They barely heard the sound of a sword being unsheathed. They were sure that, if she wanted to, she could've made it completely silent.

They were fascinated by the sword's appearance. The long handle was wrapped in leather with an intricate design below it. The guard had very intricate flower designs that could've been mistaken for a snowflake. The blade itself was curved. The underside was sharp and the top of it flat, the end of the blade coming to a point. It gleamed happily in the sun and gave off a warm light of its own. It was absolutely beautiful and fit her well.

Jaras barely breathed out. "Perfection. Seriously, the only work I've seen as its equal is well…mine, the ones you've made."

Barina blushed. "Shucks."

Jason nudged her arm. "He's not wrong."

"Wait, you were a smithy?" Ken asked. "What's your full name?" He was looking at her as if she were familiar.

"Barina Raine of Miork. My father was…"

"Adrian Raine of Miork," Ken said, cutting her off. His jaw dropped. "Holy crap. I knew of him. Never met him, but he's the only one I knew of who had been training his daughter to take up the trade."

Barina nodded, impressed. "You know your stuff. Good."

"Could you do a demonstration?" Ken then asked. He was still eyeing her sword.

She shook her head. "Sorry, no. I make it a rule not to do demos."

Ken nodded, as if he understood. "I can respect that. Who trained you?"

Before she could answer—and she was not going to say who—Aria blurted out, "Berklion of Halk, of all people. He trained Barina and Jason here."

Barina shot her a look. Jason kept his head down but didn't say anything.

"Aria, please, don't go telling everyone that without talking to me first." Barina was struggling to keep her voice calm.

"Aria." Onyx gave a tilt of his head. "You even stated yesterday that it wasn't your place to tell that."

"What's the big deal? So, someone knows. I understand why you don't talk about what you can do, but the harm of learning about who taught you, really?" She blew off their concerns in a manner that threw them off.

"Because a man with a reputation like he has," Ken began, "it could raise expectations and challenges even more than if she were to simply talk about her abilities. If someone knew what he could do, they could demand she prove herself. They could do it by threatening her or by getting to her through the people she cares about."

Barina looked grateful. "Thank you," she said quietly.

Ken nodded. He wanted her to know that he understood her reasoning. He knew that gained some points with her.

"Seriously?" Aria seemed surprised. "People would really?"

Jason nodded. "I've seen it happen to her. People believe it if they hear I was trained. It's more believable because I'm a man, but if they hear it with her, then they demand proof. It's gotten ugly when they force her to prove it."

Trya took a deep breath and looked up. "It's no different than if someone were to stab someone in the heart and have them be an inch from death, just to make you prove that you were as good at healing as everyone claimed you were."

Aria nodded. "Noted, sorry B."

"It's okay."

Ken laughed to himself. "Makes me want to ask you for a little demonstration even more, though. But I won't, don't worry."

"Thank you." Jason smiled. He and Barina eyed at each other, still leary but willing to give him a chance.

Ken saw their looks. There was still so much he needed to learn about them, but his gut was that they were people who deserved his attention and caution. Each person in this group was powerful and more than what they were saying, he could tell that. The one that got his attention the most was Barina. If she were trained by Berklion and if Jason was this protective over her, there was more to her. And he still wanted that demonstration.

Barina held back, thinking of what had just happened.

"You okay, B?" Onyx asked quietly. He was walking alongside his horse, stretching his legs for the time being.

She nodded her head. "Just, Aria really surprised me. It's not like her." Barina huffed out a breath. "Something about that guy, I can't put my finger on it."

"That surprised me too. I'm sure she didn't mean anything by it though. Come on." He smiled, trying to reassure both her and himself.

Barina squinted for just a second as she felt a sharp pain come and go. "What was that?" she hissed to herself, raising a hand to her head.

"You okay? I had a little headache earlier too."

She nodded. "I hope it's nothing."

* * *

The next few days were peaceful. Nothing dangerous, nothing out of the ordinary. The group, for the most part, had come to accept Ken. Barina and Jason were still on their guard, but nothing had given them reason to believe that he was a problem. He helped with hunting and with setting up and tearing down the campsites. He had even helped keep watch at night.

They were about halfway through the forest when they decided to make camp early. Barina found it important two days a week to stop early, before the sun started going down. This let them travel fast without getting overly tired. Aria and Arkon were tending to the horses. Barina and Jason were setting up the tents. Onyx and Twarence prepared dinner. Jaras had gone out to collect more firewood for the night.

He had also seen Ken slip away when they weren't looking. Perhaps Ken was just wandering off to have some privacy to relieve himself, but Jaras' instincts were screaming otherwise. He followed Ken for quite some time.

Ken kept looking over his shoulders. At one point, he took out a two-way mirror from his pocket and started talking with someone. Jaras got as close as he could to listen.

"What news?"

"Right on schedule, and I found some people to travel with too. One of them, a woman, was trained by Berklion of Halk of all people, and Onyx of the Hitum Mountain."

"Rutherford's apprentice and a student of Berklion's? That's an interesting group of people. Who else?"

"A scholar, a healer, an elf from the Spirit Clan, and a warrior trained by Darien Bell of Treklea. They are traveling to a school, but they could…" Ken was cut off.

"They could be dangerous. I trust you'll keep an eye on them and, if you must, you'll do what you have to."

"Yes, of course. But they seem like very nice people, so I hope it doesn't come to that." Ken sounded sincere. He put the mirror back in his pocket and, when he turned around, he saw Jaras standing with his arms crossed not far from him.

Ken didn't even flinch when he saw the warrior in front of him. "How much did you hear?"

"All of it." Jaras lit a cigarette. "Explain yourself."

Ken shrugged his shoulders and lit up a cigarette himself. "That's my father. I have to report to him every so often or he'll send out a search party." He smiled thinking about that. "He gets a little protective over me. I like all of you, and you guys are wonderful traveling companions, but what I told him is true. Each one of you in this group are very skilled and powerful in your trades and could be dangerous if you weren't good people. Keep in mind, I just met you recently, so just as you have every right to be leery of me, I have every right to be the same with you."

Jaras studied him for a minute. He didn't smell any lies on him.

"Okay, I just had to be sure." Jaras sighed.

Ken smiled a little more. "Come on, I'll help with the firewood."

Jaras held his head for a second as a sharp pain hit.

"You okay?" Ken asked him casually.

Jaras felt the pain leave. "Yeah, just a small headache for a moment."

That night they sat around the fire, everyone laughing, joking, and even enjoying some drinks. Ken was getting cozy with Aria, but the more he drank, the more he kept looking at Barina and Tyra. Twarence, Arkon, Onyx, Tyra, and Jason were playing cards while Barina was sitting back leaning against Jaras while she played her ocarina. Her and Jaras were still adding to the conversation every so often, but they were staying sober and keeping an eye out for danger while they enjoyed watching the group. Everyone else was a little tipsy—their faces red, and their eyes bright with laughter.

"Look, our kids are getting along so well," Barina joked to Jaras at one point.

He raised an eyebrow and lit a cigarette. "Our kids are drunk." He had a quiet laugh.

Barina had put her ocarina down and was now puffing on her pipe. "Well, at least we won't have trouble getting them to sleep tonight."

Jaras was laughing to himself. "I think the two of us can probably take the shifts. Let them get some rest. You and I can handle it."

She nodded. "I'll take the first one and you the second?"

"You got it. I'll finish this smoke and then lie down. It helps that neither one of us really uses a tent."

"Just one more thing to carry," she agreed.

They sat quietly. When Jaras finished his cigarette, he nodded to Barina and went to his pack. He took out the small bedroll. Covering himself with his cloak, he fell asleep quickly. Barina kept with her pipe and her journal, and was quiet while the rest of the group still hung out with each other. Jason and Tyra had fallen asleep, and the night was dying down.

"Gah, I can't wait for this to all be done with," Twarence grumbled. "I miss my books, and I really miss my bed."

Ken belted out a laugh. "That is the worst part about traveling—not getting to have a decent bed to sleep in."

Onyx snorted. "Blistering heat, freezing cold, dangerous creatures, we have all of that, but the worst is not being able to sleep in a decent bed."

"It'll all be over soon," Arkon said. "Soon. We can get that damn stone and go home."

Ken raised an eyebrow. "Stone?" He toyed with Aria's hair while she was resting against him. His eyes were lazy when he looked at her.

Aria brushed a couple of fingers along the stubble on his face. "Oh, nothing. It's part of our job as well as the school we're going to."

Ken blinked but kept his face neutral. "You picking something up? I mean stones and gems are my specialty. I might know something that could help. I hear things."

Twarence let out a yawn. "It's the Ann…" He was cut off when Barina covered his mouth with a hand.

"Don't say another word." Barina glared at him. "I think you all need to go to bed now."

It was one of the few times they had ever seen Barina borderline angry. Her eyes were doing their best to assess the situation. She didn't know if Ken knew what this meant, but there was every chance.

Twarence seemed put off by Barina's actions and moved his face away from her hand. "Overreacting a little bit there aren't you, B?"

Barina didn't say anything. She hadn't expected Twarence to almost say what he did or his reaction when she stopped him.

"We can trust him." Arkon put a hand on her shoulder. "He's decent. I just feel it. I even told him about Trekto, that's how much I trust him."

Barina gave Arkon a look of concern. "Are you feeling okay? You told him about Trekto? How much have you all had to drink?"

"Not as much as you think." Twarence stood up, brushing leaves off his pants. "But I'll head to bed all the same."

Ken's face didn't give away anything. He just shrugged his shoulders. "No worries, Barina. I don't know what you're talking about, but I know that's my cue. I can respect the fact that there are things about this you can't talk about. I can't talk about what I'm getting either beyond what I've told you. I get it."

Barina couldn't make eye contact, so she couldn't be sure.

The fire was now barely burning, and everyone had fallen asleep except Barina. Even Jaras was still asleep. Barina would wake him in a couple of hours to take a shift. They both had agreed that it would just be either of them on shift that night. They wanted the rest of the group to sleep.

Ken shared a tent with Aria, but the rest of them had gone back to their own. Barina kept the fire going and was enjoying writing in her journal for a while before she got up to stretch her legs and walk the perimeter a little bit. She found a nice spot away from everyone and the fire to look up at the sky. She could smell it earlier and now saw the rain clouds moving in. A storm would probably be there in the next couple hours.

Barina turned when she sensed someone behind her.

"Ken?"

He walked closer until he was only a foot away. "It's a nice night. Looks like it's gonna rain though."

His eyes, they were different. There was a light to them, a gleam, that made her leery.

"Listen." He rested his hand against a tree, moving closer to her. "I don't want you to worry about whatever it is that you guys are doing. I'm not interested in it, not any of it. I have a lot of respect for your group, and really for you."

Barina looked into his amber eyes. "Thanks?" She saw something else. The way he was looking at her, it left her uncomfortable.

"I wanted to tell you other things that you may not know." He smiled. His gaze was smokey.

"Like what?"

"I think you're amazing and unlike any woman I've ever met."

"Aren't you and Aria a thing? And sorry, but I'm not..."

"Shhh." He placed a finger on her lips. "I'm not finished. I've loved a lot of women, but none of them have given me as much of a challenge when it comes to gaining their trust as you have."

Barina pulled back from him. Ken put one arm around to draw her near, his other hand reaching for her backside. His lips went to hers, but before he could kiss her, Ken found himself on the ground, holding his stomach in pain.

Barina had dropped him like a bag of rocks.

"What the hell is your problem?" she hissed. "Are you high or something? First, you don't go shacking up with one girl and try to get with her friend. Aria is my friend, and I am not about to be part of some weird love triangle. Second, I have not given you any reason to think that I would be interested in you in the slightest. Now, go back to bed, leave me alone, and we can put this behind us. You try anything again, and you can take your happy ass down the road on your own. Is that understood?" Her voice was low, but he saw the steady glare in her eyes.

Ken was silent while he watched Barina walk back to the fire and add another log to it. She lit her pipe and kept her back to him.

Barina kept her senses on alert. In a heartbeat, her dagger was out, and she turned, facing Ken who was pointing a knife right at her.

"I gave you a chance," she breathed quietly.

Ken's eyes were dark and dancing, "You think so? No, I gave you a chance." He then took his knife and drove it into his own stomach and lunged at the thief, hugging her and pulling back.

"What the fuck!" Barina wasn't expecting that. Her jaw dropped. When she looked down, she was covered in his blood, as was her dagger.

"ARIA!" Ken screamed as he rolled to the ground in pain. "ARIA!"

Barina realized what he was doing. She froze.

Jaras woke up with a start. He saw Ken on the ground and looked to Barina. "B, what?"

"He set me up," she whispered. She knew how this appeared.

The rest of the group, except for Jason and Tyra, came out of their tents. Barina knew the two had drunk quite a bit and were exhausted. They wouldn't wake up for a while.

Everyone else, groggy and eyes wide, stumbled into the open to find Ken on the ground and Barina standing above him covered in blood with her dagger drawn.

"The hell?" Aria ran over and healed him in a minute.

Nobody could believe what they were seeing.

"Barina, why?" Twarence could hardly say the words to her.

"She, I came out to talk to her, and she threw herself at me. I turned her down and, when I did, well…" Ken sat up, coughing and looking grateful to Aria.

"You son-of-a-bitch!" Barina hissed at him. "I never touched him! Except for when I punched him for grabbing my ass."

Aria stood up. "What? You were going after him? I thought we were friends!"

Barina rolled her eyes. "Do you really think I'd go after your guy? Aria, come on, you know I wouldn't do that."

Arkon had heard enough. "You turned me down. I can handle that. But you have been showing me you can't be trusted at all. You know my king but won't tell me how. You've been suspicious of him this entire time when he's been nothing but good to us. You're a liar and a thief, and who knows how many people you've killed. Why should we trust you?"

Barina put a couple of fingers to the bridge of her nose. "Seriously, if I wanted you dead, I could've done it at any time. Magic doesn't affect me like it does most people, and you know that. I've never done anything but help you and look after you. I rejected you, so what? It doesn't mean I don't care about you. I just don't see you as more than a friend."

"Barina." It was Twarence who spoke up. "This looks really bad. You have his blood on you and on your dagger. It's your word against his, and the evidence…"

"He stabbed himself," Barina blurted out, even though she knew how that sounded.

Onyx came to her defense. "Barina, no. I just don't believe she would've hurt him, at least not without reason."

"I didn't hear any struggles till Ken yelled," Jaras said, thinking it through. "I'm pretty sure that if she had tried to kill you, you'd be dead already, and we wouldn't have ever found out."

Ken's face twisted with rage. "Are you saying she just maimed me and meant it? Death would've been a bigger mercy than this pain. Not just my gut but knowing that her kindness was just a sham!"

Aria was struggling to hold back her tears. She had really grown fond of Ken, and it wasn't very often that she found a man who interested her as more than a friend or even just a hook-up. She hadn't been interested in a relationship, but with Ken—with Ken it had been different. She had also become friends with Barina. She hadn't expected to go on this job and make friends with the people here, but she had. And Barina was someone she cared dearly for.

But Aria knew something else. "Barina, you're the only one between the two of you that's given us reason to believe you have a violent side. I care for you, but the evidence is here."

"Aria." Barina looked down while trying to fight back tears. "I didn't do this."

"We have no reason to believe you." Arkon turned around, unable to look at her.

"You have more reason to believe me than him." Barina snapped out of her shock. "I've been nothing but honest with you. I didn't go after him. He tried to kiss me. I made him stop, and he came after me when I walked away. I guess this was his plan. He wanted to get rid of me. I don't completely understand why yet, but he wants me out of the picture." She looked at Jaras. "Jaras is right though, if I had tried to kill him, I wouldn't have just tried, I would've done it."

Aria's face paled, and Arkon turned back to face Barina. "So you're saying that you could kill him, just like that, and not feel anything?"

"I never touched him, except when I stopped him from grabbing my ass and trying to kiss me, I never touched him. And didn't you hear anything I just said. He's trying to get rid of me for a reason. I'm a part of this group. We have a job to do."

Onyx had been sitting quietly, but he finally spoke up. "There's something to this. Why would this happen now? Why would, now, after we've been traveling together for a few days, would this happen? What's the end game? Barina, she could've turned on us anytime before now, and there's nothing any of us could've done. She could slip away before anyone could do anything, and magic doesn't affect her like it does most people." Onyx looked at Ken. "Something about this isn't right."

"Aria, I know you care about Ken," Twarence began, trying to reason it out, "but why would this happen so close to meeting his contacts? Arkon, I know you're still sore about her turning you down, but, if she could do anything, would it happen now? Why not way earlier?"

Jaras interjected. "And who *was* your contact that you were speaking with using that two-way mirror earlier? I know it was your employer, but the way the conversation was going, it sounded like you would have to end us if it seemed like we were a threat."

The rest of the traveling party turned their heads quickly to Jaras, this was the first they had heard him mention that he had seen Ken speaking with someone in his mirror.

Twarence blinked. "Wait, what? He was talking to someone? Why didn't you tell us?"

Jaras shook his head. "I wanted to monitor him before I alerted you."

"Seems too convenient that you're just now mentioning this to us." Arkon's face was turning red with anger.

"It was literally just a few hours ago, and I wanted to monitor it." Jaras gave his attention back to Ken. "Now why would Barina, even though I don't think she did, attack you?"

"I like all of you. I told Barina that I respected her, that was true. I understood why she couldn't speak about her abilities, or who her trainer was, I got it. I mean seriously, and I wasn't going to hurt any of you, not even if my employer wanted me to." Ken took off his blood-stained shirt.

"Barina," Aria finally breathed out, "I think you should go on ahead and meet up with us in Estella after he leaves the group. We need to think about all of this. I don't know if we can trust you, but I know we can't keep the two of you together anymore. We'll keep Tyra and Jason safe with us, so you don't have to worry about that, but right now..." her voice trailed off. "I just think you're too much of a wild card."

Barina stepped forward, "Aria, you can't." Barina was cut off as a ball of fire landed right before her feet.

Arkon stood between the two women. "You heard her, get your stuff and go." He held another fireball at the ready in his hand.

Onyx stood next to Barina, his staff in hand. For the first time since they had met him, the wizard was angry. "I don't think so."

"What are you going to do about it?"

"Try me."

Arkon and Onyx were in a deadlock. Barina quickly put a stop to it.

"Onyx, stand down, my friend." Barina put her dagger back in its sheath. "I'll go. You guys need to stay together and, if something happens with this piece of shit here," she pointed to Ken, "or anything else, they'll need you and Jaras. Twarence, you know the way till you get to Estella, and I'll regroup with you there."

Barina's bag was still packed. She hadn't taken anything out of it besides her journal and ocarina, so she slung it over her shoulders. "Be safe." She then looked at Ken. "If anything happens to the two people in that tent there," she pointed to where Jason and Tyra were sleeping, "or to the rest of this lot because of you, there won't be a force in this world that will keep me from getting to you."

Barina grabbed her things and quickly walked away.

Jaras couldn't believe what just happened. It all went down so fast. "No! You don't understand what you just did." Jaras went after her. "Barina!" He ran into the woods. "Barina, come back!" He searched but couldn't even find a footprint. No signs in the trees. Nothing. She was gone.

Jaras walked back. "She's gone. I mean, she's just gone." He looked down at the ground. "She was helping keep all of you safe! You have no idea how many times she's helped to keep us out of danger, and things are only going to get more dangerous the farther we go."

Arkon stepped up to Jaras. "We don't need her. All of us are capable of taking care of ourselves."

Jason and Tyra walked out of their tent, their eyes hardly awake. "What's going on? You guys are being so loud." Tyra yawned.

Jason looked around trying to assess the situation quickly. "Where's Barina?"

That woke Tyra up. She inhaled through her teeth. "Where is she? What's going on?"

Arkon walked over. "We told her to meet back up with us when we get to Estella. She attacked Ken, almost killing him."

Tyra marched up to Ken. "What the hell did you do to her?"

Ken snorted. "I didn't do anything. She threw herself at me and, after I turned her down, she came after me."

"I told her to meet us in Estella," Aria said. "I can't, it's just, I can't believe she did that. I thought we were friends." She was still trying to suppress her tears, she was so confused by everything.

Tyra crossed her arms. "That is the biggest load of crap that I've ever heard. She is not the type to go after a man if he's with someone. She also doesn't attack someone for no reason. Ken, what did you do to her?" Tyra wasn't backing down.

Jason had gone into the woods to find his friend. "Barina?" he called quietly. He reached out with his senses but knew she really wasn't there anymore. "Damn it."

Jaras had caught up to him. "I tried to go after her too. She was gone within ten seconds."

"I know. When she wants to be gone, she's gonna be gone. She was always the fastest. She's probably a mile away."

Jason turned to Jaras. "But don't worry, she's not too far if we need her."

Jaras punched a tree. "I freaking hate this. All of it is just wrong." He was pacing. "What, I mean why the hell would he do this now, why now?"

Without warning, both men found themselves on the ground, unable to move.

"A paralysis spell?" Jason breathed. "This one is powerful."

"What the hell? Onyx!" Jaras called. He was resting at an awkward angle. Calling for the wizard was all he could do.

"I'm afraid your wizard is unable to take any requests at the moment."

They looked up to see Ken walking into the brush. He had a dark smile, and his pupils were cloudy as if smoke circled in them.

"You're, you're a wizard?" Jaras snarled seeing him.

"Where's my, where's Tyra?" Jason asked.

"She's with the rest of the group, all tied up, just as you are." Ken knelt down. "She's beautiful, you know, your fiancé. Very beautiful. All of the women with you are amazing. Aria, she's about as beautiful as they get, and just a sweet girl too. Barina, she's not a beauty like Tyra or Aria, but still, she had a quality about her that was something that I wanted to enjoy." He sighed while he pushed his hair back. He waved another hand that tied an invisible rope around each man's leg, pulling them behind him to drag them back to the group.

Everyone, every single person in their group was restrained. Onyx was unconscious, as was Arkon. The rest of them were tied and gagged. Ken dropped the two men and looked at the group.

"I'm close enough to the Water Caves. I'm gonna take us all there now. I don't meet with my dealer till tomorrow, but we can wait. Besides, I want to see how long it'll take little Barina to find you."

Ken clapped his hands together, and they all found themselves suspended in the air. "Follow me. You can leave your things here. You won't be needing them."

Aria had tears and betrayal in her eyes. She couldn't believe what was happening.

"Tyra!" Jason called. "Tyra, are you hurt?"

"Jason! I'm okay!" Tyra couldn't see him since her eyes were covered, but her head moved toward where she heard his voice.

"Shut up." Ken's eyes rolled. "God, you guys don't ever shut up."

Jason could see his fellow warrior. "I can still move, but I have to wait for the right moment to act." He whispered to Jaras. "Be patient."

Jaras nodded.

"Why are you doing this?" Twearence asked. "Seriously, why? We were helping you, we trusted you." Twearence was trying to keep his wits about him. All he could think was to keep asking questions.

"I'll tell you when we get to the caves, not before then." Ken was laughing. "She was right though, I *was* setting her up. I needed her gone. You said she was stronger than you, Jason, and stronger than your teacher. If you were both trained by Berklion of Halk, and she's stronger than him, I needed her gone. The only way that was going to happen is if you guys told her to leave. Now keep quiet till we get to the caves."

Ken took them, trekking through the woods, into the dead of night. All they could do was wait to see what would happen and hope that Jason could get them out of this, or maybe Barina would come for them.

They weren't sure if it was late at night or early in the morning when they arrived at the Water Caves, but it felt like hours had passed.

The caves were enormous. Above them, a series of streams flowed. All the streams fell into a large opening at the top of the caves and cascaded into gentle and beautiful waterfalls ending in a shallow pool at the bottom. Even in the dead of night, they were beautiful with the light of the stars or the moon to illuminate them, but tonight, with the storm rolling in, there was no light.

Ken set them down on the ground, keeping them bound.

"Oh, quit with the death stares already. I'm not going to kill any of you as long as you just do what I say. So, relax and don't worry. It'll all be over soon." Ken sat back against the wall and lit a cigarette for himself.

Onyx and Arkon started to wake up.

"My head, goddamn my head is killing me. What the hell?" Arkon's voice was raspy, and his vision took a minute to come into focus. "We're in the Water Caves?"

Onyx opened his eyes and took one look at Ken. "You're with the Bask order."

"What gave me away?" Ken was laughing again.

"Your eyes, the clouds in your eyes. You've done a good job at concealing yourself till now." Onyx knew about this order of wizards all too well.

"I know you're trying to use your vision to stop me, but I slipped a little something into your drink earlier, so your powers and Arkon's, they're useless for twenty-four hours." He gave him a little wink. "I just have to wait until my guy gets here with my gem."

"Who are you waiting for? Who were you talking to with that mirror?" Jaras demanded again.

Ken's smile got even bigger as he started to explain.

* * *

Barina had hightailed it away from the camp. She couldn't quite place her finger on why Ken did what he did. With Arkon threatening her with his powers, there wasn't much she could do to speak with the group. He would've put a perimeter up around the area, so he'd sense her if she got close again. She could handle a perimeter like that, but she didn't want to at the moment. They weren't listening to her anyway.

The fact that they honestly think that I would do something so underhanded! What is going on here? I don't like any of it.

Barina made it a few miles away before she decided to rest for the evening. Jason and Tyra would be safe with the group. She'd honestly be surprised if they didn't go their separate ways in the morning after what happened. The only reasons Barina wasn't leaving this whole job behind was that she needed the money, and she had made a promise. Most importantly were the people she had come to care so much for. She wanted to be there to help them. For right now though, this was all she could do.

Barina closed her eyes. She was tired, and was glad she'd finally be able to sleep. She had hunkered down under a few bushes to give herself some cover for when the storm came. She was asleep for maybe an hour before she woke up with a start. She held her breath, sweat beaded down her face, and her eyes were wide.

No!

She realized who Ken was and why he looked so familiar. It all clicked. She had to get back to them.

Barina ran at top speed through the forest. She didn't feel a barrier when she came within range of the campsite. That didn't sit well with her. Their magic should be working. When she came to the campsite, she found their things were still there along with the horses.

"Guys!" She searched the tents. "Anyone!" She looked at the trees. "Guys!"

She examined the ground and saw the prints, the trails.

"Goddamn it! He has them!"

Darting into the woods, she followed the prints, sure she knew where they were going.

I hope I'm not too late.

The storm was starting to roll in, and Barina knew that tonight it was going to get ugly.

CHAPTER 10

At the Water Caves, Ken smiled at Jaras' question and then looked up to the sky as the rain started to come down.

"You guys really did this to yourselves. I mean, honestly, you had to mention Thoron and the Anna Stone." Ken sighed. He leaned up against the wall of the cave while smoking. "I overheard you when you were at the café in Fortania and decided then that I should probably keep an eye on you guys. Helps that you had this beauty with you." He winked at Aria. "You guys pretty much let it slip tonight too when you were talking."

"Fuck you!" Aria spat at him. "You were working for Toler this whole time!"

Ken was laughing to himself. "You could say that."

"He's more than just working for him if he's a member of the Bask order," Onyx growled. He was ready to fry him. Onyx wanted to move, he wanted to lunge at this man, to use all of his powers against him, but whatever Ken gave him was powerful enough so he couldn't lift even a pebble with his powers.

"Wait, the Bask order," Twarence said. "It's made up of six families, and they only allow descendants in. I know Toler has a brother, Agelie, so how are you involved? Are you just helping him since you're a member of the order?" Twarence wasn't able to put this together.

"You're getting closer." Ken was thoroughly amused by this.

While they had been talking, Jason had been gathering his energy. He made his move now, while Ken was talking. He jumped and hurled himself at Ken, throwing a punch followed by a strong side kick that sent Ken back about ten feet. Jason tried to get to Ken's sword, but Ken had set it aside earlier, so he didn't have a weapon. Jason took a hit to the jaw before Ken kicked him off and snapped a finger which sent Jason slamming into the wall. Ken then sent a shock wave to zap him.

Jason was still trying to stand, holding in his groans of pain while sweat beaded down his forehead and neck. He finally was able to get to his feet, even with the hits he was taking, and managed to move.

Ken didn't think that Jason would be as fast as he was, especially after he hit him with all those energy waves. He knew Jason was strong. He knew he was fast, but he didn't realize how tough he was or how deadly this man could be.

Jason could fight this guy, even without a weapon and against Ken's magic. He could fight him, and well. Even though Jason was hurting, he was still overcoming the paralysis spell. That wasn't going to stop him from doing what he had to do. *I've just gotta buy enough time.*

He sprinted toward the other side of the room, jumped, and placed a foot on the wall before darting in another direction. He jumped at the other wall, put his foot on the next one closest to it and jumped as high as he could, reaching for what he needed.

The stalactites. Hanging from the ceiling of the cave, none had been close enough for him to grab with his normal vertical jump, so he had to use the walls to reach high enough. He took hold of one and was able to punch it to break it off. He landed in a roll and stood up, stalactite in hand.

As Ken charged, Jason threw a fist full of muddy water at his face, blinding him for a few short moments. Ken's scream cut off when Jason hit him full force in the face with the stalactite which broke in half. Jason swung the remaining portion at Ken's skull, but Ken managed to put up a shield to deflect it. Jason lashed with a sweeping kick to knock Ken off of his feet completely and pushed Ken's face into the muddy water.

He just had to hold him for a few minutes, long enough till he stopped moving. He had to hold him till he knew a human couldn't recover. Even then, the fight still wouldn't be over, but he hoped it would be enough time to get everyone to safety.

Ken stopped moving, and then Jason started to count the seconds.

"Jason?" Aria spoke first.

"Don't break my concentration." He was focused, and he knew what it meant for Ken to be of the Bask order. Trying to drown a member of the Bask order was a risky move.

After five long minutes, Jason stood up and quickly went to Tyra. "Are you hurt?"

She shook her head. "You, jeez, you're a mess."

Jason had a black eye, a bruised and bloody lip, burns on his neck and shoulders, but he held a little smile. "Thanks. I've got to move all of you and fast."

She touched his arm. "Get them first."

He blinked. "Tyra."

"Destroy the wicked," she said, repeating the words that he, Josh, and Barina had made part of their reasons for fighting. "They have to be first."

Jason hated this. He hated it, but he also knew how brave and selfless Tyra was. She saw the bigger picture. It was one of the things that he loved about her. She knew that this group of people in the cave with them was key in defeating a tyrant like Toler. He could finish Ken off, and even if they didn't make it past this cave, the rest of them could defeat Toler. She knew it. And so did he.

Jason changed direction but not before he found himself crushed against the wall as a blast of energy hit him and hard. He sunk to the floor. Tyra screamed as she was unable to move to him. He turned to see Ken standing up.

"I really don't like you." Ken's cold eyes were wild now. "I might just go ahead and take you out of the picture." He started to raise his hands, but he never had the chance.

In the blink of an eye, Ken let out a yell of agony and found a throwing knife in his arm. He turned, but didn't see anyone.

Jason smiled. "Finally," he sighed.

The next second, Ken was flat on the ground with a dagger in his chest. The owner dropped from the top of the cavern and crashed onto him.

"YOU!" Ken hissed looking up.

"Surprise bitch," was all Barina said as she snapped his neck with her hands. "I will never get used to that sound."

Ken's eyes closed. He was motionless.

"Jason, can you stand at all? We don't have much time till he revives." Barina rushed over to Jason.

"I can stand, yeah." He leaned on her as she helped him to his feet.

"Wait, revives?" Arkon's jaw dropped. "But you killed him."

"You did just see him stand up after Jason drowned him, right?" Tyra asked. She wanted to move so badly, but she couldn't.

Barina shook her head. "Just once, it's not enough. Well, he's been killed twice now, but still…" She had set Jason down somewhere a little more out of the way before she rushed to Arkon, her arms around him, and pulled him from where he was. "If he were really dead, we'd know. Your magical binds are mostly gone. You can move some, but I don't know if I have time to untie you. Once I take another life, I think you should be able to move almost completely." They could hear the urgency in her voice. "I'd take his head, but that would just fuse back onto his neck. It's gross."

"The Bask order, it's their big ace," Onyx breathed. "They save the blood of the victims they kill. After one hundred kills, they drink that vial of blood after infusing it with their magic. They're given five extra lives on top of the one they were only ever supposed to have."

Barina was trying to get everyone as far away from Ken as she could with what time she had. "We have to move you guys as far back as we can. I'm gonna have a hell of a fight on my hands. He'll be at his most dangerous when he's in his last life. I don't know how many he's used up, but each time he comes back, he's more powerful than before. I need to be able to strike him down within seconds of him reviving, or it'll be trouble." She was rushing over to pull Aria back now too. "On his last life, I don't know, he'll be very powerful, and I'll need to change up my fighting.

Barina was thinking through her options out loud, knowing they weren't great. "I'd sit and wait for him to revive to take him down, but I don't dare because his powers could lash out and take me down if I were close."

"Barina!" Onyx called. He'd been watching Ken for any signs of movement.

She looked back at Ken who took a deep breath and let out a groan and stood up.

Barina threw a knife that landed in his neck, and he fell to the ground.

Her eyes studied Ken. "Damn it. Jason, get Tyra back as far as you can. I can get the rest of them back to a safe distance on my own."

"You're still helping us, after everything?" Aria couldn't control her tears.

Barina couldn't respond to her, but she gave a slight nod.

Aria looked down. "I'm so sorry."

"Barina, who is he?" Twarence asked her. "Do you know who he really is?"

She nodded. "It finally clicked, and I came running back. He's…" She was cut off when she saw him move again. "Shit."

She had managed to get all of the traveling party back to a fairly safe distance before she saw Ken finally stand up again. He threw the knife to the ground, spit blood, and his eyes were pure murder. He saw Barina, and she ran till she was out of sight. He was trying to follow her, casting bolts of energy to incinerate her, but she was too fast. He stopped finally.

"Come on, let's play." He smiled, his amber eyes trying to find her.

"Let them go, and I'll let you go home to daddy alive, instead of in pieces."

The thief walked out from behind one of the waterfalls. Barina's face was dark with a battle aura that gave every person, except for Ken, goosebumps. She walked calmly toward him, no weapon drawn, her pack still on her back. But they knew she could burst into action at any moment.

Ken's face broke a wicked grin. "You got past my barrier to the cave, and it seems like you figured me out." The clouds that swirled in his eyes were black.

"I knew you looked familiar, but I couldn't place you. It's your father. You look so much like him. You even have the same eyes."

"You're not going to bow?"

"Fuck you." Barina's voice was firm.

"Who the hell are you?" Twarence finally blurted out.

"Prince Trekenler," Barina said. "Son of King Toler, heir of Thoron." Barina was angry, angry at the fact that… "I can't believe it took me this long to figure it out. I would've killed you sooner if I had pieced it together." There was a collective inhale when Barina announced who this man really was.

Ken doubled over in laughter. He stood up, sword drawn, his eyes fixed on her. "This is why I had to get you out of the picture. I knew that if anyone was going to figure me out, it'd be you." He then looked at everyone else. "I wasn't able to get into Barina's head at all. Not her or Jason, or even Tyra. Onyx and Jaras, I wasn't able to mess with your minds either, not able to help influence how you felt about me. The rest of you, it was too easy."

"You were in…in our heads?" Arkon's face went pale.

Ken's smug smile darkened. "Of course I was. I was able to get into your minds and influence you to like me, whispering ideas into your subconscious from the moment I met you. It wasn't hard to set up a way to meet you. I compelled that man to steal your money and then..."

Aria's face turned green. "You...that's why he was so confused when I healed him."

"Of course. He was easy. It took some finesse with you, Arkon, and Twarence, but it didn't take long for me to be able to suggest to you what I wanted and influence you. Do you really think you would've invited me to join you so easily? You would've told me who trained Barina? The name of the Elven king?" He laughed again. "Do you really, honestly think that you would've believed me over your thief with what happened earlier tonight if I hadn't?"

"What we did together..." Aria felt sick to her stomach, and she was shaking. "Was anything I agreed to do with you, were those my own actions?"

Ken inhaled a breath, relishing in that. "All of *that*, I didn't need to convince you to do all of our nocturnal activities."

Twarence, tears welling up in his eyes, and looked to Barina. "Barina, I'm sorry, oh god I'm so sorry."

Barina didn't look at any of them. She kept her eyes on the prince.

"With a mind as powerful as yours, you would think that they'd teach you to protect it, wouldn't you, Twarence?" Ken was mocking him now. "Do you see it, do you see your nightmares in front of you?" He was laughing more as he waved a finger at him.

Twarence's eyes grew with terror. Ken had entered his mind and was filling it with images of what he wanted him to see. Twarence felt like he and Ken were in the same room as all of his worst fears. He felt he was living it and, even though Ken only had a hold on him for a moment, Twarence felt like he was gone for hours. If the scholar could've screamed, he would have.

That was Ken's mistake. He never heard Barina draw her sword. He never heard her pack land on the ground. He barely saw the edge of the blade as it almost reached his face. If he hadn't taken one step back, it would've taken his head instead of slicing one of his ears off.

That pain, that shock, released Twarence from Ken's mind, and he gasped, letting out a sob.

"I will kill you." Barina's voice was level, her tone was matter-of-fact.

The sword gleamed as a flash of lightning caught the reflection. Barina stepped away from Ken, emotion leaving her face, and her eyes were unlike anything they had seen. They were sure she could scare death itself.

"You do realize that I'm going to kill you and probably take your friends down too. Well, except for her." He looked over to Aria. "I'll take Aria back with me. She'll be my plaything for a few years. Maybe she'll give me an heir."

"Go to hell!" Aria screamed. "If you ever touch me again, I'll use all my powers to suck the fucking life out of you!"

"Damn, you are so, just, everything when you're angry." Ken blew a kiss to the healer.

He found another knife in his neck. It cut off his air, and he couldn't breathe as blood poured out of his neck. He acted fast, pulling the knife and healing himself within seconds.

"How many of those things do you have?" he screamed, trying to catch his breath. His eyes were wide, and for the first time, concerned.

Barina cracked a little smile. "Look at her again, and you'll find out."

"Why would you fight for them? They didn't believe you. They cast you aside. You're nothing to them."

"I care for them." She took two steps forward. "That's the only reason I need. Now that I know you're of the Bask order, I know if you hadn't rattled their brains, they would've stood by me."

Ken drew a sword in one hand and a knife in the other. "I know I said I'm taking Aria with me, probably Tyra out of spite, but you, everything I do to you, I'll do it in front of the whole kingdom." He was laughing.

He almost didn't see it, Barina moved so fast. He barely dodged out of the way as she flashed by. The only thing he caught a glimpse of was a glimmer of steel and her hair highlighted by the lightning outside. If he had blinked, he would've missed it, and the blade of her sword almost took his head again, but it left a deep gap where the muscle of his collar met the base of his neck. Blood poured from his wound and he put a hand to it to stop the bleeding and heal it.

His eyes were still swirling with clouds, and his face went dark. No more laughter or jokes.

"I've taken you too lightly." His weapons now shone with a red glow. "I was going to keep you as a trophy. Now I'll just kill you."

Barina lunged at him again. He put up a shield as she rushed him. She was able to spin around it faster than he was able to follow her. Her sword ran through the back of his thigh and sliced right through the muscle and tendons.

Ken fell to the ground screaming. His energy shield just barely stopped her next attack that would've brought her sword down to split his head open. He was crawling backwards, his leg bleeding, and she wasn't letting up. Her movements were small before she would strike, giving him no room to counter her. She was strong enough behind her blade that she was going to break his energy shield.

His leg was in agony, and he was terrified of this woman and what she could do. He knew he wasn't seeing the bulk of her power either, and that was terrifying. He could only heal himself a few more times from his injuries, and he only had one life left. Healing himself before death took him wasn't a strong option for much longer.

He gathered his thoughts and took a deep breath. Barina had been watching his eyes the whole time, knowing that the Bask order's tricks rested behind their eyes. Ken's eyes swirled to a bright teal, and she brought her blade up just as he blasted a bolt of energy. Her blade deflected the blast, but it was strong enough to push her back five feet. Some of the energy got past her sword, but she kept holding. Ken drew his sword and went after her with everything he had. Barina deflected or dodged everything.

"I've had enough of you!" Ken's breathing was deep, and his eyes cracked with red light as the walls began to move.

"She has him terrified." Onyx gave a small laugh, as did Arkon.

"He's unleashing some real power now," Arkon breathed. "Is she going to be able to fight this?"

"Let's hope." Onyx watched intently.

"I think if she were really able to cut loose, this would've been over by now." Jaras was sweating watching them. "But with hostages, she has to play her cards incredibly carefully."

Barina dodged another attack of his energies, and Ken found himself with another knife in his arm and let out a scream.

Jason got to his feet, his sword still too far for him to reach, but he retrieved some of the knives out of Barina's bag.

"I'm really sick of these knives!" Ken's eyes went into a blind rage. "And I am done with all of you!"

Jason threw four more knives at Ken, distracting him as Barina launched herself at the prince again. Ken found himself gutted with blood pouring out of his stomach, soaking the ground. He gasped for air, and he was in such blinding pain he could hardly focus. He healed himself quickly, and he knew he had to bring out the bulk of his power, and had to do it now.

The air around Trekenler grew thick and hot, and any light that was there was absorbed into him as he began to gather his powers. He changed up his tactics. Instead of going for Barina and Jason, he set his gaze on Tyra. In the blink of an eye, he pulled her to him. He wrapped his arms around her and held his sword to her neck. They could see the energy in his arms ready to be released as well.

Everyone froze.

Jason's eyes were dangerous, and Barina was waiting for the right moment.

"You take another step, and I'll kill her." Ken laughed. Tyra cringed as he placed a taunting kiss on her neck. "If you do nothing, then I'll keep her. She'll be one of my women. I'm sure she'll be a lot of fun, at least for a while."

"I'd rather die." Tyra's eyes were set.

"You'd rather die? You'd rather have the man who loves you watch you die in front of him than give yourself to me?" Ken taunted while he nuzzled her face with his own. "I can arrange that."

"I'd rather die than let you control me, and he'd rather me die in peace than live knowing that you were controlling my life," Tyra hissed. She closed her eyes before she gave a powerful stomp with her foot that loosened his hold on her just enough for her to slide from his arms and turn, punching him as hard as she could in the face. "But I will not go down without a fight!"

Ken stepped back and gave a blast of energy that sent Tyra flying back ten feet.

"NO!" Jason was able to catch her, his body taking the force of her fall. She was hardly conscious, though. Her blue eyes fluttered as blood trickled out of her mouth. She met Jason's eyes, and a smile touched her lips. He smiled back.

"I love you," Jason said, pushing her hair back. "You are such a badass."

Tyra laughed as her breathing slowed. "I learned from the best. I love you, too."

Barina kept her gaze on Ken. "Jason, stay there with Tyra."

Ken slammed a hand to the ground, his eyes swirling purple now. He was sending out an arch of energy that followed her around the room as she ran and dodged it. He couldn't touch her, she was too fast for him. He knew she was about to best him, and he had one option left.

Barina rushed Ken again. She saw him hold out his arms—one hand using his energies to hold the two people she cared for more than anything, the other entangling the entire traveling party she had been with.

The prince could see that she knew as well, that he would kill both groups in the next couple of seconds if she did nothing. She could cut off an arm linked to one group and take him down, but that would send his energy through the other arm—a fatal blow. He would still take someone with him that she cared for. The next few heartbeats, few steps, would be some of the longest of her life.

Ken's eyes swirled red and green, and Barina knew what was about to happen. She could only save Jason and Tyra, or everyone else.

Her eyes met Jason's as he mouthed, "Destroy the wicked." Barina's lip quivered. He knew the sacrifice that both he and Tyra were willing to make. Tyra's eyes looked back at her. "Do it."

"I love you both," she breathed, tears filling her eyes.

They closed their eyes while holding each other.

With a scream of agony, Barina's sword took off Ken's arm that held the traveling party in his deadly energy, and in the next movement used her sword to run it through Ken's heart. The light in the prince's eyes started to fade as she saw Jason and Tyra fall to the ground together just before they vanished.

The thief held tight to her sword as she forced Ken's body to the ground. Still laughing, she saw him start to raise his hand to heal himself. She didn't hesitate and took his other arm. Staring, she watched him bleed out—a smile still on his face.

The traveling group felt their binds disappear completely, and they were able to stand. Arkon and Onyx's powers came back fully as the man who poisoned them was now dead. They watched, unable to believe what just happened, as their thief rushed to where her two friends had been before they were taken from her.

The only thing left was the pendant that Jason had worn—identical to Barina's—and the ring he had given to Tyra. Jason's sword was still on the ground, feet from where he could've reached it. Barina knelt on the ground, trying to feel the energies her friends might have left, but she couldn't feel anything. They were gone, and there weren't even bodies for her to bury.

The others watched as she lowered her head, reaching her hands out to grab the pendant and ring and clutch them to her. Her body was shaking, her breathing was heavy, and tears were falling.

Barina could not wrap her head around what was happening. These two people had been constants in her life. Two people who she knew—just as she knew that the sky was blue—were always going to be there. They were going to grow old together, have adventures, live and laugh together. It was over.

Jason, Josh, and Barina: bound by friendship and fate, three of the strongest warriors, trained by the most unstoppable warrior in the world. They were down by one.

"I'm so sorry," she whispered to the pendant and ring. "I'm so sorry! Forgive me, stars above, forgive me! I should've done more!" She was sobbing to the trinkets she held. "How am I going to tell everyone? How? Where the hell did you go?"

She turned to where Ken lay and walked over, lifting him by his bloody neck, looking him in the eyes to see if there was any life left in him.

"Where did you send them?" she snarled.

He had one last breath left in him. "To a nightmare," he breathed, chuckling.

Her face was red with anger and pain, and wet with tears. "Fuck you." Barina dug her fingers into his neck and literally ripped his throat out. His eyes glazed over, the last bit of air escaped from his windpipe, and he hung limp before she dropped him to the ground.

She collapsed onto the ground herself and curled her face into her knees. She didn't try to silence her sobs. She couldn't. Her world was crashing down on her. For the second time in her life, she had lost a part of her family. Jason and Tyra were family. He had always been like a brother to her, especially after she lost her family. And it hadn't taken long for Tyra and Barina to develop a friendship as close as sisters when she came into the picture. This was a nightmare she couldn't escape.

The travelers watched in tears while Barina broke down and cried. They were all heartbroken. They had not known Jason and Tyra long, but long enough to call them friends. The two had been willing to sacrifice their lives so the others could live. They started to walk toward Barina, slowly, but the second she heard them moving, she stood up, her back turned.

"Don't come near me." Her tone was cold.

"Barina…" Twarence didn't know what to say.

"Save it." Her voice was barely a whisper.

Aria tried to approach, tears in her eyes and overflowing with guilt. "Barina, please, I'm so sorry."

Barina turned around, but she couldn't look any of them in the eyes. She took a deep breath before she leaned over and picked up Jason's sword. "I'm leaving first. Wait five minutes, and don't follow me."

They were quiet, all of them shedding tears or ready to. There was no way to reach her. Their thief wouldn't hear what they had to say.

Barina quickly grabbed her knives, threw on her pack, and with Jason's sword and her own in hand, left the cave. She headed back to the camp and found the tent that Jason and Tyra had shared. She looked through the tent, but most of their things hadn't been unpacked. She grabbed their bags and left the tent.

The rain was now a light mist which would make traveling easier, at least for the rest of the night. She reached a hand to Lucy's face—their faithful horse—before she strapped the saddle to her.

"It's just you and me, girl," she whispered through tears.

The horse nuzzled her face next to Barina's shoulder, letting the family friend hold onto her for a moment before she met the horse's eyes. "I'm sorry, they're not coming back. I'll get you to Estella though. Josh will be able to take care of you. You remember Josh, right? He's always liked you." She patted the horse on the back while strapping a couple of bags to her saddle. "Do you mind if I ride? I'm pretty tired."

Lucy turned so that Barina was closer to the saddle. She put her foot in the stirrup, climbed up, and rode with Lucy away from where anyone could follow her.

* * *

After they were finally able to calm themselves down, the group made their way back to camp. It felt cold and empty, even with all of their things and their horses there.

"Lucy is gone, so are Jason and Tyra's things. She just left the tent." Jaras told them in a matter-of-fact voice, "Never did like to carry a tent."

"What do we do now? What's the next step?" Arkon was barely able to talk.

Twarence took a deep breath, rubbing his face while hanging his head. "We keep going. We rest as much as we can tonight, and then we travel after first light. Once we get to Estella, we'll take a day or so to rest and regroup at an inn, then keep going. We still have a job to do." Tears fell down his cheeks and into his beard. "Toler, when he doesn't hear from his son after a few days, will most likely be sending people to look for him, so we'll need to be on high alert. We still need to finish our mission, and we have to finish Toler. If he's anything like Ken, then he needs to be dealt with."

"I'll keep watch. You guys get some sleep." Jaras sat down on the log, his back toward everyone. "I won't be able to sleep anyway."

Aria started to join him, but Onyx put a hand on her shoulder. "Give him some space, try and rest."

Aria hesitated for a moment before she nodded.

Onyx stayed with her. "How are you doing, Aria?" His eyes were full of worry. "He messed with your mind more than the others, and he, he really did a number on you."

Aria was still shaking. "I don't know how I am. I've never let a man dictate how I treat the people I care about, how I make my decisions, and if he hadn't meddled with my mind… I really hurt her."

"You know that wasn't you."

Aria nodded. "I know, but I don't know. Like, I know I said the words and felt those feelings, but there was a part of me that was screaming at me to not act like I did, but I couldn't stop it. Me being attracted to him,

215

wanting to sleep with him, that was all me, I can't deny that. But me fawning all over him, telling him who trained Barina, not even taking into question why Barina would've attacked him if she had, when I know damn well that isn't how she is, that no. All of that felt like I was, I felt like I had been drunk almost."

Onyx looked thoughtful. "I just wish I had realized what was happening. He hid what he was, that he was a Bask wizard, so well."

Aria cut him off, placing both hands on his arms. "He is to blame for his actions, and he outsmarted all of us. This isn't on just one person."

"I know." He sighed, giving her a little smile. "Are you going to be okay? I can stay by your tent till you fall asleep if it'll help."

Aria smiled. It was always his heart that seemed to Aria to be the wizard's true strength behind his powers. "I don't know if I'll be able to sleep, but I'll manage. Thank you, Onyx." She headed to her tent to try and rest. She sat with her thoughts, hoping that someday, her thief would forgive her.

The wizard sat next to Jaras, both in silence, before Onyx finally spoke up.

"I should've sensed him fooling around with their minds. It was so subtle though." Onyx sighed, he was poking the ground with this staff.

"I should've trusted their instincts, but I didn't watch him enough," Jaras added, speaking of Barina and Jason. He looked at Onyx. "I can't believe he was really messing around in their heads. It explains a lot though."

Onyx nodded. "I never would've thought that Aria would've turned on B, and even Arkon. With as much as he might have been upset about her turning him down, he respected her. Twarence and her are good friends too, so I should've dug deeper and used my magic to feel for energies when they started to question her. It's the only way those three would've gone against her. I should've checked."

"You did realize that he was lying about something. How could we have known he was messing with their minds, lightly compelling them?"

Onyx shrugged. "He got the better of us. We can't pretend that it didn't happen. It makes me worry if we're going to be in over our heads when we get to Thoron."

"Maybe, but I think we also have the best chance of anyone. We won't be caught off guard when and if we have to deal with Toler." Jaras lit up a smoke. "We just need to be more alert, cause Twarence is right. If Toler doesn't hear from Ken, he'll be having people searching."

Onyx nodded with a yawn.

"Go get some sleep. I've got this tonight." Jaras gave him a little smile.

Onyx stood up. "Do you think we'll see her again?"

Jaras met the stare of his friend. "I have no idea. If we do, it won't be until she's ready."

The group only rested for a short while before the sun came up. They packed their things up, and quietly continued on their way to Estella.

* * *

Barina, after she left with Lucy, traveled all night and most of the next day—only stopping so that Lucy could rest. She sat trying to meditate, to clear her mind, and she couldn't. She couldn't sleep, she couldn't focus on anything. Both of her old injuries opened back up and, as much as she bandaged them, she knew that they would just bleed till they stopped on their own. She had now realized, since the adrenaline had worn off, that she had hurt her ribs badly during her fight with Ken. It was hurting to breathe.

Once Lucy was rested, they kept on their way, traveling all night and into the morning till they came out of the forest.

Barina was tired but she still couldn't sleep, and her injuries still hadn't stopped bleeding. They had never stayed open this long before. Her bandages had all bled through, and blood was now dripping from her shoulder, down her arm, and soaking her shirt around the hip. She could tell the blood loss was messing with her ability to stay alert and awake. She felt her eyes drooping and her body growing weak. Even after eating, she felt as if her body was hardly able to move. Holding onto the reins was almost impossible. She could see the houses that lined the outskirts of Estella in her vision, but she was still more than an hour's ride to town. Josh's house, she had to get to Josh.

"Come on girl, just a little further." She wasn't sure if she was saying that to herself or Lucy. She leaned forward, resting herself against the horse. Her body began to slide off, too damn weak to keep herself from landing on the ground. She felt two arms catch her before she fell face first, and the only thing she could see before she passed out was the shadow of a man.

CHAPTER 11

"**D**o you think she'll wake up soon?"

"Don't know Mason. It's best if we let her rest. Is Greg coming by later?"

"As soon as he closes up the shop. We had some clients coming by, and he stayed so I could be here. Josh, can I borrow your kettle? I want to put some water on to boil and make him a cup of tea."

"Go ahead. He's been in there with her all day. He could probably use it."

Barina could hear the familiar voices of Josh and Mason speaking quietly from the other room. She opened her eyes slowly and saw that she was in Josh's guest bedroom, a place she had slept a few times before. She wondered who they were talking about.

Everything hurt. She was so tired and weak that she could easily fall back to sleep, perhaps for a month before she felt ready to get out of bed. She sat up, feeling the full pain of her old injuries that were now bandaged and had finally stopped bleeding. Her bruised ribs also had a wrap on them.

There was a strong and gentle hand on her shoulder as the owner sat on the bed next to her. "Not too fast, you'll make yourself dizzy."

Barina turned, almost unable to believe who was there with her.

He was tall, and one of the most impressive and intimidating men she had ever known, yet she knew how kind he truly was. His physique was pure muscle, bulging under his black skin. His forehead wrinkled in worry while his dark eyes looked into her own with kindness, worry, and love. He wore a pair of black pants and a black shirt. Resting on the back of a chair was his trademark cloak that was black with the inside lining of a blue so bright it hurt to look at. She hadn't been expecting to see him.

"You're still really weak. Sit up slowly." His fingers pushed some of her hair back before he kissed her forehead.

Barina's eyes met his, and she started to cry. He wrapped his strong arms around her gently and simply held her.

"Berklion," she whimpered quietly into his chest.

Berklion of Halk—the greatest warrior alive—sat holding his student, his adopted daughter whom he took in and cared for after she lost her parents. She was overcome with relief and comfort.

"It's okay, I've got you." His voice was soothing.

Berklion knew just how tough and resilient Barina was, so if she was breaking down like this, something was very wrong. He loved this girl as if she were his own. Over the years, he had held her through her tears, sat with her at night if she had nightmares, and had stayed with her when she had injuries or illness. She had done the same for him. Except for when she had lost her family and when she lost Matrikal, she had never broken down like this. He held her, smoothing her hair a bit before rubbing her back. She was tougher than anyone he knew, but sometimes, she just needed to cry.

"Were you the one who brought me here?" She looked up at him.

He nodded, wiping away her tears with his fingers. "I did. I saw you on Lucy, and you were swaying. Called to you a few times but, when you didn't respond, I knew something was going on, so I rushed to you. Caught you right as you fell." He pulled her close again. "You gave me a scare."

They heard footsteps coming into the room.

"Berklion, I'm making tea. Would you like…hey, Barina, you're awake!" Mason rushed toward her.

Mason, much like Josh and Jason, had known her most of her life. He was one of her closest friends, and she adored him. He was taller than her which, she reminded herself, wasn't a hard thing for someone to be. He had a beard and a balding head, and she always thought he looked very handsome. Over his glasses, his blue eyes looked at her with both concern and joy.

He felt her forehead. "You're a little warm. I'm sure it's nothing serious, but I'll get you some tea, anyway. You like a little honey in it, right? Be right back." He rushed out of the room.

"How long have I been out?" she asked, inhaling Berklion's scent which made her feel incredibly safe.

"The whole day. It wasn't even daybreak when I saw you, and it's early afternoon now. You lost so much blood, so you're still really pale." Berklion's words were quiet and kind. "We'll have to get some food in you here soon. Need your strength back."

Another voice spoke up. "I have tamago and gohan that I'm making to tie you over."

Barina looked up and saw Josh standing in the doorway. He was looking at her with a kind smile and warm eyes, just as he always had done. Josh had questions, she could see, but his relief at seeing her awake put those questions on the back burner. He stood, leaning against the door frame, wearing a red shirt slightly unbuttoned and a pair of black pants. He had dark brown hair, brown eyes, and a particular smile that he reserved for her. Barina was so happy to see him.

All three of these men, for a moment, made her heart forget it was broken.

Josh walked over and sat on the bed, embracing his friend, kissing her on the top of her head. She could feel him breathing in relief as he held her. "Barina, you had me worried. You're not supposed to do that." He smiled a little bit.

She looked down. "Gomen, I didn't mean to worry you."

"Baka, I'm always worried about you."

Barina smiled up at him, touching the hair on his chin, and turned her nose up a bit. "This has gotten long."

He gave her a proud smile. "It's fabulous, isn't it?"

"Just because you can grow facial hair, doesn't mean you should, or that you do it well." She couldn't help but give him a hard time about it.

"I don't complain about your facial hair." He couldn't help but make the joke.

Barina sneered a little. "I will stab you in your sleep."

Berklion rolled his eyes. "I love seeing my kids getting along so well."

"We better not let the old man hear us fight." Josh had that side-eyed grin on his face.

Berklion scrunched his face a bit before replying, "Older than you, yes. Able to still kick your ass, no question."

Barina liked this, the banter and the love that was in this room. It was like she could breathe a little bit, but she knew that this moment was fleeting. She was going to have to tell them what happened, and when she did, it would shake them to their cores.

Mason walked back into the room with four cups of hot tea. He handed one to Berklion and Josh before giving one to Barina. He sat down with his own.

Josh didn't even beat around the bush. "What happened? Your injuries have never bled like that, and you have Lucy."

Barina was holding her cup, looking into the tea, not responding.

"Barina?" Berklion held his breath. His heart stopped and his stomach sank.

Her tears started to fall again. "I don't even know how to start." Her hands were shaking, and her whole body was starting to tremble. "I couldn't…"

Mason sat on the bed as well, taking her cup from her hand and placing it on the table next to the bed.

It was then that Josh noticed the second pendant she was wearing and the ring on the chain. He reached for that pendant.

"Oh stars." He whispered, tears forming in his eyes, and his face went pale. "Jason and Tyra…are they?"

Barina broke down when she nodded. "They're gone. They're both gone, and there weren't even bodies left for me to bury."

Mason put his hands over his mouth, unable to move for the moment. His face reddened, and he didn't hide his tears. "No!" He could hardly say the word.

When that message reached Berklion's mind—that one of his students, a man he saw as at least a nephew if not a son, was gone—he lowered his head, placing his face in his hands. His body began to shake.

Josh pulled Barina close, both of them crying. Their third, their comrade and best friend, he was gone. The three of them had bonded since the first day they had met. Barina met Josh first and then, a couple years later, met Jason, and he joined their little group. They were a team, three hearts that fought as one. Now, that heart was broken.

The four of them let the tears fall and their cries be heard. There was no hiding from this pain.

Barina told them what happened, all the details, and they couldn't believe it. "They died heroes. They gave their lives to help us defeat Ken so that we could keep going, so that we could help liberate an entire kingdom.

They were heroes, they told me to do it." Barina managed to get the words out, but after that, she was crying too much to be able to say anything else.

Josh pressed his forehead to hers and held it there. He was sniffing and struggling to speak. "They did what either of us would have done, B. It doesn't make it any easier that they're gone, but they kept the vow that we have sworn to uphold."

She felt Berklion's hand on her shoulder, and he pulled her back into his hold. "Barina, it wasn't in vain. They did what was in their heart, and a lot of people, an entire kingdom, will now have a chance at a better life because of them." He touched a finger to her chin. "He knew, they both knew, and we know, that the best chance that this kingdom has, hell, that anyone has, is making sure that Toler doesn't get ahold of the kind of power this group is trying to keep him from having."

"Honey." Mason took a deep breath. "I don't think that there's anything you could've done differently. You are so incredibly talented at what you do, and I don't think anything else could've been done differently, not with hostages." Mason wasn't a trained fighter at all. His method of fighting was offering a good, as he would say, *bitch slap*. But, from listening to them over the years, he had learned enough of what kind of situations demanded what. Mason was one of the few people who they willingly discussed their fighting around.

Barina nodded. "I keep running everything through my mind, over and over, and there really wasn't anything else I could've done. I mean, if only one group had been there instead of two, then obviously the only one who I would've killed was Ken. I wouldn't have had to make the choice, but there wasn't anything else that could've been done." She sat back in the bed, pulling her knees up to her chest and huffed out a breath. "I just, I wish there could've been. There weren't even bodies for me to bury. I'm sorry, you guys."

Mason patted her leg. "Stop apologizing. We're all heartbroken, yes, but you have a decision to make now."

She let her eyes ask the question.

"Do you keep going and finish this job, or are you going to be done with it?" Mason's question was simple.

"I'm going to finish. I made a promise, and I still care dearly for that group. Plus, I won't let Jason and Tyra's sacrifice be for nothing. I'll face Toler, and that kingdom will be free." She placed a hand on her shoulder that stung, the wound open again. "I have to keep my end."

Josh went to grab some bandages. "Check her hip to see if it's bleeding, too."

Berklion checked. "It's just her shoulder bleeding now," he called after him.

Mason sat on the bed next to Barina and took her hand in his. It was a simple gesture. He just wanted to be with her and give her some of his strength for a bit. He was falling apart, but he needed to help hold her up. Barina was grateful.

"You have a plan for once?" Berklion asked quietly while he sipped his tea. "I'm intrigued." He handed Barina her drink back.

"I was gonna have Jason find me a house or an apartment when he got here, to have it ready when I was done with this job. I should have enough to open up my own shop, and I want to do it here. I mean, it would only start as a small operation, but it'd be enough to get me going."

"You'd leave Miork?" Mason's smile had grown at the idea of her moving here.

"I'll keep the cave, but it'll be more of a safehouse or place to stay when I visit my aunt and uncle. I want to be close to all of you." She leaned her head on Mason's shoulder.

Josh stood in the doorway for a minute, grinning. "You're moving here? Really, moving here?"

"Yup. I mean, I might still have to leave to take care of things from time to time, but this will be home. I might try and look for a place to rent before I set off for Thoron."

Mason smiled. "I have an apartment above my shop that you can rent out. Greg and I live in the other one above it. The one available isn't anything fancy, only one room, but it's a good start for you, and it's a decent space. I'd rent it to you cheap, too, if you want it. We can go take a look at it when you've rested more."

"I'll check it out. That might work." She smiled, her eyes closing.

Josh sat back down. "There's some land just down the way from me. If you had enough to build a house, you could do it there, but it's also good for a forge maybe."

Barina raised her eyebrows. "Maybe. I'll look at both options. If I can't afford to build a house yet, I could use it to build the forge and stay in the apartment till I could afford the house. But I am keeping the cave back in Miork. That stays."

"I only ever went to Miork to visit you, but I still might utilize that cave every so often." Berklion was happy for her. He knew she needed a more stable home. "You're one of the best at what you do. You've been able to help so many, but I think it'll be good for you to be in Estella with everyone else."

Josh pulled Barina's shirt down from her shoulder a bit while he put on a fresh bandage. "I'll start looking for some furniture while you're gone. Don't worry, I'll take care of Jason and Tyra's stuff, and Lucy. How long till you get back?"

"One month to get there, then another to travel back, providing everything goes well. So, I should be back by late fall or early winter." She wrapped her arm around Mason's. The idea of being back, and this, being with these men every day, was a welcomed thought. "I'm so glad the weather has finally cooled off. This is my favorite season."

"You like all of the seasons." Berklion poked her nose.

"I appreciate them for what they are, yes, but this is my favorite," she corrected him.

"Couple months to get things together. You should pick up some clothes while you're here. That way you have some ready for when you get back." Mason patted her hand. "You can leave them with me, and I'll keep them till you come home."

"That would be nice." She nodded, but then something occurred to her. "I just realized, I'm not wearing one of my shirts. Who changed me?" She was glaring at Josh.

Mason looked at her as if she were crazy. "As if we were going to let this pervert change your clothes," Mason said pointing to Josh. "I got you cleaned up and dressed. There was so much blood."

Berklion gave a loud laugh, and Barina joined him. Josh had a defiant pout, while Mason had a satisfied grin.

"Gross," he grumbled. "Like I'm gonna get all pervy on someone who is practically my sister." He then waggled his eyebrows. "Still…"

Barina didn't hesitate to reach out and punch his arm. While Josh would never make advances at a woman who didn't want it, and stood up for women when they needed it, he was not above enjoying the view of a beautiful woman or a stranger visiting businesses that employed risqué female workers.

"You hit way harder than you realize." Josh winced and held his arm, but he still smiled. "Damn. You've gotten stronger since I saw you a couple months ago."

Berklion laughed some more. "Good to know that you can tell her strength based on how hard she hits you."

"It's always been a sure way to know." Josh stood up. "I was going to wash everything for you, but aside from your cloak, everything is pretty much ruined. I do have a couple of things of yours. Hang on, I'll get them." He headed out of the room.

"Thanks, Josh." Barina swung her legs over the edge of the bed. Mason was propping her up with a hand, and Berklion was ready to catch her if she started to fall. Barina, slowly, stood up. She was wearing a black shirt that was four times too big, and it hung almost to her knees. "Is this one of yours, Berk?" She turned her gaze at her teacher.

He nodded. "Josh's were too short to cover your butt."

"Fair enough." She started to stretch her legs some. "So sore, but I'm okay. I need to eat something."

Josh walked back in with a white blouse and a long brown skirt in one hand and, in the other, long blue-pleated pants and a long deep-mauve piece of clothing. "I have a set of your Western clothes or your hakama and gi."

"Hakama and gi, I'll save the others for when I go out tomorrow."

"Well, I'm heating up the ofuro for you. I'll set these in the bathing room. I want you to eat and then, after your bath, we can get your injuries tended to again." Josh was very matter-of-fact, and headed back out of the room. He took her gi and hakama to the bathing room.

"Can you walk?" Berklion had an arm around her.

She nodded. "Just a little wobbly, that's all. Thank you."

Mason was close to her. "Maybe we should bring the food to you here so you can rest."

She shook her head. "I need to walk."

"Can you get her?" Berklion asked. "I'm gonna check on the food." He handed Barina off to Mason.

"Go on." Mason put a gentle arm around her. "Oh, by the way, make sure you have Josh tell you his big news." He knew that this would help distract her, if even for a moment.

Barina looked at him curiously. "What are you talking about?" She knew that Mason had some juicy gossip that she would completely appreciate.

Mason laughed with a snort. "Lemme tell you…"

* * *

Josh was with Berklion at the stove—both checking over the food when they heard Barina yell. "Are you fucking serious?" She stumbled to the doorway, her face in shock. Barina was holding onto both the doorframe and Mason. Her lip quivered before she started laughing.

Josh looked from her to Mason and rolled his eyes.

"Shit, he told you." Josh could only think of one thing that would get the look of complete and utter surprise from Barina. He sat down at the table with Berklion.

Berklion tilted his head, questioning.

"Is Mason serious?" she blurted out. "Are you really, really? His *cousin*?"

Josh nodded his head. "Yeah." He had turned bright red in the face and lowered his head, a little embarrassed.

"The absolute fuck?" She raised her hands in the air and started laughing.

Berklion raised a finger. "Somebody wanna clue me in?"

Mason helped her walk and then sit at the table. He took a seat too, obviously enjoying being a spectator for this conversation.

"Well, ummm…" Josh cleared his throat. "Ellie, Jason's cousin, was in town about a year ago when he and Tyra were here. She stuck around for a while after Jason and Tyra left. Well, we hit it off. It wasn't anything serious, just some fun, and then she left town. That fun, uhh, well, it had a serious side-effect that I found out about a couple months ago when she came back to visit." He was shifting in his seat, very uncomfortable, and his face was redder than before.

There was a five-second pause before it dawned on Berklion.

Barina started laughing when she saw his realization. She could hardly breathe. "My ribs can't handle this," she complained, but kept laughing.

"Holy shit!" Berklion laughed so hard he started to tear up.

"You have a kid!" Barina yelled. She couldn't believe what she was hearing.

Josh couldn't make eye-contact, but nodded—his face as red as his shirt.

"Way to keep it in your pants." Berklion was still laughing, "This is almost too much."

Though Mason was still getting a kick out of everyone's surprise, Barina finally managed to stop laughing enough to ask questions. "So is it a boy or a girl? Name?"

"His name is Derick, and Ellie's gonna be moving out this way in the next year so we can give it a shot together." Josh grumbled, "I was not planning for any of this."

Berklion was musing what this meant for him. "Does that make me, like, an uncle? I'm not a grandparent, am I?"

"I was gonna say great-great-great-great…" Josh made it to the fourth great before Berklion lunged and put him in a headlock. He struggled to choke out, "…grandpa." Berklion let him go, and Josh fell to the floor smiling. "Worth it," he insisted.

"I think we'll go with *Uncle Berklion*." His teacher sat back down and crossed his arms. "You're a freaking turd."

"I love you, too, Berk." Josh couldn't stop laughing. He stood back up and sat in the chair. He turned to Barina. "How long did you want to camp out here before you join up with the traveling group?"

She shook her head. "I'm not rejoining them. I'm going to follow them to make sure they make it okay, but I'm not going to be with them. I can't yet." She then added, "Oh and probably a couple days. Rest, regroup, get some supplies."

"Wait, you're not going to join them?" Mason seemed surprised.

"Hell no. I love all of them, but I am not ready to be near them, not after what happened."

That threw the men off guard.

Josh was even taken aback. "But you know that they were having their minds rattled."

"Doesn't change the fact that I need some time. Plus, if Toler knows that I was with the group, him not realizing I'm there can work to their advantage. And mine. The element of surprise." She sighed and stretched her arms. When her stomach growled, she asked, "Did you say you had some tamago and gohan?" She obviously didn't feel like talking about her plans.

Josh got up and put together a bowl of the white grain and eggs in it for her.

"I'm so glad I learned some of what you two say when you go back and forth speaking Nihongo." Mason shook his head.

"Itadakimasu." Barina was almost drooling as the bowl was set in front of her. She grabbed a set of chopsticks and didn't hesitate to start shoveling food into her mouth.

Berklion poured her some more tea. "Slow down or you'll make yourself sick."

She ignored him and kept eating with vigor. Barina hadn't realized just how hungry she was until now. It was a simple meal—just something to tie her over for a while. But it was high in fiber and carbs with lots of protein, and this had always been a quick fix for food when she had been training in Nippon.

"I made your favorite." Josh had his hands behind his back.

Barina's eyes grew to the size of plates in anticipation. "Daifuku?" she asked, inhaling from excitement.

Josh held out some cheesecloth with several round white and powder-covered buns that were filled with either a red bean paste or dried berries. "How much gohan did you bring back with you last time you went to Nippon?" She popped one in her mouth, her expression a look of bliss.

"Enough to last for a year. These are still a little warm, so eat up." He set the cloth down on the table.

Barina had a sweet tooth, and these were her absolute favorite dessert. She didn't object to shoving two more in her mouth. "You guys have some, too," she said through a mouth-full of food.

"You've earned all of those," Mason said, even though he took one to eat. "Damn, I love these." He was glaring at Josh. "I've lived in the same town as you for years, and I had no idea you could make these. What the hell?"

Josh turned red. "It's a lot of work to make them, so I wait for a special occasion." He touched a hand to Barina's shoulder. "I'm gonna check the temperature of the water. You need to soak."

Barina finished eating her food and stood up, Berklion and Mason close by.

"I'm okay." She was still holding her smile.

"I'm going to make sure you get in and out of the tub without falling," Mason said, opening the door to the bathing room. "You need to be glad that I have no interest in women at all so that it's not weird for me to see you naked."

Berklion rolled his eyes some. "She's not shy around anyone. It's not weird for anyone who doesn't make it weird."

Mason thought about it. "Truth."

Barina simply raised her eyebrows a bit. "Modesty is for chumps," she said and kept on her way to the bathing room.

Berklion and Mason were laughing as Mason closed the door after her.

Barina undressed and grabbed a bucket of hot water, a washcloth, and the soap, and disrobed.

"I've always liked the style of bathing in Nippon. Greg and I try to practice it at home, too." Mason inhaled through his teeth. "I saw how bad your injuries were when I cleaned you up earlier, but damn, you, how are you able to even stand up right now?"

Her bruised ribs were a nasty shade of purple and red from under her left breast stretching around to her back and under her arm. Her right shoulder blade, just below her old injury, was purple. Mason did a good job of cleaning her up. Barina had taken more than her fair share of bruises over the years, so she was used to them. Mostly. In the heat of battle, she would barely notice something like this. Even after the battle, she could ignore the pain decently. But these, they stung.

"I'm not going to lie," she said. "Normally I can ignore the pain pretty well, you know, work past it, but these are hurting."

Barina scrubbed herself clean, washing her hair with the white tea hair tonic she used. When she finished, she opened the small door that led to the deep, square, wooden tub. The water had steam coming up from it, and she heard a knock from the exterior wall. She could hear Josh's voice.

"How's the water? Is it warm enough, or too hot?"

"It's perfect, thanks!" she called back.

"Barina, are you okay in here?" Mason asked her. "I'm gonna grab us some drinks. I need to keep you hydrated."

"I'm okay, thank you."

Mason closed the door and walked into the kitchen where Berklion was now working on preparing dinner, and Josh was getting together an assortment of wraps, salts, and a salve.

"Did you want to stay for dinner?" Berklion asked. "You said Greg was coming by after work." He deftly sliced some veggies.

"Probably. What's on the menu?"

"I'm making a fish soup and warming some bread." Berklion put the rest of the veggies into the pot and closed the lid. "Should be ready in about an hour. I really want the flavors to mix."

Josh came into the room. "Can you help her get these wraps on when she gets out of the bath? She knows the drill. Hell, I think you know the drill by now. We need to make sure that her ribs heal decently." He placed the salve and bandages on a table in the bathing room.

"I'll take care of her. You go relax some. You've been fussing over her so much, and you need to fuss over yourself." Mason gave Josh a light pat on his shoulder. "I know you're trying to stay busy so you don't have to think about, well, what we're all trying not to think about, but give yourself a minute."

Josh gave Mason a warm hug. "You always know what to say."

"Hmm, yes, I do, don't I?" Mason had to joke.

Josh felt a tear fall down his face again and left for his own room, closing the door. Sitting on the edge of his bed, he hung his head while watching his pendant as it dangled from his neck. Josh let the tears fall. Jason was one of his best friends. He had been like his brother. Josh was sad but also proud of Jason and Tyra for what they had done and how they went out. It didn't seem real, and it wouldn't for a long time. He had brought back most of their things with him the last time he had visited everyone in Miork. Their house was bought and mostly furnished. He'd have to figure out what to do with the house. He doubted if Barina would want to live there. She'd be in the apartment. Plus, knowing that this was supposed to be Jason and Tyra's home, it would be a hard pill for her to swallow. For now, he'd hang onto it and wait till Barina got back to figure out what to do.

Barina sat in the soaking tub. The water felt so good on her bruised and tired body. She sat back and breathed in the steam from the bath. The lavender oils in the water smelled lovely, and the salts that were mixed in were already working their magic on her. If she wanted to, she could reach out her senses to feel what was happening around her as far as the edge of town. She could, if she wanted, hear everything going on in the house. She decided, for her own sanity, to tune out her senses though. Instead, she cast her gaze to the high window and into the trees.

She listened to the leaves as the wind moved them and smelled the fresh autumn air that blew into the opened window. The cold air felt good on her face while the rest of her body was submerged in the hot water. She could feel the tension leave her shoulders, legs, arms, all of her, and she smiled to herself. This felt nice. She felt relaxed.

Barina soaked in the water until her fingers started to wrinkle, and then she climbed out of the tub. She felt so much better, even after just that soak and the little bit of food she had eaten. After wrapping the towel around her hips and covering her chest with an arm, she stepped back into the room where Mason waited.

"Feeling better? Here's some water. Drink all that." He fussed about with the wraps after handing her the glass.

Barina started sipping while Mason worked in silence. Very gently, he put a comfrey salve on her bruises.

"That salve feels nice." Barina was breathing in the scent while she felt Mason's delicate fingers run over her skin. It was comforting.

Mason nodded. "Are you able to breathe okay?"

"It's hard, but I'll be okay. I think a couple days rest, and I'll be able to fight just fine. Besides, I don't have a lot of time before the others get to town."

"Yes, you do." Mason was wrapping one of her arms. "Don't you have that method the giants let you use?"

"I do, yes." She looked down. "But, I need to make sure that they can get there safely. I want to be close to them, so I will follow."

"I get that you're still upset and hurt. What I don't get is how you're still in this group but not going to be with the group. It's not like you to not be able to move past something."

"I know. I'll get past it eventually, but for right now, I can't. I mean, Jason and Tyra are gone because of Ken. I know he was meddling with their minds, but it's still hard to let go, at least for now. I think it doesn't help that they became my friends, that I trusted them. And I came to love them. I know that the words weren't all their's, but the words still came from them. I'll be okay, but I just need some time." She had another thought that she shared. "Plus, with them not knowing I'm there, it's safer. I can stay a secret if Toler does manage to get them and tries to look into their minds."

"That's fair. Here." Mason stood up and held her gi open for her.

She slipped her arms into it and tied the himo to close the gi which hung to her upper thighs. Mason handed her the hakama. She wrapped the himo around in the familiar patterns till she was completely dressed unwound the towel from her hair and combed it, running her fingers through it after. "I feel so much better."

"I always loved this look on you," Mason said. "Especially when you'd wear your sword with it."

She gave a little bow of her head. "Arigato." She looked over. "Do I have any socks that haven't been ruined?"

"Yeah, here. Don't want your feet to freeze."

Barina sat down and put on the socks. Her stomach started to growl again.

"Drink the rest of your water. Berk is finishing dinner and…" Mason and Barina both heard someone else in the main room of the house. "Greg is here."

The two walked into the main room and smiled seeing the newcomer.

Greg was about the same age as Mason, a little more-heavy set, with dark hair, a beard, and brown eyes. He was the creative side to this couple. Mason was the more logical one. They were perfect for each other, and Barina was so happy to see Mason with someone who made him happy as well. Greg's eyes lit up when he saw her, and he rushed over to give her a large hug.

"Hey there!" he said with a touch of sympathy in his voice.

"Hi Greg, it's so good to see you."

"You too. Oh, this hug feels so good. You've always given good ones."

Barina felt another wave of that sense of home and love that she always did when she was with the people she cared for the most. It showed her that this was where she needed to be after she finished this job.

"Berklion," Greg said, all smiles. "Whatever you're making for dinner it smells amazing."

"Thank you. Josh, will you take over with cooking? I need to help Barina stretch."

Josh stepped to the stove while Mason took Greg to the porch, most likely to tell him what happened to Jason and Tyra. Berklion took Barina to the backyard so he could help her with some light stretching.

When everyone had returned, Josh filled several bowls and put bread on the plates. He had made an apple pie the day before so they'd have something good for dessert.

Barina, she ate two bowls of soup, three pieces of bread, and two pieces of pie. She sat back with a smile. "I needed that."

"I can't believe how much you were able to put away." Greg was laughing. "I'm making something tasty for when you come to check out the apartment tomorrow."

"I'm already curious."

Josh couldn't contain the smile that was cracking over his face. "So you're really going to move here, like for real?"

She nodded.

"From what Mason's told me, you haven't really stayed put for more than a few weeks since you got back from Nippon. You have the cave, but you're always on the go." Greg headed to the living room with the others.

Josh poured each of them a glass of wine.

"I've been busy. I work a lot, but I'm ready to start the family business back up. I think I'll finally be able to afford it."

"Was she really as good as her dad at swordsmithing?" Greg then asked the others. "I mean, I've seen Josh's sword that she made, and the one her father made for Berklion. They're amazing. I don't know the difference when it comes to them, I do know that they're both beautiful."

"I think hers were better than her dad's." Josh's tone was matter-of-fact as he stood up. "Actually, hang on, I still have some of your dad's weapons. Not all of them were finished, but I grabbed them after everything happened, before we left for Nippon the next morning."

234

Barina's eyes almost jumped out of their sockets. "And you're just now telling me this?"

From the other room, Josh yelled, "I wanted to hear you talking about settling down before I told you."

Taken off guard, Barina looked at the others. "Did any of you know that he had some of dad's old swords?"

They shook their heads.

"He's never said anything to me, to anyone." Berklion looked as shocked as she was.

After a couple minutes, Josh came back with a large bag. He set it on the floor in front of them and took out half a dozen swords and a couple of daggers. They were all exquisite, absolute perfection.

There was one sword in particular that caught Barina's eye. The blade below the hilt was just over three feet long, just a little smaller than the average sword. It had been a simple blade with a simple polished sheath, and the hilt just as simple with nothing more than a deep purple amethyst embedded in the end.

"I remember drooling over this one when he was making it," Barina said. "I think it was the last one he created, and it was his best work, too." Barina felt that all-familiar pain in her chest while looking at these weapons. "It wasn't an elaborate design like most of the weapons we made, but it was the simplicity that made this one special."

Berklion put a hand on her shoulder. "I can't tell you how happy I am to see that you've had this sword after all these years." He pointed to it. "Adrian made this one for you, Barina. He finished it just a couple days before he passed and had planned on giving it to you when you finished your training. I thought it had been stolen, but apparently Josh did a really good job of keeping this safe. The amethyst is for your birthstone, the simplicity is because that's always been your style. I would say that you have been more than ready to carry this sword with you."

Barina's jaw dropped and she froze for a moment. "This was for me? What?" She started laughing a little. "He hated that I was learning to fight."

"He did, but I was there the morning he started working on the design for this one, and he said, and I quote, 'If she's going to learn, I want her to learn from the best, and if she's going to fight, she's going to have the best weapon I'll ever create.' I can't believe it after all this time." Berklion was patting Josh on the back.

"You did good," Greg whispered to Josh. He was in awe.

They were watching as Barina unsheathed the sword and got the feel for it in her hand. It felt like an extension of her arm. It was perfect.

"Thanks dad." She placed it back in the sheath. "Hey there, Kitty."

"You're naming the sword Kitty?" Mason laughed hearing that.

Barina looked at him like he should've guessed. "Yeah. See." She reached into her pack and pulled out her stuffed cat. "Dad gave me this the day I was born, and apparently 'kitty' was my first word. It's appropriate."

"You gonna take Kitty with you?" Mason asked while enjoying his wine.

"Fuck yeah. I'm still gonna carry Yukinohana with me, too, but it'll be good to have this."

"What does your other sword look like?" Greg asked. He held out his hand so he could look at the one she was holding.

Barina went to her bag and brought out the katana, unsheathing it to show him.

Greg stood up and held either sword. "I mean, and all three of you are able to use these things? They're so beautiful that it's hard to believe that they're ultimately made to…" he couldn't finish the sentence.

"There's nothing pretty about what they're made for," Berklion told him, "but, the three of us went into this knowing just how ugly things can get. We hate that there are times that we have to use them to end a life. If we can avoid it, we do at all costs. However, there are those who are so evil that they can't be allowed to continue their ways.

"We are slaves to our blades and servants to the people." It was obvious that the words Berklion uttered the three warriors had uttered.

"Berklion, where, I mean, I know you're not from this part of the world, but how did you get to Nippon and then to here?" Greg finally asked him. "My parents were merchants, and that's how I ended up in this part of the world."

Barina and Josh sat next to each other. They had heard this story quite a few times, but it was still fascinating. Mason had heard this story, too, but only a couple of times. Greg listened with a curious ear.

"I was taken from my home as a slave when I was young, six years old. The slavers took all of us from my tribe. They killed the old and any child who wasn't old enough to walk. Those who fought back were killed, including my father and my brothers. My mother and I were placed on the boats as we watched our village burn behind us. My mother died in transport. I'm not sure how I survived, if I'm being honest. We were packed so tight that I could hardly breathe, and the stench—people dying or already dead, blood and bile—was terrible.

"Once I was taken north, I was sold. I had no idea what the language was, no idea where I was, and I was too scared and tired to cry. One day, I was in the market with the master of the house and caught a glimpse of a man who sure as hell wasn't from this part of the world either. He saw me and waited till the master and his men were away from me. I couldn't believe he spoke my language. He asked if I was a slave. I told him I was. He then asked if I wanted to be free, to come live in the place he was from with him, his wife, and children. I didn't even have to think about it. Before the master of the house could even know what happened, he took me. Master Yuhii, he adopted me and took me to Nippon to live. He hated slavery and injustice.

"On the way there, he taught me his language and would teach me many others as well. Master Yuhii, he knew that I had a lot of pain, a lot of hate toward the men who killed my family. He taught me to work through that pain and anger, he taught me how to be able to use that energy to help others from going through what I did. The men who killed my family and destroyed my village, they died not long after. But Yuhii saved me, and because of him, I've been able to help a lot of other people." Berklion was thinking very fondly of his teacher. They could see his eyes looking off into the distance as he thought about the land he called home after he had lost his own.

Greg sipped his drink after Berklion finished. "Mason had told me a little bit but, I mean, it's amazing, and so very sad to think about what you went through. What I think gets me, though, is that you used that pain and anger to do a whole lot of good."

"That's ultimately the goal." Berklion was smiling.

"Is that why you and Barina and Jason started to fight?" Greg directed his attention to Josh.

"Barina always wanted to be able to protect the people she loved. Jason and I, neither one of us had thought about it. It was Barina who made us consider picking up a blade. I met her first. When she told me why she wanted to learn how to fight, that she wanted to protect others and be their greatest line of defense, it made me wonder if I could do the same. Jason felt the same way after he met her."

"Then how the hell did you get into this, Barina?" Greg was laughing as he finished his drink. "I mean, seriously."

She shrugged her shoulders and took a sip of her drink, all while giving him a little smirk. "My dad made weapons. I met a lot of warriors. My dad, he would only make a weapon for a person if they were fighting to help others and to protect. I always thought it was amazing that these people were willing to risk themselves to help those who couldn't do it for themselves, and I realized that I wanted to be able to do the same. The rest is history."

Greg leaned against Mason who put his arm around him. "Neat."

The group spent the rest of the evening enjoying the night and relaxing. After it started to get dark, Mason and Greg headed home. Berklion, Barina, and Josh stayed on the porch and enjoyed the cool air as the stars started to make their way into the darkening sky.

It was then that the weight of the loss was coming back to them.

"Looks like it's gonna rain. Nice we can still see the stars though," Josh sighed.

"He was excited, you know," Barina said while she puffed on her pipe and sipped her whiskey. "He was excited to be moving to Estella and about me moving here, too."

"It had been so long since the three of us had lived near each other," Josh said. "It's all I could think about after you told me earlier you were moving here." He looked down. "I thought about how great it would've been. It won't happen now, but it would've been great." His smile was bittersweet.

"I wonder if maybe I didn't teach him enough." Berklion had his eyes drawn to the night sky. "I tried to teach the best I could so that this wouldn't happen to you." He had tears falling from his eyes. "I hope he can forgive me."

Barina put a hand on her teacher's arm. "Berklion, you didn't see how amazing he was. You guys don't know just how hard he fought, and then how difficult our choices were. He did what I would've done if the roles were reversed, what any of us would have done. Tyra did the same. Tyra learned to fight some from Jason, and she didn't go down without a fight either. When it came to it, they were both willing to make that sacrifice with smiles on their faces."

"You have been an amazing teacher, friend, and mentor, Berk," Josh said. "When you wanted us to have every chance to be the best, you took us to learn, not just from you, but from your own teacher. You have loved us, cared for us, and taught us more than we could've ever asked for." He put his hand on Berklion's shoulder. "You did right by us."

Barina added, "The three of us have always held the belief we should use our strength to help others. We wanted to become the best line of defense—to protect, to serve the people who need it the most. We wanted to become beacons of hope for them. We had already been teaching ourselves how to fight even before we met you. After you came along, you taught us how to become all of this." She knew how hard this was on her teacher. She knew that he held guilt in his heart, and he shouldn't.

"We will mourn the loss of these two braves souls, of our friends." Josh stood up, as did Barina.

"Slaves to our blades and servants to the people." Berklion's voice was cracking.

"We learned together, we fought together…" Josh stopped when Barina put one hand over his heart.

She looked him in the eyes. "And forever we will be together." She couldn't stop the tears from falling.

Josh placed a hand over her heart as well before Barina took Berklion's hand. "Forever together," she said again.

They held each other, crying, before they raised their glasses to the air.

"To Jason and Tyra. Good journey," Josh breathed out.

"Good journey," Berklion and Barina said together. They nodded and emptied their glasses.

The rest of the evening, they sat telling stories of Jason and Tyra while getting a nice buzz from the bottle they were sharing.

"I think my favorites with Jason, at least one of his most badass moments fighting, was when he took on Medo." Josh smiled. "That, wow, we were twelve then, and Jason took on the rotten fish of a merman and dove into that pit to save you after Medo ran you through."

"That's when you had to go save King Megalodon, right?" Berklion was musing over the story he had heard at least a dozen times. "How many times have you been impaled?" he asked, laughing at Barina.

She scoffed at him. "Just...the one time. By the way, it really fucking hurts, in case you guys were wondering."

That got a big laugh.

"I practically had my arm cut off," Josh blurted out. "I didn't get any sympathy for that."

Berklion's face was exasperated. "Because you were being a dumbass!" He couldn't hold back. "I told you, fucking *told* you, not to..."

Josh stopped him as he downed his glass in one drink. "I know! I had no sympathy for me either." He was still rolling with laughter.

"I think some of my fondest memories were when he and I would go fishing," Berklion told them. "We'd sit and talk about life and dreams and everything. Sometimes, we'd simply sit in silence." He added his thoughts. "If there was a moment that I think defined him to me, who he was, it was probably when he heard that little girl, Kaori, had been taken by those bandits. I know he was friends with her brother, Haru. He didn't even say he was going to find her, he just left. He was gone for a week, but he found her. Apparently, according to Kaori, he got her away from those bandits within a day, but they were caught up in the mountains in a storm. He kept them huddled in a cave until it was safe for them to leave. It was his dedication and loyalty to protect and care for someone that said a lot about him to me."

Barina smiled slightly. "Poor bastard didn't know what hit him when I came up and started talking to him. I decided the moment I saw him that we were gonna be friends. I think for me, it was the morning after my family died. I remember that. I barely slept, not hardly a wink. I sat outside. The cold didn't bother me, or it was probably the shock that hadn't worn off. He came outside, bundled up, and put a blanket around me. He didn't say anything. He just sat with me." Then she smirked. "Then there was the first time I ever got completely plastered. I partially blamed him."

"Where was I for that?" Josh couldn't believe what he was hearing.

At the same time, Berklion asked, "When the hell was this?"

Barina was enjoying their reactions. "We were still in Nippon. Josh, where were you? Oh, yeah, you were out with Kinnosuke and Stephen that night. Jason, Kotoko, Hinata, Riu and I were over at Jiro's place and..."

"Did you get drunk with the Shogun's son?" Berklion was laughing hysterically.

She shrugged her shoulders. "Maybe a little bit. Maybe a lot. It was really good sake."

Berklion sat up. "Wait, was that when you two came back saying you both had a stomach bug?" He was glaring at her.

Barina gave him her most innocent look. "Maybe. Yes." She broke into a grin and winked. "Took me two days to recover from that."

"Damn kids."

Barina let out a big yawn and stretched. "I think I'm gonna get some sleep."

"Get some rest. When you get up, we'll do some training. I want to make sure you're in top shape before you go on your way to do the kind of battle you're going to do." Berklion kissed her on the cheek. "I love you."

"Love you, too." She kissed Josh on the cheek. "Love you."

Josh took her hand and squeezed it, his eyes giving her a gentle smile before she went back into the house. After closing the door behind her in the guest room, she undressed to her shirt. Barina climbed into bed and heard the rain tapping on the roof. With that sound—along with knowing that her family was outside—she fell fast to sleep.

* * *

Josh was up early the next day. He usually woke early, but even if that wasn't the case, he was restless. A lot had happened yesterday, and he was worried about his friend who was sleeping in the guest room. He had been there when she came home to find her family had been killed, and he remembered what that did to her. He had also been there, though, to see her grow and work through that pain. She had used that pain to become probably the most unstoppable and terrifying warrior he knew. He even put her above Berklion. He knew, he absolutely knew, that what happened with Jason and Tyra—while it would weigh on her mind—would become fuel for her. She would take that fuel and become even more powerful than before. He was worried about her, yes, but he was more curious than anything to see just how this would transform her.

Josh walked into the main room of the house. Barina was asleep in the guest bedroom, Berklion was in the loft. The only noise was coming from the first birds waking up outside, and he could hear both of his guests breathing if he listened hard enough. He'd let them sleep.

He felt the chill from the autumn air and headed for the fireplace and the stove. He wanted to warm the house up for them even though the chill wouldn't bother any of them that much. Still, he thought it would be nice for them to wake up to a cozy and warm home. He started to make breakfast and put a kettle on for tea.

Berklion came down from the loft and stretched. He dug through his bags to grab a shirt and then shuffled over to his student. He silently took over cooking the eggs.

"How are you holding up?" Josh finally asked him.

Berklion stopped his movements for a second then kept stirring the eggs. "I'm not sure. Not good, but I'm also trying to keep my thoughts busy. I start to cry if I stop to think about it for more than a heartbeat. I love you three as much as I could imagine loving children of my own. I feel as if a part of me is gone, and I can barely catch my breath. I feel like I need to be strong for the two of you, but I know we all need to lean on each other. I'm a collective mess." He smiled at Josh. "I've lost people, some who were very close to me, but this, it's on a different level. It hurts as much as I remember it hurting when I was taken from my home when I was a child. As much as it did when I watched the slavers kill my father, brothers, and when my mother died. It hurts. I also know that we will be able to get through this and keep their memory alive." Berklion let out a long sigh. "How are you?"

Josh shrugged. "I don't know. I haven't experienced a loss like this before. I mean, I liked Barina's family. We were always on good terms, but I wasn't super close to them. I haven't figured out how I feel yet. I don't know if it's sunk in. It has, but it hasn't. Jason was like my brother as much as Barina's my sister. I loved Tyra too. She was a good woman and was able to bring out the best in Jason. He and I, we both always promised to protect B, to keep her safe."

Berklion smiled at him. "I always had a feeling you had, even though…"

Josh grinned. "She's a better fighter than you, me, and Jason put together. This, Berk, what just happened, it's going to make her even more powerful. I mean, she was good after you first started training us. Girl has been the only one to ever make you take a knee in the sparring ring. Remember how she didn't just triple her efforts after her family died?" He was keeping his voice down.

"I remember." Berk put the eggs onto a plate. "She is one of the most terrifying warriors I can imagine when she really cuts loose, and that's only happened a few times. Hell, she's scary when she doesn't cut loose. For what happened with Jason and Tyra, her hands were really tied. It's always harder to fight while protecting hostages than it is when you just fight without worrying about the people around you. And it was Toler's son, a member of the Bask order. Nothing easy about that.

"I fought Toler alongside Rutherford years ago, and I barely escaped with my life. Rutherford didn't make it. If one of the most powerful wizards in the world and I weren't able to defeat Toler together, then Trekenler—who I'm sure learned a lot of his father's tricks—was no joke with what she was up against. I have no doubt that if it were just her and Trekenler and one of the two groups, Tyra and Jason would still be alive. But Jason was trying to keep the group safe till she got there, and she was trying to save all of them. Jason and Tyra helped her make an impossible choice. I'm proud of them. I also have no doubt that she'll be able to defeat Toler. This will add to that fire of hers." He sniffed. "Even without this fire, she'd be able to do it."

Josh nodded. "I know." He put an arm around Berk. "We love you, you know that. Thank you for always believing in us."

"I love you, too." He always saw the teenager he helped raise, sometimes forgetting Josh was now a grown man. "Go wake up your sister. I'll finish up with this."

Josh took some of the water from the kettle to put in a bowl with some salts and grabbed oils, wraps, and towels, before heading to the guest room.

Barina was resting comfortably on the bed, her reading glasses on the nightstand along with her journal. Even though she was a light sleeper, her body desperately needed to rest, and he was glad she was sleeping. He almost hated to wake her.

He reached a hand to her shoulder. "Hey, B."

Barina opened her eyes, but she didn't respond.

He smoothed some of her hair away from her face. "How are you feeling? Sore?"

243

She nodded. "Very sore, but I think I just need to stretch, and I'll be okay, I'm sure." She started to sit up, taking a deep breath through her teeth.

"I'll heat the ofuro for you after we eat breakfast. I want you to soak in it before bed tonight, too. For now," he said, putting the towel in the hot water, "lift your shirt up so I can bandage you."

Barina lifted the shirt, and Josh saw how severe the bruising was on her ribs. He rubbed on some of the oils before placing a towel that had been soaking in the hot, salted water. She held it while he used wraps to secure it in place. "I've seen you in this shape too many times for my liking," he grumbled.

"To be fair, I've seen you like this too many times, too." She barely spoke above a whisper. "It's part of the job, and you know this can't keep me down. I'm too stubborn."

"I know that better than most." He let out a short laugh. "Your hair, I have never understood how someone can have this level of magnificent bedhead."

Barina gave him a side-eyed glance and touched a hand to her head. She could feel the mass of hair that was sticking up in the back. "It's a gift. Not all of us can look as pretty as me when they first wake up."

Josh rolled his eyes and laughed. "No, no they can't."

Barina stood up, slowly, Josh helping her to her feet. "Thank you, for the wraps and everything."

Josh met her eyes but didn't respond. He didn't have to.

"I'm gonna go tinkle, and I'll be out." She headed to the toilet. She was so incredibly glad that, if there were certain Nippon styles of living they adapted for themselves, it was their bathing rooms and toilets—an indoor toilet that emptied into a box which could be wheeled to a pit once a week. It kept the odor down, and it meant she didn't have to go outside. *Thank you, Josh, for adopting this practice.*

Barina walked slowly to the kitchen table and sat down next to them. They ate in silence—Berklion and Josh each reading a book and Barina writing in her journal.

After breakfast, Josh stayed inside to do dishes. Barina went out to the back yard where he had put up a large fence that was high enough nobody would see when he was training. Josh had made a couple of Mu ren Zhuang, or wooden dummies with wooden poles sticking out of the sides so he could practice his swordplay against them. He had also wrapped rope around some very large logs to practice his melee. Each one had been well used over the years, and Barina could see that he had back ups of all of them made.

With Berklion's help, she was stretching her legs and arms more than normal. She was stiff after her injuries, and Berk wanted to make sure she regained her full movement. She rested on her back as he pushed her legs up as far as they would go. She breathed in and out as he did. Eventually she was on her stomach, letting him stretch her arms out as well. She stayed there while he gently worked out the kinks in her shoulders, arms, and legs. It felt good, but she was so sore. Barina knew she didn't have much time to rest and recover.

Eventually she stood up and could feel how much more limber she was. She still wasn't at a hundred percent, but she could almost breathe without it hurting, and her bruises didn't seem to hurt her quite as much.

Barina faced her teacher and bowed, which he did in return. In the next second, they were going hand to hand in an intense sparring match. He was attacking, she was defending. Berklion was so fast, he had always been fast, and Barina knew that he never went easy on her. For that, she had always been grateful.

She wasn't sure how long they had been at it before she felt another energy outside and saw a glint of light reflecting in the corner of her eye. She spun, caught what was coming toward her, and held her new sword in her hand. In less than half a heartbeat, Josh had tossed the weapon to her. He had also thrown Berklion his. Josh was now coming after her, too—his weapon in his hand. He didn't hold back against her either.

Quick and fierce, the men advanced, but she moved so fast that it wasn't so much a clash of metal as it was the sound of swords hitting the dirt. Or it was the grind of their weapons sliding up or down as she deflected. This was the first part of her training. Just defense. She had to get used to this new blade. It didn't take long.

The guys came from either side, faster at her than before. The men were right, though she'd never admit it. She was faster. She slid and rolled, using her still sheathed sword to knock Josh's sword from his hand before she darted past him, jumping while placing a foot on one of the poles of a practice dummy. She used it to launch herself in a spin toward Berklion.

When he raised his sword, she unsheathed her own before catching his blade in between the scabbard and her blade as she was landing. She twisted as she came down, his sword popping out of his hand, and she managed to resheath her sword before catching his in her free hand.

"Good." Berklion sat down on the steps to the back porch to catch his breath.

"Jeez." Josh was smiling. "Either I'm out of shape or you're faster." He stumbled over to the poarch to grab one of the glasses of water he brought out.

Barina shrugged for a second but then held her side, wincing a bit.

"You okay?" Josh asked. He held out a glass of water. "Did we go too hard on you?"

She shook her head. "I'll be okay, I just need a minute. It's when the adrenaline wears off that I hurt the most, but that's to be expected. I still feel better today than yesterday. I imagine by tomorrow or the next day, I'll be fine." She then gave them one of her classic smirks. "Did I go too hard on you guys?"

"Get the fuck out!" Josh couldn't stop laughing, and Berklion let out a groan.

"That was a good warm-up. How about we do more this evening? I don't want to aggravate your injuries." Berklion yawned again. "Josh, do you need to go into the shop?"

He nodded. "Yeah, I have a couple of people picking up orders today, so I need to be there for a couple hours."

Berklion stood to go inside. "Barina, how about I go with you to town? I know you need to pick up some clothes and check out that apartment. I need to do some shopping, too. I'm gonna change really quick."

Barina nodded and headed back inside to soak in the tub and then change into her western clothes. She quickly slipped into her skirt and blouse but decided she'd leave her cloak behind. The chill in the air wouldn't bother her anyway. She smiled seeing her teacher standing by the front door. Berklion was now wearing a pair of black pants and white shirt, forgoing his cloak as well.

He smiled when his adopted daughter came into the main room. She had grown beautifully, and he had a sense of pride in knowing that he helped her become who she is.

"Ready?" she asked.

He nodded and then looked at Josh who was sorting through a chest. "Josh, can you handle yourself on your own? Not gonna knock anyone up while we're gone?"

Josh didn't bat an eye at the joke. "I can't make any promises. Make sure Mason and Greg come back for dinner tonight." He tossed something to Barina from the chest. "Here. I knew I had them. It's an old pair of your shoes, but it's better than walking around barefoot."

Barina looked at her feet. She would gladly have gone barefoot, but this was much better. She put on the shoes and gave him a thumbs up. They were more dress slippers than shoes, but they were dry. She ran her fingers through her hair and took a deep breath before strapping her dagger and her coin purse to her side. "Shall we?"

Barina and Berklion left Josh's home on the outskirts of the town, and went to the center for some shopping.

Estella was a laid-back town with a lot to do. There was a library, museum, a theater, parks, all the culture and food one would find in one of the larger cities, but here it was condensed into a few blocks. There was a strong sense of community. Even with all the shops and attractions, people still took their time to enjoy themselves. The town was well-kept, lively yet relaxed, and relatively safe. There were parades and festivals, and a strong sense of community that made Estella a great place to be.

Just as they came to one of the markets, they saw Mason buying a basket of veggies. He saw them and waved, and then walked over to them.

"Hi!" he said, giving them a hug. "Just getting in?"

"Yup, gotta get some shopping done." Barina still held onto his arm, and they started walking together.

"How have things at the shop been going?" Berklion asked while they walked along the streets.

Mason yawned. "Things are going really well. I wasn't sure how well my little tea and spice shop was going to do, but honestly, business is great."

Berklion nodded. "I'll need to pick up some things from you guys before I leave. You do carry some great teas that I haven't found anywhere except back home in Nippon." He then looked down. "Has anyone given you and Greg a hard time for you, being, well, together?"

"It happens here and there, but for the most part, everyone in this town is very accepting."

"Good."

Barina put a hand on her teacher's arm, leaning her head against him. "Always looking out for everyone. I wouldn't expect anything else from you."

Berklion put his arm around her for a second. "It's what I've always known about you, too, kid."

They kept walking together, making small talk. When they came to the main streets, they stopped.

"Which way are you headed?" Mason asked. "There are some really great shops that sell clothes in that direction." He pointed down one of the streets.

"I'll probably hit up those really quick. I know which ones carry the types of clothes I need for the work I do, so I'm headed that way. I'll meet you back at your shop when I get done."

"Okay, and then I'll show you the apartment. I know of a few other rentals that you can probably take a look at."

"Great, and I wanna check out that land that Josh was talking about, too. I'm gonna need to get to work on securing it before I leave if I can. I want to start building the forge as soon as I get back, maybe see if they can even start on the foundation now." She looked at Berklion. "You coming with me, or going with Mason?"

"I'll go with you."

"I'll meet up with you both after a while." Mason waved to them and headed toward his shop.

Berklion looked over after a bit. "How are you holding up with everything?"

Her eyes glanced to the ground, she felt tears stinging her eyes again. "I don't know yet. All this, the reality of it and the heartache, it's just below the surface. I'm keeping it together, for the moment. Being with people and being distracted helps. Knowing that I have to finish this, that I have to get rid of a tyrant so that Jason and Tyra don't give themselves in vain, it's a driving force."

"You've had to endure so much." He pulled her close for a hug. "Your family, Matrikal, now this. And I'm sure there are things I don't know about even, yet you're still kind. All I want is for you to be happy."

Barina returned his hug. He wasn't just her teacher or her adopted father, he had been one of the most precious people in her life since the day they met.

"I will be, and I find ways to be no matter what's going on." She breathed in the comforting scent that was him. "I have you, and knowing you're going to be there when I need you, that helps."

"I had promised your father that if anything should ever happen to him, that I would care for you as if you were my own. Even if I hadn't made that promise to him, I would've."

Her eyes looked to his, apologetic. "You've given up so much to care for me. I'm sorry, yet, I'm incredibly thankful that I've had you."

"What do you think I've given up?" he was smiling.

"I know that you've postponed being with Miyuki and starting your own family because of me. You've held off on..."

Berklion cut her off with a look. He leaned over, so he could meet her eyes. "I have not given up or postponed anything. Miyuki, she knows that I'll be home for good someday, we just don't know when. I visit her often. She's a strong and brave woman for that, so no worries there. I have been caring for you, yes, but you've been a grown woman now for years. What I do with traveling and helping people, that's been my choice. Don't worry. Miyuki has never seen you as a reason I'm not home for good, and neither have I." He kissed her on the forehead. "I am, no matter if it's in the midst of a battle, by Miyuki's side, holding you while you're hurt or crying, all of it, I am there, because I made the decision to be there." He then held her so tight that she felt squished. "I gotta take care of my little baby girl." He was petting her head and speaking as if she were a toddler. "Yes I do, my little girl."

"Goddamn it, Berk," she croaked out. "I can't...move...or breathe."

She could feel his chest shake with laughter. "I can't hear you."

Barina started laughing and was trying to move away. "You're like the only person who knows how to keep me in a hold."

"I'd better know it. Honestly, though..."

Barina slipped away.

"I had a feeling you'd be able to break free from me."

She turned red.

"You've really improved in your fighting."

She raised an eyebrow. "I've still got a long way to go."

He opened the door for her as they headed into the clothing shop. "I don't know. I mean, I've known for a long time that you've surpassed my own skills."

Barina stopped him from saying anything else. "No. You trained me. You are the master, I am the student."

"And it is the master's wish to see their student surpass them."

"If I were so good, then I should've been able to find a way to save Jason and Tyra." She stated it as a matter of fact.

Berklion held a shirt up to Barina to see how it would look. "I've had battles where I've lost people dear to me. I always thought, if I were so good, I should have been able to save them, or I could've done something different. Those thoughts won't change the outcome, and the fact was yes, I did everything I could. Just like you know you did everything you could. I've never seen anyone fight like you. Even Master Yuhii has been left breathless by you."

Barina took hold of the shirt. "I don't need or want this flattery. You carry the mantle of the greatest, and you shall remain that, always."

Berklion pinched her cheek. "In your eyes, I know. You're probably able to take that mantle, though. You, Josh, and Jason have become three of the most amazing fighters that I've ever seen. Even before I started to train you, I knew your potential, and it was your hearts that made me willing to take you on. Jason and Josh, they're good, but with you, Barina, you've learned to fight in ways that they never picked up. I know you have been able to incorporate other styles of fighting, even without you knowing it. You've just always been able to pick up on things like that quickly, but I don't think anyone, even you, realized that you were able to add those skills to your own."

"Yeah, but I shared everything I learned with the boys."

"Yes, you shared but you also mastered it." Berklion found some more shirts. "I'm very proud of the fighter you've become. You have a better chance of taking down Toler than anyone, ever."

Barina was turning red with the compliments. This was high praise from her teacher, and the fact he was telling her what Yuhii had said about her, that was a lot. She could only hope that she'd be able to fight the way she needed to when up against Toler.

"Thank you, Berklion." She put another shirt up to her. "I don't like this one." And put the shirt back.

Berklion stopped and tilted his head as a thought occurred to him. "You've mentioned that they've asked a lot about your fighting, but have they even asked once about your skills with regard to the main reason you were asked for this job? You know, acquiring objects?" He made sure to not use the word thief or stealing. In the event someone heard them, he didn't want to bring attention.

Barina's little smirk grew, and she snorted a laugh. "Not once. Like, that's what I was actually asked to do."

Berklion shook his head, stifling his laughter. "Why were they so intent on asking after your fighting anyway?"

"I blame Vic. He mentioned that I was a fighter and played me up. I'm just sitting there thinking Vic is gonna get a foot up his butt if he doesn't stop talking. I don't get it completely. They don't really harass Arkon about his abilities, and not really with Onyx either."

"You know it's because people aren't used to seeing a woman fighting. That's probably a big part of it."

"I know, I know." Barina made a tsk noise. "By the way, how Jaras hasn't figured out how he and I know each other boggles my mind?"

"But, you hung out with him for three weeks? We were all at Darien's wedding."

"He knows that you and Darien are best friends too. He just hasn't put two and two together." Barina held up another shirt. "What do you think of this shirt?"

"Blue has always been your color," He said while she took the blue blouse. "Yellow has always been pretty on you too, oh, and so has orange. This is a nice shade."

She thought it was adorable how much he doted on her. "Thanks, Dad." She then took the reddish-orange shirt. "It is a pretty color."

"Are you going to try them on?" he asked, but he knew her answer.

She grabbed a couple of pairs of pants. "Fucking hate having to try on clothes." And she stepped into a dressing room.

The man who ran the shop walked over to Berklion. "She's feisty."

"You have no idea," Berklion admitted.

The man extended his hand. "You're Berklion, right? I remember you coming in with Josh a few months ago."

"Wow, yeah, good memory."

The man smiled. "You kind of stand out in a crowd, or anywhere."

Berklion nodded. "Not too many people with my skin color around here?"

The man was laughing. "That's a factor, but even if it weren't, you're freaking huge. So, who is she? I'm Jake, by the way, own the shop and make all the clothes."

"You do good work. That's Barina, one of my students. I was her guardian while she was growing up."

Jake looked surprised. "I've heard Josh talk about her. For some reason, she's not what I pictured."

"I hear that a lot about her." Berk scratched his head. "Then again, I hear that a lot about me."

Jake lit his pipe up. "I'd imagine it's not a bad thing to be unassuming and not what people expect."

Berklion was leaning against the counter. "It doesn't hurt." They made small talk while they waited.

Barina hated trying on clothes, but she had to make sure they fit. Every tailor was different. She traveled light when she was on business, so she only carried a few shirts and a couple of pairs of pants—taking time to wash what she could as best she could on days she stopped to rest early. She always had to have backups. In her line of work, it wasn't unusual for her to go through a half dozen shirts in a few months while on the road, leaving them in shreds, covered in blood, or both. Sometimes she had to be able to blend in better with the surroundings. When she wore pants, people would stare sometimes, so having a skirt was essential. She'd leave the one she was wearing at Josh's place.

Barina also needed to keep her clothes as free of odors as possible. Not only did she prefer it for herself, but if she or her clothes smelled terrible, it could give her away. Being clean was as much about survival as it was hygiene.

She walked out of the dressing room and saw Berklion trying on a couple of hats.

"The black one looks nice," she said as she put the items she was getting on the counter.

Berklion glanced at Jake and nodded to the black hat. "It'll be nice and warm for the colder months." He looked at Barina's purchases. "Let's see what you got. Hey, you're getting the one I thought looked nice."

Barina blushed a little bit. "It is a nice color on me, you were right." She put some money on the counter. "Could you tell me where a good cobbler is? I need to get some new boots."

Jake's eyes lit up. "Next door is my brother's shop, he's a cobbler, and pretty good. I'll pop over with you both if you want, this way I can make sure he gives you the best service possible."

Next door, she was able to find two good pairs of boots.

Jake seemed to be enjoying their company. "Berklion, do you and Barina wanna grab a couple drinks with me and my brother?"

"I still need to grab a couple things," Barina told Berk, "but you go with them, and I'll meet you back at Josh's." She bowed to him a bit before she left the shop.

She headed two blocks down to Mason's shop, admiring the sign written in beautiful letters—*Mason's Fine Teas and Spices*—hanging outside a two-story, brick building. The store was on the main floor where Mason and his partner Greg sold teas and spices that were both common and hard to find, as well as tea sets and other small wares. They lived on the second floor in a two-bedroom apartment with a rooftop patio and a balcony. There was also a smaller, one-room apartment with a small balcony that overlooked the street. Barina knew that this was a good option to rent when she returned to town. She loved the idea of living next-door to Mason, but she wouldn't mind being able to rent a house if she could afford it. Her dream was to buy or build her own home, like Josh had, close to where her forge would be. For now, baby steps.

She opened the door and inhaled the wonderful scents in the shop. The early afternoon sun gave a warm and bright feel to the room, and the shelves held all the goods in large and small glass jars that were tightly sealed. The light hardwood floors were clean, as were the shelves. The bell gave a happy ring when she opened and closed the door, and it wasn't long before she saw Mason and Greg walk out from the back room.

Greg greeted her with a kiss on her cheek. "Are you ready to look at the apartment? Mason has it ready for you to see. I also never got a chance to make those treats for you." He was beaming at the idea of her living next door.

"No worries, Greg. All ready. Can I leave my bags down here?"

Greg was already taking her things for her. He looked at his partner. "I'll keep an eye on the shop."

Mason took Barina through the shop and out the back door. They headed up the staircase that went to a little landing connected to both apartments, their front doors facing each other. He unlocked the door opposite his own and let her step inside.

Barina knew that Mason always took good care of whatever he owned, so she shouldn't have been that surprised by the rental. The room was open and airy. In one corner was a small kitchen with an island. The rest of the space was large enough for a table and chairs, a seating area, and a bed. She saw a drain on the far wall where she could have a bathtub, but she wished it was a bathroom like what she was used to back home in Nippon. The water closet drained to a far off well for waste. She was glad there was a water well at the top of the landing between both apartments. That would make her life easier. She really liked the view off the balcony, too. It wasn't large, but it was all she needed.

Mason said, "I thought about your training already. You can use the rooftop patio for it, and we have a cellar that's pretty spacious. Plus Josh would let you use his backyard. What do you think?"

"I really like this. It's really all I would need for a while. I have enough at the moment to buy some land and hire some carpenters to start building the forge. After I get back from this job, I'll have enough to buy the equipment and such. I still want to look around at a few places today, but I'll be able to let you know and give you a deposit today if I do." She leaned against him. "Thank you, Mason. You've always looked after me."

He snorted. "You're a freaking mess. Of course I look after you. But you've done the same for me." He put his arm around her. "I love you like you're my sister, but better, I think."

"Since you only have brothers, I'm guessing you don't have much room for comparison?" She poked his side.

"I have you, that's always been more than enough," he said, throwing shade.

"Hey, and I know I've said it, but I'm glad you came to Nippon the last year we were there. I know it wasn't a short trip there or back."

"No, but it was neat to travel so much and then spend time with you guys. I missed you too much and wasn't sure if I'd have another chance to go there, so I took it." He nudged her arm. "Come on, let's go look at the other places you wanted to check out."

Barina didn't find other rentals she liked, but she did see the land Josh had talked about. It wasn't more than a few minutes away from Josh's place. There was a great view of the large creek that ran along the outside of town, as well as the woods in the distance. The acreage was large enough that she'd have space for both her forge and a house when she could afford it, and the land was secluded enough that she'd be able to train in secret. If she rented Mason's apartment then, after a couple years, she'd hopefully have made enough to build her home. She could still help a lot of people, both magic and mortal, by taking jobs like this when asked. It was what she was trained to do. She had learned to fight to protect the people she loved and those who couldn't protect themselves—the innocent—and to destroy the wicked. Barina knew she could never put down her blade for good, and she wouldn't. By the same token, she had wanted to take up her father's trade since the first time she picked up a hammer at the forge.

Mason took her to meet the gentleman who owned the land. She gave him the money—a pretty penny—but she was ready to get started. With the contract signed in duplicate, the land was hers.

Next, Barina headed to a carpenter and gave him the drawing for the forge she had been carrying around with her for years. He gave her a quote, and she gave him a deposit. He offered to get a crew started on it the next week. Mason and Josh would have her permission to check on things and speak for her till she got back.

Night was starting to fall when she and Mason returned to Josh's. Greg and Berklion were already there. The men looked at her in anticipation.

"Well?" Josh asked, trying to contain his hopeful smile.

She raised her arms in triumph. "I bought the land for my forge, and I'm going to rent Mason's apartment until I can afford to build a house."

They started cheering as Josh sprang to his feet to pick her up in a big hug. "We'll be together again!"

"You started all this, you know? You moved here first cause there was a better market for your work. Then Mason found how good the place was for his shop, then Jason and Tyra, now me. Look at what you started."

Josh stood tall and proud. "I am that amazing."

Berklion raised an eyebrow. "He's always been so humble."

Josh walked back to the kitchen. "One of my best traits. Dinner's ready, come get your damn food."

They glanced at each other and headed to the kitchen.

"What's for dinner?" Greg asked. "Smells good. Oh, and I brought some dessert. Promise I made something good for you."

"I caught some fish earlier, roasted it with vegetables and picked up some fresh bread from the market."

The group sat enjoying their time together and their meal. The food was delicious, and even with the tragedy that loomed over them, for the moment, they were happy.

"I never bothered to ask, do you even know where the rest of the traveling party is?" Mason asked her while enjoying a drink.

She smirked. "They travel slower without me there, so I'd imagine they'll be stopping in town by tomorrow afternoon at the earliest, then they'll probably want to rest before heading through the Forest of Lithor. I have at least a day or two before I need to think about leaving." She leaned back in the chair, letting her body relax completely.

The men laughed as she took another drink.

"Don't judge," was all she said.

They enjoyed the rest of their evening before Mason and Greg headed home.

Barina went to bed early. She needed the rest and decided to destress as best she could while she had the chance. After she closed the guest room door behind her, she undressed and looked at herself. Her old wounds were closed for now. She wasn't sure how many more years it would be till these things healed completely, but she knew that stress could keep them open longer. Thankfully, it looked like her ribs and other bruises were healing nicely. *Silver linings*. It had been an awful week to start, but now, being here, she was feeling a little better. She simply put on a shirt, climbed into bed, and fell fast asleep.

The next morning, Barina woke up feeling a breeze on her face and could feel the light coming in through the curtains. She smiled hearing the birds chirp.

The morning held much of the same routine as the previous one. Breakfast, stretching, training, and then they all went off to do their own thing.

When the traveling party came to Estella, they would need to rest and restock. Barina would be able to spot them easily. Dressing in a gray skirt with a long-sleeved white blouse, she tied her hair in a braid and covered it with a scarf. She borrowed Josh's blue jacket, pulling the hood up over her head as the rain came down.

She walked into town and headed to the clocktower in the square. Nobody noticed when she picked the lock to go in the side door of the tower. Inside, it housed the gears and the large staircase that led through and up to do repairs. At the top, she found a hatch on the roof that she was able to prop open and look out toward the Green Forest in the distance.

Barina wasn't waiting long before she spotted them walking out of the dense trees and into the clearing, following the road into town. She slipped back out of the clock tower and waited, unnoticed, till they walked not more than twenty feet from her. She followed them to a nearby inn.

The group looked rough. Admittedly, they had been through hell. Some had had their minds tampered with, and all of them had lost friends. She was sure that, from the looks of it, Jaras had a cold. His eyes were still alert and sharp, but she could see his face was flush with a fever. Aria looked pale, too. Barina wondered if she had been eating. She wanted to reach out to them, but she wasn't ready. Not yet.

Arkon's eyes weren't their normal pale blue, but a deep, almost indigo color, and he had bags under his eyes. Had he not been sleeping? She could see that Twarence and Onyx were both looking over their shoulders, searching. Barina knew what they were looking for, or rather, who. She listened.

"We won't see her unless she wants us to." She heard Jaras sigh while he helped Aria off her horse. "Come on, you need to eat something. You have to have your strength."

She nodded. "It's just, I don't have an appetite."

"I know, but you've got to at least drink some milk, something." Jaras was trying to plead with her as they headed into the inn. They could hear the congestion in his voice.

"Arkon, you have to rest," Onyx told the elf. "I can put a spell on you to help you sleep. You'll be no good to anyone if this keeps up."

Arkon's weary face gazed at nothing. "Can you make it so I don't dream?"

Onyx patted him on the back. "Yeah, I can."

The elf hung his head. "I see them every time I close my eyes."

"I've gotcha. Go with them to the room, and get yourselves settled. Twarence and I will get the horses in the stables, and we'll be up soon." Onyx let out a sigh when Arkon closed the door behind him.

Onyx and Twarence shared the same concerns.

"Jaras is sick, Aria can't eat, and Arkon can't sleep," Twarence said. "Since she left us, I keep looking to see if she's around. I know she was going to be coming to Estella." Twarence lit up a cigarette.

"Jaras is right, though. If she doesn't want us to see her, we won't." Onyx took a flask out of his traveling bag. "What's the plan now that we're here?"

"I know we're on a timeline, but we need to be healthy. I want to wait until Jaras feels better, and same with Arkon and Aria. Once they get their strength up, we'll keep going. So probably the day after tomorrow, if we can." Twarence sat down, exhausted. "We can restock while we're here, hatch out the last portion of this road and, maybe, if we're lucky, maybe Barina will even find us."

"She's gotta know we'll be here. If she wants to, she'll find us." A thought occurred to the wizard. "Are you having second thoughts about the rest of this mission?"

Twarence shifted uncomfortably. "A little. I mean, she knows the roads. She's the one intended to steal back the stone, and I don't know if Jaras is going to be able to go up against Toler without her. I don't know if Arkon can tame a beast like Uraki. There are so many variables and, without her here, a lot of these scenarios that we're going to encounter just got more difficult."

All the wizard could do was agree with him. "You know, when Rutherford fought Toler, he was fighting alongside Berklion. They fought together, and it was everything Berklion could do to get me out of there after Rutherford was killed. It was three days before Berklion could leave my home because he was injured so badly."

Twarence laughed a little bit. "You're not helping this case at all."

Onyx had to share his laughter. "No, I'm not. Let me put it this way. I know, I absolutely know, just how dangerous this situation will be once we get to Thoron. I've met Toler, and I've seen Uraki and what he's capable of doing.

"Toler took down one of the most powerful wizards I've ever known and almost killed the most feared warrior in the world. I know the stakes, I know better than anyone what we're up against. I'm still going."

"Do you think we can win?"

Onyx looked straight ahead. "I think we're the best chance that kingdom has had in a long time. I have to try, and with all of us, we have a great chance. I also haven't given up hope that Barina will be there. She still loves us. She knows what Ken was doing to you and the others. She just needs time to get over it. I think, or at least I hope, she'll still be there. If she shows up, then yes, I think we really can defeat him."

"You don't think Jaras can…" Twarence was cut off.

"I can't defeat him. I'm not that good." Jaras walked into the stables. "I'll do everything I can, no question. I might be able to give him some scratches, but if Darien isn't up to fighting him, I know I'm not. If Berklion couldn't beat him…" He held his hands open.

"Shouldn't you be resting?" Twarence asked.

"Yes, but I needed some air. I got Aria to drink some milk and eat a little bit. Arkon is trying to sleep, but he's gonna need that spell from you." Jaras sat down on a haystack. His eyes and face were red, and every muscle in his body hurt. "I hate being sick."

Onyx got up to head inside. "I'm rather fond of it, said nobody ever. I'll go get Arkon to sleep. Get some rest."

Jaras waved at him and then turned to Twarence. "Really worried, aren't you?"

"Doesn't even scratch the surface. I mean, I know that I now have to guide you guys and then ultimately have the final say on what the main plan will be once we get there. That was always the plan. But, I don't know."

"Don't doubt yourself. Don't doubt us. We need to have complete confidence that all of us working together will be able to do what nobody else has been able to do since Toler came to power, with or without Barina." Jaras looked at his cigarette and put it away. "This thing doesn't even look good right now. I'm with Onyx though, I haven't given up hope that she'll be there when we really need her."

"Jason said she was better than Berklion. Even though we lost Jason and Tyra in that cave, I mean, watching what she was doing, how she fought, I can believe she is."

"We still haven't seen what she's really capable of if she were to completely let go." Jaras sneezed. "When there's other people to keep safe, like what she was having to do, you have to change up your game, and a lot."

Twarence leaned back. He had a lot on his mind. "So many variables. Uraki is something that worries me just as much as Toler does. Arkon still isn't sure if he'll be able to use his powers on him. He needs to be able to focus his strength, and he just doesn't know if he's strong enough."

Jaras closed his eyes while thinking.

Without them noticing her, Barina marched past the two men and right into the inn.

"Uraki is something that we really have to plan for. Arkon, I think, is strong enough to hold him but not completely shut him down. Arkon's the strongest elf for the job. I don't even think their king could take down a dragon. But that might give us enough time to strike Uraki down. We need to really look at all of our options, and I don't even know if B had a plan for him. I'm sure she had an idea, but no plan."

Twarence glanced at Jaras. "Do you really think she ever seriously had a plan? I don't think she ever does."

Jaras had to laugh at that. "She wings it more than anyone else I know. That girl knows the layout but won't know how to assess the situation till she gets there. Cracks me up. But no two jobs for her are ever the same. It makes sense." Jaras yawned.

Twarence scratched his beard before reaching his arms up in a large stretch. "I'm gonna try and eat something, then get some rest. You coming?"

"I will in a bit. The cool air feels good."

Twarence patted Jaras' back and headed into the inn.

Jaras stood and headed out of the stables. He saw a creek that ran behind the inn. He took a seat at one of the benches along the shore and simply watched the water run by.

A cup of something hot was shoved in front of his face. "Drink this. It'll help."

Jaras' jaw dropped as Barina took a seat next to him. She left the hood of the blue jacket up. The moonlight would light up her hair like a beacon if the others came outside. He wasn't used to seeing her dressed like this either. A blouse and a skirt, it was a different side of her. But her eyes were alert, and she was ready to spring into action if need be. She looked straight ahead, holding the mug for him.

"Seriously, drink that. It's hot water with honey. It'll help."

Jaras took the mug and sipped the contents. "This is tasty and very comforting," he said as the drink warmed him. "I wasn't sure if we'd see you."

"I wasn't sure if you would, either. At least not yet." She watched her breath in the cool night air. "I'll be there when you fight Toler. I'm still going to do my part. I love you guys, that hasn't changed. I just need some time before I can be around everyone again."

"How long have you been here?"

"Saw you guys come into town. Followed you here. Sat out and listened to Twarence and Onyx while they were talking. I'd appreciate it if you don't tell the others you saw me." She was still looking forward. "If you tell anyone, you can tell Onyx. You two were the only ones who didn't go against me."

Jaras was about to speak, but she stopped him. "Yes, I know their minds were messed with, doesn't change that I'm still kinda pissed and hurt. Thing is though, if you guys happen to get captured, it means your minds, you and Onyx, can't be tampered with or read. I won't be detected if Toler or another member of the Bask order happens to be there and tries to get into your heads. It serves a dual purpose."

She put a hand on his forehead. "Your fever is pretty bad. I'll be by with some herbs for you tomorrow. I'll leave them at the front desk. I'll also have some things to help with Aria not eating and Arkon not sleeping. I'll be back here tomorrow night to check on you. You or Onyx can be here to meet me, preferably him if you're still sick." Barina stood back up.

Jaras took hold of her wrist before she left. "I don't think you know what it means to know you're still here with us."

Barina gave her fellow warrior a kind smile and placed a hand on his shoulder. "The same as it means to know you all still care for me. Oh, and yes, I have an idea for Uraki. Just an FYI. Get some rest."

Jaras shook his head and watched as the thief walked away. He knew if he turned around, she would vanish. Just then, a horse and carriage went by, blocking her from view, and sure enough she was gone. He knew she had probably hitched a ride on the unsuspecting carriage.

He took a few more minutes to finish his drink and headed back in. At the bar, he saw Onyx staring into a bowl of soup and drinking some water. It was the first time he had seen Onyx look worried. He was so good about keeping his emotions hidden until he didn't think anyone was watching.

Jaras sat next to him. Onyx glanced up, giving a feeble smile.

"I just saw her. She's still with us."

Onyx almost dropped his spoon and let out a sigh of relief. "Thank the spirits."

"We can't tell the others."

Onyx took a spoonful of his soup. "Makes sense."

Jaras smiled as the bartender gave him another hot water and honey mix. "How do you figure? I know why she said that, but what's your guess."

"She's still hurting. But since you and I didn't turn our backs on her, she believes that our minds can't be controlled. Not easily anyway. She will make herself a secret weapon if needed."

"Yeah, that's what she said." Jaras sipped his drink. "She's bringing some herbs for me tomorrow, as well as stuff for Arkon and Aria. She'll also be out by the creek tomorrow at the same time, if you want to see her."

"Good." Onyx sipped some more of his soup. "Go get some sleep, if you can. I'll be up soon."

Jaras requested water for a bath and then took his mug with him up to the room.

Onyx finished his soup quietly and then followed. Aria and Twarence had fallen asleep, and Arkon had been able to drift into a deep and dreamless sleep with Onyx's help. Jaras must have been in the bathing room, still. Onyx felt better knowing what he had hoped—that they weren't alone, that they had an ace up their sleeve. Nobody, save for himself and one other, understood just how much this battle would depend upon Barina. He changed out of his robes and climbed into the bunk.

The next day, the group spent time healing and recovering. Jaras slept most of the day. Onyx answered the door when the clerk brought up a package of herbs that were left. He gave Arkon, Aria, and Jaras the herbs meant for each of them, and it wasn't long before they were all starting to feel it working. Aria's appetite came back, and Arkon was able to feel at ease and rest. Jaras was simply able to breathe again and fall asleep.

Twarence had opted to go walking the town, picking up supplies that they would need when they got back on the road. Besides enjoying the sites, he hoped that he'd see Barina somewhere. Maybe she was in Estella, or maybe she went on to Thoron. Maybe she went back to Miork. He didn't know, but he could hope.

He spent most of the morning and a good portion of the afternoon shopping. The town was beautiful, and Twarence could understand why so many people loved this place. He found an interesting shop and he went in. The aromas of all the spices and teas hit his nose. He inhaled a deep breath and basked in the warmth of the scents and the sunlight coming in the window.

"Hi, how are you today?"

Twarence saw a man walk out from the back room. He was about the same height with a balding head, blue eyes behind his glasses, and a beard.

"I'm good. This shop you have is really neat. Where do you get all these things?" Twarence looked at the teas on the shelf. "Are these really from Nippon, these teas?"

"Yeah, I've been there. Lovely place. I have a couple suppliers who are able to keep me stocked."

"I have a friend, she lived there for years. It's really neat to be able to see some more things from there." He was looking at the water paintings on the wall.

"Would you like to try a cup of one of the teas? I'll brew one up for you."

Twarence was surprised by the offer. "Yes, actually. Which one would you recommend?"

"I really like the Shincha. It's going to be a little sweeter in flavor naturally, and they pick it earlier in the season than any of the others. I really like Hojicha, too. It has a lovely rich flavor."

"I'll go with the first one. I'm Twarence, by the way."

"Mason. Have a seat. It shouldn't be too long." Mason turned his back and set the kettle on the stove while he took the tea down from the shelf. He caught a glimpse of Barina in the back room and could read her eyes. This was one of her travel companions. She put a finger to her lips and vanished from sight.

"Are you just passing through?" Mason asked.

"Yeah, I'm just here for a couple days. The rest of my party is at the inn resting, so I thought I'd get supplies. Then I found your shop."

Mason nodded and brought over a couple of scones and a pot steeping with the tea.

"That smells fantastic. I'll buy a couple of bags of that to take with me."

Mason smiled. "Excellent." He sat down with him. "How long have you been on the road?"

"Couple of months. A rough trip. Heavy losses."

"Sorry to hear that. Hopefully the rest of your trip won't be too much."

The scholar shrugged. "If only. We're more than halfway there and then, well, when we're done we can go back to our lives." He watched as Mason poured the tea. The aroma was soothing.

"Sounds like it really has been rough on you, hasn't it?" Mason took a bite of one of the scones.

Twarence nodded, sipping the tea. "Damn, this is good. For the moment, this tea and this shop, they are helping me relax a bit, so thanks."

"I'm happy to be able to help."

"You wouldn't happen to know Barina Raine, would you?"

Mason nodded. "I do. She's my childhood friend. I'm friends with Josh, and I already heard about what happened with Jason and Tyra. Barina's come and gone already." That wasn't a lie, she had come and gone. He just didn't specify from where to where. Mason gave Twarence a reassuring smile. "Hey, listen. She told us about your minds being messed with. She still cares about you guys, she just needs time. That's what she told me anyway."

"Do you know where she went?" Twarence asked. "I'd like to see her, just to tell her how sorry I am for everything, even if she doesn't forgive me."

"She forgives you. She just needs time. No, by the way, I don't know where she's at." Still not a lie. Mason had no idea where she had run off to for the day.

"If you see her, will you tell her that I'm sorry, and I miss her?"

"I will." Mason leaned in. "She's a tough girl and very compassionate. She also, when she loves a friend, loves them completely. Don't worry, it'll work out."

Mason and Twarence had a nice visit about the town, and the shopkeeper invited him to visit again once everything in Thoron was over.

After Twarence left, Mason went out the back door of the shop. He found Barina walking up the stairs, carrying a chair above her head. He saw another one still on the ground.

"I found a small dining table and some chairs," she called to him. "Figure if I can find some things to furnish the place now, I might as well take advantage of it." She hadn't even turned to look at him when he came out.

"I hate it when you can just tell I'm out here."

Barina didn't miss a beat with her response. "I smelled you."

Mason grabbed one of the other chairs. "Whatever, Stinky. How do you think I knew you were here? The smell." Mason was still following her, a little nervous. "Should you be lifting that with your injuries?"

"It hurts, but I've got it."

Once in the apartment, he saw that, while he had been working, she had been bringing up furniture. Not only did she have a dining set, but a rocking chair by the wood-burning stove in the living room and some dishes she had found.

"Didn't tell him I was here, right?"

"No, but I told him I knew you. I love that you're really going to be moving in."

Barina very casually replied. "As long as I survive the fight, yup."

Mason snorted. "I love how you're so calm about it. I know I shouldn't laugh, cause I get that you're serious, but damn."

Barina gave him a little wink.

* * *

At the inn, Twarence came into the room quietly. Jaras and Arkon were sleeping peacefully, and Aria was reading a book while eating a large bowl of soup. Twarence went to the balcony and looked out to the creek. There he saw Onyx, sitting and reading, needing some peace and quiet from everyone. The scholar could relate to that. He finally went inside to eat and, without realizing just how tired he had been, he went to bed early that night.

Onyx sat on the bench outside, reading, but hoping Barina would show up. He waited for over an hour before he heard her voice.

"How's the book?"

Onyx jumped. "Don't scare me like that."

Barina gave him her usual smirk. "Worth it. Are they feeling better?"

"Not sure. We'll be able to tell by tomorrow morning. They've all been resting, thankfully."

"You should get some rest too. You've been doing well keeping yourself together, but rest. I would imagine that you'll be leaving the day after tomorrow."

"Probably."

"Very well. I'm not joining you, but I'll be following you. You won't have to worry about too much." She placed a hand on Onyx's arm as she stood up. "Get some rest, my friend."

"You rest, too. I know you got hurt pretty badly, so you rest and get to feeling better." His brown eyes peered through his glasses. His face did not show much emotion, but his words spoke volumes.

"I will."

* * *

The next day Barina spent training with Berklion, making sure that she was back up to speed. They used the better part of the last half of the day to simply meditate. They had a quiet evening with Josh, enjoying dinner, and Barina went to bed as early as she could. She knew that this last month of traveling, while it would have its challenges, was nothing compared to what she was about to face when she got to that final destination.

In the morning, she awoke before everyone, even the birds. She put on a pair of black pants, a dark blue blouse, boots, and her cloak. With her new sword at one side, dagger on the other, she shouldered her pack—Yukinohana still in her bag. She was ready.

Josh had gotten up early to make her breakfast and, after she ate, he and Berklion gave her a bittersweet goodbye.

"Come home to me," Josh whispered to her. "Your forge will be waiting, and so will I."

Berklion squeezed her tight. "I'll be back here by the time you get done. I'd tell you to be careful, but that's silly, so just be the best you."

Barina nodded and walked out the door and to the inn where the group was staying. She found a comfy spot behind some bushes to hide and waited. It wasn't long before the group left the inn. They took the road to the Forest of Lithor, the last stretch till they would come to the Kingdom Thoron.

CHAPTER 12

Only two days had passed since they had left Estella and, thankfully, they learned that the Forest of Lithor had few dangerous creatures to worry about. It was a peaceful area and quite lovely, for the most part. There wasn't anything magical about it, but the forest had a charm about it all the same.

The autumn leaves were falling and covered the ground red and gold. It almost seemed like a path of treasure as they walked along. The crisp, cool air would chill their faces, but the satisfying sound of leaves crunching below their feet and the occasional smell of a campfire in the distance warmed their spirits. The forest was enchanting all on its own.

Jaras, though, became anxious from the lack of activity. "I am so bored," he finally groaned while crossing over a small creek.

"I am going to take a moment to fully appreciate that sentence," Aria said, teasing him.

"There really isn't anything to worry about besides some bandits here, right?" Arkon looked over his shoulder.

The scholar scratched his beard. "Not really. I mean, it's common knowledge that this place is generally a haven for thieves and other criminals, but they don't come out much during the day. It's an unspoken law that, from dusk till dawn, if you go off the path and even when you're on it sometimes, you understand there's a chance you could get robbed. I think there's an inn and an outpost halfway through the forest that's considered neutral ground. No crime is allowed, and the keepers are left alone. Even the supply carts are left alone."

Arkon nodded at that. "Talking about thieves makes me wonder how she's doing."

While they made small talk as they crossed the river, they had no idea how close they had come to trouble. It was a good thing Barina was tailing them. She watched as six men appeared from the tree-tops, all between the ages of nineteen and maybe twenty-six or so. They were armed and, while she could see they were all well-trained, they wouldn't stand a chance against her or those in the traveling group if they targeted them.

"I recommend that you leave them alone."

The bandits spun around when they heard someone speak. They laughed when they saw Barina. Their leader—an attractive man in his mid-twenties—stepped forward. He was tall with dark hair that almost fell in front of his eyes as it framed his face. Behind his hair, his gray eyes seemed to have a particular gleam when he saw her. His dark red shirt was a stark contrast to his pants, cloak, and boots, which were all black. At his sides, he carried his sword, a rope, and two rolled-up links of chain. She had to admit, he was probably one of the most attractive men she had ever seen, but it didn't matter. He wasn't going to touch her friends.

"Are you lost? Go home before you get hurt," he said while walking toward her.

Barina stood still with her arms resting at her sides. The leader seemed enticed by her calm. Most people he had met, even grown men, would run from his group. This young lady didn't seem bothered in the slightest.

"You'll have to get through me," was all she said as he stood not even a foot from her.

He grinned when his eyes met hers. He found her attractive in an uncomplicated way. Her hair was in a simple braid—strands escaping to play with the wind. He was impressed by the fact that she seemed confident enough to wear men's clothing and no makeup. But maybe that's what he liked. Attractive or not, she wouldn't keep them from their goal.

He reached up to pull a leaf out of her hair. When he leaned forward and lightly touched her waist, he whispered, "I don't want to hurt you, my lady."

Barina could feel her face turn red. *Don't get distracted by him B. Damn it, I'm enjoying this too much. Course, two can play at this.*

She placed a gentle set of fingers on his chin so he would have to look her in the eyes. "I won't be the one getting hurt," she said, surprised that she was flirting.

He met her eyes and couldn't breathe for a moment—his heart skipping a beat, maybe two, as he was drawn to this woman. Her eyes went soft and her lips curled slightly. He thought he saw her cheeks turn pink. He hoped it wasn't simply from the chill in the air.

That smile. Those eyes could hypnotize a girl if I'm not careful.

"Are you sure you won't back down?" His eyes pleaded with her. "Please, back down."

Her smile faded, and he saw the light change in her eyes.

"Only if you leave them alone," she replied.

"Damn," he said as he walked back to his friends. "You're not worth our time." The gleam he had earlier was gone, replaced by a cold stare.

Barina stood still, her eyes focused. Then, in the next moment, she put one hand on her hip. "Just so ya know," she said, flicking her other wrist forward, "that group has one of the greatest fighters in the land—an elf of the Spirit Clan who is set to become a general. And then there is the most powerful wizard in the world. Oh, and a healer who is strong enough to suck the life out of you if needed." She crossed her arms. "I'm really doing you guys a favor by stopping you."

That made the man tilt his head. "How do I know you're not bluffing?"

She crooked the corner of her mouth just a fraction. "You don't." Her eyes locked with his again, but he couldn't read them. She knew they would challenge her if she didn't stand down, but she could easily win against them.

"You honestly think you can go up against us," the leader said. "You must think you're pretty good, unless, of course, you are really good. Either way, you're still cute." He chuckled to himself. "I really don't want to hurt you," he admitted. Turning to his companions, he said, "Stew, would you take care of her for me please?"

Stew stepped forward. He was tall with a wild look about him. His brown hair twisted into thick dreadlocks that went to his shoulders, and his playful blue eyes smiled at her. He was as tall as the man who called him to challenge her. She genuinely wished that they were all meeting under different circumstances. They'd probably be friends, even if their way of making money was questionable.

Stew drew his sword. "No problem, Kevin."

Kevin grabbed the water flask and took a drink while Stew rushed Barina. She didn't move a muscle until he was within inches of her, and then she simply stepped aside, stuck out her foot, and he went tumbling to the ground.

Barina turned toward him, giggling privately. "You okay?"

Stew had to laugh a little. "Clever." He got back to his feet, turning to advanced again. Barina quickly grabbed his wrist, squeezed to disarm him, and caught his sword in her free hand. Her left foot met the side of his head, knocking him to the ground.

Stew looked up at her, laughing. "Not even mad," he said, and then passed out.

The five men still standing were amazed. She hadn't drawn a weapon or even taken off her pack. What really concerned them was that, next to Kevin, Stew was as good as they had in their group.

Kevin stood, trying to figure her out. They should be able to win against her, slight as she was, but she had just defeated one of the best fighters he knew.

"I can take her down, Kevin," one of his men offered, his eyes cold.

Kevin shook his head. "No Truman. You, Brodrick, Casey, Mel, don't hurt her, just make her yield." He wasn't taking his eyes off her. "You're not going to draw a weapon? Shouldn't you set your bag down at least?"

She shook her head just a bit. "I'm good, thanks."

Only due to curiosity did Kevin nod the four men forward. They attacked her all at once. Barina used nothing more than her sheathed dagger to disarm them before she sent strikes to each man, knocking them out cold.

Kevin stood silent, open-mouthed. He dropped his water flask. This woman, she hadn't even taken the sheath off of her dagger. She was sparing their lives and could've killed them if she had really wanted to, even without a weapon. He watched her, eyes wide, as she walked up to him. He took a defensive stance and reached for his sword. She leaned over and picked up his water flask, handing it to him.

He took it with a shaky hand. "Thanks."

She put her hands in her pockets. "You can try if you want. Having your friends fight instead of you, that's smart."

Kevin took a step back, his gray eyes narrowed, offended by the comment. "If I fight someone, they get hurt. I meant it when I said I don't want you hurt. It'd be a shame to see someone like you go to waste."

She wasn't sure how to take that. "Thanks?"

"I guess that didn't sound that great." He rubbed the back of his neck, his face heating up. "You're incredible. I don't know if I've ever been so impressed in my life. I would, however," he stepped up and took her hand in his own, lightly kissing it, "like to try my luck." He noted how small her hands were. He also felt a shock wave through his body when his lips touched her hand.

Barina would've preferred not to fight at all, but to just sit and talk with him. "I guess I won't knock you out like I did your friends," she joked.

He scoffed again. "I appreciate that. And if you beat me, I'll buy you a drink."

Barina shook her head, looking down while hiding her facial expression.

"What?" he asked her.

"Nothing."

"Fine, what do I get if I win?"

She gave him the sweetest smile. "I'll buy you the entire bar."

Kevin let out a quiet huff. "Oh shit. I'm about to get my ass kicked, aren't I?"

He advanced toward her, but she didn't move until he was within a foot of her. She dodged each attack, and still didn't bother with her weapons. She was fast—faster than anyone he had ever seen. The way she moved, the way she kept her cool seemed almost identical to a man he had met once—a man he knew might've killed him if he hadn't befriended him first. This woman's style was the same.

"Damn, you're wonderful," he said, stopping for a moment to catch his breath. He lowered his sword and propped himself on it.

"Thanks." She leaned against a tree. "Take your time. Would you mind if I took a minute to put a salve on my side? If not, I can wait till later."

"Go ahead."

"I'm actually enjoying your company, too," she said.

"Likewise." He moved a little closer and took a drink from his water, watching as she set her bag down and dug out a jar with a salve. "So, do you come through here often?"

"Why? Hoping to see me again?" She nudged his shoulder before she took her cloak off and set it on her bag. She was joking, but part of her was also hoping.

Kevin shrugged. "What if I am? I mean, if I have to buy you a drink, I need to know when it's a good time." He tried to be as charming as possible. It was working.

"After I get done with my job, I'll be moving to Estella if you're in the area."

"I think I could make a trip to see you." He surprised himself how much he was flirting. It had been years since he had found an interest in anyone. "Where are you headed to, if you don't mind me asking?"

"It's safer if you don't know." She sat down. He saw her close her eyes as she did, trying to hide a wince.

"It's just, if you keep going that way, you're headed into Thoron. I'm sure you know just how dangerous that place is. Word is that Toler's forces have been spilling over into the forest to catch and question anyone they find."

Barina nodded. "I appreciate the info."

"Ah, so you're going to Thoron?"

She didn't answer, but her blue eyes said she wouldn't even if he was right. She unscrewed the jar of salve, took a large dab, and moved her hand up her shirt, putting it on her ribs. "Sorry, don't want to do this here, but since we're taking a break, and you didn't mind…" Her voice trailed off, and she exhaled.

"What's wrong?" He sat down next to her, putting his sword on the ground.

"I bruised my ribs badly last week. They're still a little tender, so I've been trying to put this on when they get sore."

"Can I get you anything, anything to help?" He started searching in his pouch. "I might have something…" He felt her hand on his, gently stopping him.

"It's fine, thank you though." She ruffled his hair. "Besides, aren't we in the middle of a duel?"

Kevin raised an eyebrow slightly, enjoying her fingers in his hair. "Duel shmuel. I really just wanna see if your skills surpass my own, which I'm pretty sure they do." He handed her his water flask. "What will you be doing when you get back to Estella? How long till you're there?"

"I'll be back in a couple of months, and I'll be starting the family trade back up." She took a drink from the flask, handing it back to him, moving closer still.

"What's that? Maybe I can bring you some business?"

"Weapons smith." She felt oddly comfortable with him.

He raised his hands in the air, a shock on his face. "That is in no way the answer I expected to hear."

Barina feigned innocence. "Surprise." She was enjoying Kevin's laugh.

Kevin watched while Barina put the jar back in her bag. He liked that her movements were calm and simple. He could spend the rest of the day with her and not feel like it was enough time.

She stretched a bit and stood up. Kevin did the same.

"Well, my dear, shall we continue? I promise, we will get that drink, too."

Barina bowed slightly. "I certainly hope so."

Kevin walked about ten steps back. "Will you humor me? Please, use your sword."

She nodded.

He rushed toward her. She quickly pulled her blade and hit his blade, his sword flying high into the air. In the next second, she put her own back in its sheath. He was so shocked at the speed that he fell over his own feet. Barina caught him before he met the ground. She grabbed the sheath of his sword and held it in the air so his sword fell back into it. She rested the sword back at his side.

"Are you hurt?" she asked, brushing his hair out of his face and standing him upright.

Kevin was left breathless while he watched her put her cloak on and sling her bag over her shoulder. "Who are you?" he asked.

"I'm someone who fights to protect those I love. The people you guys would've gone after, I love them."

Kevin froze. He couldn't move.

Barina touched a hand to his shoulder. "I have to leave. Try and keep yourself out of trouble. We'll have that drink when I get done with this job. Take care." And she ran off into the forest, vanishing when he blinked. She hoped maybe they would get that drink someday.

Still stunned, Kevin thought over her last words. *Are you really her? Blonde hair, grayish-blue eyes, a fighting style identical to his, and you fight to protect those you love. You have to be her, after all these years. Finally.*

"I wondered if I would ever meet you, Barina," Kevin said, hardly able to contain his excitement. "I've waited a long time for this."

He saw something glittering in the sunlight. Pushing away the leaves, he found a chain through a pewter pendant with a single line on it, along with a ring. He knew it belonged to the woman he'd just met. *It's as good a reason as any to go after you.*

He waited until his friends woke up. They had no injuries at all, they had just been knocked out. She knew how to hit them just right. It wasn't until the next day, when he knew that they were okay, that he set off to find this girl again. A girl he had wanted to meet for years, someone he had only heard about once in a story.

CHAPTER 13

It didn't take long for Barina to catch up to the group. They were still traveling, enjoying the beautiful fall day, and that's what she wanted for them. For the next couple of days, things were peaceful and smooth.

The group stopped when they came across a group of men blocking the road. Their eyes were dark, and they looked as if they wanted blood.

Jaras stepped forward, putting his cigarette out under his foot. "May we pass?" He knew the answer.

"For a price." The largest man stepped forward. The men behind him snickered, the smallest one licking his lips. "For a price," he said, mimicking his boss.

"What's your price?" Jaras already knew what they wanted. He just had to hear them say it.

The man directed his eyes toward Aria. "Let us have her for a while, and we'll call it good."

Aria scowled as the men in her group drew closer to her. She drew her bow, ready to fire if anyone got too close.

Jaras didn't hesitate as he threw a hidden knife into the man's shoulder. In the next second, he had his sword drawn and launched himself at their attackers. He moved like water with a fury so deadly that there might only be a handful of people in the world who were as good.

Onyx kept a close eye on the fight. If it looked like he would need to intervene, he would. Arkon was doing the same. Even Twarence had his weapons drawn. With Jaras in such close range of them, they didn't want to risk doing more harm than good.

A distance away, Barina had climbed into a tree just above the group, watching.

Jaras took down the largest man, the one who had spoken with him. There were three equally good who circled Jaras, attacking all at once. Jaras didn't miss a step. Within a matter of seconds, he had killed all three. He hated to kill, but he also knew that these men would not stop till they took Aria. He was sure they had done this to other women and would do it again if they weren't stopped. The burden of their deaths was the price of preventing other rapes and murders.

The other four moved on those protecting Aria. As they approached those still on horseback, Onyx and Arkon both lit up their hands and didn't hesitate to fry two of them. Twarence swung his axe at another. One slipped by, putting his hand on Aria's leg to grab her from her horse. He used his sword to pull her bow from her hands.

She met his gaze, anger in her eyes, and a fury she had never felt went through her body. His ugly and dirty face grinned while he licked his lips again, knowing he was close to taking her. It would be the last thing he would ever think.

Aria leaned over and put her hands on his face. She did something she'd never done before, even though she knew it was possible. Something that went against everything she'd been trained to do. She used her powers to suck the life out of him.

He let out a scream of sheer agony—one that she ignored. Her companions watched in shock as the color drained from the man's hollow face, his eyes rolling back. Blood began to pour from his mouth. Aria pushed him away, a look of disgust on her face.

Onyx, Jaras, and Twarence had always known of her abilities, but they looked on with a mix of admiration and horror, seeing what she had done.

"That was terrifying, but absolutely amazing," Arkon told her.

"It was too good a death," Onyx spat.

Twarence nodded in agreement.

Jaras looked around. "There's one missing."

The next second, the small one—the one who had been mimicking the largest man that Jaras had taken down first—landed on the ground about five feet behind him. The little man still had a smile on his face, as if he didn't know he was dead.

"Never mind, found him."

His neck was broken. In his hands, though, he held a blow gun loaded with poisoned darts ready to fire. But he never had the chance.

"Did he fall?" Twarence asked.

Jaras nodded. "He must've slipped while he was up there and broke his neck while falling." He met Onyx's look. They both knew the truth. "Let's keep going. These guys stink, and we need to cover more ground before nightfall."

Twarence led the way, Aria behind him, Arkon still staying close. Onyx and Jaras traded looks before looking up into the trees. If she hadn't waved at them, they wouldn't have seen their thief hiding in the high reaches. She met their gazes and darted away.

"Thanks, B," Jaras whispered. He looked down till he felt the wizard put a hand on his shoulder. Onyx gave him a simple nod of his head while getting back onto his horse. They caught back up to the group, nobody the wiser that their missing member was in hiding.

Aria rode at the rear, waiting for Jaras. "Thank you, Jaras. I know that everyone stepped up, but you really, you didn't hesitate" She whispered out the words.

"You're welcome," Jaras said, knocking her booted foot with his fist. "How are you?"

"Shaken. I've never had to do that before. You know, take a life."

Jaras nodded. "I know."

Aria held back her tears. "How do you live with it?"

"You just live. You know that you had to do this to live, to survive. Those men were as bad as they get. I wouldn't lose too much sleep over them, Aria. It's hard to do, I know, but it'll get easier to deal with."

She nodded her head. "To be fair, I don't think Twarence has ever had to do this either."

"He has a couple times, but it was before he met us. Oh, and there were those giants," Jaras added. "When he was younger, some assassins came into the university to try and kill his mentor, the head of the university. Twarence stopped them just in time. He was only eighteen. Same thing as you after he did though—he had a hard time sleeping for the first couple nights. But those guys would have killed his teacher who is a very good man."

She looked forward, setting her mind, and kept riding.

That night, they stayed close to each other, but they were quiet for a long time. The fight earlier had made them realize a lot of things, and they mulled over all of them. They had become friends on this mission. Close enough friends that they each knew they would lay their lives down for the other. They also knew, because of what happened in the Water Caves—in the fight that cost two people their lives, and one of their number to leave completely—just how much was at stake.

They knew that their own lives were on the line. They weren't just going to retrieve the stone. They weren't just going to oust a king and tyrant. They were trying to save an entire kingdom. It hit them that they were going to have to win or die—those were the options. They realized some time ago that this was their real mission. To save a kingdom. They understood—as close as they were, as great as these friendships had become—that the kingdom could be snuffed out, along with their lives.

Aria sat in front of the fire, staying close to Jaras. She wasn't scared, she was uneasy and not sure how to deal with the fact that she had taken a life for the first time. She felt better being next to him. She could handle her own, with her arrows, or as another option, her own powers. She knew that while she wasn't anything spectacular in hand to hand combat, that wasn't her role either. She would fight if she had to, but she had to make sure that she could stay alive to save her friends.

Arkon had kept to himself more than any of the others. He had been doing so since the Water Caves. Today though, he put the feelings of shame and sorrow aside and focused on what was going to happen.

He had the ability to tame animals, to calm them. He could talk to them. It was one of his really strong gifts. Uraki though, this was a beast unlike anything he had ever worked with. While dragons were beasts, they also had the gift of speech, and their intelligence far surpassed any other being in the world. When dragons were young, he could influence them and their thoughts, but not control them. When they got older, it was impossible for him to even influence them.

Uraki was too ancient for him to connect to. His only other option— which is something he hated to do—was to freeze the beast's movements and then kill him. He didn't like to do that to any creature, even one that was evil. It felt underhanded and wrong.

Uraki, though, this was a dragon as bad as they came. He hated humans, hated elves, hated everything. He stayed on with Toler because Toler was just as strong, and Toler gave him power and the freedom to kill when he wanted. Arkon—while he hated to kill a creature that he wasn't going to eat—this was more than self-defense, and the number of people this would save would outweigh the guilt he would feel.

Onyx had been feeling nervous since Barina had left the group. Knowing that she was still close by if needed, put his mind at ease. There was something that felt very serendipitous about him and Barina taking on Toler. It had been their two teachers who had fought him together but lost. Hopefully, he and Barina, along with these others, would be able to win. Toler hadn't had Uraki with him then, though. But Barina said she had an idea, and if there was one thing he had learned about her, it was to trust that she would come through. How the hell she thought she could handle a dragon, he had no idea, but he'd have to trust her.

Twarence sat just a little bit away from everyone, wanting to be away from the fire. He was smoking and thinking, looking at the stars and the sky lit by a quarter-moon. In three to four weeks they would be in Thoron. He wondered how they would retrieve the Anna Stone. He didn't know the first thing about stealing, especially how to go about taking something from a place that was so well guarded. He wanted to talk to Barina, ask her for some advice. He wished he had their thief here. She was always good to mull these things over with and to lighten the mood. He hoped that one day she'd come back, and they could still be friends. He missed his friend, simple as that.

Twarence worried for good reason. He knew the rest of the route to Thoron, and he knew what kind of things to expect on the way there. He had the names of the best inns, who to talk to, who they could trust, how they should dress, how they should even go about getting into the palace. Everything down to where the stone could be, he knew it. But it was one thing to read it, to be told it, and another to execute a plan.

Jaras was the most grim out of any of them that night. He stayed close to Aria, knowing that she still felt uneasy about what she had done. He kept trying to read a book he had brought but losing his focus. He worried that he wouldn't be able to handle the last bit of this job when they got to Thoron.

He was a gifted fighter. He always had been, and he knew what he was about. He also knew that Toler was one of the most powerful warriors alive. Even if he wasn't a member of the Bask order, he'd still be a force to be reckoned with. Jaras also knew that, while Barina was following them, any number of things could happen on their way to Thoron. He had to plan as if she wouldn't be there.

Even if all they could do was take the Anna Stone as far away from Toler as possible and not dispose of him, that would be a win. It would mean that he wouldn't be able to expand his powers to the entire world. If they could keep that from happening, then someone could still live to fight him another day.

When nobody was looking, Jaras glanced over his shoulder and looked out to a hill about a half mile away. There, under some trees, he saw a very small figure leaning against a tree. He knew she was letting him see her, even there.

The body falling from the treetops wasn't the first thing he had seen to indicate that she had helped them. He had woken to signs of struggles at the perimeter of their camps, but there wouldn't be a sign of anyone. It was her, looking out for them.

Jaras and Onyx knew that she was right and smart in thinking that she needed to be kept a secret. Toler knew that his son had been traveling with Onyx and Jaras both. He also knew that there was one who had been trained by Berklion. With Barina in hiding, he could believe she was gone if someone read the others' minds and these two kept that secret to themselves. If anyone had a chance of getting that stone and getting it the hell out of there, it was Barina. Jaras finally drifted off to sleep hoping that everything would be okay in the end.

Barina watched the traveling party from a distance. It was a peaceful evening, and the cool autumn winds blew—a beautiful night. She leaned against a tree and took a deep breath.

The group was nervous, she knew that. She would be there in the thick of the fight, and she would take Toler head on. None of them really had to fight him. Ultimately, all they were required to do was get the stone and leave. But if they thought they could and win, they would take on Toler.

Barina had been training her whole life to stop the wicked. She felt it was an obligation. And Toler was as bad as they came. She had fought some of the darkest creatures known to the world, and he made that list.

She took her hair down and, while running her fingers through her locks, she had another thought. For the last few days, she kept feeling as if someone was closing in on her. Were they following her? Did they just happen to be on the same path? Barina didn't sense a dangerous or malicious intent, all she knew was that they were getting closer—within walking distance.

Her attention came back to the now. With a sigh, she turned her head slowly. "I really don't feel like dealing with this right now. Could you guys please leave me alone?"

Nine men stepped out from behind the trees, one of them less than twelve feet from her when he showed himself. Barina stayed calm as she casually put her hair back in a bun.

"Little lady, don't you know it's dangerous to be out all by yourself?" one of them asked.

"If I had a bronze note for every time I heard that, I'd be able to retire by now," she mused out loud. "I really just want to have a peaceful night."

The men laughed to themselves. "After we're done with you, we'll leave you be." They drew their swords and knives.

Barina heard a faint rustling in a tree, then another, and then another. There was something, or someone, going from treetop to treetop, and they were getting closer. She felt sure it was whoever had been on her trail. They had caught up to her at last, and they were on her side. That was all she needed to know.

"Do these lines really ever work?" Barina crossed her arms.

One of the men blew a kiss at her. "Doesn't matter if it does or not. They're all ours in the end."

Her eyes grew dark. "I considered just knocking you all unconscious, but now, I've changed my mind."

The men laughed even harder at that. "I was thinking of letting you live after we get done too, but now…" His eyes looked her over. "We might just keep you as a toy for a while, then kill you."

Barina drew her dagger, her stare was ice. "Try it, and you'll be left with little stumps to piss with."

"You have weapons, but nine against one is not in your favor, is it?" The man drew his sword, and he and his men started to close in.

The man closest to her found himself on the ground, out cold, as someone dropped an elbow on his shoulder after jumping from the high branches of the tree Barina had been standing under.

"It's unfair for all of you," the surprise guest growled, grabbing another man by the collar and pushing him back. He looked over his shoulder, his gray eyes sparkling when they met hers, and winked at her. "Mind if I crash the party?"

Barina was pleasantly surprised to see who stood beside her. "Kevin! Glad you were able to *drop in*."

Kevin groaned. "Should've expected that. By the way, you are really hard to follow."

"How the hell were you able to track me?" She sent a hard punch to one of the men that ran toward her and kicked the other in the stomach.

Kevin headbutted another attacker and picked up a third to drop him hard on the ground. "You were amazing at covering your tracks. I've just always been really good at figuring things out. If I'm being honest," he admitted, "I followed your group, and it led me to you."

Barina elbowed one man in the face and pushed another into the tree hard enough to knock him out. "Why were you following me?"

"You dropped something when we met. Wanted...," he punched the last guy out, "to give it back to you." He squinted his eyes, gazing toward the woods in front of them. "Oh, hey. They have more friends."

They looked at each other.

"Would it be okay if we discussed this later?" He nudged her elbow with his own.

"Sure. How do you wanna play this? They have, like, twelve guys coming to join us." She pulled a leaf out of his hair. "I can take them, not a problem."

"I know that we could probably fight them off, but do you want to? Let's change the venue a bit. There are too many corners here."

She tried not to laugh. "If you really want. Wanna go left, or right?"

"Left, we can lose them at the suspension bridge just over that way."

She nodded.

Kevin led the way, and they took off running past the men, the men giving chase.

"I know you can take them on your own, but I couldn't sit back and do nothing." Kevin sounded apologetic for interfering.

"You really think I'm offended by someone helping?"

"Well, no. The only thing that I was really holding back on was snapping their necks for what they wanna do to you." His eyes went dark. "I still might. But it's really what made me jump in."

"I try to avoid bloodshed if I can," Barina said, "but rapists, I wouldn't bat an eye if they disappeared." She didn't have to think twice about it. "They'll do this to others."

"Noted." He turned to a man who was catching up and punched him as hard as he could in the throat. "Good luck breathing, bastard."

Barina cut in front of him as two more men drew their swords. She didn't hesitate to slice both of their necks with her dagger. "Baka."

Her fellow thief glanced at her. "What was that?"

"I called them idiots."

"He said you could speak in other languages too."

"Nani?"

"There you go again." Kevin motioned ahead and said, "Oh, here, we're at the bridge."

"You have some explaining to do."

"I know, and I will."

Barina hated that his smile—and him in general—became a weakness for her.

She stopped in her tracks when she saw where they were. "You call that a bridge?" She stared at an unstable suspension bridge that had to stretch at least one hundred feet over a large canyon. The canyon was as deep as a ten-story building. The ropes that acted as a railing across the bridge were frayed and moldy. Barina was pretty sure that the single large tree trunk—old and cracking—was the only post connecting the bridge from one side to the other. It looked as though, if just one more termite had a snack, the tree would topple over.

"Are you afraid of heights?" he asked, laughter in his voice.

"Hardly." She pouted. "Just not a fan of falling from them."

"The pout though, that's cute." He leaned in a little bit closer. "You comin' with me or not?" He poked her nose lightly with his finger.

She blinked. *Not the worst decision I've ever made.* "Let's go," she said then, sighing to herself. "I can fight these guys just fine. Why am I following?" She didn't realize that Kevin heard her.

"Cause you think I'm a stud." He couldn't help but give her cheek.

Barina hit his arm. "Shut up." *That is a factor,* she admitted to herself.

They kept close together while they rushed over the bridge. Once on the other side, Barina and Kevin both turned to cut the ropes, and half of the bridge fell.

Barina turned and pushed Kevin aside as four more men who had been waiting in ambush on this side of the bridge jumped them. She took down one and two. The third one, though, threw a bag of something at her. She batted it away, but not before some of the powder hit her in the face. Barina breathed it in by accident.

It would have worked instantly if she hadn't trained herself over the years to slow down the effects of various powders and potions. She felt as if sleep could take her at any moment, but she kept her focus, fighting to stay awake. A man ran toward her with an axe over his head. Barina flung her dagger and struck him in the neck. She grabbed her dagger back and staggered, trying to stand.

"Barina?" She could hear Kevin call to her. "Shit! Barina!"

Her body felt weak. She knew this powder wouldn't kill her, but it would knock her out for a while. She had to keep it together till she could get a safe distance from these men, someplace hidden. She also had to make sure Kevin would be safe. She would wonder later how Kevin knew her name.

Kevin overpowered the last man and rushed to her. Her breathing was heavy, and he knew she didn't have long before the powder would completely take effect. He was impressed that she could still fight against the knockout powder that these men must have used to drug the people they attacked. Anyone else would have fallen over in an instant.

"Kevin," she breathed, raising her head while propping herself against a tree. She reached out to touch his face. "Kevin. Daijoubuka?"

She and Kevin looked to the bridge. The remaining men were throwing ropes to the other side and starting to line the gap with large branches.

Kevin knew that he and Barina could travel through the forest, lose them that way, but there was always the chance the attackers would find them, or go for the people she was trying to protect. Kevin had another idea.

"Do you trust me?"

She gave him a sideways glance. "Kimi ni inochi wo azukeru."

"I'll take that as a yes." He took the chains and rope off of his sides. "Climb on my back." He knelt down for her.

Questioning, Barina put her arms over his shoulders. He stood up quickly and tied the rope around both of them, securing her to him. "Just in case that stuff knocks you out before I get us to the bottom."

Barina didn't argue and held on. What he did next would impress the hell out of her.

He threw the chains around the large tree that held the bridge up and then jumped off the side of the cliff. Kevin swung with her in the air until he found another landing that brought them closer to the bottom of the canyon. When they were about to hit the wall of the canyon hard, he managed to maneuver her in front of him, letting his back hit the wall. He had put a foot out to take some of the impact, grunting from the pain and breathing out slowly to work through it.

"Are you okay?" Barina asked, worried. "I could've taken the brunt of that," she said, slurring her speech. "My pack would've absorbed the shock."

He shook his head as he pressed his forehead to hers. "I'm fine. Not gonna let you get hurt."

Barina thought he smelled nice, and she almost forgot that she had been hit by knockout powder and they were both suspended over fifty feet in the air. She tried to wrap her arms around his shoulders, and he tightened his arm around her waist.

"Thank you."

Kevin brushed a hair out of her face. "I'm gonna swing you around again. I need both hands to get us to the bottom."

She gave a sharp inhale as if she wasn't quite ready for the movement. He shifted his body and, in a second, she was resting on his back again.

"Why is he doing all of this for me?" she asked aloud.

He looked over his shoulder, his gray eyes soft and warm.

The next thing she knew, he was swinging them to the next landing. He did this a few more times before they touched the ground. When he looked up at the bridge, the men were still watching and laughing.

"We'll still find you!" they yelled. "We still want her! You could make this really easy on yourself and just leave her!"

"Fuck them. Fuck all of them," Kevin mutter to himself. He propped Barina against the canyon wall. "Be right back."

Kevin didn't draw his sword until he was at the tree post. With one powerful swing and a kick, he took down the tree that held the bridge. He quickly put Barina on his back again and ran as far away as he could—away from the debris and the men who screamed as they fell.

He ran until they were about a mile away before Barina slid off. She stood on her own, though not easily. Kevin quickly wrapped up the chains and rope, putting them back on his side.

"What you did with those chains, that was pretty incredible." Barina smiled up at him. She took her hair down from the bun and let out a big yawn.

"Thanks, how are you?" He could see her eyes droop, and she started to sway.

She shook her head. "I don't have long." She was slurring more.

"Barina?" He looked her over, studying her. He honestly didn't know how she was still standing.

"How do you know my name?" Her legs began to shake as sleep finally started to win. She felt her body going numb. "Damn it, I need to move to someplace I can hide and be safe till I wake up." Her legs gave out. She would've fallen to her knees if it hadn't been for Kevin.

He saw her legs buckle and quickly caught her as she fell against him. She tried to place her hands on his arms, but couldn't. She couldn't even lift her head to look at him. Instead, she rested her face on his chest, breathing against his shirt. He had one arm around her and used his other to lift her face up.

"I have a safe place to go. I'll get us there." He pulled her cloak around her as the rain started to fall. He knelt down again and secured her body to his with the rope.

The rain started coming down harder, plastering Kevin's dark hair to his face. He slipped on leather gloves and lifted her legs so he could walk quickly. Barina, plus her pack, made it a little more difficult, but he knew it wouldn't be long until they reached safety.

"You okay back there?" he asked her quietly.

"Mhm," she answered, watching his breath in the cold air. "How do you know who I am?"

"We have a mutual friend. You don't have to fight the sleep anymore, I've got you."

Barina couldn't keep her eyes open any longer. She knew that, with Kevin, she would be safe.

CHAPTER 14

Barina woke up groggy, unsure where she was or what had happened after she fell asleep. She was in a tiny, one-room house, lying on a mattress on the floor and tucked in under a warm quilt. In the room, there was a cabinet that doubled as a table with a couple of mismatched chairs on either side. A chest and shelves against the far wall held plates, cups, dried food, and a kettle. A small wood burning stove kept the room at a comfortable temperature—still a little chilly, but not unpleasant. Kevin's shirt hung on a line nearby. There were windows with curtains drawn on three of the walls, and she could hear a light rain tapping on the glass. A door stood open on the fourth wall.

She saw Kevin at the door, sitting on the floor and keeping a sharp eye on the outside world. His sword was in his hands, ready to move at a moment's notice. She could see a nasty bruise forming on his back and an angry scrape on his shoulder. She remembered that Kevin had taken some injuries as he swung them to each of the landings, hitting his back hard on the wall of the canyon.

Then she noticed something else. Out the door, she saw tree branches at eye level. Kevin tossed something from his hand—a twig or pebble—and she didn't hear it hit the ground for a few moments. They were in the trees. This was an honest to goodness treehouse.

She watched him for a few moments. The rain must've been really heavy on the way here. He had on different pants too, his other pair drying as well. He had hung up her cloak, taken her boots and socks and set them aside.

Barina felt like she had known him for years, even though they had only met a couple times. She trusted him, without a doubt. There was that, and she felt safe with him. For someone like Barina—used to being the protector—it was a big deal that someone wanted to keep her safe.

As she stood up slowly, Kevin laid his sword by the door and stood as well. "Hey, you're awake."

She stumbled a bit as she walked and—in two steps—he was there, catching her before she could stagger another step.

"You shouldn't stand up so fast." His voice was quiet while they met each other's gaze. "The powder hit you hard. You're just coming out of it. Be careful."

"It's worn off. I'm just a klutz." She could hardly respond. Barina really liked being in his arms. His skin felt cool from the fall breeze, and his hair was still a little damp from the rain, though his chest hair had dried. She liked how it felt under her fingers. She tried to hide her blush. She had to stop thinking like this about him.

Kevin helped her to one of the chairs, and he sat in the other. "Are you feeling okay?"

She nodded. "I am, thank you—both for bringing me here and for taking care of me. So, the chains, is that what you really use them for?"

He nodded. "Yeah, it's how I get through the forest a lot of the time, climbing in the trees. But I can fight with them, do a lot of damage if I use them for that."

"And is this a freaking treehouse?" She was in pure delight.

He had a feeling of pride go through him. "Yup, this is my home. I have a couple of other safe houses set up in the forest, but this is my actual home. It was the closest one to where we were, so I brought you here. We're pretty high up, and we blend in perfectly with the trees. Nobody can find us. The only one who knows how to find this is my friend Stew. I'll give you a tour in a bit. Did you want something to eat, anything to drink?"

She shook her head. "I do need some bandages and some astringent or something."

He tilted his head, confused, but he opened the cabinet and handed her what she asked for while she grabbed her salve out of her bag.

"Give me your wrist," she said, "and then I want you to sit in front of me so I can get your back fixed up."

His eyes softened while he held out his wrist. "Thank you."

They stayed quiet while she bandaged his wrist, and then he sat in front of me as she cleaned the scrapes on his shoulder and used her salve on the bruises on his back.

"Thank you, you didn't have to do that." His tone was low and quiet. Whatever she used on his back felt great. He started to rest his head on her thigh and wrap an arm around her leg. He hardly noticed what he was doing, and Barina wasn't objecting while her fingers played with his hair.

"Kevin." She finally broke the silence.

"Mmhmm?" Kevin was certain he could fall asleep if she let him.

"How do you know who I am? I mean, you even know that I can speak other languages. How?"

He sighed. "I did promise you." He moved from the floor to the chest on the other side of the room. He grabbed a dry shirt and a couple knitted blankets, wrapping one around himself and placing the other around her shoulders. "Don't want you to catch a cold."

Kevin closed the door and sat back down on the chair next to her. The blanket was warm and now, with the door closed, the small stove warmed the room up nicely. "It's a bit of a story, but I'll tell you everything.

"Okay, so a few years ago, I worked for a man named Corbin Hansen of Marklyin. I was a bodyguard. It was an easy job, and the money was good. I had been really well-trained, and I needed work, so I figured it was a win-win. It wasn't even a few days into the job, and I started to realize what kind of man I was working for, what kind of monster he really was.

"I started to hear stories about what he had done. A couple weeks before I joined, he had killed an elfin family, leaving only the oldest son alive to watch as his little sisters were forced to feed a poison to their parents and then drink it themselves. Corbin did things like this for sport. He would take orphaned children and sell them as slaves, and nobody would dare stop him. I didn't think this was real until one day, a group of mercenaries he had hired brought in a prisoner. It had taken over twenty men to bring him in.

"He's still the most impressive man I've ever met. Six foot five, black skin, shaved head, brown eyes, a massive man. He wore all black, except for the inside of his cloak which was such a bright blue that it was hard to look at. They had him in large chains and weights on his feet. I stood my ground, knowing that I was supposed to protect Corbin if this man escaped. Then I learned who this guy was, and I knew at that moment that I would do everything to help him escape."

Barina interjected. "Berklion? He was captured at one point?"

Kevin nodded. "Yeah, I couldn't believe it. I knew the stories about him and how good of a man he was. I couldn't for the life of me figure out why he was there. I listened to the conversation carefully, and hearing that, well, it would change everything for me. It's how I would meet him and learn of you.

"Corbin laughed. I can't forget this conversation. I remember it word for word. 'Berklion, finally, I have you here, the great Berklion of Halk. Why have you been so insistent on killing me?' Berklion was pissed. 'You killed a family over a sword. You killed them over a goddamn sword! Adrian had told me about his confrontation with you the day before you had him killed. I had hoped they had just been thieves and murderers, but I did my research when I got back to this part of the world and learned it was you.'"

Barina's eyes widened, and she froze. Kevin knew what this story would do to her, but she deserved to know. He could tell she had never learned. He put a hand on hers, trying to be of some comfort as he continued.

"Corbin's smile went dark. 'I never did get that sword that I wanted. It was gone before my men could go back for it. I didn't realize you knew them. What of it? Why did it take you so long to try and avenge the death of a family that's all gone?' It was Berklion's turn to smile. 'You didn't kill the entire family. I was training his oldest daughter to become the most fierce and deadly warrior the world has ever known. I took her to continue her training. Both myself and my teacher worked to fine-tune her. Barina, the daughter of Adrian Raine of Miork, is unlike anything anyone has ever imagined. She will end evil like you if I don't.'

"I had never seen fear grow in the eyes of a man like I did in Corbin's face. I even saw him break into a sweat. 'Does she know about me?' Berklion had laughed. 'No, and pray that she never does.' Corbin had Berklion thrown into a cell that night. He was going to hang him the next day. Corbin had placed a dozen guards by his cell too.

"I knocked out every guard and opened the door, taking the chains off him. Told him I was there to get him out, and he thanked me. I led him out of the manor and away from Marklyin. I traveled with him till we arrived in Fortania, and then we went our separate ways. He told me all about you while we traveled. I kinda pestered him for information on you, if I'm being honest. I mean, come on, someone learning to fight under the greatest warrior of all time, and a woman, no less. I had to know who to look for if I ever saw you.

"He told me a lot about you—what you looked like, what kind of sword you carried and your dagger, your personality. When I met you in the forest not long ago, I recognized your fighting. I knew there was something familiar about you."

Kevin knelt down in front of Barina. He held both of her hands in his. "I knew it was you by the way you fought and how you acted, how you looked. What really hit me was when you told me you fight to protect those you love, Barina. I don't think you understand the power those words had on me. Since I learned about you from Berklion, I always hoped I would meet you. And when you dropped this…" He reached in his pocket and held out the pendant and ring. "It gave me a reason to track you down, even though I would've found another one."

Barina blinked as he put the jewelry in her hands. "This pendant had been Jason's, my best friend," she said, "and his fiancé's ring. I didn't realize they fell out of my pocket. Thank you. But Kevin, this story you just told me, I mean, what? Are you saying that my family was killed over a sword?"

Kevin nodded. "I had hoped that Berklion would've told you about Corbin. Obviously he hadn't, but yes, that's why they were killed. When I heard that story, Barina, I was done with that man. I had never wanted to put an end to someone so badly. I knew I'd have a better chance at it with Berklion. Plus, like I was gonna let the greatest warrior in the world be hanged. I didn't really think that he couldn't get out anyway, but it was probably smarter on my part to make friends with him."

Barina took a long deep breath, letting all of this sink in for a moment. "They were killed all because of a sword. While I'm glad that you and Berklion finished him, it should've been me."

Kevin couldn't hide the truth in his eyes.

"What aren't you telling me?" she asked, not angry or demanding.

"He's not dead, Barina." Kevin had no idea how to read the look in her eyes. "We went to kill him that night, but he had left for business. I'm sure he found out that Berklion was free, and so he never came back. We never learned where his safehouse was. We went looking for it, but he's still out there." He saw the light in her eyes change. "Are you going to go after him?"

Her eyes locked with his. "I don't know. It won't be until I'm done with this job. That's all I know. I wish Berk had told me all of this."

Kevin took a deep breath. "He said he had thought about it, but he didn't want you to fight for revenge. Thought you had been through enough, and he didn't want to burden you with that. If he had taken out Corbin, he was going to tell you everything, but not before. I know it weighed on his mind. I wouldn't be too hard on him."

Barina nodded. "I understand." So many emotions ran through her that she didn't know sure what to think. At the moment, she decided to push everything aside and sort them out later.

"You okay?" he asked. He saw the light change again to one of calm.

She nodded. "Yeah, I am. I'm glad you told me, and I'm grateful to you for helping Berklion. He raised me after my parents were killed." Her voice was barely audible.

They were quiet for a moment. When Kevin realized he was still holding her hands, he let go quickly, an apology in his eyes. Neither of them said anything while looking away from a very awkward moment.

A loud growl in Barina's stomach broke the silence, and her eyes went big, but Kevin just laughed.

Standing up, he said, "I'll make us something to eat, and I did promise you a tour. Come on."

Barina stood and cautiously followed him.

"This is my home." He flourished a hand around the room.

She snorted as she rolled her eyes.

Kevin's jaw dropped. "Did you just snort? Wow."

She shrugged it off. "It's one of my more endearing qualities."

He shook his head. "Go with that." Then he asked, "And what's the deal? Berk said you had a different sword than the one you're carrying."

"Oh, I have that one with me." She reached for her bag and took out her katana. "Yukinohana. Snowflower." She handed it to him so he could look at it better.

Kevin took hold of it, impressed, and unsheathed it. "Whoa." He seemed giddy. She took a few steps to the side, so he could move it about. She enjoyed watching him as he sliced the air with simple movements. He was very precise, and she could see even more now that he was extremely well-trained. He put the sheath back on the blade and handed it to her. "It's almost as impressive as the person who wields it."

Barina looked away while setting the sword back in her bag.

"When did you get the other one?" he asked, pointing to the one by her boots.

"I just got this. My friend Josh has been hanging onto this apparently since my family was killed. It was the last one that came from my dad's shop, made…"

Kevin blurted out, "He made it for you!" His eyes widened.

Barina read his thoughts. "Holy fuck! Do you think this is *the* sword? The one they were killed over?"

Kevin nodded. "If your dad wouldn't make one for him, he probably demanded this one. But what Berklion told me is that your dad wouldn't let him have any weapon from his workshop. My guess is that Corbin demanded this one, and your dad refused."

"I get why he refused," Barina said. "It was one thing to make weapons for someone who was working to protect. This guy, if dad knew about his reputation, he'd never make or give him a sword knowing what he'd do with it, how many people he'd kill with it." Barina wasn't sure how to process this.

"At least I know that Corbin will probably get that sword in the end," Kevin joked. "It'll be his ending."

Barina's eyes were amused. "Your jokes are as bad as mine." She scratched the back of her head. "But you have been helping me, so I guess I'll let it go."

He poked her nose. "It's appreciated. Come on, there's a lot more to this place than just this room."

Barina followed him out the door and saw that there was a wide deck that led to a set of stairs headed up above his treehouse. There were three different platforms built above the house—the branches and leaves trimmed to give him plenty of space.

"What on earth, this is amazing!" she breathed and went poking around.

On the lowest platform, a cover sheltered a small fireplace he had built out of rocks that served as an oven and a grill. Next to it sat a couple water barrels and a table with chairs. The other two platforms appeared to be for training. He had a set of weights, a bar for pull ups and, she saw, a couple of training dummies that had seen better days.

"Thanks. I spend a lot of time out here, even when it's cold. It's easier to cook out here. Keeps the smoke out of the room. And yes, I have thought about trees and cooking with fire. I have built and planned for it. With those two platforms, I can train by going between the trees and just practice in general." He headed over to the fireplace and quickly got a fire going. "I'm hungry. I have some fish up here that's been salted. Are you a picky eater?"

She shook her head and went to look around the platforms. Kevin set to making them something to eat. She studied the practice dummies and looked over the markings that were made. It told her a lot about his abilities and what he was able to do as a fighter. She could also see marks in the trees that showed where his chains had wrapped around. She felt sure he could hold his own with the very best of the best.

Kevin joined her on the platform with the practice dummies. "I take it you like it?"

"This is really neat. I'll have to show you my place back in Miork. I showed some of the guys I was traveling with the living area but not my training area."

"I thought you said that you were moving to Estella after this?" He was amused as he observed her checking every inch of the practice dummies.

"I am, but I'll keep my place in Miork too. It's a good safehouse. I've made some enemies over the years, some very powerful ones, and it'll be good to have a place to hide out if I need it. Plus, well, I really like my home there. Too bad I can't pick it up and move it, but caves are so immobile."

She inspected the dummies again, impressed. "You are a really gifted fighter. I think that if you and I had fought for real, not just in a duel like we had, I think…"

"You still would've kicked my ass."

She blushed. "Looking at all this, and from what I've seen, I'd put you right up there with Darien Bell of Treklea."

He inhaled, taking a step back. "That's one hell of a compliment. And coming from you, I'm humbled."

"Did you train with a master of the Willow?" she asked him. "Some of these hits look like it."

"Yeah, I did." He could hardly believe that she could pick out his style just from looking at the marks. "I was Master Franklin's last apprentice before he retired."

"You trained some with a couple other styles, too, but yeah, damn you're really good." She looked more closely at the marking on the dummies.

Kevin was speechless for a second before his own stomach growled. "Let's eat. You need to get your strength back."

She followed him to the fire where he had placed a couple of plates with grilled fish and veggies. They had a nice meal, sitting under the overhang by the fire. It was chilly but nice where they were, and she enjoyed his company. They talked about many things they had in common. He was very kind and caring, and he had a way of making her feel she had known him for years.

"What?" she asked at one point. She had to know what he was thinking.

"It's just, finally meeting you face to face, I'm still not over it. You're not what I expected," he said while he stood up to put the fire out.

"Oh." She wasn't sure how to take that.

With his back still turned, his attention on the fire, he added, "You are so much more, much better."

Barina smiled at that and stood up. "Thank you for that. Hey, where, um, I have to pee."

He pointed toward a set of stairs that led down and away from everything. "I actually kinda built an outhouse up here."

"Neat, be right back."

"Okay, I'm gonna head back in."

In the house, Kevin added more fuel to the stove and thought about this woman in his home. He had decided a while ago what he was going to do, and he knew their story was just beginning.

Barina came back inside and let out a yawn.

"What time did you want to be up in the morning? I figured we want to get an early start." Rubbing his eyes, he set to packing a traveling bag.

That got her attention. "We?" She put her hands on her hips.

"Yeah, we're going to Thoron, right?"

She glared at him. "Uh, no. *We* are not going to Thoron. You are not going anywhere near this."

He didn't stop what he was doing. "Sure I am."

"What makes you think you're coming with me?"

His answer was simple. "Because I am."

"You don't even understand why I'm going or what I have to do, how incredibly dangerous it is."

He tied up his pack and stood in front of her, his eyes studying hers. "Then tell me, and let me decide for myself."

Her eyes refused to give away her real emotions, the wall came up quickly. Barina studied him for a moment. There wasn't a part of her that didn't trust him, and she would be lying to herself if she said she didn't want his company, but she didn't want him to get hurt.

"I have to go to Thoron to retrieve the Anna Stone that was taken from my kingdom," she said. "It was stolen and given to King Toler. If I'm able to, after getting the stone, I need to dispose of Toler as well. He's a tyrant, a monster, and he must be stopped. I've already had to confront his son. Ken took Jason, the original owner of the pendant, he took Jason and his fiancé Tyra from me. He took them from me, and I killed him for it, so there's every possibility that Toler will know that someone is coming for him. It's going to get very dangerous once I get into Thoron. I'll have to be on high alert the whole time.

"So, there you have it. I have to infiltrate a palace, steal back what's been taken, and kill a king. I don't have to kill the king, but I know what he is, and he must be stopped. Oh, and he has a dragon, Uraki, with him too, and I'll probably have to deal with him."

Kevin listened to her, his mouth open the whole time. "Holy shit. That's pretty heavy."

Barina seemed relieved that he quickly grasped the seriousness of what she was doing. "So, you see why you need to stay here."

His expression softened. "I do, I get it." He pulled a stray leaf out of her hair.

"Thank goodness," she whispered.

"Still doesn't answer my question." He went back to packing his bag. "What time are we leaving in the morning?"

"Are you kidding me?"

"I can hold my own, and if this is gonna be as dangerous as it sounds, an extra set of eyes and an extra sword might not be a bad thing." He tied his bag. "That should be everything that I need."

"You barely know me. Why would you want to risk yourself for this?"

"I'm not entirely sure," he said, thinking about it. "Part of it has to do with, well, since I heard about you from Berklion, I've wanted to meet you, to fight alongside you. There's that, and I know how bad Toler is, how much pain that kingdom has been in since he took to the throne after his father died. And let's be real, we all know he killed his father."

"I appreciate that you want to fight alongside me and that you understand how dangerous and terrible Toler is, but this isn't your fight." She was desperately trying to keep him safe.

"Why not? It should be everyone's fight. The people of Thoron are terrified. He is so powerful in magic, might, and his damn forces that most have not dared to confront him. People have tried, I know that there have been wizards and warriors who have fought him and…"

"And they all lost." She was firm.

"But it's different with you. I don't know how it is, but it is. The air, it feels different this time, and all of my instincts are telling me that I need to be there with you."

Barina grabbed her cloak and reached for her boots.

Kevin crossed his arms. "I was able to track you before, I'll be able to do it again. What makes you think I won't just head to Thoron myself and wait for you by the palace?"

Barina wanted to pull out her hair. "Fine." She grabbed one of the ropes on the table and, in a heartbeat, she tied him up sat him in the chair.

Kevin said, teasing, "Bondage is okay with me. Is there a safe word?" He didn't struggle to get free. That should have been Barina's first clue.

"Cute," she said. "Maybe when I get back. This should hold you till morning at least. I'll cover my tracks to the point you can't find me. When I get done in Thoron, I'll find you, but you need to stay back."

She turned and grabbed her boots again.

"It's really sweet that you're this concerned about me. To be fair though," Barina was not expecting to feel Kevin's hand on her shoulder, "that concern goes both ways." Kevin stood close to her, the rope she had used tossed behind him.

"How…whoa." She was both at a loss for words and impressed.

He poked a finger to her nose again. "Not to brag, but I've always been a pretty good escape artist." He placed his hands in his pockets. "Do you really not want anyone, not want me, to go with you?"

"It's not that I don't want you there. I do, I just…damn it, Kevin, too many people." Her voice was quiet and her eyes began to show fear.

He was starting to break through the mask that hid her emotions, and he finally saw what was going on. Kevin studied her eyes more intently. Very gently, he touched a hand to hers. "Barina?"

There was no use in hiding what happened. She told him everything about her traveling companions, about Jason and Tyra, and how it nearly broke her.

Kevin listened carefully, and when her story was done, he looked at her with the deepest sympathy. "I'm so sorry. I wish, I wish there was something I could do."

"The pendant and ring that you brought me, they were Jason and Tyra's. If something happened to you too." He could see fully the worry in her eyes. "I don't know if I could handle it."

His smile was soft. "I understand."

She nodded and breathed a sigh of relief. "You'll stay then?"

He shook his head. "Not a chance."

"But you said you understood."

"And I do. But I still can't sit back and do nothing. So, I hope you don't mind some company." He was calm and kind with his words.

Barina laughed to herself. "Damn it." Her eyes held Kevin's. "My company could be worse, I guess." She nudged his arm and set her boots back down and hung up her cloak. "Not sure how, but it could be worse."

Kevin started laughing. "Cute." His laugh turned into a yawn. "I am exhausted. How about we get some sleep? Will you close the door? It's gotten pretty chilly out there. And don't turn around till I tell you. I'm changing."

Barina closed the door and waited for a couple minutes. "Okay." When she turned, she saw Kevin was shirtless and wearing a pair of baggy pants to sleep in. He was lying on the only mattress in the room. She knew it was innocent, but she still appreciated the view.

Kevin rested on his side, propping his head up on an arm and posing. "I know you want this body," he said, waving his free hand over himself, "but you will have to do all the work. I am just too damned tired. And do be gentle. I'm delicate."

"Oh my god!" She could hardly stop laughing. "Keep dreaming."

He covered himself up with the blanket. "Trying to take advantage of a sweet, innocent man like me."

"Shut up and turn around while I change." Barina was not used to having someone give her a run for her money, but she got a kick out of his sense of humor.

Kevin turned to face the wall. He turned back around when he felt the blanket move. Barina wore a pair of baggy-short pants and a comfortable-looking shirt. She climbed under the blankets next to him.

"If you're not comfortable with me next to you," he said quietly, "I have a hammock I can get out." Barina could hear sleep already taking him.

"Don't worry about it," she whispered, watching his eyes close. In the next couple of moments, he was sound asleep.

Barina normally had a hard time falling asleep, but for some reason, with him there, she closed her eyes and fell asleep quickly.

* * *

Kevin woke up early the next morning and looked at Barina curled up next to him. One of her hands rested on his arm, and her forehead touched his shoulder. She looked very peaceful, so he moved carefully so as not to wake her. He threw on a shirt, a pair of warm pants, and his boots and jacket. He lit a small fire in the stove to warm the room for Barina.

He grabbed Barina's boots and headed outside and up to the first platform. He lit a second fire and set a kettle on to boil, and then started to work breakfast.

Kevin had never met anyone who had this kind sway over him. He had always wanted to meet her, ever since Berklion told him about her, that was true. How could he not? She was trained to fight by both Berklion and his teacher. And she learned to fight for the best of reasons—to protect those she loved and those who couldn't protect themselves. She was orphaned but never lost her heart, or even her smile it seemed. Berklion had talked her up quite a bit while they traveled together. He began to wonder if every blonde woman he came across was her, to watch for signs. Kevin always figured that Barina would become someone important to him—a team member, a friend—but he didn't think he'd feel so deeply for her.

Or did he? He was partially terrified when he first realized who she was. He hadn't known how much he had anticipated this, and now that he had met her, she wasn't what he had expected. She was much shorter than he thought she'd be and unassuming. He never expected her to fight the way she did. This was the first woman he had taken an interest in since Berklion told him about Barina, and it made him happy to know that this woman just happened to be her. He would've come after her to give back the pendant anyway.

The fact that she was unassuming and not what he had expected made her more than he could've imagined. It was her heart—the love she had for the people in her life—that warmed his own heart most of all. She was funny too—quick with a joke or a pun that kept him on his toes. Kevin was very glad that she was now a part of his life, even if it was for this short time while they traveled together. If he played his cards right, who knew what would happen?

He wasn't lost in his thoughts long before Barina sauntered onto the platform. He was impressed with the level of bedhead this girl had. Wrapped in her cloak, her eyes were only half opened as she rubbed the sleep out of them. She didn't even acknowledge him as she walked past him to use the toilet.

He set out their plates and piled on the eggs, sausages, bread, and the cups of tea as she came back and sat down in front of him.

"Not a morning person, I take it?" he asked quietly.

She let out a yawn before taking a bite of her eggs, her eyes still mostly closed.

"I'll remember that."

"Thank you for breakfast," she mumbled. The only visible part of her from the neck down was her right arm as she used it to hold her fork. "Did you take my boots?"

"Sorry." He turned a little red. "Didn't want to chance you bailing on me again. So, I took precautions."

"Smart, I wasn't going to leave, but that's smart. Still…"

Kevin jumped when he felt something icy on either leg.

"My feet are cold," she said.

He immediately put his cloak over his legs. "I think you froze my legs off."

She stuck her tongue out at him, satisfied, and went back to her eggs.

After breakfast, they finished getting ready. When they headed out the door, Barina looked down for a moment. "Soooo, how do we get down?"

He pointed to a rope ladder that folded over itself, and then he pushed it over the edge. "Follow me."

As they climbed down, she couldn't believe how high up they were. She could hardly see the forest floor. At the bottom, Kevin pulled what looked like a length of ivy, and the ladder raised back up about half-way. Wrapping the ivy back around the tree, he adjusted his traveling pack and looked at Barina. "Ready?"

She nodded. "You sir, are one smart cookie. I'm really impressed with everything you've done with your home."

"Thank you. We'll probably camp out for a good portion of the next few weeks, but I do have a couple of little safe houses, and there is the outpost where we can crash for a night too."

"Sounds good."

He adjusted the pack on his back. "Lead the way."

CHAPTER 15

Over the next couple of weeks, the traveling group was thankful for the peace, and even more thankful that they came across a small inn still a week outside of Thoron. The weather was getting cooler by the day, and the nights were cold.

Barina and Kevin continued to follow about a half mile back, keeping an eye out for trouble. Barina reassured him that, with the likes of Jaras, Onyx, and Arkon, they would be plenty safe. She kept an eye out for impending danger they wouldn't realize otherwise.

"You did warn them about this inn, didn't you? About what can happen there?" Kevin couldn't believe the travelers were planning on staying the night.

Her face turned red. "It might've slipped my mind."

He tried not to laugh, but he couldn't help it.

"To be fair, I haven't spoken with them since the Green Forest. They'll be okay. And I'm not going near that place. It gives me the creeps." She looked up at a window and saw Jaras looking back at her. "They're all set here. Let's go."

Kevin tugged on one of her braids a little. "Finally, something in this world makes you uncomfortable. I'll keep that in mind."

"Not just uncomfortable. Like, literally freaks me out. I can stop in for a bite to eat, but I'd be out before the sun goes down." She kept her voice light, but he could tell just how serious she was.

Kevin's smile was gentle. "Really freaks you out that much, doesn't it?"

There was no apology or embarrassment in her eyes. "I wouldn't stay there even if I was with them. Did you want to head to the outpost a couple miles that way? I need to pick up a couple things."

"Sure. Mags, her cooking is the best." Kevin's eyes looked in the distance, hopeful.

"I love Mags! Oh and Milo, her husband. They're both just good people."

"What are the chances we know the same people?" he asked. "Though you do travel a lot, so I'm not *that* surprised. Come on, let's go. Oh, and don't worry. I have a safe house not far from here if we don't stay at the outpost."

"Excellent."

While Barina and Kevin headed for the outpost, the travelers went into the inn. It was warm and relaxing, with only a handful of people there. The fire crackled happily, and the food smelled great.

"Welcome, how can we help you today?" a cute young woman came into view from the kitchens. "Were you needing a room for the evening?"

"Yes please," Twarence said. "Your inn is pretty far off the beaten path. Is this the only inn in the whole Forest of Lithor?" he asked while lighting up a smoke.

"The one and only. I'm Anna. My family runs this inn. If you need anything, please let us know. We have a room with enough beds to suit everyone in your party unless you would like two rooms."

"One room for all of us together, please. What's on the menu today?" Jaras could hear his stomach growling.

"We have barley soup, roasted beets and carrots, fresh bread, and chestnut pies. Just a moment and we'll have someone take you to your rooms." Her smile seemed to light up the room. "Excuse me."

Anna went into the kitchen and, a moment later, a man walked into the room carrying a load of firewood. He was tall with a large beard, kind eyes, and nodded to them when he saw them. "Be right with you." He set the firewood down and walked over. "One room for all of you?" he asked. "Just for tonight?"

They nodded before following him up the steps.

The room was small but cozy and warm, with six twin beds that looked very inviting. Arkon lit the wood stove, and it didn't take long for the chill from outside to dissipate.

"I'm Arnold. Hope you like your stay here. I'll have Mary and Josh bring some water to the bathing rooms so you can wash yourselves if you'd like."

"Thank you," Aria said. "I know I could use one for sure."

"Take your time, and we'll be downstairs whenever you're ready for dinner. Let us know if you need anything." Arnold left them alone. They set their bags on the beds, and each of them let out a sigh, excited to finally have a night in a bed and not on the road.

"Know anything interesting about this place?" Aria directed the question to the scholar while she hung her traveling cloak on a peg on the wall.

"I feel like Barina told me something, but I can't remember what." He scratched his beard and reached into his bag for a clean shirt, heading behind the changing screen.

"She always had vital information and plenty of useless but fun facts about the places we were going and what to expect." Aria looked at the ground, her smile fading. "I miss her."

Onyx put a hand on her shoulder. "We all miss her, and who knows, maybe someday we'll be able to make amends. She seems the type to be willing to give a second chance." He was trying to keep their spirits up. "I'm worried, even with Jaras, Arkon, and myself, how we're going to fair when going up against Toler, though. Aria, you're going to be more vital than you can imagine. I know that we're going to sustain heavy injuries."

Aria nodded. She was still so filled with guilt, and she was ashamed of how smitten she had been with Ken and how he had made her act. She knew he had manipulated her the easiest. "I still can't believe that Ken, no, Trekenler, was Toler's son, and that…he took Jason and Tyra from her. I mean, there was nothing left of them." Aria tried to hold back tears. "Couldn't even bury them."

"At least she killed that bastard," Arkon growled. He had more resentment than anyone about what happened. "If I had only listened to her. God, this is all my fault." He couldn't hold back his tears. "I was proud and judgmental, and it's all my fault." He wanted to put those feelings aside, but it was so difficult.

"You didn't betray us," Twarence told him. "You didn't take them away, you didn't try to kill everyone in this room. It wasn't you."

"No, but I influenced everyone into betraying her, turning their backs on her, and she still came to our rescue. To my rescue. She knew what she was doing. I don't know if you guys saw it, the look her and Jason gave each other at the end. It was Jason telling her to make the move she did, the one that would save us and not them. He knew he was probably going to die. They knew what was about to happen, and they still…" Arkon's sobs kept him from speaking further.

"She fights to protect those she loves," Twarence said, "and to destroy the wicked. Trekenler was just as evil as his father. Jason and Tyra knew he had to be destroyed, and they also knew that we are key in defeating Toler. They knew the stakes were high." Twarence was trying to reason with him, but it didn't do much.

Onyx finally spoke up. "She knew Ken had messed with your minds. She knew it. It's not you, Arkon. Barina knows full well it was all Ken's doing. She just needs some time."

It had been hardest on Arkon. He had waves of guilt and remorse for how he had treated her and for his lack of trust. It took the better part of a half hour for Arkon to calm down before they left to eat.

What Barina had left them with, though, was information. Thankfully, she had told Twarence a lot about what to expect when they came to Thoron itself. They were making plans and going over them again and again as they traveled through the forest. They felt they would have a good chance of succeeding in this mission.

What Jaras and Onyx wouldn't tell them was that Barina still tailed them, was still with them. Jaras had spotted her. He knew that she allowed it. If she didn't want to be seen, she wouldn't be. He knew there had been times where she had fought off danger. He could just sense it, and he knew that she was still planning on doing her part. He wondered who the guy was that seemed to now be with her. Most of all, he knew she still cared for them all.

Jaras and Onyx would both see her. And there were times, like now, when the others were hurting because of her absence, and Jaras wished he could clue them in. While he looked out the window, he saw Barina and her traveling companion looking up at the inn. She caught a glimpse of him in the window, and then walked away. That meant that Barina was satisfied that they were safe, and she was taking care of other matters.

"Arkon," Jaras sighed. "Barina and Jason fought to give us a chance to recover the Anna Stone and destroy Toler. Don't think for one second that the three of them would do that differently." It was the first time he had addressed the elf on the issue since it happened. He missed his fellow warrior, that was no secret. He had been angry, very angry about what had happened. He had spoken with Arkon about trivial matters, but not about that night.

They all took time to bathe and change into clean clothes before they headed down to the dining room. They sat at one of the tables closest to the fire and welcomed the warmth.

"What can we get for you tonight?" Arnold asked, walking over to them.

"Well, Anna told us that you had some stew tonight, right?" Aria asked with a yawn.

Arnold blinked and held his breath for a moment, then he nodded slowly. "Sure do."

"I think we'll all take that, some bread, and some wine if you have any." Jaras lit up a cigarette.

Onyx and Arkon both got a chill and shivered in their seats.

"Do you feel that?" The wizard looked at Arkon with a feeling of unrest.

Arkon's eyes said it all. "How did we miss it when we got here?"

"What is it?" Jaras asked.

"I didn't feel it, but I saw the look in the innkeeper's eyes just then," Twarence said quietly. "Something's off."

Arkon closed his eyes, reaching his senses out farther. "There's a chill in the air, and not from the weather." He tilted his head, feeling more. "There's something here that shouldn't be here." His tone was hushed. "It doesn't feel dangerous. It's just, I think this place might be haunted."

"I feel it too," Onyx agreed. "Like he said, though, it's not a malicious spirit, but it's here. Nothing to be concerned about really." Onyx pulled his robes tighter. "I'm surprised we just felt it now."

Arnold came back with a tray full of glasses and some fresh bread for them to share. "Stew is being fixed up right now."

"Sir, may I ask," Twarence began, curious, "the look you had when we mentioned Anna. What was that about?"

Arnold sighed. "Probably won't believe me."

"Try us. These two both feel something. Is there a connection to that?"

Arnold sat down with them at the table and nodded. "Anna. There's nobody alive by that name living in this inn. She is, however, an ancestor of mine whose family did own the inn years ago. Thankfully, she's very kind, but rarely does she show herself when it's still light out, which means she must like you. She really likes children and animals. Always did, and if she sees someone who is troubled, she'll comfort them.

"One night a year though, on the night she died, she wails in agony and despair. She was supposed to have a grand life. She married a king, gave birth to three children, a boy and two girls, then she was killed when the powers the king held went rogue one night."

Everyone's eyes went wide. Aria almost dropped her glass, while the glasses Onyx had taken off to clean fell to the floor.

"Do you mean Anna?" Twarence asked. "THE Anna, the wife of King Theodore, the founding king of Larindana?" He could hardly say the words.

Arnold nodded, impressed. "You know your history. Yes, she's the same. They say the king roamed the old castle in Fern up until about ten years ago. Anna though, I wish she could rest, too. I would like to see her go home."

"You said she doesn't always show herself. Does she see everyone here?" Onyx asked.

"No. She sees my son, or did, but he might be too old for her to see him now. She can see children and some travelers for whatever reason." Arnold looked up. "I understand if you don't want to stay here tonight."

"We'll be okay. We were just curious." Twarence let out a long breath. "Tonight is that night, isn't it?"

"Yeah, that's why I wouldn't be upset if you decided to leave," he told them. "If not, then make sure you're in your rooms and stay there from eight till at least four in the morning. She won't go into the rooms, but she'll wander the grounds and the common areas. She sees everyone at that time, and she does not look like the beautiful and charming woman you saw earlier. She looks like she did when she was killed, and it's not a pretty picture. I've tried to talk with her a couple times, tell her where she is, what happened, but she doesn't understand. She simply wants to find her husband and her children, and to have the pain stop." Arnold sighed again while he stood up. "I hope she does find peace someday. Anyway, I'll go check on your dinner."

He stood up and left the group to themselves.

"Explains why she can see us." Onyx gave a little grin.

They all smiled. "Given our mission, that'd be a safe bet. Might be hard to sleep tonight if she's wailing." Jaras couldn't help but smile.

"I can put up a barrier so it'll keep the noise out," Arkon told him. "Look."

They glanced out the window and saw her. They saw Anna. She smiled and watched the birds with a peaceful gaze. She looked so incredibly kind and sweet. They really did hope that one day she would find peace.

Twarence had something else on his mind, something about the whole situation that made the loss of their thief even more dire than before. "I had forgotten about this until recently," he said. "Ten years ago, Barina, Jason, Josh, and Berklion all came to visit the university at Fern where I was studying. I was there. I met them. We hung out, and they were a lot of fun. Berklion had to speak with Julius, my teacher, about some things, and the night they stayed there, from what Julius said, the ghost of King Theadore did appear to Barina and her friends.

"The old palace was turned into a university when they built the new palace. And it was true, the king did haunt that place. I never saw him, but plenty of the workers and scholars had. I guess, after that night, when he went to see Barina and her friends, he never roamed the halls again, his spirit was at peace. Something about that meeting—something about meeting them—it put his mind at ease."

"Well, he was meeting three people being trained by Berklion," Aria mused. "That would be enough to put anyone at ease. Knowing that there are three others who can take on the evil of this world when needed." She took a big drink. "This is great wine."

"Has everyone here, did all of you guys meet her too when you were younger?" Twarence finally asked.

"She came in once with hypothermia and a broken leg," Aria said. "It was about ten years ago. Her sister had been kidnapped by trolls and, when Barina caught up to them, she killed the trolls. But they had thrown her sister into the river, so she dove in. It was winter, and she didn't even think twice. Berklion brought her in with her father, your teacher Jaras, her sister, as well as Jason and Josh." Aria looked thoughtful. "She didn't remember meeting me. She wouldn't, she was unconscious, but Jason and I talked about it. I healed her leg, and my aunt took care of the hypothermia."

"Berklion brought them to the Hitum Mountain twice," Onyx told them. "Once, just so they could meet us. We had dinner. Josh wanted a plate of garlic, and Barina and Jason requested desserts. I obliged. Also might've made them levitate."

"Levitate? How'd that go?" Arkon was grinning.

"Jason and Barina were not phased at all. Josh freaked out. They came there again to take a portal to Treklea after her family was killed. I really liked them even then." Onyx thought fondly of the memory.

"I'm pretty sure I met them once," Arkon spoke up. "They were in the Forest of Elves, and my friends and I came by three youths who we thought were dead. I poked them with a stick. Nope, they were alive. They tried to practice speaking our language, and didn't do a bad job either. That was a little over ten years ago or so."

"I just don't remember…" Jaras scratched his brain.

Twarence threw his hands in the air. "Seriously, how do you not remember? Barina was waiting for you to pick up and remember, but seriously? You got to know her, the guys, and Berklion for three weeks after her family died. Berklion and Darien are best friends. They were at Darien and Kate's wedding, for crying out loud."

Jaras's mouth fell open before he leaned forward shaking with laughter.

"He remembers," Aria said, laughing at herself now.

"That funny?" Arkon laughed at Jaras' reaction.

"She always did like the waltz." Jaras was shaking, he was laughing so hard. "How did I *not* pick up on this?"

They tilted their heads, all curious to know more.

"She kicked my ass in the sparring ring, twice! The first time she sparred with me was because Darien insisted that, just because my opponent is a girl, I should never underestimate her. She told me then that fighting was like a dance, and she liked the waltz. The second time, well, let's just say, I didn't really like her for the first few days I knew her. I hated the idea that I was beaten by a girl. My pride got the best of me, especially since I knew she wasn't fighting as hard as she could. I harped on her for another match, but she kept refusing. Jason and Josh offered, but I wanted to fight her. Finally she accepted, pissed off, and she took me down with one freaking move. I was even more angry and tried to continue to fight her after she used that one move. Before I could draw my sword again, she landed one hell of a right hook on my jaw." He felt his face. "Girl can throw a nasty punch. But after that, we became friends. I don't know why I didn't remember that till now." Jaras felt his face even more. "Damn, it still hurts when I think about that punch. I deserved it."

It was the first time in weeks they shared a genuine laugh with each other.

"I never would've pictured you as anything else than the mild-mannered and calm person we know," Aria said, beaming, and just as amused as the others by this information.

"Oh no. I had a hell of an ego about myself. Darien had squashed that out of me after I started my training, and anytime it would surface. I had been doing well, but then she showed up. The idea of a girl being better than me, that a girl was being trained by Berklion even, how could he be wanting to train a freaking girl?" Jaras' eyes lit up when he saw the stew. "I'm starving. But yeah, I couldn't handle that idea and Darien decided to have her knock me down a few pegs. I got rid of that ego completely after all that."

Arkon laughed hard. "I would've loved to have been a bug on the wall."

"So she and the boys really had a visit from the ghost of the king?" Arkon found that tidbit fascinating. He leaned in to hear more.

Twarence nodded. "They did. Julius and Berklion saw him that night after he had been to see the boys. Julius said the king went to Barina first, and then she bolted from her room and ran to stay with Jason and Josh. They woke up again later with his ghost standing in front of them. He spoke to them. I don't know much of the conversation, but I know that he touched a finger to each of their foreheads. When they woke up, they saw they had some kind of marking on their backs, just below the base of their necks." The scholar scratched his beard. "I can't remember what, an animal."

Jaras, his eyes wide, hissed, "A dragon."

Twarence snapped, "Yes, thank you. A dragon that has features that resemble a turtle."

Jaras froze hearing this. His hand was shaking and he dropped his spoon. "The hell?"

"What? What's so important about that?" Aria yawned, trying to stay awake.

"It's just, I thought it strange that she had that small silver dragon with blue eyes on her back, on that spot when I saw it. Just below the nap of her neck. A warrior would have to be really stupid or really sure of themselves to get a tattoo like that. Are you telling me, that's not a tattoo? I saw the same marking on Jason, but it was a gold dragon with green eyes. I figured they were tattoos. Now you're telling me this. Holy hell."

"Apparently. Why?" Twarence burned with curiosity, and so did the rest of the party.

Their guardian took off his glasses and rubbed a hand over his face. "Stars above, she can't?" Jaras took a moment to compose himself. The group had never seen him come close to losing his cool, not like this.

"Jaras, what's going on?" Aria leaned closer.

Jaras kept his hand over his face. "Onyx or Arkon, put up a sound barrier."

Onyx waved a hand, putting up the barrier.

Jaras shook his head as he put his glasses back on and lit a cigarette. "There are stories about what I'm going to tell you that've been written down in only a handful of manuscripts. Every warrior that's been in the game, even if they weren't formally trained, hears some version of them. I've heard some, and I've read some of the manuscripts.

"There's tales of a handful of warriors who are gifted, either by birth or magic, with a small dragon marking on the base of their neck. It's not clear if it's really a dragon, but that's the closest thing they resemble. The markings have a unique gift and abilities that can be tapped into when the need is greatest. The warriors will gather all of the energies around them, and those close by will feel the air pressure change, and the warrior will change, tapping into their full potential.

"Their eyes will glow a brilliant shade of purple and, for a short time, they become unstoppable. The only thing they can't completely fight against is magic. But might is no match for them. That part is a legend with all warriors.

"The second half is a myth, and I say that because there have been accounts of elder retired warriors who have claimed to have seen those with purple eyes. The *myth* is that there are those who are so powerful that, when they channel all of their energy, not only will their eyes go purple but their hair will change to blue. This makes them invincible to might and magic both. The darker the color of blue, the stronger the resistance to magic. There have only been pictures drawn, and no first-hand accounts in over two hundred years.

"Darien—now that I'm remembering her and I met—told me about Berklion's students having those marks. But I didn't think anything of it.

314

Not until I saw it on her in the steam caves and caught a glimpse of one on Jason. I'd bet money that Josh has one too." Jaras started laughing, "She just might be one of the warriors with the purple eyes."

They sat with their mouths open, unable to completely believe this.

"That's not a real thing," Aria finally blurted out.

Arkon sat back. "I mean, how can a mortal have magic if they haven't trained to become a witch or wizard? Yes, some have a natural spark of magic that's stronger than others to work, but most have to learn it from nothing. Could they still be considered mortal at that point?" The elf was curious about how this worked.

"They're mortal." Onyx took a long drink. "Wizards know about these tales. I've met with three different wizards who saw the same person whose eyes changed. The wizards were able to project their memories so that we could all see the person. That warrior didn't survive after the transformation."

Twarence nodded. "That part of the tale is also used as a warning to those who might carry that gift. They won't survive if they use it."

Jaras wiped sweat from his brow. He held his cigarette in his mouth while he spoke. "Right. That kind of energy gathered by a mortal will turn in on the person. They'll be their most powerful, but for a price. Those who have the mark, most of them learn what it means. They also understand what could happen if they become strong enough to tap into that." Jaras put his smoke out in the ashtray. "It takes time for them to gather their powers like that. Which is probably why we didn't get to see Jason use it in the caves. I also don't know if his abilities were at that level yet."

"What about B? Do you think hers are?" Aria sipped her wine. This information was fascinating, but she couldn't think about Barina losing her life.

"I don't know," Jaras said. "I fully believe that she has the potential to do it someday. I just don't know if she's at that level now. I haven't seen her fight enough to make that assessment." He took a long pull on his drink. "Holy shit. I never thought I'd have the possibility of seeing this in my life."

"Let's talk about something else. I can't think of her getting hurt." Arkon's face had paled. "We need to plan what to do once we're in Thoron."

Onyx's expression seemed to match the elf. "How much longer till we get there?"

"Probably going to be about another two weeks," Twarence said, "and it shouldn't be too bad on the way there, honestly. We'll have the look of travelers, obviously, so we'll be able to blend in. I have the names of a couple of inns that don't ask questions. B told me the best ones to stay at. I have blueprints of the palace—one of the few things I was asked to bring on this assignment. There's a list of the best ways to get in and around.

"The stone, when it gets there, is going to be in one of three places. The most obvious would be on or with Toler himself, and then we'd have to find him. From what I understand, he spends most of his time in the throne room or his war room. He likes to look over his kingdom and practice his powers.

"One of the other places would be in the vault which is just beyond the throne room. The passage to it is literally a door in the ground behind the throne itself. There are spells on it that are some of the most nasty and dark magic known." Twarence took a piece of paper from his pack and showed it to the magic men.

Arkon and Onyx took one look and both inhaled sharply.

"Spirits above!" Arkon hissed.

"This is…" Onyx had to hide his unease. "This is some of the darkest stuff I've ever seen. These are some of the spells he used on me and Rutherford when we were there, when Rutherford was killed. I can counter them, but it won't be easy. But I can break those spells."

"Good to know." Twarence lit a smoke for himself. "And the third most likely place the stone could be is…"

Aria cut in. "Let me guess. With Uraki."

Twarence nodded and looked to Arkon. "Do you think you can handle him?"

"Going up against a dragon doesn't happen often, and Uraki is a rare case. He's just a terrible being. Dragons on the whole, they're kind and keep to themselves. He's been out for blood for the last four or five years, and when he met Toler a few years ago, he got a pretty sweet deal. But, I'm able to tame the Comuhing, so who knows? Maybe I can do some work there." Arkon grunted. "When we get to Thoron, I'd like to have a few hours to prepare myself for this. It's going to take a hell of a lot of energy out of me. I don't think I can tame him or bring him down. I doubt even my king could do it, but I think I could immobilize him long enough for us to be able to slay him or do some serious damage."

They all nodded.

"I think we're all going to need to prepare for it," Onyx agreed.

"And I'll want to scope out the area," Twarence said, lighting up another smoke. "We'll make sure we give ourselves a good amount of time to get ready and to rest."

"I'll go with you when we check out the perimeter," Jaras told him. "His soldiers, the soldiers of Thoron, they're some of the best fighters that have ever been seen in our part of the world."

"I've heard stories about them as far away as Cirus." Aria looked into her wine glass. "From what I've heard though, a lot of them are fighting because they're forced to, not because they're loyal to him." Her eyes were worried. "I really don't want to hurt people who are being forced."

"We'll try to avoid as many casualties as we can," Twarence said, trying to reassure her, "but we may not have much choice in the matter either. Who knows, maybe they'll fight with us."

The group spent hours discussing what they would do once they came to Thoron and how they would arrive closer to the kingdom. They'd have to get their act and stories straight so as not to draw suspicion.

Finally, they headed up to their room and got ready for bed. Arkon and Onyx set up a barrier so that they wouldn't hear the wails from the spirit of Anna that evening. They were tired, and it didn't take long before they all fell asleep soundly and comfortably in their beds.

* * *

Barina and Kevin walked away from Jaras' sight. They made their way to the outpost not far from the inn. It would give them a chance to eat without having to hunt or forage, and they could pick up some supplies that they really needed.

"Did you want to see if Mags and Milo can put us up at the outpost tonight, or did you want to stay at the safehouse?" Kevin asked with a stretch. "Either way, it'll be nice to sleep under a roof tonight."

"Oh, I think the safehouse is fine. Besides, they don't have a lot of space."

"They're going to offer though. You know that, right?" He smiled thinking about the sweet couple that ran the outpost.

Barina was smiling too. "I know, but I hate to inconvenience them."

They found their way to a small, two-story building. The ground level was a shop where people could buy or trade for goods as well as get a bite to eat. The shopkeeps lived upstairs.

As they walked in, the bell above the door dinged, and it felt good to get in from the chill.

"Hello!" Barina called to the room.

"Barina, is that you?"

A woman walked out from the back room. She was petite—not much taller than Barina—with long, dark hair which she had in a bun. Her eyes were dark brown and friendly. She was about fifty years old, and everyone who came through here saw her as a kind, motherly woman.

"Hi Mags!" Barina smiled brightly.

"Milo! Come out. Barina is here and...oh Kevin, Kevin is here too!" she called over her shoulder as she gave both of the visitors a big hug.

A tall and portly man came out of the back room. He had a thick, red beard, dark brown eyes creased with crow's feet from all the smiling he did. His red hair was now mixed with white. He looked from behind his glasses, and his face brightened.

He extended his hand to Kevin. "Kevin, how have you been?" He then hugged Barina. "And you, young lady, it's been a while. Are you two traveling together?" Milo and Mags were looking between the two.

"We happened to meet each other a while ago, and I decided to tag along with her." Kevin couldn't stop grinning. "We wanted to say hi and get some supplies."

"Are you hungry?" Mags asked. "I have some fresh bread and pheasant stew. The stew will be ready in about an hour, but come, I want to catch up." She started to pull Barina by the hand. "Come with me, dear, come on."

Barina gladly followed Mags to the kitchen, and Kevin stayed with Milo.

"So, are you and Barina, are you two an item now?" Milo asked as he followed Kevin toward the supplies.

Kevin's face went red. "Well, no. I mean, we've only known each other for a couple weeks really."

"Doesn't mean you don't like her." Milo waggled his eyebrows. "You two look good together. Just sayin'. They don't make women like her very often."

"I know that's for damn sure." Kevin looked in the direction of his thief. "She's something pretty special."

"What kind of supplies were you needing?" Milo asked.

"Dried food, extra pipe-tobacco, and her and I will need to make ourselves blend in more when we get to our destination. So I'll need to look through your clothing."

Milo held up a finger and went to get something. He came back with a small bag and, when he opened it and held out his hand.

Kevin raised an eyebrow. "You're kidding, right?"

"It's the easiest and most convincing disguise in the book," Milo told him simply.

"I'm gonna love the look on her face. Gonna wait to do this one," Kevin said, trying to hide his laugh. "You're probably right. Yeah, I'll get those too. How have you been, how have things been here?"

Milo nodded. "I'm well. Things here are pretty good for the most part. There were a lot of scouts coming through the area from Thoron. They don't say that's who they are, but I know scouts when I see them, and I know enough to know where they're from. Be careful with them. They've been a little rough with travelers."

Kevin nodded, "Good to know."

In the kitchen, Mags took Barina's bag from her and forced her to sit down at the table.

"How have you been doing, Barina? You look healthy, maybe a little tired, but that's just you traveling all the time I imagine."

Barina sat back, fully taking comfort in Mags' hospitality. "That pretty much sums it up. I'm doing well even with traveling as hard as I am. What about you, how are you?"

Mags took the lid off of the pot of stew to stir it.

"We've been keeping quite well, thank you." Her eyes darted from Barina to the front room of the shop. "How did you find Kevin? He's such a sweetheart. I've always hoped he would find a nice girl. Every time he's here, he'll help us out by chopping some firewood, doing some cleaning, or something, just a good man. Let me tell you, if I was a single woman, I don't care how much younger he is than me, I'd go after him in a heartbeat." Mags blushed thinking about him.

That got a huge laugh out of Barina. "I freaking love you Mags! We're not together like that, just traveling together. He's becoming kind of one of my favorite people though." Barina could feel her face heat up a little, feeling a rare touch of shyness.

"If you've made friends with him, he's the type to have your back till the very end." Mags obviously thought very fondly of the man Barina was traveling with.

"I've been learning that about him." Barina gave a little yawn.

"Still, I saw the way the two of you were looking at each other. I know there's something there. You like him, don't you?" Mags did her best to keep her voice down.

Barina looked down, trying to hide her blush, before she nodded. "I do."

Mags poured her a glass of wine and sat down. "Really? I've known you for a long time, and I've never heard you flat out admit it even to yourself, let alone anyone else."

She shrugged her shoulders. "He's different from any man I've ever met. Guy like him though, he could have any girl he wants. I doubt that I'm what he'd be looking for. He might not even be looking. Hell, I wasn't looking, and he just showed up in my life." She smiled at that thought. He did seem to appear out of thin air.

"In the time I've known him," Mags began, "which is almost as long as I've known you, I've never known him to even have a slight interest in anyone. He's never spoken about anyone anyway. I've only ever seen him in here with a couple of the guys from his group. If he's traveling with you, that says something."

Barina shook her head. "It's, well, it's kinda difficult to explain why he's with me. He met my teacher years ago, and Berklion told him about me. When I met Kevin, we kinda had a duel, and he remembered my style and some about me, so he tracked me down after."

Mags almost dropped her wine glass. "*You're* the girl he was telling us that was trained by Berklion? I never knew, otherwise I could've directed him toward you."

Barina looked up, curious about what Mags meant.

"Barina, he's waited a long time to meet you. No wonder he wants to follow you."

"Just cause of me being taught by Berk?"

Mags lightly tapped the top of Barina's head with a wooden spoon. "No silly. You're the woman he's dreamed about meeting for years. I'm sure he hasn't been disappointed."

Barina felt the shyness even more. "I don't know."

Mags touched a hand to Barina's shoulder. "You are always so confident about yourself with everything, why not about this?"

Barina tried to piece together the right words. "Just trying not to get my hopes up too much."

Mags nodded. She understood that.

Barina changed the subject. "How have the kids been?"

The two women sat talking for a little while before they were interrupted.

Kevin popped his head into the kitchen. "B, come help me?" He met her eyes.

Barina nodded and joined him in the other room.

"I'm pretty sure that I have most of the supplies we would need, but I wanted to double check if you needed anything else."

Mags waved her husband to her as soon as Barina and Kevin had their backs turned.

"What?" Milo asked while pushing a strand of hair behind his wife's ear.

Mags grabbed Milo's arm and squeezed it with excitement. "She's the girl that Kevin's always been talking about. The one who was taught by Berklion."

Milo got a big grin on his face. "What? Are you serious? He's mentioned wanting to find her for years, I can't believe it's Barina. He never did mention her name, though. I guess we never knew she was trained by Berklion."

"Wish he would've told us her name or that we knew she had been trained by Berklion. We could've maybe helped him track her down." Mags put her arms around Milo and smiled while she watched the two thieves talking to each other. "They're good together."

"There's definitely something there. I think they both realize how they feel for each other, just not sure about how the other feels for them."

Kevin stood close to Barina, their eyes meeting. He then leaned in and said something.

Barina glared before pushing him away. "Fuck off!"

Kevin laughed at both the joke he had made and at her reaction.

"She needs to work on her flirting," Mags said, rolling her eyes.

Milo tried to stifle his laughter. "I think it works for them though." He kissed his wife, "I'm gonna get a couple of the bathtubs ready for them. Even if they're not staying, I want them to relax a bit before dinner."

"Why don't you wanna go with that dress when we get to Thoron?" Kevin was still laughing. "I wouldn't argue."

"That's not a dress, that's not even a shirt." She threw the tiny corset and skirt back at him.

He caught it and set it down. "And the problem?"

"I also lack the cleavage to make that work for me." She started sifting through the other outfits.

He raised an eyebrow. "I'm not going to respond to that other than to say I think your proportions are perfect." He raised his hands indicating he was backing away from that topic. "I'm sure whatever you pick, it'll look amazing on you." He knelt down next to her. "By the way, Milo said that there have been scouts from Thoron in the area." He kept his voice quiet.

He saw her register that in her mind and nod slightly. "I'll just have to keep both my swords hidden if we see them. They wouldn't think twice about me carrying a dagger while traveling, even with a male companion." She was thinking out loud again. "Course, if they're good, we won't realize they're scouts." She met his gray eyes for a heartbeat. "It's all the more reason for us not to stay here tonight. I don't want to put those two at risk."

Kevin nodded his head slightly in agreement. "I'll let them know that we'll really have to leave before too long."

"Not before you both have had a bath and we've fed you," Milo said, walking over to them. "I have one of the bathing rooms prepared, the other will be shortly."

Kevin tugged on one of Barina's braids while winking at her. "You go ahead and use it. I'll get the other when it's ready." He walked to the back of the shop.

Barina found a simple dress that would work as they got closer to Thoron. A woman in pants wasn't normal there, and she didn't want to stick out. "This is pretty much everything," she told Milo.

"Barina, are you able to tell me what you're traveling for?" Milo asked when she got to the counter.

She shook her head. "All I can say is that I'm trying to make life better for a whole lot of people. This job is going to make a lot of things better, I hope."

He looked at her with his kind eyes. He knew that she was always on the go, trying to do work to help others. He also knew that she faced a lot of dangers while she was out there.

"Let's hope that you're able to." He then pointed. "Do you remember where the bathing room is?"

Barina nodded and handed him payment for their items. She had to admit, a bath sounded nice. She was tired, and she knew better than to turn down all of their hospitality. She didn't take long in the bath. They weren't going to have that kind of time. She scrubbed herself clean before climbing into the tub and soak only for a few minutes before she dressed and went to the kitchen.

"That didn't take long?" Milo looked up from his wine glass.

Barina shrugged. "It's just, I don't want to linger too long after we eat. If there are scouts around, no matter what we're doing, I don't want them to give you trouble for us being here."

Mags crossed her arms. "We can take care of them. Even they know better than to harass us."

"Easy dear." Milo touched a hand to her arm. "We have to let these two leave if they have to."

"When did Kevin start his bath?"

"He hasn't yet." Mags nodded her head toward the backdoor. "He's been out chopping firewood for us."

"We've always told him we don't need it, but he doesn't listen. Goes and does it anyway." Milo looked at Barina thoughtfully. "He cares about you, you know. Thinks very highly of you."

Barina looked down to hide her blush. "I'll tell him to bathe before dinner is ready."

"Tell him not to take long. Dinner will be ready soon." Mags smiled kindly.

Barina headed through the kitchen and out the back door where, sure enough, she found Kevin at the block, splitting firewood. He had a calm way about him as he swung the axe and stacked up the firewood. Kevin stopped when he saw her.

"Already get a bath?" He touched a finger to her wet hair. "Figured you'd take longer."

"Normally I would, but we can't be here too long. Why don't you get cleaned up?"

"Is dinner ready?" His question was simple.

"Almost."

He nodded and went to a barrel of water where he washed his hands off as best he could and used some to splash on his face.

"Sweet of you to chop this wood for them." Her tone was quiet.

"They're good people, always been very kind to me. I like doing something to help them out when I'm here."

She shook her head ever so slightly. "What kind of a thief are you? I had to stop you from robbing my friends but yet, here you are."

"Well, you know, I really only do that with groups who I think can afford to lose some gold. And we never take more than what we need. That was a special case. I let Truman decide who we were going to hit next. Didn't really want to, but hey, it led me to you. I don't steal from stores or businesses or homes, though." He thought about that again. "Well, can't say I haven't taken a couple of things here and there when we knew the ass had already taken it from someone else."

Barina raised her eyebrows. "So there's some reason."

Kevin opened the door for her and gave a little bow. "Yes and, as I said, it led me to you, so I'm okay with it."

Barina didn't have words for that, so she didn't respond.

"Hurry and clean up, Kevin," Mags said when she saw them. "Dinner should be ready pretty quick. I want you to have enough time to enjoy your food before you head out." Mags poured herself another glass of wine.

"Where'd you put my bag?" Kevin asked quietly.

"I think Milo put it in the room for you already."

"Do we have everything we'll need?" he asked Barina.

She nodded.

"Are you okay?" He touched her hand. "You're quiet."

She knew that her silence had always been a sign that she wasn't herself. "I'm just a little tired, that's all."

"Did you want to stay here tonight? We can. No sense in being exhausted."

She shook her head. "I'll be fine. I think I just need to eat. That'll help." She then looked down. He was still holding her hand. "You get your bath, stinky."

He mussed her hair and headed to the bathing room.

Barina went back outside to get some air and light her pipe. She was tired, yes, but she put her senses on high alert while they were at this outpost. She didn't feel anyone near, nor could she hear anything. She closed her eyes and listened. Birds chirped, and a squirrel jumped from one tree to another. A nearby stream gurgled in the distance. Nobody was in that area either. They were safe for now.

It wasn't long before she heard, even from outside, Kevin's footsteps walk into the kitchen. She could hear Mags pour him a glass of wine and hand it to him, and him say thanks. Barina heard the lid of the stew pot come off and a few seconds later, smelled the savory scents it carried.

She stood up and headed back inside, her stomach rumbling.

Kevin watched her while he tried to piece her together. For the most part, she was an open book. She was funny, and they both had great stories to share from their travels. They shared a lot of the same views. He was drawn to the side that was just her, not a warrior. Just a woman who was passionate about the things she loved in life and didn't take little things for granted. He often caught her enjoying the feel of the breeze, the sun shining on her skin, or the colors of the leaves that were changing with the season. It was as if these things charged her. She sought beauty in the world around her. Even if it was as simple as a leaf, she cherished it.

Then there were moments like this, where she would say she was tired, and that was true. He also knew that she wasn't telling him everything. Sometimes it was because she didn't know how to word what she was feeling. Sometimes it was because she hadn't wanted to alarm him to danger nearby. This was a mixture it seemed.

He poured some wine into the glass she had used earlier and set it at the table. Her smile said thank you before she grabbed a bowl and helped herself to a large serving of stew and a couple of slices of bread.

The four of them had dinner, catching up, and Kevin recounted the story of how Barina and he met, and how she proceeded to kick the asses of every man in his group. Mags and Milo were getting a kick out of it.

"There isn't much that'll intimidate this girl here." Milo laughed and patted Barina on the back. She blushed.

"I did learn that she won't stay at the inn up the road." Kevin was poking fun.

Barina pouted. "That's different. I don't like ghosts. I imagine that's what it's like for people afraid of spiders or something like that."

Mags looked thoughtful. "I think...Barina, I think tonight is her wailing night."

Barina dropped her spoon. Her eyes widened, and her face went pale. "What? That's tonight? I love you both, but the farther he and I can get out of earshot, the better."

"It's not too bad here," Milo told her. "We have extra wind chimes to drown her out."

"I know, but still, she can roam this far. I don't want to risk seeing her." Barina gave a weak smile. "I'm sorry."

"It's okay," Milo said. "We know how you feel about it. You should go though, before the sun sets." He stood up.

Kevin was already grabbing their things. He wasn't afraid of ghosts, but he knew it bothered Barina. He wouldn't downplay this fear she had, not if she needed to know she could trust him. Within ten minutes, they had said their goodbyes to Milo and Mags, and headed into the forest again.

"How far away is your safehouse from that inn?" Barina asked him.

"Probably take us about an hour to get there." He could see her trying to calculate that distance in her head.

"Good," she said. "We'll be out of earshot."

* * *

At the inn, the group finished with their meals before retiring to their rooms that evening. Arkon and Onyx put up barriers in hopes of keeping the wails of a restless spirit from reaching their ears. Everyone was quiet and taking time to themselves, reading or trying to let sleep take them finally. The wizard and the elf sat up, startled at the same time, looking at each other.

"Geez, you felt that too?" Arkon breathed out. "I can feel the vibrations of her screams."

Onyx nodded. "Her cries are almost powerful enough to get through the barriers, both of our barriers." He raised an eyebrow. "That's a lot of energy."

"Do…do you think we should try and talk to her?" Aria asked. "She saw us earlier, maybe we can help her. Maybe if she knew what we were doing, it would help ease her mind some."

The group looked at each other. Reluctantly, they agreed.

Onyx stood next to Arkon as they both nodded and took the barriers down. It was quiet for a few seconds, then a shriek, unlike anything they had ever heard, pierced the night. It made their skin crawl, but it made them sad too. Anna was hurting, and she was desperate to find the people she loved.

Arkon took a deep breath and opened the door.

Standing in the hallway was one of the most horrifying sights they had ever seen. No longer was Anna sweet and full of love, or the beautiful figure they had seen earlier. She stood before them, her face covered in dried, blackened blood, her hair matted. Broken bones in her arm stuck out of the skin. Her head tilted and twisted on a broken neck, and her eyes were foggy. But she saw the people in the room.

"Where are they!"

"Anna! Anna, be still!" Arkon tried to call to her. "Anna, be still!"

He reached out a hand, expecting to feel the mist that came with ghostly forms. He touched cold, dead skin, and felt the warm blood on his fingertips.

"How?" Arkon didn't think it was possible.

She looked at him. "You, elf." She blinked. "Can you make the pain stop?"

"I'll try. What can I do to help you? What do you need?" he asked her.

"I saw you. I saw all of you earlier. You have the power to stop those who would hurt others with my namesake." She seemed to calm down some, though bloody tears fell from her eyes. "All of you do, though you are missing one."

"She left the group," Twarence said.

Anna took a breath. "How do I not feel pain right now while I speak with you?"

"Anna," Aria asked her gently, "do you remember what happened to you?"

Anna closed her eyes, thought about it, and remembered. "Teddy lost his temper while talking with a prisoner. The stone, the one named after me, took that energy and unleashed a fury." She shook her head. "Teddy loved me, and his people. He never would have been wearing the stone if he knew it would've done this. I've been in such a nightmare for so long, but I think with all of you, I might be able to rest soon." Her form began to change shape. The blood was disappearing, her injuries healing, and in her eyes was hope.

"We hope so," Twarence said. "We want to make things better for all who need it."

"Warrior, wizard. Step forward," she requested.

Jaras and Onyx walked up to the spirit. They watched ast she began to revert to her peaceful and beautiful self, not the blood-covered spirit they had just seen.

Anna placed her hands on the two, and only they could hear her now. "She still travels near, yes?"

They nodded.

Anna turned and walked away with a purpose.

"What just,...what?" Twarence could hardly believe what had just happened.

Jaras closed his eyes, fighting back the tears that started to fall. *It all comes back to her, doesn't it? I just don't know how.*

Arkon's skin tone went gray, and he tried to fight back his own tears that were now indigo. "Even she knew that we needed Barina."

"What are the chances that she's gonna march right up to Barina and tell her to get her ass back here?" Twarence asked, laughing at the thought. "I would be okay with that."

"What did she say to you?" Aria asked, looking at Jaras and Onyx.

"Just some extra tips that might come in handy. We can't talk about it. It would give away the element of surprise, but she believes we have a chance," Onyx said.

Jaras put a hand on Arkon's shoulder. "It's going to be okay. Don't worry. One day Barina's gonna come back. Have a little faith in her, and have a lot of faith in yourself and us."

Arkon's skin tone went back to normal. "Hearing this from you, considering how close you and Barina were, it means a lot."

Jaras gave him a reassuring look. "She wanted us to stay together. It's why she allowed herself to be separated from the group before everything in the caves. She knew that we needed each other, and I believe that, too. Don't worry, we're going to be okay."

Arkon's eyes were crystal blue again. "Thanks." His smile, for the first time in weeks, was genuine.

* * *

Kevin and Barina hurried away from the Outpost, Kevin leading the way to his safehouse.

"So, what kind of place is this safehouse of yours?"

"You'll see when we get there." He looked up at the sky. "It's gonna be dark soon, and we don't have much time to outrun her screams. I've never heard her screams." He could see Barina's face was focused and her breathing controlled.

"Be glad. I only have once. I saw her too when I stayed at the inn, before I knew that kind of thing happened. She's a very kind spirit. She even saw me, which, according to the innkeeper, is rare. She only sees children and animals, but she saw me. She waved at me. When she's wailing, she sees everything though. That's what he told me. The moment I walked into the inn, I knew something was there. I ate my meal, her sitting across from me, watching me, and then I booked it out of there as fast as I could. But not before I could hear her screaming later that evening." She started to shutter. "It was awful." Barina looked at the sun. "My watch is in my bag. I'm not sure what time it really is. Geez, we may not make it, but we won't be in range for long. I'll take it."

Kevin kept a playful gaze and nudged her with his elbow. "I won't let the scary ghost get to you."

She didn't skip a beat. "I won't hesitate to use you as a human shield."

"Good to know that I can somehow aid the unstoppable Barina Raine." He bowed to her.

She turned her nose up at the word. "I'm not unstoppable." Her face fell for a brief moment, but then her smile returned.

"You are humble though, and…" He cut himself off as he saw Barina stumble and almost trip. He went to help, but she had caught herself pretty quickly.

Her face turned pink, and she sighed. "Definitely not unstoppable."

Kevin, no matter how many times he had seen her trip over her own two feet, just couldn't get over it. "How the hell are you able to walk half the time, let alone fight?"

"I was just testing the ground to see if it was level. It's not." She tried to play it off.

Kevin's gray eyes were thoroughly amused. "Do you need me to carry you for a while? I could."

"Baka."

This time he didn't hold back his laughter. "I know what that means when you say it."

She stuck her tongue out, satisfied.

He shook his head and looked down. "Damn it, you're adorable," Kevin whispered to himself, unsure if she heard him.

Barina sat her pack down and rummaged through it. He watched her for a moment. Her hair, in twin braids, frizzed from the misty weather. Her cheeks were pink from both the cold as well from being happy, and she had a look of determination on her face. The mist turned into a light rain, and he admired that she closed her eyes, inhaled deeply, and seemed to become more content, enjoying the rain.

"What are you looking for? Better shoes?" He knelt down next to her.

"There's not a pair of shoes in this world that can help me." She poked him on the chin, then found what she was looking for. "I just remembered that I picked something up at the outpost for you."

She held out a pocket watch. "Here. You said you liked mine, so when I saw this, I figured you might like it."

It was a simple pocket watch made of silver tied to a piece of leather.

"They didn't have a chain for it, but leather is quieter when you move around." She was looking up at him.

He didn't respond for a moment, not expecting this, then he grinned ear to ear. He took the pocket watch and appreciated its simple elegance. Kevin looked into her eyes for a long moment. The rain touched her hair and face, but she paid it no mind. She checked for his reaction.

"This is really, I mean, wow. Thank you." He was having a hard time trying to find the words.

Barina's eyes were bright, happy to know he liked the gift.

"What's the occasion?"

She thought about it. "It's not your birthday anytime soon, is it?"

"No."

She shrugged. "Then just because."

Kevin leaned over and kissed her on the forehead. He put the watch in his pocket, attaching the leather to his belt.

Barina swung her bag over her shoulder. "Let's go." She nudged his arm and kept walking in the direction he had set earlier.

Kevin took a chance and reached over to take her hand in his. She didn't let go.

They hadn't been walking for more than a few seconds before Barina felt the hairs on the back of her neck rise just before a blood curdling scream filled the night air. Her face went pale, and she looked over her shoulder, hoping they could get away.

When Kevin saw her terrified expression, that was all he needed. He pulled her by the hand. "Come on."

They ran until they came to a large tree. It looked like all the others except for a couple of silk flowers at the base. Kevin twisted a hidden latch and pulled open the door that was camouflaged in the trunk. He let her go first, down a set of twisting steps, and pulled the door closed behind him, locking it. He lit a match and grabbed a lantern off the wall.

"Keep going down the stairs," he said.

The steps turned away from the roots of the tree and down about five feet. There was just enough room for him to squeeze ahead of her. The ceiling was so low that even Barina had to duck as they walked. She could see boards propped up along the walls.

"Don't worry, I've reinforced this tunnel so it shouldn't collapse," Kevin said. "This is going to take us to a cave. And there's another way out once we get there." In another couple of minutes, he pushed aside a door that looked like a large boulder, but it was light and easy to move.

Once on the other side, they were in a large cave that was almost as big as the main room of Barina's home back in Miork. It looked like it hadn't been used in a while. There was a little stream that ran through it, so there was water and a small fire pit with a supply of wood. She saw a cabinet and a chest, but that was all in the way of storage or furniture. She could see a small hole in the ceiling that opened to the sky, and there was what looked like another hidden door on the other side of the cave.

"You can't hear her here." Kevin set the lantern on the chest and went to light a fire in the pit. "At least I can't, can you?"

Barina listened. "No, I can't." she leaned against the wall, sighing in relief. "Thank you for getting me away. I can deal with that kind of thing if I really have to, but I'd rather not."

He glanced over his shoulder while he worked on the fire. She went to the little creek and splashed water on her face and the back of her neck, taking a drink while she was there. She was still shaken.

Kevin finished lighting the fire and headed to the cabinet. He found a bottle of brandy and, touching the bottle to her arm, he offered it to her.

"Bless you." She stood up and took a long drink. "Strong stuff, but tasty." She handed the bottle back, and he took a little sip.

"Figure it takes the edge off. You want more?" he asked. She shook her head, so he put it back. "How about some tea? I still have some stashed in here."

"Yes, please. Actually, I have some really good tea I picked up from my friend Mason's shop before I left Estella. Oh, and I have something I want you to try." She reached for her bag. She handed him the tea, which had a really great scent of rose and chamomile, while she found something else for them.

"What's this?" He accepted a small bottle of some type of alcoholic drink.

"It's from Nippon, where Berklion took me to train. Sake."

He took a sip and coughed. "Jeez, that is strong, but I like it." He gave it back to her and put the tea on. "That tea smells great."

"Mason always has the best." She took a drink of her sake and put it back in the bag. "Save the rest of this stuff for a special occasion."

They went through the motions of quietly getting themselves settled in for the night. Kevin worked the fire and got some tea going for them. Normally, Barina would set out the bedrolls and check the perimeter. Her job was easy tonight. She laid the bedrolls by the fire and sat down on hers while Kevin finished up the tea, handing a cup to both of them.

"You feeling alright?" He sipped his tea, glancing over. He was a little ticked at the ghost for simply ruining the moment he and Barina had been having earlier.

She gave a little shrug. "I will be. You being with me, it helps a lot."

"Did, umm, did you want me to stay right next to you tonight?" Except for the first night in his treehouse, they normally kept their bedrolls close, but not touching.

Her smile was weak as she nodded her head. "I'd feel better, yeah."

He saw Barina's eyes widen and her face go pale. She froze. He felt a tingle on the back of his neck before he stood and spun around.

An adorable woman stood silent, looking at them. Her eyes were glassy and unblinking, but not unkind. Her hair was wild and floated around her, and her pale, dead complexion brought a chill to the air.

She looked at Barina and started to come closer, but her legs didn't move. She floated. When she came within a couple feet, Kevin stepped between the two women.

"No," he said to her.

The ghost met his eyes. "I understand your feelings for her, but I need to see her for myself. So, move." She waved a hand, and Kevin found himself thrown against the wall and held there.

Barina stood up, her eyes matching the stern warning she gave. "Stop!" Her voice was firm. "You *will* let him go. Don't think I can't take on a spirit, Anna. What do you want?" Her concern for Kevin's safety made her push her fear aside.

Anna let Kevin go, and he slumped to the ground with a groan.

Barina wanted to go to him, but she stayed still—hoping she could reason with the spirit.

"I wanted to see you for myself," Anna said, coming closer. "I know why you're going through these woods, where you're headed to, what you seek to do." Anna placed a cold hand on Barina's chin, tilting her face to look at her. "You can set me free. You and the rest of your group can do it. I believe in you."

Barina wasn't expecting to hear that, but she nodded.

"The scouts won't harm you." Anna then looked at Kevin. "Stay by her side." And with that, Anna vanished into vapor.

Barina rushed over to Kevin, kneeling down to place her arms around him so he could sit up. "How bad are you hurt?"

He was trying to catch his breath. "I'll live." He tried to reassure her, but he could hardly talk, let alone sit.

"It meant a lot that you stood up for me like that," she said. "Thank you."

He finally managed to stand, though not well. "For you, anything."

She held him up, his arm around her too. "Where does it hurt the worst?" she asked.

She hadn't heard what he just said and Kevin kept his eyeroll to himself. "My back and my side," he said, though she didn't hear.

Barina's face twisted with worry as she helped him to his bedroll. She removed his shirt and then laid him on his stomach. She winced seeing the red marks on his right side. "Damn it." She went to her bag and got the salve. Thankfully she still had some left.

"Don't you still need that for your ribs?" Kevin wasn't about to let her use something she needed for herself.

"I'm all healed up. You need this more. She could've just pushed you aside or walked past. She didn't have to freaking hurt you." Barina was pissed as she started to gently put the salve on his back.

"That stuff works like magic. Feels so good, and you can keep rubbing my back all you want." He was enjoying the feel of her hands on his back.

Barina laughed a little. "I'll see what I can do."

She was glad he couldn't see her face—sure she had turned red while her hands were feeling his back and side. He was in great shape, able to climb with his chains and fight in the style he'd learned. His strength was impressive. Kevin was a fully-trained warrior, so he knew the importance of making sure he was strong, fast, and able to do what he needed to do. He was also humble and didn't try to pretend to be more than he was.

For some reason, he wanted to help her. She didn't understand it, but she was very glad he was there with her. In just this short time, he had become one of her favorite people to be around, if not her favorite. She was almost certain that he felt something for her, but even if he didn't, she had made a very dear friend.

"Tickles." He whispered. He started to fall asleep.

Barina took that to heart and lightly ran her fingers along his side, trying to tickle him on purpose. She couldn't help herself.

He squirmed and laughed. "I'm injured and delicate." He grabbed her hand in his and pulled it close to his chest, pulling her to the ground next to him. Holding her breath, she laid on her back and looked into his sleepy gray eyes. He reached out and gently touched his fingers to her face, brushing her hair behind her ear. "I'm sorry."

"For what?"

"I tried to stop her from getting to you. Obviously that backfired." He seemed disappointed in himself.

She shook her head. "Indaiyo. Gomen, anata wa kizutsuite iru."

He struggled to smile as his eyes closed. "I don't know exactly what you said, but it sounds like you're not angry with me, or even disappointed."

"I keep doing that. I said *it's okay*. Then *sorry, you got hurt*." She blushed. "I don't mean to keep speaking another language. I guess it's because I'm so comfortable with you I slip, I think."

He made one last slow movement, taking her fingers in his again, and lightly kissed them. In the next moment, he was asleep.

Barina sat up and covered him with his cloak, more worried about him now than about the ghost. She pulled her bedroll closer to Kevin. He was in a deep sleep, and she would doze off a little but woke up to put more of the salve on his bruises. As much as she faced her fear, she was still on edge.

The next morning, Barina slipped away and made them something to eat. Kevin woke to the smell of food and saw Barina at the fire, cooking sausages and heating water for the tea they never had the night before. He enjoyed watching her simply sitting by the fire, keeping herself warm while the food cooked. He heard her humming a little tune to herself—one she hummed every so often without realizing she did it. It always made him smile hearing it. He felt brand new after a good night's rest.

"How do you feel?" she asked.

Kevin jumped in surprise. "Holy crap! Didn't think you saw me move."

"I didn't." She glanced back, asking her question again. "How do you feel?"

"Good. You?" He moved to sit next to her.

She nodded then handed him one one of the sausages. "Did you want to rest today? Or we can get a late start."

"I'll be okay." He glanced over while taking a bite and sipping some tea. "Is that your way of saying you want to rest?"

She gave him a look that answered that question. "We should've just stayed with Mags and Milo last night. If I would've known Anna would show up, we could've stayed in bed."

"Well, if there are scouts out, we still did the right thing." He leaned in, a playful gleam in his eyes. "Are you saying my cave isn't up to your standards?"

She stood to gather her things. "You should see my cave." Then she thought about what she'd said. "That's not a metaphor."

Kevin gagged on his tea and almost spit it out. "You can't do that to me. I just about died." Still, he laughed.

Barina winked before she turned to pack her bag. She headed over to the little creek, splashing water on her face and taking some time to brush her hair before putting it in a bun on top of her head.

Kevin sat back, eating and looking up through the hole in the top of the cave. It was still very early in the morning. He could see just a little bit of light but still see some stars. After he finished his food, he put out the fire and then put a shirt on. There was a chill in the air, but it felt nice.

He glanced over at his companion and saw that she moved just a little slower than normal. He wondered if she had slept the night before. "You okay?" he asked. He could see her doing her best to hide her fatigue. He'd let her, but he'd keep an eye on her to make sure she was taking care of herself.

Barina could hear the worry in his voice. She felt his hand on her shoulder, but still she nodded.

Kevin gathered his things and asked, "How much longer till we get to Thoron?"

"Couple weeks. A small village, I think it's called Tricen, is what we'll hit first. Then a day of open road, then we'll be into the capital city of Lavenbo. That's when shit's gonna get very real."

Kevin nodded and led them out of the cave and above ground. In the distance, they could hear her traveling group. The two knew that they would follow in whispered voices when they were this close, but they were ready. And they were that much closer to Thoron.

CHAPTER 16

Two weeks went by quickly and, thankfully, without incident on the way. The days were getting cooler, but it was still pleasant and peaceful. The group had no idea just how fleeting that peace would be once they stepped foot into Thoron.

The morning brought them to the first village, and they could see smoke rising in the distance. They felt uneasy.

Behind them, Barina eyed the smoke. "Kevin, we need to get ahead of them, and quickly. There's enough cover, but we need to go. Whatever is happening, it's, oh it's bad. No, I think it's already happened. Stars."

Barina and Kevin took off at a dead run.

The group knew something was wrong, and they rushed toward the smoke as well. Nobody was prepared for what they found.

The entire village had been burned to the ground—nobody had been left alive. The buildings and houses were charred ruins, heat still coming from them. What was worse, as the group walked along the streets, they saw the blackened or partially-burned bodies of the people—people who had been running for their lives, searching for cover that didn't exist. Shear terror was still on their faces, and the fire had gotten so hot that there were imprints of their shadows on the brick walls. Even some of the bricks had melted.

"What in all of that is..." Jaras was at a loss for words, tears falling down his face. The entire group was stunned.

"This kind of heat, only one kind of creature." Arkon had a growl in his voice. "Uraki, he did this. I'm gonna do everything I can to put him down. This kind of thing can't ever happen again."

"This is what Toler does. He allows Uraki to have reign to destroy some of the smaller villages every now and then. Toler cares nothing for his people, and Uraki knows it." Twarence's face turned green from the smell alone.

With a gasp, Aria stopped her horse. "I feel it!" She jumped down and ran into the remains of a building that could fall at any moment. The men followed.

She found a young woman, barely moving. Aria rushed forward, trying to get to her, but the woman was trapped under bricks and beams. Blood poured from her forehead, and she couldn't move. As the group ran toward her, the woman's eyes widened, and her face twisted in pain and sadness. She knew that no matter what anyone did, she was about to die. All she could do was give one last request.

"This has to stop." She reached her hand out.

Only feet away, Aria yelled to her, "Hang on!"

The woman's eyes glazed over. "This has to stop," she said again, and her head went limp.

"No!" Aria climbed over the rubble and ran to her. "Hang on! No! No!" She put her hands on the woman, trying to save her, but it was too late. She was gone. If the woman had had at least one last breath, one heartbeat, Aria could have saved her.

The healer knelt down, angry that there was nothing she could do. "We end this. Toler will not, just no."

Twarence sat next to Aria, closing the woman's eyes. "It might be more of a mercy. Her whole family was probably killed, too. The trauma might've been enough to make her life hell."

Aria stood up, furious. "Toler's reign ends by the end of this week. Get me close enough, and I'll do it myself."

The men shared a look.

"Keep that fire for when we get there," Twarence said and nodded. "There's nothing we can do here. We should go."

They walked away and headed back to the road that led them to Lavenbo—the home city of a tyrant and his monster.

A short distance away, Kevin and Barina moved through the ruins as well. Her face was red with anger, and she couldn't fight back her tears. Kevin felt sick.

"I have to stop him and Uraki, no matter what." Barina knelt down to the blackened remains of a man holding his two small children. "I will stop them."

Kevin stood close and put his hand on her back. He needed to feel the warmth of a living human. They both knew it was Uraki, that he had been allowed to destroy a village, most likely taking a few of the people to feast on later. Kevin didn't know if being close to Barina was to reassure her or himself.

"After this is done, I'll be back to bury all of you," Barina said, covering the man and his children with a piece of tattered cloth. "You deserve that much. I'm sorry I wasn't able to be here to save you. It'll all be over soon."

Kevin was amazed, but not surprised, by the promise she was making to the whole kingdom.

"If only I had been stronger sooner, I could've come to you."

"Barina?" There was a deeper question in Kevin's heart.

"I haven't tried to end Toler sooner because I didn't think I was strong enough. I don't know if I am yet, but I'm gonna try." Barina stood up, closing her eyes to allow a calm to come over her. When she looked over her shoulder at Kevin, she didn't say anything, but simply motioned for him to follow.

It wasn't long before everyone had left the remains of the village. Kevin and Barina went into the woods along the road, while the group used the path that was before them. Barina took a moment to slip a skirt over her pants. In Lavenbo, a woman wearing pants would draw notice. The civilians wouldn't care, but soldiers would notice, and it could bring unwanted attention.

* * *

It was early the next morning when the travelers finally came upon the city. Lavenbo itself was a mixture of rich and poor. There were the estates of the nobility—most of which were well cared for—and some of these men were almost as bad as Toler. Others barely held their names and estates. These were the ones doing their part to help the people as best they could, even with their lives on the line.

The group passed by a wall just beyond the entrance of the city. There, men, women, and children who had been executed, either by hanging or beheading, were lined up. Among them, two noblemen who had been hanged with their families. A notice stated that they were killed for treason—the treason of helping prisoners who would be fed to Uraki escape. The noblemen were killed, and the prisoners they tried to save were still fed to the dragon.

The group saw that this is what happened to those who tried to help, who tried to do more, who saw what was wrong and spoke out. Another two women had been hung in cages and killed for refusing the advances of the king. A man was beheaded for not giving the king his ten-year-old daughter to be groomed as one of the king's women. The girl was dead, too. There were elderly men and women deemed too thin or fragile to be fed to Uraki. They had simply been beaten to death.

The group kept to the streets, going toward one of the inns that Barina had suggested. The townspeople tried to go about their daily lives as best they could. They kept their heads down, their smiles reserved for indoors. The city itself was immaculate, at least from the outside. Toler wanted to give the impression that his kingdom was perfect. The exterior of every building looked to be in great condition. On the inside, unless one was wealthy, the buildings were mostly falling apart. Clean water was only for the rich and for the inns where travelers were to believe what they saw—though all travelers knew better. Everyone else got their water from their neighborhood wells and boiled it, hoping that would be enough. The group saw that the people were malnourished, and many were sick.

Despite that, there was happiness to be found in the city. People loved and cared for their families and friends. Behind closed doors, they felt safe, even if food was sparse. The city played host to restaurants, a theater, and shops. The citizens just had to adhere to the strict rules that were enforced. Street performers tried to bring happiness to those around them, and the people seemed to really enjoy what they saw.

"You'd only notice how bad things are if you really looked for it," Twarence whispered. "Nobody will even look at us. They're scared."

"In this case, that's a blessing," Arkon said, letting out a sigh.

"Oh stars!" they heard Aria gasp. "This is,...what the fuck is wrong with this guy!" She hissed quietly, "I will kill Toler." Aria seethed at so much death and pain.

The men followed Aria's gaze, more than a couple miles away.

The Palace. The enormous fortress easily took up over a mile of land. It would almost be beautiful if it wasn't for the heads impaled on spikes and placed every one hundred feet along the top of the palace walls. Not all were human. There were heads of animals too. Some fresh, some not. They appeared to remain until they fell off from rot.

Behind the spiked walls, the palace had fifteen turrets—the tallest reaching a hundred and twenty feet. A guard stood on every turret and in every tower. Just outside the wall, there was a twenty-foot drop to the moat lined with jagged rocks in the shallow waters at the bottom. It would be a thirty-foot jump to the other side where the ground slanted away from the wall.

The guards and soldiers of Thoron were known to be some of the most highly-trained and skilled of their craft in this part of the world. The gray stone bricks of the palace were large, and not one of them looked as if it would crumble anytime soon. Toler was a stickler for defense and demanded that every part of his palace would be able to withstand an attack.

"How the hell are we supposed to get into that?" Arkon could hardly whisper the words.

"Barina gave me tips and some routes to look for.." Twarence kept his voice down. "We can review them once we get to an inn."

"I've been in there before, so I have a couple ideas, too," Onyx told them.

"Let's hurry to the inn. We don't want..." Jaras hushed when they saw people being pushed to either side of the street. They followed suit. "What's going on? Keep your heads down," he suggested.

They could hear guards yelling for people to move as a long procession came through the streets. The guards marched in formation five rows deep, five guards in each row. Behind them were a dozen women and girls as young as twelve and ranging into their mid-twenties—each stunningly beautiful. Their heads were down, but terror showed in their faces. Two of the girls were obviously pregnant. Each had red ribbons tied around their necks and linked together, and the ribbons led to the man who held them while riding in his open carriage pulled by the most beautiful stallions that could be bred.

The man was massive—just under seven feet—and he was built of pure muscle and might. His long, dark silken hair blew in the wind while his amber eyes looked down on everyone he passed. His clothes were made of the finest silks and leathers while, upon his brow, a golden crown adorned with rare jewels and a large Black Diamond rested. Everyone knew who this man was. Everyone knew his word was the ultimate law, and anyone who tried to disobey him died, if they were lucky.

"That's him?" Aria scowled, hardly able to believe it.

Onyx held back a growl in his throat. "Yes, that's him." His hands tightened on his staff, his knuckles turning white.

Jaras put a hand on his sword. He could do it now. They could end this man now and put a stop to the misery. As he started to draw his sword, Onyx began to gather his powers, both felt something hit their weapons—two small darts, one in each. Both looked across the way and saw Barina take the hood of her cloak back just enough for them to get a look at her. Her eyes fixed on them, and she shook her head slightly, warning them not to take action.

She was there, just as she had promised. She wore her cloak over her blue blouse and a gray skirt, weapons hidden. Next to her stood the same man they had caught glimpses of with her off and on.

Barina touched her neck and forehead, and then motioned to Toler with her eyes.

"Shit!" Jaras hissed out.

Around Toler's neck rested a small peach-colored stone wrapped in a silver coil and attached to a chain made of the same. On his forehead glowed a bright silver star—a symbol that was connected to the stone.

"He has the Anna Stone!" Twarence exclaimed, breathing heavily. "Fuck, he can use the damn stone."

"What's the plan?" Arkon asked.

"We play it cool," Twarence suggested. "We can't do anything right now. I want to, but we have to make our plan."

Jaras and Onyx looked back at Barina. When she saw that they understood the warning, she and the man she was with slipped away into the crowd.

As soon as the king passed, the people went back to their lives, and the traveling group headed to an inn.

When they arrived, they booked a room for the next two nights. Once upstairs, they closed the door, and the magic men put a protection around it to keep anyone from hearing their conversations.

Onyx threw his staff against the wall and kicked a chair. It was one of the few times they had seen him in a fury. "DAMN IT! If he didn't have that stone, I could've killed him!"

Jaras was angry too, his face red with fury. "I could've challenged him. We could've ended this!"

Crossing her arms, Aria contradicted them with a stern glare. "Do you really think that you could've challenged him with all of his guards there?"

"And we have no way of knowing if there are other members of the Bask order out there," Arkon told him. "You could easily have been outnumbered."

Twarence said firmly, "We are not doing a damn thing until we have plans A through Z hashed out on how and what we're doing to get that stone back. We get the stone first, and then we take him down. But only after we have the stone."

"If I have a shot at killing him, I'm going to," Onyx spat at him.

"But we have to be smart. I know you want your shot at this, but you can't do anything while he wears the Anna Stone. That thing literally gives him the power to do whatever the hell he wants to do." Twarence wasn't bending on this. "We follow the plan, whatever that is."

"Let's get our plan together then," Jaras growled.

Rubbing his forehead out of frustration and exhaustion, Arkon suggested, "Let's eat something first. Get our thoughts together, and then we can talk about it. We've had a few very long and hard days, especially with what we've seen since we came into this kingdom. Let's take some time to catch our breath."

Aria stood next to the elf. "I'm with him. You two will be no good in planning if you're all emotional."

They agreed to eat and rest before planning how the hell they would break into the most heavily guarded castle in this part of the world and go up against the most powerful king, who just got more power.

* * *

Kevin and Barina slipped away as soon as they could when Toler passed.

"That was too fucking close," Kevin hissed after they made it into the alley. "What were those two thinking?"

"They weren't. They were seeing a chance to end this now, but it meant they didn't see everything. They didn't see that he had the stone. Even I know what the star on his head means—that he can wield the powers the stone holds. This just got about a million times harder." She rubbed her face in her hands for a moment.

"Are you saying it's impossible?" Kevin felt his stomach sink and wondered if his face had gone pale with the thought.

"No." Barina focused and thought about the steps she would have to take to make her job work. "It means that I have to be smarter, faster, and stronger than normal. And I still have to deal with Uraki. I'll need to meditate on this."

Kevin smiled. "It's not impossible. I'll take it." He looked around. "Let's get to an inn."

She nodded and pointed. "I know one just down the street from where the others are staying." It was then she saw Kevin yawn for the fifth time in just a few minutes. "You okay?"

"I'm just tired. Might take a nap once we get to our room. Did you want one, too?"

She shook her head. "As tempting as that sounds, I have work to do. Then I might get a little shopping in and definitely a bath. I also have a friend I'm gonna track down."

He raised an eyebrow. "Shopping? What did you need to get?"

"Well, I'm not sure yet, but maybe a couple things to take back to Estella. Remember, after I'm done with this, I'm gonna put down some roots there."

Kevin looked at his shirt sleeves. "I should probably get some new clothes. Everything I have is about at its limit." He ran a hand through his hair that was now long enough he had tied a scarf around his head to hold it back.

"Did you want to go with me?" Barina asked.

"Yes, but I really want to get some sleep. Don't know why I'm so freaking tired."

Barina felt his forehead. "You're not warm or anything. Sorry if I pushed us too fast."

He put an arm around her shoulders, pulling her closer and poked her on the nose. "I don't mind. It just means I need to toughen up and get on your level."

She blushed, not used to all the compliments. Then her expression became thoughtful.

"What is it?" he asked.

"I just don't know. Some inns and people wouldn't think twice about a man and a woman sharing the same room, while others would turn us away. I just hope they don't care."

Kevin held a finger up. "Hang on. Milo suggested this to help us blend in once we got here. In his words, it's the easiest and most convincing disguise in the world." His face heated up when he reached into his pocket and held out two, polished-wooden rings.

Barina's face turned red as well. "Well, I mean, he's not wrong." She took the smaller of the two rings, slipping it onto her left ring finger. "Still, pretty big on me."

Kevin took her ring back and used a bit of thread from his shirt, wrapping it through the bottom of the ring a few times before giving it back to her.

"Much better," she mused.

"Forget how small your hands are sometimes," he stated, slipping the other ring onto his left ring finger.

"These are simple, but they're really pretty." Barina met Kevin's stare and saw he had been watching her for a moment. "What?"

He shook his head. "Nothing, let's go honey."

They walked a few blocks, putting some distance between them and the palace. She had told Twarence that travelers who stayed too close to the palace were treated with suspicion. There were inns, but aside from merchants who came through the area on a regular basis, anyone else would be questioned by guards who noticed.

They found a suitable inn and went to the front desk where a woman who seemed like the sweetest grandma greeted them.

"Hello, how are you today? I'm Marsha, what can I do for you?"

"We're doing well, how are you? I was hoping we could get a room for the next few days?" Barina's smile was warm and her manner cheery—something Kevin loved. She never pretended to be someone she wasn't. She had different sides, no question about it, but she was true to herself in all aspects.

"Absolutely, how many days?"

Barina thought Marsha was adorable. "Probably four days?" She looked at Kevin, hoping he would play along as if they were visiting for longer than they intended.

"Sure thing. We have our honeymoon sweet that's available. You two are such a cute couple. How long have you been together?" Marsha beamed, looking at the two of them.

Barina's face turned beet red, and Kevin had to suppress a laugh. But he jumped in where Barina was caught off guard.

"No matter how long we've been together," he said, placing a hand gently along her face, "my heart still skips a beat every time I look in her eyes."

Barina froze, not daring to breathe, and found herself wishing that he meant what he said. His thumb was lightly rubbing her cheek, and she didn't want that moment to end.

Marsha gave a heartfelt sigh. "That might be one of the sweetest things I've ever heard." She looked at Barina. "He's a keeper, for sure."

Barina didn't lose eye-contact as she placed her fingers on his hand. "I know."

"Well, we'll have dinner ready after four, and we'll be serving it till ten, but the dining room will be open for drinks till midnight. Tonight, we even have a small musical group coming in, too."

Kevin took Barina's hand in his. "Wouldn't mind hearing some good music tonight." He then looked at the price on the ledger and counted out the coins to pay her.

"Excellent. Follow me, and I'll take you to your room." Marsha headed toward the stairs.

They climbed three flights to the top floor and to the room at the end of the hallway. There were two other doors on their floor.

"What's in those?" Barina asked as they walked.

"Oh, one is the bathing room, and the other goes to our roof. It's quiet up there, and the views are beautiful." She winked at them. "It's a nice place for couples to get a good look at the stars."

Marsha opened the door to a spacious well-kept room. There was a large bed with a comfy quilt and big fluffy pillows along the far wall. Two nightstands sat on either side with lanterns on them. A small wood-burning stove sat between a couple of cozy chairs. On the entrance side of the room was a small dresser with a standing mirror and a changing screen. Across from the stove was a door that led to a small balcony.

"I hope this is to your liking." Marsha stood at the doorway.

"It's great, thank you." Barina bowed her head a little when Marsha handed her the keys.

"If either of you need anything, please, don't hesitate to ask," she said. "Oh, I didn't get your names."

"Barina and Kevin." She found no use in giving false information, she sensed nothing malicious about this woman.

Marsha gave a little bow and closed the door behind her.

Kevin didn't immediately let go of Barina's hand. Instead, he gave it a little squeeze. "I'll get the fire going. It's kinda chilly in here, but the room is nice." He set his pack down on the floor, taking Barina's for her too, and headed to start the fire. "I can sleep on the floor tonight, but would you mind if I used the bed for my nap?"

Barina lightly punched his arm. He turned his head in surprise and saw Barina looking at him as if he was crazy.

"I'm not gonna make you sleep on the floor."

"You're not making me, I just don't mind. You're sure as hell not going to, not with what you're up against." He turned back to the stove. The fire started to burn, and it felt nice.

"Kevin. There's no reason why the two of us can't sleep on the bed."

This time he was the shy one. "Are you sure?"

"It's not like we didn't sleep next to each other in your treehouse. If you plan on helping me with this crap that I'm about to get into, you'll need all your energy too."

He could not help himself. She saw the playful gleam in his eyes. "If we need all of our energy, then we *definitely* shouldn't sleep in the same bed." He tried to stifle his laugh. "I know you won't be able to keep your hands off me."

"You're acting like you hate the thought of that. I guess I can be a good girl and behave myself if that's the case." She walked to the doors of the balcony and looked out at the view.

Unable to stifle another yawn, he finally sat on the bed to take off his boots, socks, and his shirt. Kevin had just enough energy to take off his pants, leaving him in his small clothes. It was then that she saw just how tired he really was. There was an audible moan of relief as he was finally off of his feet.

She came over and tucked him in, taking his headband off. "Feel better?"

He nodded. "How long do you think you'll be gone?" His eyes started to close.

"Not sure. A couple hours maybe."

"Will you wake me when you get back if I'm not already up?" She ran her fingers through his hair. He loved how that felt.

"Sure. Unless I decide to take a nap too." Barina started to stand, but Kevin put his hand on her waist.

"Do I get a kiss?" He touched a finger to his cheek. "It'll help me sleep."

Barina rolled her eyes, but she still leaned over and gave him a little kiss on his cheek. He closed his eyes while curling up with a pillow. By the time Barina made it to the door, Kevin had fallen asleep.

Barina closed the door behind her, locking it, and first made her way up to the roof. There, she could get a good outline of the streets and scout the best route to get them to the palace without causing alarm or suspicion. She already saw three different ways, and that was her starting point.

She went down the stairs, leaving the inn, and out onto the city streets. Barina walked all three routes, testing them out, seeing how they felt. Each one was good—all lined with vendors and people going about their day-to-day lives. She was able to blend in, which was what she wanted.

Barina did her best, once she was in view of the castle, not to let her stomach turn at all the heads that had been impaled along the walls. She said some words of respect for the dead to herself. Not one of these people or animals deserve this fate.

The moat—even if it wasn't a short drop to a quick death of jagged rocks—was a no-go for her. The last thing she needed was to be soaking wet and to leave a trail of water, or make noise, or make her feet and hands slippery. Plus, she knew what kind of waste was in that moat. *That's a big no from me.*

Barina smiled when she saw an old friend. He was one of the highest-ranking guards in the palace and an extremely skilled fighter. He had just come off duty and stood outside the gate at the main entrance, out of uniform. The man caught her eye and nodded to her. She made sure he saw her walk to a café. Barina sat down at a table and ordered a pot of tea with some tea cakes.

She wasn't there long before he walked in and found her. His face broke into a large grin, and she stood to greet him with a hug. "Oh, it's good to see you B!"

"Kyle, how are you?" She was happy to see her friend.

"Hanging in there." They sat down, and she poured them their tea and put a tea cake on each of their plates.

"How's your wife? Her name is Kelly, right?"

"Yeah, she's doing well. I mean, as well as anyone can do here. We're expecting our first kid." He beamed.

"Congratulations!" Barina beamed and clapped a little. "You're going to be such a great dad."

"I hope so."

They were quiet for a moment. "Barina, things are worse than ever here. I can't even leave if I want to. I stay because I care about the people of this kingdom, but the things that…the things that *he does*…" Kyle couldn't finish his sentence.

"Kyle, I've known you forever, and I can't imagine what it's been like living here."

He shook his head. "My parents said things here weren't bad when his father ran the kingdom, and we all know he killed his dad. They said after Toler took over that it got so bad. And as time goes on, it gets worse. Nobody is allowed to leave, not ever. I was allowed to go to Miork so I could study under Gregory with the Ash School for my training. That's the only reason, but I had to come back after I finished or they would've killed my parents."

Barina sipped her tea. "I remember you telling us about that." She knew that Kyle had never had the choice but to come back to Thoron. "I also know that you still do what you can to keep many from a terrible fate by smuggling them out of the kingdom when you can."

Kyle let out a deep sigh. "I know that you're probably just coming through on business or whatever, but B, if you ever think of a way to help, clue me in."

Her eyes met his while she peered over her tea cup. "Something's in motion."

Kyle did his best to stifle a gasp and to keep his eyes from getting wide. His dear friend had just given him a glimmer of hope.

"What do you mean?" He could hardly whisper the words.

"There's a reason I'm here. There's a reason a few others are here. I'm telling you this because I trust you, and I know how much you care for the people."

He took a bite of his cake. "What do you need from me?"

"I would appreciate some help. Not me personally, I can handle myself. It's for the others in on this. They could use some help getting in."

"How many are there?"

"Five. There's four men and one woman. There's a scholar, wizard, elf, warrior, and a healer—all the best of the best. They're staying at the Owl Inn. If you decide to help them, go there and ask to see them. They can know that I alerted you to find them, but don't tell them that I'm here. Jaras and Onyx can know, if they ask. Their minds can resist a member of the Bask, just like yours can." Her voice was soft, and her expressions gave way to talk of friendly matters so as not to draw attention.

"Got it." Kyle followed her lead, so he acted as if he heard her tell a joke. "Do you really think that this will work?"

"I sure hope so, or I'll be dead. What do you say?" Her smile wasn't for show.

"I'm all in. What are you planning on doing?"

"What I do best."

Kyle gave a genuine laugh before he leaned in and quietly said, "That means you either found something to obtain, are kicking some ass, or both."

"Little bit of both, my friend." She gave him a kind look. "I'm going to do everything in my power to make things better. When will you move to speak to them?"

"I'll head there now. Where can I find you?"

"The Burr. I'll be back there in about an hour and a half. Tell them you're my cousin. I'll let them know to expect you when I get back."

"Got it." He finished his tea and stood up. Barina followed him out the door.

"I'm grateful for your help." She gave him a big hug while saying quietly, "I have no desire to put you in harm's way, but I know that you want and are able to help your kingdom. So am I."

Kyle held her for a long moment. "I want to give my family a real chance at a future. We can't keep doing this. None of us can."

Barina nodded. "Be careful."

"You too."

They went their separate ways.

Even if he hadn't been able or willing to help, she had been glad to see him. She could still get her traveling companions in, but this would make it so much easier.

Barina headed toward the clothing stores. She was happy to find some nice things to wear when she got back to Estella and, after her shopping was done, she walked closer to the palace. She looked like she was on a stroll—taking in the sights while carrying her shopping bags. In reality, she was scouting the best entry into the palace.

She had never seen a place more heavily guarded. Guards were not in short supply, and they all appeared extremely well-trained. She could handle them, but she'd rather not have to. Many were like her friend Kyle—doing this work because they had to, their families threatened with death or worse if they didn't serve.

Then she saw it—the best way in! It was the only blind spot along the entire palace perimeter—a very narrow window of opportunity—but it was just enough. She saw a couple of alternative ways as a last resort, but this was the best. Barina wanted to test it.

Branches from a row of trees near a corner building intermingled from there to the palace grounds. Kevin would appreciate that. Barina watched the timing of the guards. Once on the grounds, they would have about one minute to land on the rooftop of the stables and then make a running jump to the wall, climbing up three windows before jumping onto the lowest turret. From there, they would move down into the smokestack. She didn't know where it would lead them, so she needed to find out.

Staying calm, Barina checked to make sure nobody was looking. Then, in the blink of an eye, she climbed the tree. She hooked her shopping bags on a limb and headed through the branches until she came to the roof of the stables. When the guard on the wall walked the opposite way, she took off in a sprint, running along the rooftop. In her gray cloak, she made it to the wall, climbed up the three windows, and jumped onto the lowest turret. She came to the smokestack that was, thankfully, not in use and climbed in. Using the rope she'd borrowed from Kevin—she would apologize later for not telling him—she secured one end to a hook on the smokestack, thankful that the colors blended together. She secured a small mirror with a length of sewing thread and then tied the rope around herself and lowered her body down the stack. Once she was close enough to the ground, she propped her legs on either side of the stack and lowered the mirror. Using it to peek around corners, she saw that she was near the chambers for all the women that Toler had made his concubines. She could hear their quiet sobs but knew, for the moment, she couldn't do anything for them. She'd be back though. Barina would come back and rescue them from that life.

This would be their best way in. These women wouldn't give them away. Barina took back the mirror and climbed up the rope. At the top, she used her mirror to watch the guard and repeated her steps to where she had left her shopping bags.

Except for a bit of soot where her cloak had fallen off, nobody would know that she had gone on a little side quest. She was tired though, and figured she had a little time before Kyle made it to the inn. Plenty of time for a nap.

Barina hurried back to The Burr, nodding at Marsha when she walked in. "Hi Marsha. Hey, my cousin Kyle is gonna stop by after a while, so if you could just send him up when he comes in…"

"No problem," she said. "Did you or Kevin want us to draw a bath for you?"

"After my cousin gets here would be a good time. He's just popping by really quick. Till then, I'm going to rest a bit. Kevin is probably still asleep." She smiled at the thought.

"If I may, Barina, where did you find a gem like him?" Marsha leaned over the counter.

Barina turned beet red while rubbing the back of her head. "We found each other."

Marsha laughed. "Cute. I'll send your cousin up when he gets here, then get the bath ready."

"Thanks." Barina headed up the stairs, fully feeling how tired she was now.

Once in the room, she saw Kevin still asleep. She set her bags down, hung up her cloak, and changed out of her clothes and into a nightshirt. She climbed into the bed and pulled the blankets over her. It felt so good to get off her feet and let her hair down.

She could feel her eyes close and heard the calming sound of Kevin's breathing. Barina smiled when she felt Kevin wrap an arm around her and pull her close. She hadn't expected that, but didn't protest. He spoke quietly, still half asleep.

"Find anything nice while you were shopping?"

"Yeah. Got some nice clothes, met up with a friend, and found a way into the palace." She positioned the pillow more comfortably.

He laughed. "You were busy. Why do you have soot on your arms?"

"Part of the way in is through a smokestack. I had to make sure it'll work." She settled herself down to sleep. "It will."

"You really found a way in. I sometimes don't quite understand just how good you are."

Barina could feel the stubble on Kevin's face—almost a beard—lightly touching the back of her neck. She wondered if he realized what he was doing, and if this was him showing affection or trying to keep the conversation as close to them as he could to not risk others overhearing.

"How was your friend?" he asked.

"Good. He works at the palace, and he's gonna help get the others in." Her voice was fading. "He's gonna be by later with an update. After he stops by, I'm gonna get a bath, but first, a nap." Barina let out a frustrated sigh.

"What is it?"

"Too bad I can't just go kill the bastard in his sleep." She seemed disappointed.

Kevin opened his eyes wide, propping himself up on his elbow. "Holy shit, could you? I mean, could you really do that?"

She met his gaze with a little nod. "I think so."

"Why the hell don't you do that then?"

She yawned. "I'm tired. If they were waiting beyond tomorrow to strike—which is my guess—I would do it tomorrow night. For something like that, I like to be well rested. I mean, if I had no choice but to spring into action tonight, I would, but if I can get a good night's rest, it's a much better option."

The man looking down at her couldn't believe what he just heard. He watched as she closed her eyes and moved her head closer to him. That was enough for him to curl back up next to her. He didn't know how else to respond, so all he could say was, "Sweet dreams," before they both fell asleep.

* * *

At the Owl Inn, the group had been in their room for a couple of hours, trying to hash out a plan on how to get the stone, where to find Toler, and plans for Uraki.

"Okay, so we have about a dozen really great plans." Twarence was pretty happy with the progress they had made.

"Only trouble is, we still don't know how the hell we're going to get in there. She left some great suggestions, but until we get a closer look at the palace…" Aria sipped on her wine. "I just, I mean, it's so well fortified. I don't think there's a way in."

"This is where we could use our thief," Arkon grumbled. "She would've had a few good ideas. Maybe we should split up and go take a look at the perimeter."

"May not be a terrible idea." Twarence stood up. "Can everyone keep their heads down? I want us to go in groups. Aria and Arkon, you two come with me. Jaras and Onyx, don't do anything crazy. This is just to check things out."

As they gathered their cloaks, they paused when someone knocked at the door. Jaras opened it as the others stood cautiously behind him. In the doorway stood a man of average height with short, dirty-blonde hair and blue eyes.

"Can we help you?" Jaras asked.

"I think *I* can help *you*. We have a mutual friend, and she got word to me to find you. May I?" he asked, motioning to come in.

Jaras stepped aside and let him enter, closing the door. "Who sent you?"

"Barina. She contacted me and suggested that there would be people here who would need my help. I'm Kyle."

"Is she here?" Arkon looked out the window.

"No, she's not." It wasn't a lie. Arkon hadn't specified where 'here' was. Barina was in Lavenbo, but not the inn. "But she suggested I track you down."

"How can you help us?" Aria sat back down at their table, listening eagerly.

"I have a high rank in the military, so I can get you into the palace. Many of us want him gone. I know that this is our best chance—maybe our only chance—so I'm going to help. I'll get you as close as I can to Toler."

"What's your plan?" Arkon asked. He seemed relieved that there was an option.

"I'll bring you in as recruits for training. Miss," he said, looking at Aria, "we'll have to dress you in men's clothing. Spirit elf, we'll need to cover your ears. Don't use magic unless you absolutely must. Toler will pick up on it otherwise." He looked around at the group. "When did you want to make a go at it?"

"Tomorrow," Twarence suggested. "We're going to rest tonight and go in tomorrow afternoon. It'll give us time to make sure we're prepped, but we want this to be done with." He lit up a smoke. "Is that enough time for you?"

Kyle nodded. "Yeah. I'll come get you guys tomorrow around two, and we'll head to my house. You can prep there." He stood and walked toward the door.

"Do you know if he's always wearing the Anna Stone?" Onyx then asked. It was all he needed to know.

Kyle shrugged. "No clue."

"Hey," Onyx said. "Thank you. We'll do everything we can to make things better."

"I know. Get lots of rest, and I'll see you tomorrow." Kyle left the room.

"I wonder if she sent a letter ahead," Aria wondered aloud, her eyes drifting. "She's still looking out for us."

"Even if she isn't here, I feel a lot better knowing that she at least tried to give us a way in." Arkon smiled more than he had in weeks.

"Well, Aria, come on," Twarence said, standing and grabbing his cloak. "We'll pick something out for you to wear. I'll go with you so that nobody thinks twice about you buying men's clothes."

Arkon stood as well. "I'll come with. I need to make sure I can hide the fact that I'm an elf."

"You two coming?" Twarence looked at Jaras and Onyx.

"Nah, I'm gonna grab a snack and rest a bit." Onyx smiled back at him.

Jaras shook his head. "I want to do a small workout and some training. Make sure I'm ready for tomorrow."

The others left the room, leaving Jaras and Onyx to themselves.

"We really will have a chance," Jaras said.

"I hope so. I'm worried he has the stone on him. We'll hope he takes it off at some point. I don't dare reveal my powers unless I must if he's still wearing it."

"We have a dozen great plans, and there's still a thousand things that could go wrong, but we have to try." Jaras sat on the ground and started to do some sit-ups.

Onyx left to find something to eat and to read a book. He wanted to clear his mind for a while. So many things could go wrong. They just needed one of their plans to go right. He was nervous and excited about the next day, and he hoped he could make his teacher proud.

* * *

Barina and Kevin woke up to a knock at the door. She answered while Kevin ducked behind the changing screen to dress.

"Hey Kyle." Barina smiled.

"Hi, did you enjoy your nap?"

She nodded. "Come on in. So, what's the word?"

"I'm meeting them tomorrow at the inn at two p.m. and then taking them to the palace after we go by my house. They want to strike in the afternoon, so yeah. I would say be at my place by three if you want to follow them. You do your thing when you get there."

"Okay. I appreciate your help with this."

Kyle could hear someone moving behind the screen. "Are you on your own?"

"Nope. Kevin, say hi."

Kyle saw a hand wave. "Hi."

"Hi." Kyle laughed and shook his head, raising an eyebrow at Barina.

Kevin stepped into view the next moment and shook Kyle's hand. "Nice to meet you." He then put on his boots. "B, I'm gonna get some new clothes and take a bath when I get back. Do you wanna go somewhere for dinner tonight?"

"Sure."

He nodded. "Dress nice." He went to the door. "Nice to meet you again, Kyle. I'll see you when I get back, B." Kevin headed out the door.

Kyle leaned into Barina, nudging her arm as soon as she closed the door. "Dang girl. You didn't tell me you had company. Even I think he's attractive."

Barina smiled at him. "I know. He's going to be with me when I go in."

Kyle wasn't expecting to hear that. "Really? You normally fight alone." He gave her a wicked grin. "You hittin' that?"

"NO!" She punched his shoulder, and her face turned bright red. "Totally wouldn't be angry about it if I was." She couldn't help but smirk. "Back on the other subject, I don't like him coming with me, but he wants to help. He's going to be good help, too." Barina leaned against the dresser. "I hate it cause I don't want him to get hurt, but I would be stupid not to bring all help I could get. And he was insistent."

Kyle scratched his chin as he ran a number of scenarios in his head. "B, how far are you going to take this? What is your endgame?"

She crossed her arms and looked at him. "Hopefully, you'll be looking for a new monarch by the end of tomorrow night."

Kyle took a deep breath. "I really hope you have a great plan."

"I have a few ideas."

Kyle let out a groan. "You never do have a plan, do you?"

She gave him a full-on toothy grin. "That's the plan."

Kyle laughed loudly, and then gave her a big hug. "I can never take you seriously. It's one of the most endearing things about you." He pinched her cheek before he went for the door. "None of this is going to be easy, is it?"

"Nothing about what I do is ever easy. If it was, everyone would be able to do it." She hesitated. "I still don't know if I can pull it off, but I'm going to give this my all and more." Barina placed a hand on Kyle's shoulder. "Your family, they will live. If I fall, it won't be safe for you. I will make sure that Kevin gets you and your family out of here."

He nodded. "I know, but if things don't change, there won't be a life for my family at all here. This is worth the risk."

"I'll do everything I can."

"That's why I'm doing this. I'll see you on the other side when this is done." He nodded as he opened the door. "Be careful, Barina."

"You too." Kyle and Barina regarded each other one more time, and he left.

She sat down on one of the chairs, taking a few seconds to clear her mind before she heard another knock on the door.

"Barina?" Marsha called to her. "Your bath is ready. I put a robe in there for you, and fresh towels."

Barina answered the door. "Bless you." She took a few coins from her pocket and handed them to Marsha. "I need this."

Marsha accepted them with a humble bow. "You didn't need to give me that, but thank you."

When she left, Barina grabbed her hair tonic, soap, and a sponge, and made a line for the bathing room. One of her favorite things in the world was having a good soak.

She closed the door behind her, dimmed the lights on the lanterns, and got herself set up. Barina bathed in the Nippon style—grabbing the bucket next to the tub and filling it with water. She used it to scrub herself clean of all the grime, dirt, and soot. Even while traveling, she would find a creek or some source of water so that she could at least clean herself somewhat and change her clothes, washing them as best she could. In her profession, keeping any kind of odor to a minimum could keep her from being detected and save her life. Plus, she just liked to be clean.

She scrubbed her body, rinsed off, and then washed her hair with the tonics. She loved the way it smelled—a hint of lavender and tea—and it felt wonderful on her scalp. After she brushed out her hair, she wrapped it in one of the towels and climbed into the bathtub, adding some dried flowers to the water. Barina sat back and breathed in the scented steam.

She had a lot to think about. Tomorrow was going to be big, and it could be her last day. She knew full well what she was going up against and how dangerous this was. She worried about the others, but she had things to worry about herself. She wasn't a hundred percent sure that Arkon would be able to handle Uraki. He might slow him down and hold him, but it might not be able to do more than that. He was one of the strongest elves she had ever met, aside from the king himself. Uraki was a monster of a dragon that had killed a lot of elves.

Barina had an idea how to defeat Uraki, but she knew there was also the chance she would have to take this dragon head on by herself. She came close to fighting him years ago, but the timing wasn't right. She had fought a couple of terrible dragons before, she knew she could do it, but it would be deadly. It didn't help that those dragons she killed were Uraki's friends. He knew who she was. She would have to stay out of his view until there was no other option. One wrong move and she'd be dead, and a lot of other people would be too. Fighting a dragon required skill, strength, with a whole lot of crazy. At least she knew she fit the last part.

In addition to Uraki was Toler himself. He killed Onyx's teacher and almost took down Berklion. She wasn't afraid for herself, but she knew that there was every possibility this might not end well. With Onyx on her side, as well as Jaras, Aria, Arkon, Twarence, and now Kevin, they had a great chance. If Toler was wearing the Anna Stone, she'd have to take it from him before trying to fight him. She could do it, it was just going to be very tricky.

Barina didn't want to think about this. She wanted to relax and think about the here and now. When she thought about the present, her mind went to the man who had been traveling with her. Automatically, her lips curled into a smile. She knew without a doubt how she felt about him, and she wasn't afraid to admit that to herself, but she wondered if he felt the same. If they were to become more, how would that work? She couldn't ask him to give up what he did, and she was ready to settle in Estella and start up her work. Could they find a middle ground? All she knew was that she wanted to stay close to him. She was happier, she felt safe, and he had become her closest friend. She loved him, and she wanted to keep him in her life.

She finished her soak and dried herself off, putting on the robe. It was a little chilly in the bathing room, so she wanted to hurry back to the room where, hopefully, the stove gave off enough warmth. When she opened the door, Kevin was standing in the hall getting ready to knock.

"That worked out." His eyes showed surprised and amusement. "I was just gonna let you know I was back and not to go running into the room naked."

"Thanks?" Barina looked him over. "You got a shave and had your hair cut. You're just one of those guys who looks good no matter what style you go with, aren't you?" She noted his face was now clean-shaven, and his hair was shorter than it had been when she first met him.

Kevin hadn't been expecting the compliments. "I don't know about that, but thank you." They headed back to the room. "Is the bath water all gross from you climbing in a chimney?"

"No. I cleaned myself before I got into the tub. The tub is just relaxing for me."

"Huh, that's really smart. Is the water still warm?"

"Yeah. You're gonna get cleaned up?" Barina was going through her shopping bags to figure out what to wear.

"Well, yeah. I'm taking us out to dinner, and I got tickets to the theater. Apparently, there's a really great play that a troupe is putting on. I thought you might like to see it." He was nervous to ask her for a real night out.

Barina's face lit up. "Abso-freakin-lutely! Thanks, I wasn't expecting that."

Kevin set his bags on the bed and grabbed a fresh change of clothes. "I'm gonna get cleaned up then, and we can head out." He took off his boots and set his cloak on a hook.

"Alright, there's clean towels in there, and I think a spare robe." She grabbed some clothes and stepped behind the changing screen.

"Be back soon." Kevin took his clothes with him. He was eager to get this evening going.

Once in the bathing room, he undressed and tested the water in the tub. It was still very warm, almost hot. Climbing in, he took his soap and scrubbed himself clean, even washing his hair. He wanted to put his best foot forward tonight and was pulling out all the stops.

Kevin knew how he felt about this woman. He hoped he could steal her heart, but she was ultimately the better thief since she stole his first. The more he was with her, the more he fell in love with her. He wanted her to know he loved her and, hopefully, she would feel the same. He wasn't trying to get her into bed—though he wouldn't argue if she wanted to—and he wasn't even trying to get a kiss. Again, he wouldn't argue. He simply wanted to see if she'd want to give him a chance and take it from there.

Kevin climbed out of the tub, drying himself off, and looked in the mirror. He ran the towel through his hair, combing it a bit then letting it do as it pleased. He dressed in a pair of black pants and a black, long-sleeved shirt.

Once back in their room, he saw Barina standing on the balcony, taking in the view. Her hair was down, and he loved the way the setting sun made it glow. She had donned a dark brown skirt and a reddish-orange blouse. The combo looked good on her. Kevin took out a trinket that he had found while shopping and went to join her.

"It's a nice night," was all he could think to say.

She nodded. "It really is."

He held his hand out. Barina looked down and saw a barrett with five tiny little flowers, each made with a different color of glass. It was simple and very pretty.

"What's this?" she asked, surprised.

"It's for you. Found it when I was in the market." He felt her fingers take it from his hand and watched her put it in her hair. She then wrapped her arms around him, and he returned the hug.

"It's beautiful, thank you."

When their eyes locked, he could see her face heating up, her cheeks turning pink. Kevin leaned over and kissed her forehead. "You're welcome."

She rushed back into the room and took a moment to look in the mirror, making sure she had the barrette where she liked it. She smiled back at Kevin who stood in the doorway of the balcony, simply smiling and watching her. He seemed happy, and this was when Barina noticed how nice he looked. She would be hard pressed to find anyone who could catch her eye like he did.

He handed her her cloak. "It suits you." Kevin put on his own cloak and took her hand. "Shall we?"

The two of them had a really great evening. Dinner was fantastic, and the play they saw was funny enough that Barina was in tears. Kevin laughed at the play but also at hearing her snort with laughter a couple of times. It started pouring down rain, so they rushed back to the inn.

There was music playing in the dining room to a small, but lively crowd.

"Why don't you find us a table," Kevin said, "and I'll take our things upstairs?" He took her cloak and headed up to their room.

Barina found a table along the wall and sat down. She enjoyed the music, the scenery, and the people-watching. From the corner of her eye, she saw a man take notice of her and start stumbling in her direction. She rolled her eyes—not in the mood to deal with a drunk. He plopped himself down in the chair opposite hers.

"Buy you a drink, missie?" He tried to hold back a small belch.

She turned up her nose at his body odor. "No, thank you. I'm also with someone." Barina wasn't worried. She could take care of him if he was annoying. If he turned violent, and sometimes that happened, she had her dagger well hidden—not that she would need it to handle him.

He leaned forward. "You sure about that? I don't see anyone. I'll buy you a drink, and then we can get one of these rooms upstairs." His eyes looked her up and down, and his tone wasn't asking, it was telling.

Barina rubbed the bridge of her nose. "Go home and sober up," she groaned. "I'm not interested."

His face went sour before he reached a hand to grab her wrist. "You fucking bitch, I said…"

His hand never made it close to her. Kevin grabbed his wrist and forced it onto the table with one hand while holding a bottle of wine and two glasses in the other.

Barina watched Kevin, impressed. Kevin let him go with his eyes fixed. "Leave," was all he said to him.

"What are you gonna do about it, pretty boy?" the drunk snarled while standing up.

Kevin leaned within a couple inches of the man's face. "Meet me outside, and I'll show you." His tone was dark, but Barina detected something else in it.

The drunk huffed out a breath and stormed out into the rain.

When the door closed, Kevin sat down across from Barina, putting the wine glasses on the table. She started laughing.

"Not going outside, are you?" She leaned toward him.

"Hell no. It's cold, and it's raining. He's drunk enough he won't remember what he went out there for in the first place, and hopefully he'll stumble on home." He grinned while he poured each of them a glass of wine. "I can't leave you alone for two minutes without guys trying to hit on you."

She took a sip of her wine, trying to give herself a second to think of what to say. The sweet look he gave her then could've stopped her in her tracks.

"First, thank you for getting rid of him. Second, even if that was a common occurrence, and it's not, jealous?" she joked. She wasn't expecting his response.

He met her eyes. "A woman like you doesn't come around but once in a lifetime. I'm not about to let you slip through my fingers."

Barina let a tiny breath escape before she cracked a shy smile.

Kevin took a large drink of his wine and stood up, holding out a hand. "Wanna dance?" He tried his best to control his nerves.

She took another drink before she placed her hand in his, and they joined the other couples on the dance floor. The band had just begun a fast-paced song, but they were keeping up. Barina looked at Kevin. "You're a pretty good dancer. Where'd you learn?"

He spun her, pulled her back, and answered, "My sister taught me. You're not half-bad yourself, where'd you learn?"

"My great uncle is a dance instructor. He even gave lessons to royalty. He taught me what he could. I'm nothing great."

Kevin leaned in. "I don't know. We won't win any competitions, but we're not too shabby."

"I second that. Your sister, older or younger?" Barina realized they had never talked about his family. She was curious.

"Jenny was older by a couple years. What about you? I know you had a brother and sister." The music changed up with a slower song playing.

He pulled her closer, and they moved slowly in the dance.

"Tobi was two years older and Anya younger by about a year and a half. Do you have any more siblings?"

He nodded. "I have a younger sister, too. Sarah lives in Fern with her husband, and they have a daughter now."

Barina tilted her head. "What about Jenny? You used her name in the past."

"We lost her a few years ago."

Barina's face fell. "May I ask what happened?"

"It wasn't pretty, what happened. I'll tell you another time."

She nodded. "I'm sorry." She toyed with a button on his shirt.

Kevin shrugged. "It's okay, it was a long time ago. Still sucks, but what do you do?" To change the subject, he said, "In case I haven't told you, you look stunning. You always do, but tonight, there's just something a little extra special."

Barina blushed, looking down a little. "Thanks. You're playing this bit as my partner better than I could've asked."

He let out a sigh while touching his forehead to hers. "This isn't a bit. This is just me, and I've meant every word I've said."

She kept her forehead against his, trying to control her breathing. *Fighting is easy compared to asking him about this.*

"After all this is over, what're you gonna do? Head back to your companions?" She looked up, fidgeting with his shirt a bit more.

He cleared his throat, steadying his voice. "I was thinking of heading to Estella."

That got her attention, and she felt his hand bring hers to his chest.

"There's this girl I've met. I'd like to see where things go with her, if she'll have me. I'm pretty tired of being on the go, so why not change it up."

Barina tried not to get her hopes up. "What would you do there?"

"Don't know. Maybe teach, do maintenance. I'll figure it out. I just hope she won't mind if I follow her."

Barina closed her eyes when he touched his fingers to her hair. "Do I know her?"

His smile was playful. "Nope, I don't think you've ever met." He laughed when she slugged his arm. Kevin took both of her hands. "Barina, would you be okay with me coming to Estella with you? I'd like to give us a real go."

She nodded. "I'd really like that."

Kevin saw the light in her eyes change ever so slightly. "What is it?"

She stopped dancing. "You do realize that tomorrow, well…ashita inochi wo ushinau kanousei ga…Konkai makereba." She looked down, her happiness now in limbo.

He raised an eyebrow. He had learned to recognize the language she spoke though he didn't understand it. "What was that?"

"Sumimasen. Sorry, let's go somewhere quiet. We need to talk where others can't hear."

They grabbed the wine and their glasses, and headed up to the roof of the inn. Once there, Kevin poured them each another glass, and they stood under the overhang, out of the rain.

"What's going on?" he asked, leaning against the building.

She downed half her drink in one gulp. "It's just, well, there's a very real chance that I could be killed tomorrow. I don't know if it's fair to you to set your future with, um, well. It's not fair for you to not have a backup plan. I love the idea of you coming to Estella, but what if I don't make it tomorrow?"

Kevin hadn't even considered that idea, if for nothing else than he couldn't. Hearing that made him stand up to his full height. "Like hell you'll get killed. You are ten times better than that fucking tyrant you're going up against."

"You don't know that. He's good Kevin. I mean, he's really good. I've heard stories from Berklion of how strong this guy is. He went up against him with Onyx's teacher and Berklion barely came out of it alive. Onyx's teacher didn't. These are two of the best in their field, and they couldn't defeat him. Others have tried too, and they've failed. He now has the stone, and with it, is way more dangerous to fight than even when Berk and Rutherford fought him." She paused to take a drink. "I'm going to go at this with everything I have and more, but I also go into this knowing what the outcome could be. I need you to understand that too."

"Those people who fought him, they're not you. You'll be okay." Kevin was becoming unglued as he finished his wine and poured them each, another glass.

"How do you know?" Barina finished her second glass in one drink.

Kevin drank his quickly before he answered, filling their glasses with the remains of the bottle. He tried to piece his words together while they finished the wine. He placed their empty glasses on the ground, next to the bottle.

"A number of reasons," he finally said, his tone quiet but firm. "You are a freaking bad ass when it comes to fighting, more than anyone I've ever met. You have instincts and abilities that are far above anything that I could imagine, and that includes what I've seen of your teacher."

"You've only kinda seen me fight a couple times."

"Doesn't mean it wasn't the most impressive thing I've ever seen. And I know you weren't even going at a fraction of what you're able to do, were you?"

She didn't answer, but her silence said everything.

"Didn't think so. Another thing. Do you really think that when we're in there, that if I saw for one second that something was going to happen, I wouldn't do everything in my power, right down to my last breath, to stop it? I know you don't need someone to rescue you, to save you, but if I see something, even if it means it gives you a chance to run, I'll do it."

Barina looked up, her face not happy. "You are not going to interfere with a damn thing while I'm fighting. I don't like you going into the castle in the first place, but if you try to get into this fight while I'm going at it…"

"Try and stop me."

She shook her head, visibly frustrated. "I can't look out for you too if I'm fighting. Do you know what it would do to me if something happened to you because you were in the thick of it and I couldn't help you?"

"I'm not asking you to look out for me. I don't need you to."

"But you are asking me to accept you jumping in to protect me but not the other way around, and that's not how it works. The guilt would eat me alive."

Kevin ran his hand through his hair, "I know you don't need me to protect you. I'm just saying that I can't sit back if something is about to happen and I know I can stop it. And yes, I'd take a blow for you, so what? You'd do the same for me, I know you would. We're a team, a damn good one, and I can't sit back when I know I can help. Just like you can't."

Barina looked down, quiet for a moment. "Kevin, I just. I get what you're saying, but still, you have to keep in mind that I may not…"

He cut her off, his hands in the air. "Yeah, I get it. Fine." He headed for the door, storming down the stairs before she could say anything.

"I didn't…" She stopped when the door closed behind him. She hated to upset him, but she needed him to wait till tomorrow to think about planning a future.

Barina headed back down the stairs and to their room. The room felt cold. Kevin's things were still there, except for his cloak. Barina knew that hoping he really cared for her, that he loved her, hadn't been wishful thinking. He cared for her too. She knew, though, that bringing up the reality of the situation—that she might not live and needed him to wait to see what tomorrow would bring—might be a deal breaker for him.

She took the barrette out of her hair, leaving it on the vanity. If she fell asleep and it was gone when she woke up, she knew that would mean Kevin would be gone too.

Stoking the embers in the stove, she got the fire going again and then walked out onto the balcony to watch the rain for a while. She hated to argue with the people she cared for. She wasn't one to raise her voice or anger easily. That wasn't saying she didn't stand up for others or herself, but this was a different situation. He had to understand the risks she took and that this could be her last night. She didn't want Kevin in between her and danger. The idea of him getting hurt to help her, it made her sick, but it also made her feel loved.

Barina blinked, surprised, when her focus went blurry. She put her fingers to her cheeks to wipe away the tears. She had to stop this, to get herself together. This was not the time for her to be wrapped up in her thoughts.

She headed to the front desk to request a candle, which Marsha gladly gave her. Once back in the room she grabbed a pair of baggy black pants and a white shirt to sleep in. Looking at herself in the mirror, she shook her head. She'd be lying to herself if she said she hadn't dressed nicer earlier to impress Kevin. She changed out of her clothes and into the pants and shirt that hung past her waist. Fussing about her looks wasn't her style anyway and it was generally the least of her concerns.

Barina had to get her mind back on the task at hand. Tomorrow was a big day, and it was going to take her being completely at the top of her game to fight Toler. For a fight this big, she needed to clear her mind of everything.

She closed the curtains and put a pillow on the floor with the candle on a holder in front of it. Barina stretched, focusing on her breathing, before kneeling on the pillow. She placed her katana on one side of her, her new sword on the other, and her dagger behind. She lit the candle, gazing into the flame, clearing her mind. When she meditated, she was everything and nothing. She felt peaceful and more in tune with the world. She just was. Barina lost track of the time. She could feel her breathing, and she could feel her mind stealing itself for what was to come in the next twenty-four hours.

At some point, her old injuries—the ones that never healed—opened again. She paid them no mind.

Even though he didn't make a sound, she sensed when Kevin walked into the room. She paid him no mind, she had to keep her mind clear.

When he saw her, kneeling in front of a candle, in a very deep trance, he thought she looked beautiful. He had always thought so, but right now, it was another side of her he was seeing. When he moved closer, he saw her right shoulder and her lower hip. They were bleeding through her shirt. That raised an alarm in his head.

He quickly reached into his bag for some bandages and ointment, putting a water kettle on the stove. He hadn't been gone for that long, maybe a couple hours, just to clear his own thoughts. The idea that she had been in trouble in the time he was gone, bothered him. Once the water boiled, he poured it into the basin and carried it, with a couple of towels, bandages and ointment, over to Barina—still out of her way—and sat on the floor himself. He leaned against the bed and waited for her to finish. He watched in awe when her meditation became a way of connecting herself to her weapons.

She took hold of her katana in one hand, stood up and, with her eyes closed, held it vertically in front of her for only a second before she moved into action. She and the blade whirled in small controlled movements that would be lethal at any point. Barina made a thrust with her katana before she ducked as if avoiding an attack and grabbed her other sword. Both swords were so different, so the movements with each were different, but so controlled and powerful. In her last couple of steps, she reached a foot back, kicked her dagger up, dropped both swords behind her before taking the dagger in one hand with the sheath in the other and struck forward. It took only a minute, if even, but it was impressive.

Kevin watched her bring out her full potential, proving that she was ready. He had guessed right. The little bit of fighting he had seen from her wasn't even a fraction of what she was capable of. He wondered what she would really be like if she was to fully cut loose.

"They won't stop bleeding for a while." She blinked, finally coming out of her meditation, and sheathed her weapons before kneeling down on the pillows again to blow out the candle.

He moved closer. "Did something happen while I was gone?"

"No. They just open up every so often," she said quietly. "They take a long time to heal completely, if they ever do."

Kevin tried to process that information. "Woe, wait. What? There's only one kind of being I know of that can leave injuries that never completely heal. Are you saying those are from them?"

She nodded.

"You can fight them on your own?" He lifted the side of her shirt and started to clean and bandage her side. She didn't stop him.

She nodded again. "I have a feeling you can too."

"I've done it once, and I'd rather not do it again. How many times have you fought them?"

"I don't know. I lost count."

"How many can you fight at once?"

She blinked, thinking hard. "The most I've ever taken on at once was about, well, a lot."

"Stars, Barina." He shook his head. "I can't even. I fought three at once, and I still get nightmares." He lowered her shirt back down and then started to work on her shoulder. "How are you not screaming all the time? When did you get these injuries? I mean, how many were there?"

"The one on my hip was about three years ago. There were fifteen. The one on my shoulder was four years ago, and there were.... " She looked down. "I don't know, I lost count after forty."

Kevin didn't see any fear in her eyes for the creatures she had fought. Instead, it seemed that the reason for fighting was what made her face fall. She seemed to be fighting back tears.

"May I ask, well, why?"

"Three years ago, they stole an artifact from the giants. The other..." Her voice trailed. "I, I really can't talk about that one. Not today anyway."

He heard how her voice changed and knew that something still haunted her. It was a stark reminder that she was human.

Barina appreciated that he was tender while working on her shoulder. It stung the most. She could feel his fingers moving softly as he pushed her hair aside and bandaged her shoulder.

"Berklion can fight them in multiples," she said. "He can do this, and he barely came out alive fighting against Toler. This is the level of danger I'm going up against tomorrow." Her voice softened. "I'm not afraid to fight him. I know what I'm about, and I already know how I'm going to have to fight. I figured that out when we saw him in the street earlier. He's good. He is really good, and it's gonna take everything I have. It's also why I know I very well could've seen my last sunset today. I do, however,..." her voice was barely a whisper, "I worry that, if I'm killed, the others in my group will be in very real danger. Would you help get them out if anything happens to me?" She looked him in the eyes. "Even before you told me you were able to fight the same creatures, from the moment I first saw you draw your blade when we dueled, I've known what you can do. You're already putting yourself at risk by coming with me, but since you are, I would take it as a personal favor if you would look out for them."

Barina inhaled a breath. "Woe," she whispered to herself, surprised, then continued. "I mean, if you're leaving or don't want to, obviously, you don't have to. And I won't hold it against you. I understand if you want to leave." She put her hand on his leg. "I don't want you to think that I don't want you with me. It's very much the opposite. I just have to be realistic about what tomorrow might bring."

Kevin finished with the bandage. "I'm not leaving. Just needed to gather my thoughts earlier." He set the rest of the bandages and ointment aside, and pulled her close, having her lean against him while they sat on the floor. "Have a little faith in me, I'm not going anywhere." He wrapped his arms around her, a leg on either side of her as well. "Yes, I'll look after them while you do your work."

She smiled a little. "Thank you."

He wasn't about to tell her that he'd come back for her after he helped her friends, if it came to that. That would just make her worry, and she needed to know that his focus would be on her friends.

"What was that little, woe, for earlier?"

Barina enjoyed the way his hand felt as he rubbed her arm. It was soothing.

"I don't talk about my fighting with, well, anyone aside from those who learned with me or taught me to fight. I never do. I can with you."

He met her eyes, trying to read them. "Really?"

"I trust you that much. I trust you with knowing things about me, about the darker side of me." She relished in knowing what she could tell

370

him. "It surprised me, and it says a lot about you." An air of calm came over her with that realization.

Kevin felt his cheeks heat. He understood that level of trust. It wasn't something that happened with just anyone. It showed him what he had known about them since they first met. He laughed to himself, shaking his head.

"What?" She tilted her own head.

He placed his hands gently on either side of her face, his fingers twinning in her hair, then his lips touched hers. It left her breathless for a moment.

Barina laughed a little.

"Was it that bad of a kiss?" he asked and kissed her again.

"The worst." Barina didn't skip a beat and gave a little side-eye.

Kevin let out a tsk, his face level, but he also knew she couldn't resist the joke.

She shook her head. "No, it's just, this, all of this with you. I wasn't looking for anyone. I wasn't expecting you."

"Surprise." He kissed her cheek. "To be fair, I wasn't sure what to expect with you either, so we're even."

Barina rested one hand on his shoulder, and with the other, her fingers fidgeted with a button on his shirt. "You really wanna go with me into that castle tomorrow and then to Estella?"

He kissed her again. "I don't care if we're in a castle about to take on a king and a fire-breathing dragon or enjoying the peace and quiet on a night like this. The only place for me is with you."

Barina buried her head in his chest, trying to hide her blush. "I think I'm gonna keep you."

Kevin had to laugh as he ruffled her hair. "Now that we have that settled, we need to get some sleep. Big day tomorrow."

Barina gave him a kiss before she stood up and tripped over her own feet, catching herself on the bedpost. "I am so smooth."

"The hell girl?" Kevin had to sit down, he was laughing so hard.

"Yup, I'm ready to go into one of the hardest fights, maybe the hardest fight, I've ever faced. Perfect."

"I have nothing but faith in you," he said, but he couldn't look at her before his laughter would creep back up.

Barina went to the changing screen to put on a shirt that wasn't soaked in blood while Kevin put more wood into the stove. He then grabbed some clothes to sleep in from his bag. When he looked over his shoulder, he saw Barina running her fingers in her hair while climbing into the bed. He changed, then climbed in the bed next to her. He wanted to do more than just give her that kiss, but he also knew that they both needed to save that energy for the next day. That, and the knowledge that she might not be ready to go to that level. He would wait for her to let him know she was ready.

When she felt the weight of the bed shift, Barina found herself watching his movements. She didn't know that she could be so fortunate to find a man like him. Or did he find her? At that point she wasn't sure, but she didn't care. All she knew was that he was staying by her side.

Once he was next to her, she moved closer. She fought the urge to suggest some other activity. She wanted to, and she was pretty sure that he did too. But she needed to keep her energy for the following day. Plus, her old injuries were very sore. She settled for feeling his arms wrap around her and pull her toward him. She felt him kiss the back of her neck, and then his breathing fell into the steady rise and fall of him sleeping. Barina found herself drifting off into a peaceful sleep.

CHAPTER 17

In the morning, Kevin woke up to find Barina standing on the balcony, sipping on a cup of coffee while watching the sunrise. She was dressed in her black pants and a dark blue blouse from which she had removed the sleeves. He noticed that this was something she had done with a lot of her clothes, and assumed it was easier for her to move. Her feet were still bare, and her cloak hung on a peg by the main door. Her hair was still down for now, and the crisp fall air played with her locks. She took a deep breath while raising her face a little bit toward the sun as it peaked through the clouds. Her eyes scanned the trees of the outlying forest, enjoying the changing colors of the leaves. It was quiet moments like this where she enjoyed taking in the little things in life that Kevin enjoyed seeing the most. He could sense that she was also clearing her mind.

He stood up, wrapping the blanket around his shoulders, and grabbed some coffee before he joined her on the balcony.

"Good morning." He kissed her cheek. "Sleep okay?"

She nodded. "You?"

"Yeah." He yawned a bit. "Heavy for your thoughts?"

"Mh-hm, but they're crystal clear."

"You're way more calm about today than I think anyone should be."

"Does me no good to fret."

Kevin had to agree before he turned to the door. "I'm gonna see about us getting some breakfast."

"Actually…" Barina looked over her shoulder just as Marsha approached with a tray of food, startling Kevin.

"Good morning, Kevin!" She was all smiles. "Barina asked if we could bring up something to eat."

His eyes lit up seeing Marsha. "Perfect timing. Come on in." Kevin stepped aside.

Marsha sat the food on the bed. "Anything else?"

"No, thank you." Kevin gave her a couple of coins.

Marsha nodded her head and left the room.

"You think of everything, don't you?" Kevin took the towel off the tray. "Damn, this looks good."

Barina walked past him and grabbed a plate, loading it up with eggs, sausage, bread, cheese, and fruit. Kevin did the same for himself.

"What time did you want to leave?" he asked her.

"Kyle's gonna be at their inn by two and said we could meet him at his place at three if we want to follow. I want to be there when they leave. I don't want any mistakes. Gonna watch their every move till they get into the palace. So soonish."

"Noted. What's our plan once we see that your friends are in?"

"We make our way along the route I found. It'll lead us to the chambers of the women Toler has taken for his own." Her eyes lowered. "We'll have to make sure that they're alone before we go in. They don't like this, they hate what they've had to become, so they'll stay quiet."

Kevin looked up. "You sure that they'll stay quiet?"

Barina looked stern. "If you were forced to be a sex slave until you popped out a baby and then killed if you didn't produce a son, you'd want him dead, too."

Kevin looked as if he might get sick. "Yeah, I would." He forced himself to take another bite. "What's the plan after that?"

"I have some ideas, and I'll know where to go and what to do when we get in there."

Kevin shook his head with a laugh. "You really do just wing it most of the time, don't you?"

"Plans don't mean shit in my line of work." She gave a tiny wink. "You just follow my lead, then trust your instincts when we have to split up."

"When will that be?"

"Don't know." Barian pressed her lips together. "You are asking questions that I don't have answers for, sir."

"Fair enough." Kevin seriously had no idea how she kept her nerves with so many unknown variables, but she appeared to.

They finished their breakfast, and then Kevin dressed for the day. Black pants, a black shirt, and his cloak.

Barina finished hooking up both of her swords and her dagger. She also made sure she had a few other tools of the trade in her pouch before putting on her boots. She tied her hair, putting it into twin braids.

The final touch was her cloak. "I'm set. Go downstairs, and tell them I don't feel well and not to disturb me. I can't let them see me like this. It could put them all in danger if they did. I'll meet up with you."

When she put her hood up, the transformation in her demeanor was shocking to him. It was still Barina, still the woman he had fallen in love with, but this was a much different side of her than he had ever seen. Different than when he first met her and sparred with her, different than when they beat up those guys who chased them across the bridge.

This was her about to bring the highly trained and deadly warrior, and obtainer of lost or stolen objects, into full action. He knew that, in less than half a heartbeat, she could become a person's worst nightmare.

Kevin nodded and went to the door, but when he turned around again to say something, she was already gone. He closed the doors to the balcony and left the room, concealing his sword, chains and ropes under his cloak.

"Hi Marsha." He waved when he walked to the front desk.

"Kevin, hi. Where's Barina?" She was looking for her.

"She's not feeling too well. She has a pretty nasty headache and wanted me to request that she be left alone. Noises and bright lights are bothering her a lot right now. I'm even stepping out for most of the day, so she can rest. She'll come down if she needs anything, or I'll check for her when I get back." Kevin gave her his sweetest smile.

Marsha was genuinely concerned. "Poor girl. Well, I'll let everyone know to give her some space today. What are you going to get up to?"

"I'll figure something out. I might go see her cousin and hang out with him if he's free. Marsha, I'll see you later." He gave her a little wave before heading toward the door.

"Bye Kevin. Be careful out there."

Kevin left the inn and started walking. He wasn't sure where to look for Barina, but he knew she'd find him, so he started on his way to the inn, stepping into the alley next to it. He wasn't sure where she had been but Barina now stood directly behind him. He didn't turn around, he didn't want anyone to know someone else was there.

He felt her hands lightly take hold on his cloak, and she guided him further back into the alley and then into a doorway.

"You can turn around." She whispered.

Her eyes were happy to see him.

"When they leave, we're going to follow like this. I'll make sure you can see me, periodically. But you follow on the ground, I'll take the rooftops. I have to hide myself since I'm dressed like this." She stretched her arms over her head. "Everyday people wouldn't care, but guards and soldiers would take notice. I'm assuming you know how to follow people without being seen."

He nodded and lightly took her hand in his fingers without realizing he was doing it. "I'm assuming that you'll let me know when you want us to regroup."

"I will." Her gaze for him was warm. "Be careful, and I'll see you even if you don't see me." She stood on her toes and gave him a kiss on the cheek.

He blushed as she took three steps back into a darker shadow and vanished. It happened so fast, he was impressed.

Kevin found a couple of crates just outside the alley to sit on. He pulled out his pipe, put his hood up, and sat back, waiting. He even took hold of some flyers on the ground, taking a moment to scan them. What he read was very concerning—laws that had become effective some time ago that were absolutely insane. He wasn't sure how people survived here. Tax increases that, if they couldn't be paid, their possessions would be taken or they'd be arrested, and the taxes were the highest he had ever seen. Citizens were required to have a portrait of the king in their home and have a shrine in honor of him. If their home was randomly inspected and the shrine wasn't there and perfectly cleaned, a person would be arrested. There was a large statue of the king in the city square and one in each city and town in Thoron. If a person didn't bow when passing or leave a gift on his birthday, they'd be arrested if not struck down immediately. Women could be taken at a moment's notice if the king or one of his noblemen took a fancy to them.

Kevin knew things were bad in this kingdom, but he sometimes didn't grasp just how terrible it could be. Nobody in this kingdom was safe. Everyone here was at the mercy of the king and his men. There were plenty of soldiers, like Barina's friend Kyle, who tried to do what they could to help by serving at the front lines to keep them safe when nobody was looking.

On the opposite side of that, there were plenty who enjoyed using the fact that their king was a monster. It gave them the right to act on his behalf, knowing he wouldn't stop them. Barina and the group she was with were going to put an end to this, or die trying.

It wasn't long before Kevin saw Kyle approaching the inn. Kyle caught his eye and gave a slight nod of his head. Other than that, he gave no indication that they saw each other.

As Kevin waited while Kyle went to get the group, he was pretty sure he heard a flute playing not far off. It was a beautiful melody—one he recognized—and the only feeling he could describe was *safe*.

Twarence finished his lunch at a table downstairs when he saw Kyle walk into the inn and wave at him, walking casually to join him.

"You ready?" Kyle sat down at the table.

"I think so. Let's get the others."

Twarence led the way up the stairs and to the room they were staying in.

"Guys, Kyle's here." Twarence took a deep breath, trying to keep his nerves in line.

The group looked at him, all of them ready for what they were about to do.

"Any news on if Barina is here or not?" Arkon asked. "I'd feel better if I knew she was gonna be there."

Kyle shook his head. "I don't have any news, no." That wasn't a lie. He honestly didn't know if she'd be with them, even in hiding, before they got to his house.

"I'd feel better if she was around," Twarence said. "She needs to steal the stone back. It has to be her. I don't know the first thing about stealing, and if she's as good at this as Vic thinks she is, we need her."

"She's good," Kyle said. "I've seen her in action before." He thought hard on what he just said. "Well, honestly, no, I didn't see her, cause you don't see it happen. She just does it."

Aria leaned in. "Can you please elaborate on this for us? It's, you know, we pestered her so much to learn about her fighting that we never bothered to ask her about how good she was at stealing and what she could do."

Kyle started laughing hard. "You didn't ask about the really big thing she was brought here to do? Classic!"

They all laughed at themselves.

"We did kind of skim over that tidbit about her, didn't we?" Onyx was just as guilty as the rest of them.

"No, remember when we saw her fight the giants back at the dragon lair?" Jaras asked. "I mean, we saw how she could disappear and reappear in no time."

"True, but that was when she was fighting," Aria blurted out.

Jaras shook his head. "She was stealing the dragon eggs back."

"She was hiding to get there," Onyx said, "but once she had them, they saw her."

"That was probably because she knew she didn't have time to take the eggs to where they needed to be and to fight at the same time," Kyle explained. "If she didn't think she had to fight, they wouldn't have seen her. I know her style."

"Then tell us. Do you have a good example?" Aria asked him again.

"When I was in Miork for my training, after she was back from Nippon, there was an incident where my teacher had been robbed. An heirloom, an old ring that had been passed down for generations, was stolen by a former disgruntled student. My teacher asked Barina if she could get it back. She agreed of course, and he insisted that I go with her. Barina said she didn't need the backup. She wasn't kidding, but let me join her anyway." Kyle couldn't stop smiling thinking about this memory. "That girl, my gods, when we got there, she actually decided I'd make a good distraction. Told me to go inside and start up a conversation with the student, acting as if he and I were just catching up, and she'd take care of the rest." Kyle shook his head in disbelief. "She took the ring off the guy's damn finger without him noticing, while he and I were talking! We were sitting in his study, both having a drink, and he was wearing it on his finger. At one point he hung his arm over the armrest of the large chair, and the ring was on his finger. When he brought his hand up, the ring was gone."

Kyle laughed again when he saw the shock on their faces. "It was everything in my damn power not to have my expression give me away. He didn't even notice it was gone till after I had left and we heard him yell. When I think back on the room, there was no indication that anyone had been in there. She told me later that she walked in through the front door when she saw us walk out of the entry way. She would listen to our conversation from there to hear where we were going. When he said we'd sit in his study, she hid in there. She had lightly oiled the doorknob to the room, making his fingers slick. I remembered seeing him rubbing his fingers after opening the door, which just distributed the oil. That's what she wanted.

"She climbed to the top of the large bookcase and waited for us. Once we were seated, she hopped off the bookcase, climbed behind his chair and waited for him to lower his arm. She took the ring from his finger, and simply waited back on the bookcase till he left the room."

Everyone's jaws dropped.

"Stars, that's impressive. It's smart and just... I mean, the oil is smart, the rest of it is just, well, skill." Arkon could hardly believe what he had just heard.

"She's really good at what she does," Kyle assured them. "If she's there, she won't show herself unless she has to or unless she decides to flat out fight him. I wouldn't put it past her to just stab him in the back if she got the chance." He stretched his arms.

"Wait, she would stab someone in the back?" Onyx seemed shocked but slightly impressed. "Not the whole noble thing of fighting face to face?"

Kyle laughed. "Shit, I've known her to take down a target in their sleep. She did that to some men who had taken a few young girls from Miork to sell into slavery. She waited till nightfall, walked right into the compound, killed the one drunk guy who was on watch before he saw her coming, and slit the throats of the rest while they slept. She saved the girls and took them home. I asked her about that, cause almost every warrior I know believes in a fair fight. She was just, like, 'Why the fuck would I give them the chance to kill me?' She fights plenty head-to-head, but if she can finish a fight fast, especially when it has the potential to be a very difficult opponent, she does it. Her work can get ugly fast. She has to be faster." Kyle smiled, shaking his head thinking about her. "Let's get to it, you guys. I need to get you to my house so you can change."

As they gathered the things they would need, Arkon turned his head, looking toward the window.

"What is it?" Twarence asked him.

Arkon tilted his head, listening. "I heard a really pretty melody on a flute playing. Something about it. There's a magic to it. Nothing harmful, just," he began, smiling to himself. "Never mind. Let's go."

Twarence was nervous. He held the ultimate secret about what they were walking into, and the only other one was the wizard who walked beside him. He had no idea how this would turn out. They had made over a dozen plans, all good, but there were still thousands of things that could fail, leaving them to make things up as they went. But he had hope that they would be strong enough, that their thief would be there to help.

They followed Kyle out of the inn, keeping themselves casual so as not to draw attention. Kyle explained that, due to his high rank, nobody would bat an eye at his actions. Fifteen minutes later, they arrived at his house.

"I had my wife go to her parents for the next couple of days," he told them as they crossed the threshold. "I didn't want them too close in case things went bad."

Kyle's home was a humble, well-kept house. The living room, dining, and kitchen were all in one large room. Off to one side was the room where he and his wife slept, a small crib close to their bed, ready for the new baby. They kept their washtub behind a screen, and the outhouse was just out the backdoor. The home was small but warm and inviting.

"Aria, these are for you." He handed her a bundle of clothes. "Go change in my room. The rest of you, except for Onyx, you're okay with what you're wearing. They won't blink since you'll be recruits. Onyx, you have to get rid of the robes. I'll keep them in my bag for when we get inside if you want. Your staff—transform that to look like something else. Arkon, good. You've covered your ears well, and you scruffed your face to look more human."

"I did what I could without magic," Arkon said. "My hair's grown long enough that it covers them easily." In fact, the elf's hair had grown well past his shoulders, and he was able to tie it in place over his ears.

Onyx changed his staff into a ring with an onyx stone. He could change it back with the right words.

Aria stepped out from the bedroom wearing black pants and a green men's shirt. She had wrapped her chest to hide the most obvious sign that she was a woman. Kyle then had her tease her hair some before letting it hang closer in front of her face. He snipped off just a little bit of her hair, not even an inch of one lock, and used some type of glue to attach the hairs to her chin and under her lip.

"Looking better," he said while working on her appearance. "If I brought a woman in there for any other reason than her being arrested or to be taken as a plaything for the king, it'd be suspicious."

"Do you think this will work?" Aria asked, holding still.

"I certainly hope so, or I'll be dead before sunset." He gave her a reassuring smile before he stood and patted her on the shoulder. "Take a look." He gave her a hand mirror.

Aria could hardly recognize who she was. "Stars, you do good work."

"Let's see." Twarence walked over as Aria turned around. "You look more like a guy than Onyx does," he said, laughing.

Onyx could hardly believe it. "Thanks for that, but honestly, you'd never know you were a woman."

Jaras looked over his shoulder and did a double take. "I thought you guys were exaggerating. Damn, I couldn't pick you out of a crowd. How many times you done this?"

Kyle leaned against the kitchen counter, his arms crossed. "I've done it mainly to help smuggle women out of the palace and kingdom. Women who go into the palace don't leave, not alive anyway. It's hard as hell to leave the kingdom even as a man. Impossible for a woman who is from here. Aria, I'm not exaggerating when I say you don't know how closely you've been monitored since you've been here. You're not a citizen, but if you caught the eye of the king or a noble, it'd be everything in your friends' powers to get you out." His eyes were serious. "The best way for a woman to protect herself here is to not be one."

The group felt his words, letting them sink in.

"We need to stop this," Jaras said. "Thing is, what'll happen if we defeat the king?" he asked, taking a deep breath.

Twarence looked out the window. "They get a new monarch. Since there's so many nobles who are dirty, it shouldn't be them who decide. Perhaps our king would choose since he had someone send us." He scratched his beard. "We'll have to cross that bridge when we get there."

Kyle put on his armor while listening. He strapped on his sword and shield, the crest of the white dragon on both. "You guys ready? Don't speak unless someone speaks to you. You're recruits for the army. I'm taking you right into the palace grounds where I'll take you to the dorms just by the armory. Once there, I'll give you directions, but you'll be on your own. I'll have to keep my distance without bringing attention to myself or you.

"Uraki is in the second highest tower. The whole tower is his. The throne room is the most central room in the palace, and it's huge. Toler's personal chambers are in the east wing. He has his war room which is just off the side of the throne room. Those are the most likely places he'll be, and if he's not, he will be eventually. I have to make my rounds once I get you to the dorms, but this is the best I can do. I'll join in on the fight if it comes to it. Like I said, this might be our best and only chance at being liberated from him, so I'm all in." Kyle put his helmet on. "I told my wife what was happening and that, if I wasn't there by morning, to run. She knows the roads and the drill, so I've got her covered."

"You're putting your life on the line for all of this and standing with us," Twarence said, giving him a grateful look. "Thank you."

Kyle gave a thumbs up. "Let's go."

* * *

Barina watched as the door to Kyle's place opened up and her friends started walking down the street. She noticed that Kyle's disguise for Aria was amazing. She could see Kevin keep a safe distance, tailing them, and none of the group was the wiser.

They were getting ready to enter the palace, and she really wanted to let them know she was there, that they weren't alone. Barina also knew that keeping herself a secret could work in their advantage. She watched anxiously as they made their way to the main gate and then took a deep breath when they disappeared inside.

She headed down to the streets, finding Kevin standing by an alley again, checking his watch. Barina grabbed him by his cloak and pulled him back into the alley till they were on the other side of the building.

"They're in. This is really it." Kevin could feel himself steal his nerves. No matter how often he had to go into a fight, it could be nerve racking. He was trying to read Barina's eyes, but there was no sign of fear or nerves.

She gave him a grin. "Take a breath, and follow me."

Kevin followed as she moved casually until she came to a large tree. She checked to make sure nobody was watching and then she jumped into the tree so thick with branches and leaves that no one could see her. Kevin made sure he wasn't being watched and followed after her.

"What next?"

"We have to get from here, through all these branches, and then to the tree that's right there by the roof. When the guard walks away, we'll have about sixty seconds to run from the roof of the stables to that smokestack." Barina took the rope from Kevin's waist and attached her hook to it. "Follow me."

In the next second, she went from branch to branch. Kevin followed a second behind her so as not to bend the branches too much. They made it to the last tree before coming to the roof of the stables, staying just out of view from the guards.

"I have to go in first and check with my mirror to make sure it's safe. Wait a couple of moments before coming into the room. I'll need to reassure the girls that we're not going to hurt them." Barina glanced at the guards.

Kevin put his hand on her shoulder. "Barina."

Her eyes met his, and he pulled her close and kissed her. It was a slow, deep kiss that, if they were on solid ground, she was sure she'd find herself being lifted off her feet. One set of his fingers twined into her hair while the other ran the length of her arm before he locked his fingers with hers. For a moment, nothing else in the world mattered to Barina.

When he pulled away, they both had to catch their breath. He kept his forehead against hers, his fingers clinging to her as if he was trying to hold her and never let go.

Barina let out a sigh. "What was that…"

"I love you." He had to tell her at least once.

Barina didn't move or speak for a couple of seconds while those words rang in her ears. She touched her fingers to his chest and then felt his face. "Kevin."

"I love you. Get out of this alive." He gave her another kiss and poked her nose.

His beautiful gray eyes made her melt before she kissed him, too. "I love you, Kevin. Don't worry, it'll all work out the way it's supposed to. Oh, and staying alive, that goes double for you."

When Kevin heard her say those three words, there wasn't a single part of him that didn't believe they wouldn't get through this. "Let's go help save this kingdom."

Barina squeezed his hand and then turned back to wait. As soon as the guard turned and started to walk in the opposite direction, Barina ran, holding Kevin's hand, to the smokestack. She hooked on the rope and climbed in. Kevin climbed down after her. He was really glad she had pulled him by the hand—she was so much faster than he was.

He noticed she had everything on herself tied in place as she slid into the chimney. She lowered a mirror so she could watch the room as she crept closer and closer to the bottom. She listened to what was happening.

Barina dropped into the fireplace and climbed out into the room.

As she did, over a dozen women turned, frozen in fear when they saw her. These women were beautiful, all from the ages of twelve to twenty-five. They were miserable. All of them were in tears, shaking, and it wasn't from the cold. Something was very wrong.

Barina gave a bow to them. "Ladies."

CHAPTER 18

Kyle led the group through the main gates of the palace and toward the dorms of the recruits.

A man waved at him while they passed. "Kyle, are those new rookies?"

"Hey Mark, and yeah. They're impressive. Each of them is talented in their own way," Kyle told him. "How are Linda and the kids?"

"They're good. The twins have their birthday next week. You guys should come by."

"Just let me know the time, and we'll be there."

"Oh, and be careful. *He's been in a mood these last couple days.* Apparently even though he got his treasure, his son hasn't come home yet or even checked in. It's made him cranky," Mark said in hushed tones.

Kyle nodded. "Thanks for the heads up. You be careful, okay. Tell the rest of your unit to keep away from him as much as they can for a while, and I'll let my men know, too."

Mark had a curious stare. "Do you know something I don't?"

Kyle shrugged, shaking his head. "No, I just don't want anyone to get in his way if he's in a bad mood. With his new toy, he's more dangerous than ever."

Mark nodded. "I know. See you at the rounds." He then waved to the group. "Good luck, rookies." And he left them.

Kyle motioned his friends to follow. They walked for another few minutes before they came to the dorms.

"Okay. I have to leave you here and make my rounds, but I'll find you. Mark, he's a good man. Most of the men in his unit are good. If something happens to me, get him. He can at least help get you out or point you in the direction of *him*." He met eyes with each of them. "Remember, no magic unless you must. Good luck."

Kyle gave them one last nod before he left them to their own devices.

"How do we want to play this?" Aria asked the group.

Twarence took the lead. "We go as if we're making rounds till we find the stone. We then wait till the right moment to take it. We get the stone the hell away from him before we do anything else. That has to be the first order of business, *even* if we see a chance to take out Uraki or Toler. We can't do anything unless we have no choice—not until we have the stone."

He turned to Aria. "You stay close to us. We need to make sure that you stay safe. No magic from anyone unless you have no other choice. Don't draw your weapons unless you're being attacked. We have to blend in."

They all nodded, and the group headed out of the dorms and for the main corridors of the castle.

"Do we split up or stay together?" Onyx asked as they took another turn.

"We stay together. We keep to the story that Kyle gave us. We're new recruits and are learning the layout of the grounds so that we know how best to protect the king." Twarence led the way, heading to the war room first. "My guess is that he'll be in his war room or the throne room. I doubt he'd be in his chambers at this time of day, and Uraki wouldn't be of interest to him unless he was personally feeding him or letting him go crazy in the kingdom, which he already did this week."

"Seems like the best plan. Let's go," Aria said.

They made their way through the palace, occasionally asking others where they were heading. Acting as new recruits, it gave them the freedom to get familiar with the surroundings.

They made it to the war room, walking in slowly and looking it over. The stone wasn't there. There was no indication that Toler had been in there that day. The next probable option was the throne room just through a set of doors from the war room. They opted to go through the main hallways, as it would be less suspicious if they made their way through the palace like everyone else.

Heading through the castle, they noticed that the servants—maybe slaves at this point—were all starving, scared, and exhausted. They were terrified of what a wrong move could bring them. Aria and the group listened to the whispers in the halls.

"Did you hear what they did to him? He was killed for that. She had her food rations taken for a week because she wouldn't let him look up at her…"

Some of the things the friends heard made them sick.

They came into the throne room, and there it was. On a pedestal just in front of the throne itself was the Anna Stone.

The triangular, smooth, peach-colored stone rested on a pure white pillow. It gave off no light nor looked like anything special. It had a silver coil wrapped around it that led to a silver chain so it could be worn. About the size of a cherry, this stone, to the right holder, could give powers beyond anything a person could dream. Toler was one of the few people who could yield it. They had to act while they could.

"This has got to be a trap," Twarence hissed.

"It is, but we have to try and do this now." Jaras's hand twitched for his sword.

"How do you want to play this?" Aria asked again, looking to the scholar.

"We walk in as if we're just checking out the room," Twarence told them "When one of us gets close enough, take it. Tap the ground three times with your foot if you get it, and we'll know to get back here and book it out of the room. We get it somewhere safe then we come back for the second half of the plan."

The group moved into the room—Onyx and Twarence going right, Arkon down the middle, Jaras and Aria to the left.

Onyx was closest to the stone. He reached out a hand, but then he saw something, rather two someones, just in view. There were cells in the room, behind the throne, where the most high-profile prisoners were being kept. Stunned, he froze in his steps. When the prisoners saw him, their jaws dropped, too. They looked malnourished, beaten and bruised, but they were *alive*!

The man in the cells mouthed *Run!* trying to shoo him away.

Nodding, the woman mouthed *Get the stone and run!*

Onyx tilted his head for a moment before he nodded to the two prisoners and he grabbed the stone, tapped the ground three times with his foot, and started to spring back to the entrance with the others.

"That was cute," was all they heard as the doors sealed themselves shut.

Onyx spun on his heels first, turning to see that Toler was now in the room.

"I'll be taking that back." He held out his hand, pointing at the stone.

"Like hell!" Onyx raised his hand and blasted Toler with as much energy as he could.

Toler blocked it. Arkon was using his powers on him now, trying to make a dent, but Toler blocked them, too.

"Give it back." He ordered.

"No." Onyx smiled.

"It seems like you know a couple of my prisoners. I was trying to think why my son would've sent them to me, but I think I know why now." Toler was laughing. "They made too much noise, so I haven't let them speak, but it's good to see that they'll have company."

"Jason! Tyra!" Onyx yelled.

The rest of the group stopped short.

"They're here?" Aria's eyes filled with tears. "They're alive!"

"They're here, and now I think…" Toler waved his hand and tried to pull the stone from Onyx's hold, but the wizard's hold was too strong with a shield of magic around it. "I think I want to play with this wizard a bit," the monarch said.

Onyx blasted Toler again, knocking him to his knees, and Arkon sent his energies to him as well, trying to buy time.

"Get Jason and Tyra!" Onyx yelled. "Reveal!" And the ring on his finger changed back into his staff as he slammed it on the ground, charging it with energy.

Jaras ran as fast as he could behind the throne. "Shit, you're really here. Hang on."

Tyra shook her head, pointing, her fierce eyes saying, *Get the stone and go!*

"We're not leaving without you," Jaras insisted, shaking his head.

In the next second, Jaras and the others except for Onyx, found themselves in the same cell with Jason and Tyra. Toler had used his energies to move the cell closer toward the main doors of the throne room.

Toler grinned at them. "This way you can get a better view while I kill your wizard." He held Onyx by the front of his shirt. "I remember you. You were Rutherford's apprentice, weren't you? Don't tell me you've come for revenge."

Onyx snarled. "Revenge is an added bonus."

Toler punched Onyx, breaking his nose, and took the stone from his hand. "You want to try your best shot against me? That's adorable. Well, little boy, if you want to play, we can." He then pointed to the star on his forehead. "Of course, since I can use the Anna Stone, it might be a little tricky for you, but we'll play." Toler set him down.

The group wanted to help, but they couldn't get out of the cage that was magically reinforced while Toler still had the stone. They didn't even know if all of their powers and abilities combined could stop him.

Onyx didn't hesitate for a second when the king set him down. He sent a blast of powerful energy that threw Toler into the throne. Toler didn't get a chance to stand before Onyx raised his fists, slamming them down, creating two bolts of lightning that came down on Toler. Toler put a single hand up which barely blocked the attack. But when Onyx waved a hand, Toler was knocked back by a blast of wind that pinned him to the wall.

All the light in the room went out. Onyx waved his arms in a wide circle before bringing his hands together in a crushing movement. The others could hear Toler grunt in pain, crushed under the pressure of Onyx's power. They heard the king give a defiant yell, break the hold that Onyx had on him, and a force of energy flung Onyx to the ceiling. The wizard managed to shield himself from a direct hit before he crashed onto the floor, managing to barely cushion his fall.

* * *

Barina held out her hand to Toler's women. "Ladies." She tried to give them a reassuring look. "Don't be afraid, I'm here to help you. I have someone else joining me. Don't worry, he's good."

Kevin landed in the fireplace the next moment.

One of the women started crying uncontrollably.

"What is it?" Barina knelt down by her, gently touching her arm.

"They…they…they took my sister and her baby!" She had trouble breathing. "She gave birth to a daughter, and they took them both to be fed to Uraki."

Barina stood up. "Who took them?" She had an idea and made her way to a wardrobe.

A young girl, perhaps twelve, answered. "One of the noblemen. He enjoys doing it. He likes to watch as Uraki feeds.".

"How long ago did they leave?" Barina grabbed a dress from the wardrobe.

"Just before you got here," she said.

"I'll be right back. Kevin, stay with them." Barina slung the dress over her shoulder and marched out the door. She rushed through the corridor, climbing up into the rafters, and made strides to catch up to the girl and her child. She knew where Uraki's tower was, and she knew how much time she had. Barina could hear a woman screaming and a baby crying. It was heart wrenching.

When she came into view of them, she could see that this disgusting excuse for a human, this noble, had the woman's arms tied up and was dragging her with one arm while holding the baby in the other. The woman was weak and was having trouble walking. She still had yet to be cleaned of the afterbirth on her nightgown, and the baby hadn't been washed. Barina suppressed a growl in her throat.

"I can give someone else to Uraki if you want to come home with me," the noble offered. "Toler picked a fine woman to try and give him a son. You failed at that, but there is another option. You can be one of my women. I can send another prisoner to the dragon." The man leaned in toward her. "We can't have this little bastard with us, though. We can feed her to the dragon, then start over again."

"I won't leave her!" The woman was sobbing and trying to get to her daughter, but with her arms bound. She knew it was useless.

"You women never do leave your daughters." He kissed the woman, and said, "So be it." He licked his lips. "I'll still have you before I feed you to Uraki." He pushed her as he started to tear her gown off.

Barina didn't hesitate. Jumping down, she gagged the man's mouth with a leather strap while slamming his face against the stone wall before kicking to break one of his kneecaps. She swiftly caught the baby and cut the ropes tying the woman. "Here," she said, handing the woman her child. It happened so fast that the woman barely had time to blink. Barina tied the man with his own ropes and had him pressed against the wall.

"Miss, I need to ask you to stay close to me. Don't panic, and don't scream." She met the woman's eyes, and the young mother seemed to listen.

"You sir," Barina said, giving the noble a wicked smile, "are fucked on so many levels." She pulled his shirt off, slipped the dress she had brought on him, and—after cutting eye slits—covered his head up with his shirt.

"You have fed, how many, to Uraki? You've killed how many?" she hissed at him. "I know who you are, Lord Griu, and I know what you've been doing over the years. It's over. I want the last thing you see to be the same thing your victims did."

Barina kneeled down beside the mother clinging to her baby. "I won't have you see the dragon, but I do need to keep you close. I'll have you back to your sister soon." She looked at the newborn. "She's beautiful. Don't worry, things are about to get better."

The new mother fell against Barina, trying to catch her breath. "Thank you!" she whispered, crying into Barina's chest. "Thank you!"

Barina smoothed her hair, trying to comfort her. "Shhh, it's okay to cry. You've been living in hell. What was going to happen to you and your child, and what happened to others, was awful. It ends today. What's your name?"

"Morgan," she croaked out.

"And your daughter?"

"I didn't think I'd get to give her a name." Morgan started to smile through her tears. "I'll have to think of one."

Barina nodded understanding. "Can you walk at all? I know you shouldn't since you just gave birth, but can you?"

"I can walk some, yes."

"Okay, hold tight to your girl, and follow me. By the way, I'm Barina."

Barina helped Morgan to her feet and then dragged Lord Griu to his feet, putting her dagger against his back. "Move." Her tone turned dark again.

She marched him through the hallway and into the tower that housed Uraki. As much as Barina didn't feel anyone deserved to be eaten alive, she was going to make an exception with this man. He had fed plenty of people to Uraki himself over the years. Not only that but...

"Uraki will be expecting to be fed today. You probably already told him he'd get a snack, so we can't leave him hanging." Barina was still pushing him.

The man struggled and tried to speak.

"You don't deserve last words. You don't deserve another day. You were going to rape and then kill this woman and her child. You've done this to countless others, and you've never shown mercy. I heard you even fed your own daughter to Uraki when she didn't produce a son for Toler." Barina read him his crimes while they made the walk.

Once they reached the final steps, Barina looked at Morgan. "Rest here for a moment. I don't want you to get any closer than you have to."

Morgan was shocked at the different way Barina acted toward her and toward the man who would've sealed her fate. She went from sweet and caring—Morgan knowing that she could trust this stranger with her life—to a person who could probably make Death cower in a corner. The new mother was really glad that Barina was on her side.

Barina pushed the man down the steps that curled to the middle of the tower and to the only door that led into Uraki's lair. The roof of the tower lifted with a lever that only Uraki himself was strong enough to control—him or Toler's magic. Barina had ways around it, but she didn't need them.

She opened the door that was never locked because nobody was stupid enough to go through it. Dragging Lord Griu in with her, she ignored his whimpers and his shaking body as they walked onto a small ledge by the door—the ledge where so many had been pushed off to meet their maker. There she could smell the old blood and the new soaked into the walls and the floors. She could make outlines of the bones and half-eaten bodies scattered on the floor.

Stories have told that dragons preferred to rest and sleep on treasure—gold, in particular—and a few did, but it was more of a fetish for them. They liked the smell and the feel. Most dragons preferred to rest on the soft grass and leaves in their lairs, staying near nature.

Uraki was different from all of them. He preferred to use the bones of the people he had eaten. He would start with the head, taking it off, then he would literally suck the flesh, organs, and blood from a person, leaving only the bones. He had enough under him to cover the floor three feet deep. It turned Barina's stomach.

A deep hissing voice echoed around the wall. "I smell a woman. I smell fear and blood." The dragon stayed below in the shadows, but Barina could see the glimmer of his crystal blue eyes. She kept herself out of his sight since they had a history.

Barina knew he smelled her, but the fear and blood was from Lord Griu. "Do you feel that fear," she whispered to the man next to her. "Do you feel that? Do you feel what you've made so many feel over the years?"

He was shaking, and she could hear it as urine trickled down his leg and onto the stone floor. The gag muffled his sobs and whimpers.

"I'm going to give you greater mercy," she whispered, "than you ever gave any of these people. I'm going to take out this gag, and you're going to tell him that this woman has decided to go with you and that you'll have a snack for him later. Then, I'm going to let you go. You will leave this kingdom. You won't go home, you won't look at anyone, you will leave. You don't deserve this mercy, you don't deserve it at all, but I'm giving you one chance. If you so much as say anything other than to tell him this, I will push you in and not lose a moment of sleep over it. Nod if you understand."

He nodded.

Barina removed the gag but not the shirt from his head.

"I'm afraid, your grace..." His voice was shaky, "that I do not have a snack for you at this time. This woman has decided to become mine, but I will bring you a suitable replacement shortly."

"You actually managed to convince a woman to be with you? What of her child? I hear no babe crying, nor do I smell one."

"The babe was too small. It didn't even take one breath. I felt it would be an insult to give you something so pitiful. Don't worry, I have a cell full of small children who you would just love for dinner."

There was a hissing laughter. "Very well, make sure they're screaming, it makes them more tender."

"Yes, your grace."

Barina pulled Griu out of the room and closed the door.

"I'm going to see you hang for this, you fucking bitch!" he snarled at her.

"Nope." Barina punched him in the throat, opened the door to Uraki's tower again, and pushed the man over the ledge, closing the door when she did.

All she heard was a delighted Uraki hiss out, "She changed her mind!" and the man let out a scream that was cut short.

Barina walked back to Morgan. "Lean on me."

The mother put her arm around Barina's shoulder and found the strength to walk with her. The corridors back to the women's chambers appeared empty, but she still had them move as quickly as she could.

Barina opened the door and heard the sound of a sword being drawn.

"It's me." She saw Kevin at the ready with his weapons, sword in one hand, chains in the other. His stance relaxed when he heard her voice.

Barina closed the door behind her, and the woman who had cried for her sister earlier stood in disbelief.

"Morgan!" She ran to embrace her sister and niece. "And the baby, the baby's alive!"

"Megan!" Morgan sank into her sister's hold.

Barina went to Kevin. "We need to head to the throne room. Thank you for watching over them."

Kevin put a hand on her shoulder. "What happened to the man who was taking her there?"

Barina had a wicked grin on her lips again. "Uraki didn't go hungry."

"Good." Kevin's eyes held a moment of disgust for the man. "Did you see Uraki?"

"Just his eyes. He didn't see me," she said. "I can't let him see me, not yet. We have a history."

"I know you said you've encountered him, just what does that mean?" Kevin asked, touching one of her braids.

"He used to have two other friends who were just as bad as him."

"Used to. The operative words, right?"

Before she could answer, Barina felt the arms of all the women trying to hug her.

"Ladies, I'm glad I could help. Please, I need you all to stay in here. Things are about to get really nasty. I have to take care of that bastard of a king. If I fall, Kevin or Kyle will be back to get you out of the kingdom. If they fall, run like hell." It was all she could say.

Then the youngest looked up. "Do I get to go home to my parents?" Her big brown eyes welled with tears that slid down her bruised cheeks.

Barina put a hand on the little girl's head. "I'm going to do everything I can to make sure you do. Stay here, and be strong."

Barina and Kevin left the room and jumped back up into the rafters. As they approached the throne room, Barina felt the hairs on her arm stand up. It made her slow down.

"What is it?" Kevin asked, noticing the slight change in pace.

"I think it's already started." Her eyes widened and her breathing got short for a moment.

"What do you need me to do?"

Barina had him follow as they climbed even higher, slipping into the throne room through one of the small decorative windows.

"He has them all in a cage. He has them." Barina's eyes went dark. "And he has Onyx. Shit. Oh stars!" She fell back when she saw who else was there. "Jason, Tyra? They're alive, oh stars, they're alive!"

Kevin peered farther into the room. "Wait, the ones you thought had been killed by Ken?"

She nodded. "They're here. He sent them here. Holy shit!" She smiled brightly for a moment before putting her game face back on.

"You tell me what to do, and I'll do it."

They both cringed when they saw Toler pick up Onyx and throw him to the other side of the room.

"Can you get down to those in the cage?" Barina asked. "Can you get them out? I'm sure it's magically reinforced, but here…" She reached into her bag and gave him a golden key. "This can open any door, magic or mortal made. Open it and get them back as far as you can." She slipped on a set of leather gloves that had short metal hooks on them. "I want that key back."

Kevin blinked and looked at the key. "I don't think I want to know how you got a key like this."

She twitched a lip. "We don't have time for that story."

"Yeah, I got them," he said. "What about you?"

She squinted when her wizard and the king collided their energies in one blaze of light. "My job,…getting that stone." She glanced at him quickly. "I'll see you on the flip side."

Kevin reached fort his chains and ropes to start climbing, and when he turned back, she was gone. He positioned himself by the nearest tapestry close to the cage and barely caught a glimpse of Barina doing a vertical climb down the wall behind the throne itself, ducking behind another tapestry.

Toler—with the stone resting against his skin—knew it gave him power beyond his dreams. Onyx knew it, too. He also knew that Toler was playing with him, but he still had to fight. He got back to his feet, wiping blood from his face where he now had a gash above his eye. He continued wielding fire and ice, sending a tidal wave from his staff. Toler would simply hold out a hand while trying to hold back his laugh. Onyx brought down the massive chandelier that hung above the king who dodged out of the way just in time.

"I've never seen…" Arkon could hardly speak, "in all my years of magic, I've never seen the kind of power that Onyx is bringing. Even though Toler has the stone, he might be able to bring him down."

"Come on, Onyx." Jaras watched on the edge of his seat with the others.

Aria had her arms around Jason and Tyra, both hugging and healing them. "I can't believe you're both still alive. If Barina could see this. Can you still not talk?"

They shook their heads.

"Let me see." Aria placed her hands on their necks, focusing her powers. "It's no good. It won't let up unless Toler is dead or lifts it."

"So, when he's dead." Twarence had to make the joke.

"Which hopefully, won't be too long now." It was a voice of someone they didn't know.

They all turned their heads to see a man hiding behind them, kneeling on the ground, and working on the lock to the cage.

"Who are you?" Arkon asked.

"I'm Kevin. We have a mutual friend."

"I've seen you," Jaras blurted out as Kevin finished unlocking the cage.

Kevin nodded. "I was asked to help you and give you a way to run if needed. I'm here to guard you, but I'll join the fight if she wants me to."

"Wait, are you talking about Barina?" Twarence could hardly get the words out. "She's here?"

Kevin crooked a lip, but didn't respond.

"And you knew that she was around?" Aria spat at Jaras. "You never told us?"

"No," Jaras said simply. "She agreed that Onyx and I could know because a member of the Bask order couldn't mess with our minds. It was more for everyone's safety than anything."

"I figured because she was still pissed at us." Twarence looked down, rubbing his arm.

"There's a little of that, too," Kevin said. "But we've been following not more than a half mile behind you since you left Estella. Get down!" he cried.

They all ducked as a line of fire streaked over the wall, narrowly missing their heads, and melted some of the metal of the cages.

"Arkon, can you do anything to help?" Twarence asked.

"Yes, but there's still Uraki. I will need my energy for him!"

"Toler is MINE!" Onyx roared while light crackled around him. His staff absorbed all the light in the room before he sent it hurling toward Toler, knocking the king off of his feet and into the wall behind him. Toler landed about five feet above where Barina was hiding behind the tapestry and then fell to the floor.

Perfect timing Onyx. Now that Toler was on the ground and close enough, Barina was going to make her move. She covered herself with her cloak.

Toler started to stand, laughing to himself. "You do have a fight in you. Power much more than what Rutherford ever held." He waved a hand and lifted the wizard off his feet. "Still not as good as me, but better than him." He pulled Onyx toward him slowly, his eyes swirling with red clouds. He waved a hand, freezing everyone else in their steps. Even Jason could barely move.

"You, though," the king snarled at the wizard, "will meet the same end he did."

Onyx could feel Toler's breath on his face and, when the spit hit him on the chin, he said, "I will see you dead." Onyx showed no fear as this man stood over him.

Toler flung Onyx to the ground in front of his throne before he walked over to sit in it. "If you kiss my boots, I'll give you a quick death." Toler was still laughing to himself.

"You'll meet death just like your son did." Onyx laughed to himself when he spoke those words.

Toler paused for a moment. "You speak nonsense." The king began to smile again. "Now kiss my boots."

Onyx didn't waver in his gaze.

"Very well." Toler stood up again. "I will show you what real power is." He reached his hand to his chest to touch the stone. It was then, as he did this movement and touched his chest, that everyone finally noticed.

"It's gone!"

Twarence started laughing. The stone no longer rested around Toler's neck, the star no longer upon his brow. The stone was gone, and Toler hadn't even noticed.

The king stood up looking around him, unable to believe. "Where is IT!!!" His bellow shook the walls, his face twisted in rage. He stood up in a fury of anger, raising his hands with all the energies he could muster to strike down Onyx.

A sword emerged from Toler's chest, piercing him from behind as it was thrust through his heart. In shock, he tried to glance behind him, but instead felt a blade run along his neck. He gasped for air, holding his throat as he fell to the ground.

Barina pulled her katana out of his back, flicking the blood from it, and wiped the blood from her dagger before turning her attention to Onyx.

"Can you and Arkon protect the others while I fight?" She held her hand out to help him to his feet.

Onyx stood up with some difficulty, nodding.

Barina held him close, steadying him. "Lean on me." She looked back to Toler. "Fuck, that didn't take a life, he's already healing." She put Onyx's arm around her shoulder and rushed him back to the others.

Everyone beamed at her. She wanted to hug them all, but this wasn't the time for emotion. She nudged Twarence with her elbow and said, "I missed you, buddy," before rushing back to Toler. Barina blew a kiss to Kevin before she went back to work.

Onyx knelt for a moment, letting Aria heal him quickly. He met eyes with the elf. "Arkon, we have to protect them."

Arkon raised his hands to put up a shield, and not a moment too soon. Toler raised a hand, sending a large ball of fire at those by the cage. Onyx blocked it as Barina kicked Toler in the face.

Holding his jaw, the king turned his focus to Barina. "You bitch!"

She jumped back, dodging one blast and side-stepping another. Toler got to his feet as Barina watched his every move, a little smirk on her face.

The doors to the room burst open, and Kyle led a group of soldiers as they filed in around the walls. They were all ready to fight, ready to do what they had to do to help Barina and her friends if they gave the word. The last to enter were the women that Toler had enslaved. Morgan, her sister Megan, all of them, holding anything they could find as a weapon. They were shaking and afraid, but ready to fight.

"Morgan," Kevin called from where he stood. "You should all be trying to get out of here."

She shook her head with the rest of the women. "There's no life for us if we have to run. If we can somehow help her win this fight, help all of you win this fight, we're in." Morgan was holding her child close.

Megan gasped. "He was injured!" She could see the blood staining Toler's shirt and neck.

"It's not enough yet," Aria told them, making a line to the women. She looked at Morgan. "You've literally had this baby today. Sit down," she ordered and set to work checking the new mother over.

Toler was too angry to notice that his soldiers were refusing to help him. They watched, trying not to attract too much attention to themselves. Even with two magic men holding up a shield, there was no telling what Toler could send their way.

Barina ran toward the king, moving out of the way at the last second before a blast of his magic could touch her. She rushed in and kicked him in the chest, sending him flying back over a dozen feet. She ran past him and jumped to the walls, climbing up them with her hooked gloves just as fast as if she was running on level ground. Toler sent a piercing line of fire after her. She ducked behind a tapestry which was now ablaze.

"Missed me!" She poked her head out from behind another tapestry.

He set that one on fire, too.

Barina appeared from behind another. "I'm up here!" She waved this time and swung from the tapestry before ducking behind it again.

Toler didn't just set the tapestry on fire, he set the wall ablaze. "Where is the STONE?" Toler yelled. "Where are you?"

He was startled by a tap on his shoulder and turned to see this woman jump up, meeting him face to face.

"Boo," was all she said to him before she dug two hands clad in hooked gloves into his neck. She ripped his throat open while simultaneously flipping him onto the ground.

Toler was back up on his feet in seconds, healing his neck. Barina saw the lights in his eyes change as he attempted to put a paralysis spell on her. She shook her head while she walked over to sit on the throne.

"Those spells don't work on me," she said, swinging her feet. "FYI, magic doesn't hurt me like it does everyone else. That information's a freebie for ya."

Seething with rage, Toler stared at her. "Who the fuck, are you?"

"Do you really care?" she asked calmly.

"Humor me."

She knew what her name would do. "Barina Raine."

Toler laughed to himself. "My son mentioned your name, too. The one trained by Berklion of Halk." He then eyed her up and down, "I was going to kill you for sitting in my chair, but I don't think I will."

Barina raised her eyebrows, looking thoroughly amused. "What do you think you're gonna do? I mean, you won't get to kill me cause I'm gonna kill you. But tell me, I'm curious."

Toler nodded from Barina to the two women who were her friends. "I think I'll save you and your friends—Aria and Tyra I believe he said their names are—I'll save you for my son. Your healer was disguised well to look like a man, but if I look closer, I can tell she's a beautiful woman."

Barina's laughter was dark. "Oh, honey no. No, you won't get to do that."

"What makes you so sure?" He eyed her more closely now.

"Because he's dead." Satisfaction laced those words.

Toler's smile faded, his eyes became wide, and he didn't move for a moment. "You're lying."

"It's been, what, a little over a month since you've heard from him? He was in the Green Forest last time you spoke, right?" She looked at her katana. "You should check the Water Caves. His body is probably still there. He'll have some wounds that were made by a blade that looks like this one," she said, indicating her katana, "except for where I literally ripped his throat out." She took her gloves off, putting them back in her pouch. "I wasn't even wearing these gloves when I did it. I used my bare hands."

"Fucking savage," Kyle hissed trying to hold back a smile.

"Who the hell is this girl?" one of his soldiers whispered. "She's like a cat playing with a mouse she caught."

"An old friend," Kyle responded.

"You're lying!" Toler's eyes went magenta. Barina knew what that meant.

She lifted her blade directly in front of her as he created a large molten boulder and sent it her way. She sliced it in two, the halves blowing out the wall behind her. She didn't bother to stand up.

"You kill me, and you might destroy your precious Anna Stone. Then your son will have died for nothing. Well, no, not for nothing. He was a piece of shit." She put her hands to her face, pretending to be worried. "And then what will you do? I mean, you've already seen that your magic isn't as effective on me as you'd like. What if I strike you down so many times you won't be able to keep healing yourself? How awful. I mean, how terrible for you if you were to get struck down by a girl with no magic of her own."

Toler's eyes still swirled with rage, but he steadied his breathing as he thought about her words. "What do you suggest?"

Barina stood up, her face stern. "No magic, just steel."

Toler threw his head back in laughter. This small woman going up against him, he thought it was a joke. "Are you serious? You think you can really take me?"

His laughter was cut short when he landed on his back, and it was lights out. Barina had pounced from the throne, using her sword to slice his face almost in half as it went through his nose and out the back of his head.

"What do you think?" Barina knew he wasn't in his last life. She walked a few feet away and waited for him to revive. She flicked the blood from her sword again before sheathing it.

"Onyx!" she called to him. "Did Rutherford or Berklion take any of his lives? I don't remember."

"Rutherford did get one." Onyx glowed seeing the man who killed his mentor on the ground. "Now he's down by at least two more lives."

"Is she really going to fight him?" one of the soldiers asked.

"If anyone can do it, it's her." Jaras told him.

Jason nodded before he cleared his throat. "Finally! Damn, not being able to talk was a pain in the ass. She got a new sword, too, but she's still using her katana."

"Its name is Kitty!" Barina called to Jason while she kept her eyes on Toler. "Josh had it this whole time. My dad had made it for me!"

"Are you serious? And he never told anyone?" Jason looked surprised.

Tyra coughed, trying to use her vocal cords again. "That new sword is really pretty."

One of the soldiers asked, "How can you be so sure she can defeat him? We know he has more lives left, and he gets more powerful each time he taps into a new one. Kyle, what have you gotten us into?"

Arkon stared dumbfounded at the man. "You guys have been paying attention since you walked into the room, right?"

Aria patted the soldier's back. "You did see her literally slice whatever it was he threw at her in half and not flinch? She didn't even stand up. And she has taken one of his lives."

"Like I've told Jaras, Barina is stronger than me and stronger than Berklion," Jason said. "He trained both of us, and she's really good."

"What about the dragon?" Megan asked. "What do we do about him?"

"Apparently," Kevin said, grinning to himself, "she killed two of his friends back in the day. So, just saying."

"And there's me." Arkon raised his hand.

"How can you help?" Morgan asked with a curious smile.

Tyra pushed Arkon's hair behind his ears, revealing the fact that he was an elf.

"That's how you can help," Morgan said, her eyes wide.

"Cute baby," Arkon said. "She's not even a day old, is she?"

"No. Thanks to Barina, we're both alive. We were supposed to be fed to Uraki."

Twarence looked at Onyx. "Do you know where she might've put that stone?"

"I don't. It could be anywhere. My guess is in her pocket, but I don't know if she'd keep it on her." Onyx suddenly looked curious. "Wouldn't it?"

Twarence cut him off. "No, it doesn't work like that," he whispered.

Tyra looked over. "What are you talking about?"

Onyx shook his head. "Nothing. Toler's getting back up. Everyone look alive."

Aria wasn't convinced that something wasn't going on with those two, and then it clicked. "Can someone else here use the Anna Stone?" she asked under her breath.

Twarence nodded. "Yes. Has to be skin to stone contact."

"Do they know they can use it?" She could hardly say the words.

"No, nobody knows who they are but me and Onyx. I haven't dared say anything, and I won't unless there's not another option. Barina, she's another option without resorting to the stone. We have to see if she can win." Twarence held his breath. "He's up."

Barina had been waiting patiently, not daring to listen in on the conversations of others. She needed to keep her focus. She wasn't afraid, not even now as the king got to his feet, but she knew that she couldn't afford to make one mistake.

Toler used his powers to fuse his face back together and wiped blood away at the same time. He took his sword from his side and stood at the ready.

"I guess I should take you seriously." He had a growl in the back of his speech. "I'm going to murder you but not before I rape you so that the entire kingdom can see it. Everyone will know what happens when they try to defy me."

Barina didn't flinch hearing his words.

"Let's see how well Berklion taught you."

Barina gave a slight bow of her head, taking a stance, her hand on the handle of her sword, ready to move.

Toler rushed her, but she moved aside, sticking her foot out and tripping him.

Kevin laughed. "I've seen her use that one."

Toler spun in the next two steps, and his blade came crashing down. She lifted her own and let his slide down her blade till it touched the floor. She came at him—her blade in such a frenzy that he could barely keep up with her movements.

"I always did like the waltz," Barina said while attacking him to make him move the way she wanted. "One two three, one two three, and lunge." She slashed his side, drawing blood. They both bounced back and then came running at each other again. This time, their swords hit and even made sparks. Barina kicked his legs out from under him, but when she went to strike him down again, his eyes swirled blue. She deflected the magic attack with her sword, just in time. It gave Toler enough of a moment to swipe at her with his blade before he rolled away, getting to his feet.

Barina was poised and waiting when Toler started to laugh. "Does it hurt? I'm surprised you can hold your sword."

Barina glanced at her arm. "I'm not even bleeding."

Toler saw she was right and ran toward her again, angry that she made him look foolish. She deflected his sword and pushed him—aware that neither was using all of their strength.

His long sword in one hand, Toler brought out a short sword from behind his back. Barina took out her dagger to use in sync with her katana. More sparks flew as metal hit metal. The king became increasingly angry that he couldn't put a scratch on this woman. He sent strike after strike to her neck or heart, but she was too fast and too strong. He used not only his weapons but his eyes swirling pink this time. Barina spit in his eyes to stop the magic and then buried her dagger in his neck, following him to the ground with it. She knew this didn't take one of his lives, but each time he had to heal himself, it weakened his magic in general.

Toler wiped his eyes, looking at Barina. "I don't need to deal with the likes of you."

"You don't, or you can't?" Barina asked while sitting back on the throne. "You have an option right now. You can surrender."

Toler's eyes went dark, and he raised a hand, waving it to ring a bell behind the throne. It was loud and shook the walls, startling everyone in the room aside from Toler and the thief who didn't move a muscle. She registered what this bell was for and caught her breath.

"I don't even care if *I* kill you at this point."

Barina's eyes went wide, and she jumped off the throne. "TAKE COVER! ARKON!"

Arkon's face went pale, and he knew. "Oh stars!"

The ceiling and the walls around them came crashing down, exposing the throne room to the whole city when the beast landed. Arkon and Onyx held their shields up as strong as they could to protect everyone from the falling debris.

Uraki made his entrance. His thirty-foot body was pure white except for the scales on his underbelly and the curled horns on his head shining gold. His crystal-blue eyes were hungry. He let out a screech that it would've made their ears bleed if it wasn't for Arkon.

Toler kept a shield over himself and used his powers to swipe the debris off the ground. He laughed in delight seeing Uraki.

"Toler, what do you want? I was sleeping." Uraki seemed only mildly irritated.

"I have a feast for you." Toler pointed to everyone near the cage.

Uraki licked his mouth. "Oh and even a baby!"

Arkon raised his hands, his body becoming almost transparent. His eyes changed from blue to clear as he directed all of his power at Uraki. "Like hell!"

Uraki hissed, spitting at the air, while he found himself in the hold of this elf. "Spirit elf!"

Arkon tried with all his strength to bring Uraki down. But the dragon was so strong and had so much power that the elf struggled just to hold him. Though Uraki couldn't speak, he growled and thrashed until Arkon splayed the beast's legs and forced his belly to the ground.

Arkon's body began to glow a bright red, and his eyes turned to a shade of orange—a striking contrast to Uraki's blue eyes. The elf met the dragon's stare and began using his powers to siphon energy from him. Uraki froze, unable to move from Arkon's powerful gaze.

The elf felt all of the anger and hate that this beast held for all living beings of this world. Arkon could find no reason for it. It seemed Uraki was just a wicked creature who wanted to dominate all other beings. Arkon circled the dragon's body in a thin red veil, and Uraki's blood began to heat up. The dragon could do nothing to signal distress or defend himself.

Toler still wasn't worried about his dragon. His eyes searched for Barina. "Do you see, woman!" Toler yelled. "Either you're hiding or you're dead! Uraki will kill them if you hide and kill them if you're dead!"

Kevin scanned the area, but there was no sign of her. "I've gotta find her."

Jason and Jaras put a hand on him. "Whoa there. You don't really think something like this could take her down, do you?" Jason gave Kevin a wink.

"She might need me." Kevin was ready to search the room.

"She might, but she'll let you know if she does."

Toler looked over in shock seeing Uraki's head slammed to the ground, and he finally realized that his dragon was going to lose its life if he didn't act. "No!" he yelled and sent a piercing stream of fire toward Arkon's heart. Jaras ducked in front of him and deflected the line with his sword, sending it back to Toler who narrowly escaped.

Arkon didn't break his concentration, but Uraki gathered enough strength to strike at the elf with his tail. It sent Arkon flying against the cage, breaking an arm and causing a large gash in his forehead. He slumped to the ground, unable to move.

"Arkon!" Aria cried, and she and Tyra hurried to him, tending to his wounds.

Onyx was sweating and struggling to hold up the shield. "I don't know how much longer I can hold this," he whispered. "I don't know."

"Let me help you with that." Toler sent a shock wave at Onyx, and it put the wizard on his knee, his shield around the group shaking.

"I can hold against a few more hits from Toler," Onyx said in a shaky voice, "but not from a dragon."

Uraki came to his feet, shaking his head and limbs, angry at what almost happened. "Which one shall I eat first?" he asked, getting closer. His chin hovered only a few feet above the ground to look at them. "Ahh, a mother and her little daughter. I'll start with you."

Kevin and Jaras moved to stop him, but Uraki's tongue slithered out of his mouth and would get to her before they could help.

Suddenly, Barina slid out from under Uraki's mighty chin and drove her sword into his tongue, pushing it through to the ground. The dragon let out a cry while she sliced through half of his tongue. He held it while Toler used his magic to heal the dragon.

A bruise began to form on Barina's face and blood dripped down her arm from a gash, but she hardly seemed to notice.

Uraki looked down at the woman who was now running, drawing his attention away from the group. "Hey Uraki, how ya been?"

The dragon's face twisted in anger and rage. "BARINA RAINE!" He inhaled a breath and blasted out a wave of fire, following her as she ran.

"He remembers her," Jason said, smiling to himself.

When the fire subsided, Barina turned to look him in the eyes. "You still mad?"

Uraki glared at her. "You killed them both!"

"You were destroying villages!" she spat at him. "Only reason I didn't finish you was because Usami and Medole dragged me from the fight." She looked at her pocket watch. "Should be any minute."

"What's that?" Uraki asked her.

"I had an idea earlier," she said, teasing him. "But until I see if it pans out, we can get reacquainted." She then ran toward the dragon, driving her new sword and her dagger into the beast's side. Before he could react, she climbed onto his neck and ran to his head. "Now you see me." She met one of his eyes before she stabbed it with both blades. "Now you don't."

Uraki screamed in pain again, flinging Barina to the ground. She landed hard, sure she hurt her ribs again, but she didn't have time to worry as she stood back up. Toler was busy enjoying the show, even with his dragon maimed. The king waved his hands and fixed the dragon's eye.

"Toler, you're really making this a pain in the ass," Barina grumbled, hurling a throwing knife that landed in the king's neck. Toler pulled the knife out to heal himself.

Uraki snapped his jaws at Barina, and she rolled out of the way twice. He lashed at her with his tongue, but she sliced it again.

"Didn't learn the first time." She glared at the dragon before running straight into his mouth.

"The fuck are you doing?" Jason and Kevin cried together.

From inside, Barina used one sword to pierce the roof of Uraki's mouth and the other to cut a handful of his long, thin and razor-sharp teeth clean off. She ran out of his mouth as he began to yell.

"I'm going to kill you if it's the last thing I do!"

Barina took off her cloak, tossing it aside.

"Son-of-a-bitch!" Jason inhaled. "That's a big risk for her."

Barina was still jumping, predicting Uraki's movements. She was so much faster without her cloak.

While she fought head to head with Uraki, Toler turned his attention back to the group. He drew his sword.

"Now that she's distracted, who wants to play with me?" He was grinning. "All my women? Morgan, I see you had a girl. You should be dead by now. What happened to Lord Griu? He was supposed to have taken you to Uraki."

This time, Morgan had a dark smile. "*She* happened." The young mother pointed to Barina. "Uraki got to taste nobility."

Toler's face went red. "I'll kill you and the girl myself." The king had talked too long, not paying attention as Jaras' sword came crashing down onto Toler's shoulder, almost taking his arm off. He turned with a scream, healing his arm and rounding on Jaras.

"You!" he yelled. "Jaras Luca, trained by Darien Bell, you don't really think you can win against me, do you?"

"I don't have to win," Jaras snarled. "I just have to keep you busy till she can fight you again."

"You think…" Toler was cut off again. This time, an arrow landed in his shoulder. He saw Aria holding her bow, drawing another arrow.

"You can hold hands with me if you want."

Toler laughed, waved his hand, and drew the healer near. "I'll end you quickly enough." He bared his sword, ready to strike her down.

Aria dropped her bow and dodged out of the way of his blade before she lunged at him—one of her hands holding his. He dropped his sword and cried out in terror and shock, trying to inhale a breath. His eyes were sunken into the back of his head, and his body started to shrivel into a lifeless husk on the ground.

Aria leaned over the king. "I know this isn't your last life. But I really hope that hurt." She kicked him for good measure before she picked up her bow and went back with the others. They were quiet, watching the healer with admiration.

"I enjoyed that way more than I should have!" Morgan said, delighted.

"LOOK OUT!" Arkon bellowed. He had run in front of everyone and raised his shield just as a blast of deadly energy came from Toler's body while he reanimated. The elf threw blasts of his own at the king while the others readied for their next attack. In the next moment, he lowered his shield.

Toler barely saw it as a double-bladed ax flew in and dug into the back of his thigh. Twarence had joined the fight with Jaras. "Aria, you stay with Onyx and Arkon. Kevin, Kyle, keep watch on the rest of them. Jaras, you and me."

The pain was blinding for the moment till Toler healed his leg. He sent a kick that threw Twarence against what was left of the wall, but the professor got back up. Jaras went after the king, delivering blows and strikes, but nothing landing. Toler was fast and powerful. Even when Twarence came back, using all his might and strength, it wasn't enough to strike the king again. They just knew they had to keep him busy for a while.

"It's everything in me not to jump in right now," Kevin said, anxious. "But I know the best place for me is here with you guys."

Jason walked over to Kevin. "You're new. I have never heard her talk about you. How did you and her meet?"

Kevin shook his head. "In the middle of all this, these are the questions you wanna ask me?"

Jason shrugged.

"Hey, I'm curious about you, too," Kyle said, putting an arm around Jason. "By the way Jason, I'm really glad that you and Tyra were just brought here. Not, you know, what Barina was led to believe."

"Same." Jason then looked back to Kevin. "My question still stands."

Kevin had turned his attention back to Jaras and Toler, watching to see if he'd have to step in. He felt a tap on his shoulder. Jason and Kyle were leaning in.

"Woe, um, you're still on that." Kevin turned red. "We met in the Forest of Lithor right after she left Estella. I'm moving there with her after this is over."

Jason's eyes widened. Even Tyra looked up from tending to Arkon.

"We're gone for a little over a month and, well, it seems a lot happened." Tyra glanced at Jason.

"I was asking her about him yesterday," Kyle said. "Good for her." He turned to Kevin. "Can you fight? Obviously, you can. Where did you train?" He poked at Kevin's arm. "Got some springy muscle on him."

"Willow, last apprentice of Franklin before he retired," Kevin said, a little confused but finding their interest endearing. "Let me know when you finish inspecting me."

Barina had come running from Uraki's fire again. Toler didn't notice when she ran right behind him, slicing both of his knees open, and kept moving. Toler fell to the ground in agony and almost didn't put his shield up in time to block Uraki's fire that came down on him.

"That shouldn't be funny," Onyx chuckled as he blocked Uraki's fire. Arkon was still being healed. Uraki let out another ear-piercing screech that brought everything to a halt. "I really hate you!" he cried as he and Barina stood still in the middle of the room–her ready to move, him watching to anticipate what she'd do.

"I'm aware," she said, catching her breath. She twitched an eye barely a fraction as she noticed among the rubble of the room that a fire was still lit in a fireplace. She spotted a flicker of movement in the flames. She'd worry about that later.

"I'm surprised you're not running anymore." Uraki's face was now level with hers.

She showed her teeth.

"What is it that makes you smile?"

"My idea."

Uraki looked up to see a shadow before something landed right behind Barina. It let out a roar so powerful it made Uraki recoil his head in fear. With a wicked grin, Barina stood unmoving with her arms at her sides as the roar shook the ground.

Jason laughed when he saw who had shown up. "She always does have some crazy good ideas."

"Explains the music I heard earlier," Arkon said, impressed.

"Na'imah!" Uraki could hardly whisper her name. He cowered back.

There was a growl in her voice. "Uraki."

"You. How. Why are you here?" Uraki's eyes held fear. Na'imah was much larger, and he had to think how to fight her.

"Barina has friends in high places." Na'imah's eyes narrowed.

"Nice one," the thief said, smiling back at her. "Would you mind teaming up? I mean, I can take him myself if you can't, but if you…" The human didn't need to finish.

"Not at all." Na'imah's brilliant orange eyes narrowed as she set an arm down. "Climb on. Uraki and I have a history to settle and, apparently, I'm in debt to you for more than just helping in the lair."

"Traitor to dragons!" Uraki called and launched himself at Na'imah just as Barina climbed from her arm onto her back.

Barina held onto Na'imah as the dragon was pushed back and then knocked Uraki hard enough that he flew out of the room. The next thing Barina knew, they were flying into the skies, her sword out and ready to fight.

Toler whispered, "Who the hell is this bitch?" He couldn't believe that she had managed to bring in another dragon. He turned his attention back to the group as Jaras and Twarence went back to fighting him.

"You're all pathetic," the king declared. "You really think that you can get rid of me? I cannot be defeated. So many have tried and, as you should remember Onyx, so many have died. You will join them. None of you can beat me."

"You think so?" Jaras asked. "You're not a little worried?"

"You're joking, right? Berklion couldn't stop me. What makes you think you could? Rutherford couldn't stop me. Onyx definitely can't."

"But all of us together." Twarence threw his body into Toler, knocking him off of his feet. "And the girl that's about to take down your dragon. Admit you're terrified of her."

Toler sent a shock wave of energy toward Twarence. It would've killed him if Kevin hadn't stepped in, deflecting the energy wave with a large piece of broken metal. He knelt in front of Twarence and reflected the energies back toward Toler. The king barely dodged out of the way of his own spell.

"I'm not afraid of that fucking whore!" Toler snarled.

"Sure you are." Twarence got to his feet.

Kevin pulled out one of his chains. "And you should absolutely be terrified of her." He lashed out at Toler, wrapping the chain around his leg and pulling as hard as he could. Toler was on the ground and being dragged as Kevin pulled him closer. "Twarence!"

Twarence swung his axe down hard, but Toler rolled out of the way just before the scholar was able to take off one of his legs. Toler swept his leg, Twarence backed away.

Kevin then pulled harder on the chains, enough to lift Toler off of the ground, and flung him over his head. Toler almost slammed into what was left of the wall but stopped at the last moment by putting up his energy shield.

"I like this guy," Jason said, impressed with Kevin.

Toler landed on the ground, kicking the chain off of his leg, and turned his attention to Kevin. Kevin locked his cold gray eyes with Toler's amber ones.

"Who the fuck, are you?" Toler asked while menacing his sword.

Kevin pointed to the sky. "I'm with the girl that's gonna end you and Uraki."

Toler's jaw was set. "I'll make sure you have a front row seat to watch everything I do to her. She'll be ruined and broken, but I'll let you both die together when I finish with her." He licked his lips. "I bet she's delicious. The strong and stubborn ones always are."

Kevin took a breath and tried to control his emotions. Toler never saw him move. Kevin lashed out with his chain again, this time wrapping it around Toler's neck. He pulled, snapping bone. The king fell to the ground, a smile still on his face.

"One more life down," Kevin huffed, wrapping his chain back up.

Jaras walked over and shook his hand. "We don't know you Kevin, but I think we all like you."

"That was, wow," Aria said, finally finished with healing all the women and Arkon.

The elf got to his feet. "Kevin, right, thank you."

He nodded before he looked up to the sky and flinched. "Things are really heating up with those dragons."

* * *

Barina held tight to Na'imah when they took to the skies. She wasn't a novice to flying on a dragon, thankfully, and she climbed from Na'imah's back to the top of her head. "If you get me close enough, I can get on him and do some damage!"

"You got it." Na'imah took off after Uraki.

"So, what's your beef with him?"

"When his true nature came out and he first turned for the worst, he went on a rampage through my lair. He's killed many dragons, including several of our young. He tried to kill my son. And he later would try to kill my brother." Na'imah was gaining speed.

"He was always like this?"

"We had hoped he was just still learning. But he believed that dragons need to be at the top, not living in peace and harmony with the rest of the world. When Usami was selected to represent the dragons in the Circle of Greats, it made him bitter."

"That makes no sense," Barina said. "Why wouldn't the leader of the dragons be selected to represent dragons in the Circle. And I thought it was only the last four years or so that Uraki's really been out for blood. The Circle has been around for hundreds of years."

"He carried that grudge for a long time. What set him off was, well, when they brought in a human member, five years ago."

Barina groaned. "Was this before or after I had taken down his friends? And to be fair, all three of them had set fire to several villages."

"You took down his friends and we detained him after that for as long as he could. When word got to him about a certain human being brought into the Circle, he went crazy with anger."

Barina looked down. "I have to stop him." She felt a wave of guilt go through her entire body. "Stars, I'm so sorry."

"This is not your fault, dear. He made the decision to be a monster."

Barina nodded. "Hey, who is your brother?"

Na'imah smiled. "The other reason I owe you for more than just helping in my lair. Medole."

"Get out of here! Is he really?"

"Thank you for saving my brother, twice."

"My pleasure." Barina looked up. "Here we go," she warned. "He's bringing the heat!" She slid down Na'imah's neck a bit to offer herself some protection from Uraki's fire as he came flying toward them.

Na'imah let out a roar that, even from as high up as they were, still shook the ground below them. The city was watching.

When everyone first saw Uraki fly from his tower and go barreling into the throne room, the civilians had all taken cover. Now they watched with caution from partially cracked windows. Aside from Na'iamh's ground-shaking roar, the citizens were watching in awe as she flew after Uraki. Another dragon was challenging Uraki.

With the walls of the throne room blown away, many people could see the energy and magic being thrown around. They realized that, not only was there a challenge against Uraki, but against Toler as well. Many also noticed a small figure riding the challenger.

When Uraki came rushing toward her, Na'imah turned just in time and grabbed him by the wings, sending a powerful swipe with her tail. Uraki turned around and rammed himself into her. Barina held on tight as the force almost knocked her off.

"Give me the human!" he screeched, breathing fire at her again. "Give me Barina, and I'll let them live!"

Na'imah dodged the attack. "Over my dead body!"

"That can be arranged!" Uraki sped toward her in a moment and slammed Na'imah into the side of his tower. He dug his jaws into Na'imah's neck, biting down hard. Na'imah was trying to push him off, but Uraki had her wings pinned down as well.

Barina dodged being trapped between the tower and Na'imah just in time, but her friend was now in danger. She launched herself at Uraki's neck, using her katana and her new sword to climb up onto his head. There, she stabbed him in one eye again. It was enough to make him scream and to give Na'imah a chance to bring her large wings crashing down on Uraki.

Barina had to get him away from Na'imah. She had been able to maim him which was more than enough to help her out.

Na'imah slid down to the ground, holding her neck, trying to breathe. She looked up, relieved to see Uraki's attention elsewhere. "Get him Barina."

"Now you have to deal with me," Barina hissed at him. She stabbed the top of his head.

"I will *kill* you Barina!" Uraki tried to shake her off, but Barina had dug her swords deep into his head.

"Neash ta!" *You first*, she yelled in his language, and she pulled back on her swords buried in his head.

Uraki started to fly, haphazardly, back into the sky. He landed on top of his tower, shaking his head, trying to reach back to grab hold of the human.

Barina flipped around beneath his head, driving a sword into the underside of his chin, and sliced it about four feet. Uraki almost managed to grab hold of her—one of the tips of his sharp claws scratching deep into her left side. She hissed out in pain. She climbed higher onto the back of his neck, but not before he blew fire onto the roof of the tower, setting the whole thing ablaze. Flames large enough to catch hold of Barina's clothes threw large sparks and fiery debris on her. She climbed to Uraki's head so she could roll around to put her clothes out—her pants singed and burned up to her knees. Debris hit her left arm, and it burned enough that she could no longer feel those spots. She could still move it, thankfully. She managed to block the rest of the debris.

Uraki flipped his head up, and Barina went flying into the air. She turned to look down and saw the dragon opening his mouth.

"I will burn you alive!" He inhaled to let out a fire blast.

"I'll take your damn head!" Barina was filled with her own rage. She pointed both swords in front of her, hoping her body would fall directly into the middle of his fire. She knew that the center of a dragon's breath was a hollow tunnel. She could dive into it, avoiding the flames. Still, the heat was unbearable, and she had to close her eyes and mouth. She couldn't breathe or see, but she knew where she was going to land.

She used both swords as she dove into his lower jaw, her whole body going right through the soft tissue under the tongue and chin, and back out the other side of his flesh. Uraki was lashing and screaming in agony. Barina then dug her swords into the underside of his throat, slicing in a curve, and managed to flip herself onto the back of his neck.

Uraki tried to fly while blood poured from his neck and jaw. He desperately wanted to get back to the throne room where he knew Toler could heal him. Na'imah was on her way back toward them.

Barina jumped from Uraki, Na'imah catching her in her hand.

"Throw me up in the air," Barina called out. "I need to get some speed under me." Na'imah held out a hand and threw the thief high.

* * *

In the throne room, the group stood back when they saw Toler get to his feet. Na'imah landed, holding her neck to try and stop the blood. Aria hurried over with Arkon, and they began to work on healing where Uraki had bitten her.

"Thank you." Na'imah rested her neck. "Barina should be back any moment."

An angry Toler, his eyes swirling in a rage, could hear the shrieks and looked up to see his dragon struggling to stay alive.

"Uraki! Come back to me!" he ordered.

Uraki was trying. He came closer and closer, flying just above the throne room. Everyone heard Barina yell as she fell, her katana bared. When she landed on Uraki, she used the curve of her blade and her own momentum to pull her sword all the way around the back of his neck and around to the other side. They could hear the cutting of bone and scale before the beast's head came away from his body and crashed onto the ground outside of the room; his head landing in the throne room.

Barina managed to be on top of Uraki's head when it landed, and she made a line for Toler. She sent half a dozen throwing knives from her pocket before she even hit the ground. She came at him, both swords dancing, to take him down once and for all. Toler could barely get away.

"You killed my dragon!" he roared.

"You're welcome!" She kicked and slammed him into what was left of the hard, crumbling stone wall behind him.

Injured as she was, Barina was faster, fiercer, and stronger than before. The intensity of this fight between her and Toler brought out everything they both had. He tried to sweep her legs, she sidestepped him. He sent a wave of magic and his sword down on her at the same time. She dodged that too. For what seemed like forever, but was barely a minute, maybe two, the battle between them raged.

Barina was no longer on the defensive. Every strike she sent was one that could've killed Toler if he hadn't blocked it or moved just in time. He didn't want to play with her anymore. She was too dangerous to be left alive, and he needed her dead.

"Are you ready to see your son again?" Barina's wicked grin grew when they locked swords.

"I don't need him. With the stone, I can live forever."

"Good luck with that."

Toler brought his blades down, but Barina moved close enough to him that his swords missed. Hers remained true. Yukinohana went into his heart, while Kitty went into his neck.

The room went silent. Nobody even dared to breathe.

The king couldn't move or even gasp for air. He couldn't believe it. The room was spinning, and blood poured from his mouth as this woman who stood over a foot shorter held her blades inside him.

Barina pressed her swords deeper as his knees buckled. Leaning into him, she said, "Tell your son I said, 'Go fuck yourself.'"

She put a foot on Toler's chest, sliding him back, her swords bursting out of his chest and neck. He fell to the ground, not moving, his eyes starting to glaze over. Her piercing gaze locked on his.

Barina flicked both of her blades to get the blood off them. She put her new sword back at her side and held her katana still. She took a moment to let the adrenaline wear off as she leaned on her katana before turning to look at everyone. The others were just beginning to realize that it was over.

"Hey guys." She was catching her breath.

"Barina," Twarence began. "Where did you put the stone?"

She gave him a tired nod. "Check your left pocket."

Twarence did just that and grinned when he pulled out the small stone on its chain. He realized she must have slipped it in there when she nudged his arm earlier.

"We did it." Aria couldn't help but smile. "It's all over," she said, leaning back against Na'imah with a sigh of relief.

Arkon turned to Kyle. "You weren't joking. You don't see her act when she steals something."

Kyle nodded. "Honestly, on the off chance she didn't want to fight, she would've been out of the kingdom by now, and we never would've seen her. Let's be glad she's the type that steps up to the fight when needed."

Barina met eyes with Kevin and took a step toward him. The sky went dark on her next step, as if someone extinguished the sun. The ground began to shake, and all of Toler's former women found themselves unable to move. Toler stood up, barely teetering to life, only to look at these women with dark and crazed eyes.

"I just need to kill all of you," he said, panting, "and that will replenish my power. I'll start with Chelsea." He pulled the twelve-year-old girl toward him, her screams filling the air.

Barina ran back toward Toler.

"Barina!" Twarence yelled. "Catch it!"

Toler looked just in time to see Twarence throw the Anna Stone toward Barina, barely feet from the king. The king knew exactly what that meant. The stone was in reach, Toler held out his hand to grab it.

In one swipe, Barina took his hand clean off with her dagger while taking hold of the Anna Stone in her free hand. During the next half heartbeat, Toler would look in horror as he saw death come for him.

Barina's bare fingers took hold of the stone, and she felt a surge of energy like she had never known before go through her body. It was strange but familiar all at once, and she knew what to do with it.

In Toler's eyes, she could see her reflection and the silver star that was now upon her forehead. Toler's eyes started to swirl red in a last-ditch effort to try and save his skin.

"You're done," was all Barina said, her eyes glowing with a bright white light.

In the city, people flinched when the white light burst from the throne room. None had ever seen power like that, and it shook the ground below them.

When she spoke her last words to Toler, Barina engulfed him in the light. She took the entirety of his life force from him, his body shriveling into skin and bones. He couldn't even scream.

Toler fell to the ground as a lifeless shell, his crown clinking to the ground, rolling away. His power gone from his body. All of his life was exhausted.

The king was dead. The people of Thoron were free.

CHAPTER 19

Barina looked at the stone and put it in her pocket, not daring to trigger its powers again just yet. She held her injured ribs on the side that had been ripped open by Uraki. It had stopped bleeding, thankfully. She wasn't sure when she had sprained her ankle, but the pain was setting in. Still, she didn't care.

Leaning on her sword, she turned her attention to Chelsea–the little girl Toler would have killed–who was sitting on the ground with her knees curled to her chest, crying from fear. Barina held out her hand to the little girl. "Are you hurt?"

Chelsea looked up and threw herself into Barina's arms, sobbing.

Barina smoothed over the child's hair. "I got you."

"I was so scared." Chelsea couldn't stop crying.

"I know," Barina said, trying to calm her. "It was very scary. It's all over now." She knew this little girl had been living in hell for so long, and she just wanted to hold her and let her know she was safe now.

Barina's friends—from the traveling party to Jason, Tyra, and Kevin— were silent. The guards and soldiers, the women in the room, and Na'imah. All of them stood quietly, letting this moment sink in.

They had won. Nobody could speak or move. No words could express this feeling. It was as if the entire room—and soon the entire kingdom when they learned of Toler's demise—would let out a sigh of relief.

There was one who seemed to know what to do next.

As Chelsea cried in Barina's arms, Morgan's eyes were set on the woman who helped save them. She handed her baby to her sister to hold. If it weren't for Barina and the people in this room, they'd all be dead or worse. Morgan grabbed the crown off of the floor and walked over to Barina.

"Yeah, this seems right," she said, her eyes starting to leak.

Barina looked at her. "Huh?"

Holding the crown, Morgan knelt in front of Barina. "My queen."

Chelsea's smile was full of excitement, before she knelt as well.

"Yoooo, what?" Barina was taken aback and completely confused. "No thank you."

Kyle let out a breath. "Yes." He walked over to help, taking the crown from Morgan's hands and placing it on top of Barina's head.

She squirmed, trying to get away. "What are you doing?"

Kyle's long arm managed to place the crown on her head. "Just...hold still."

"This thing is heavy and too big." It sat crooked on her head, and she was still trying to take it off.

"Wear the damn thing," Kyle protested.

"But, what? Why? Stop!" Barina shook her head and then stopped, listening to what he had to say.

Kyle nodded to her. "You defeated Toler. You helped save us from his wrath and tyranny." He took a knee and bowed his head. "I will gladly pledge my loyalty and my service to you."

Barina froze, not even daring to breathe as she looked around to see the rest of the soldiers, guards, and the women kneeling. It didn't seem right. She wanted to run.

Her friends stood frozen, smiling as they saw what was unfolding before them. Barina was relieved none of them knelt. This was already weird for her.

Twarence walked over and let out a loud laugh. "You defeated the king. That's kinda one of the ways it works to become, well, a monarch." He placed a gentle hand on her shoulder and then gave her a warm hug. The rest of the group walked up next to Twarence, little grins spreading over their faces. They also snickered at Barina's expression of shock.

Even Na'imah gave a nod of her head, approving of this transition of power.

"But, I'm not..." Barina tried to find words. "I had plans for after this."

"Plans aren't your style," Kyle said, joking. "You freed us from Toler, and you can control the powers in the Anna Stone. Barina," he began, making her look him in the eye again, "I can think of nobody better, then you. I *know* you. I know that you won't abuse this authority. I know you can and will use the power behind the crown for good and for what's right. I know you will protect these people."

Morgan spoke up. "If it wasn't for you, I'd be dead and so would my daughter. The rest of us would be waiting to die while that bastard continued to rape us until we gave him a son or kill us when we didn't. He did things to us," Morgan said, nodding to Chelsea. "He did things to all of us that nobody should ever have to experience. Every woman in this kingdom has always been in danger, no matter their age, if they were married or not. It didn't matter. He and his nobles would take us."

"I know with you that we can finally be at peace," Kyle said. "So I say it again. Your majesty, I pledge my loyalty and service to you."

Twarence spoke up again. "Barina, you have the stone. You can do pretty much anything with it. It can give you the power to do great things. You should test it."

Barina gave him a wry smile. "How long have you known I could do this? I mean, you held the biggest secret in this whole thing."

"I was suspicious after you said you knew Julius. I remember a story he told me involving you and the stone. I knew for sure after we crossed Rose Lake. Some of the water got in your mouth during the storm and, when it did, the star appeared on your forehead for a couple seconds." Twarence had a sheepish grin. "Sorry I had to keep this from you."

"I understand why you did. It's all good."

"What are you gonna do now?" Jaras asked. "You gonna be the queen?"

She leaned on Jaras, quietly telling him, "I don't really want this, but I know I can make a difference. I know I can help a lot of people." Barina propped herself up a little more using her sword to walk. The large crown lopsided on her head, she took the stone out of her pocket and held it in her fingers. As she did, the star appeared on her forehead, giving off a soft glow.

Barina hobbled to the edge of the floor where the wall no longer existed and looked over the city. She closed her eyes and focused on not just this city but the whole kingdom. She asked the stone to clean the water, to make the fields fertile again, to repair and fix all buildings that were broken, and to bring health to all those who had suffered. She asked that the people in the village who died in the conflict be buried, the stone putting up markers by each grave.

The palace was no longer a terrifying fortress. All the heads that had been on spikes were now with their bodies and buried. The moat was gone completely. The bricks on the palace shown white and clean, and she changed the structure of it. It became a beautiful storybook castle. The gardens grew lush and green. All the rooms were bright.

Life was coming back to the kingdom.

She rebuilt the throne room in pristine white stone with large colorful stained-glass windows in every color of the rainbow. The throne where Toler had sat was gone, and a simple chair of light polished wood with blue cushions took its place. Dark blue drapes in between the windows and tapestries depicting different magical creatures now covered the walls.

She would eventually have to think of a new crest for the kingdom. For now, it was the beautiful white snowdrop flower that was the inspiration for the name of her katana with a dark blue backdrop.

There were no more signs of death and destruction. No more signs of torture. Barina got rid of them. There was no place for this anymore, not in this kingdom.

Barina did have one feature that she kept—the ability to open up the ceiling. She was a friend to dragons after all. At the moment, she had it open. She took the crown and handed it to Na'imah. "Would you be able to give this to the gnomes of the Black Mountains when you get back? This black diamond needs to be with them."

Using the stone, she made herself a simple white-gold diadem to circle her head.

"Of course." Na'imah tucked the crown under one of her scales. "I understand why Usami talks so highly of you."

"Are you still injured?" Barina was intent on checking her over.

Na'imah gave a little laugh. "Barina, I'm fine. Arkon and Aria were able to fix me right up. And it's not as if I would've let Uraki get the better of me." She purred. "I'm sure I will return soon to see you, and I wouldn't put it past Usami or the gnomes to have messages for you once they all hear about this."

"Thank you for everything." Barina nodded, bowing her head. "Valata."

Na'imah bowed her head. "Valata, your majesty." The next moment, she flew out of the room, Barina watching her fondly.

Barina felt a number of arms wrap around her, and she looked to see Jason and Trya had moved close. She leaned against them, trying to lift her arms to hug them back. "You're both alive," she said, finally able to breathe. If she hadn't been exhausted, she would've cried tears of joy.

Tears fell down Jason's face. "We knew you'd come. We knew you'd be here."

"And we knew you'd get us out of here," Tyra whispered.

"We sold your house," Barina said, giving them an innocent look.

Both of her friends went wide-eyed before they realized she was joking.

"Goddamnit." Jason laughed.

"Don't worry. Josh held onto it, and Lucy is with him, too."

"Your new boyfriend," Tyra began, looking over her shoulder at Kevin, "we like him." She stepped back a bit so Kevin could move in.

Kevin had been waiting patiently to stand next to Barina. He cupped her face in his hands, rubbing her cheek with his thumb. They shared a look while she leaned her face in, relishing the feel of his touch.

"Looks like the family approves of me," he said.

All she could do was lightly kiss his hand before turning her attention back to Tyra and Jason. "How…how did Ken send you here?"

Tyra rocked a hand in a so-so motion. "He didn't really send us here. The spell put a cloak on us that left us both paralyzed and shackled. We were there, but you couldn't see us or hear us."

Jason's face showed struggle. "We saw what this did to you. But we were under the cloak until dawn. Once the sun came up, we were visible again but still shackled at our wrists and ankles. A man showed up, he would be the guy who originally took the stone. When he saw us, he put a hood over his face so we have no idea what he looked like. He picked up pretty quick that, since Ken was dead, he was supposed to bring us here."

Barina looked guilty. "You were there, and I…"

Tyra's hands went to Barina's shoulders. "Stop right there. There is no way you could've known, so don't you dare give yourself a guilt trip."

"She's gonna do it anyway," Jason said, nudging Barina's arm. "Really though, please, try not to worry about it. You have bigger fish to fry now."

Barina blinked. "Guess we get to test your theory on if I'd be good at this queen thing or not."

"I'm already taking bets on how you'll do," Jason teased as he stepped aside when Onyx approached.

Onyx gave her a slight nod. "You did good."

"You did, too," Barina admitted. "You all were absolutely amazing."

He handed Barina her cloak while quietly adding, "Wanted to make sure you didn't lose this. Handy Haluex you have here."

Barina's eyes sparkled with amusement. "I know I shouldn't be surprised you figured this out, but I am impressed. Thanks." She took her cloak back.

"You, you took down the king," Jaras said. "You really are a force."

"I didn't do this alone," Barina corrected him. "All of us did this."

"Barina." Aria looked her in the eyes for the first time in weeks. "I'm so sorry for everything. I hope you can…"

Barina was already putting her arms around her in a warm hug. "Aria, it's okay. All of it. I love you. I forgave everyone pretty quickly. I understand what happened. But, after a while, I decided that it would be smarter and safer if I was to stay hidden so that Toler wouldn't know I was around if he read your minds."

"That was smart on your behalf," Arkon agreed. "I hope you know that we wouldn't have said and done what we did if Ken hadn't been messing with us."

"I do, yes." Barina started to slump.

Kevin stepped in and got an arm under her. "You need to rest, my queen," he whispered softly in her ear.

She shook her head at hearing him refer to her as queen, but she smiled. He wasn't speaking to her as if she was in a position of authority. It was just a nickname. She nodded, then looked at Aria.

"Could you maybe do your thing for me, Aria? I'm starting to feel everything now that the adrenaline rush is gone. I could use the stone to heal myself, but I think, until I get the hang of it more, I don't want to chance messing something up. Oh, it all hurts."

"Of course, hang on. Kevin, keep hold of her." Aria placed her hands on Barina, but before she could start, the doors to the throne room opened.

Twelve men walked into the room—each dressed in the best clothes money could buy, and each had angry faces.

"Who are they?" Barina asked Kyle.

"The lords of the region. Toler's right-hand men." Kyle stood beside Barina and added, "Be on your game. They're gonna have a lot to say about you taking over instead of one of them. There had been thirteen, but you fed one to Uraki earlier."

Barina leaned on her sword again, ignoring the pain pulsing through her body while limping to approach the men.

The lords rushed in, shocked by the new surroundings, and stopped in their tracks when they saw the shell of their former king.

"What is the meaning of this? The king, he…he's…" The man looked from Toler to Barina and then noticed the star on her forehead. "You, did you do this! Did you kill our beloved king?"

"Sure did," she said, taking full responsibility. There was a tone of annoyance in her voice.

"And now, you wear a crown upon your head and control the stone like he did," another said. "What is this?" The look on his face made it seem like she had insulted all of his ancestors.

Kyle stepped forward. "Say hello to your new Queen. Her Majesty Barina Raine."

The first lord seemed appalled. "New Queen? I believe I was next in line if anything was to happen to the king and his son."

"She defeated Toler," Kyle explained. "She bested him with her swords and again with the stone. Do you want to challenge her? It has been decided by all here, and I'm sure that the rest of the kingdom would agree that she is who we want. She has already shown that she is fair, caring, and willing to risk her life for the people of this kingdom." He gave them a cold stare. "She stays. Do you have an issue with that, Duke Ferwall?"

"This is,… what, no," Duke Ferwall stuttered. "We won't stand for this. A woman, we've never had a woman lead us in over two hundred years and we're…" He was stopped.

Kyle's friend Mark, who was also with the guards, stood up, along with the other soldiers and guards in the room. "I think we're due for a change."

"We will all contest this," another lord told them. "We will all challenge this. Things were running just fine with Toler. We had everything we wanted."

"*You* had everything you wanted, Baron Harl," Megan spat at them. "Tell me, all of us being raped until we produced a baby and then killed if it wasn't a boy, killed even if it would've been? How was letting this little twelve-year-old girl and others like her be raped over and over okay?" Megan was in tears thinking how heartless these men were.

"You knew he needed an heir," the baron replied. "So what if he took his share? The lords of this region, we kept things running smoothly."

He and the other Lords pulled their swords. They didn't get to take two steps.

A throwing knife became embedded in each of the sheaths, pinning the blades and making it impossible for the lords to draw their swords.

Barina stepped forward, her eyes dark. She still used her blade for support. She was tired, which made her temper short.

"If any of you want to challenge me, be my guest. Don't worry, I won't even use the stone, just to keep it fair." She drew Kitty, holding it firm. "You have two choices at the moment. We can hold you in the cells until I figure out what to do with you, or I can let you follow him." She made a motion to the shell of Toler's body.

Each of the men went pale.

"Where, what happened to Lord Griu?" Baron Harl asked, still the only one not completely phased by their new ruler.

Barina pointed. "Uraki's body is outside. If you wanna look between the dragon's stomach and intestines, you'll find Griu there."

Harl froze. "What? What do you mean, you whore?" He could barely whisper the words.

"I fed him to Uraki," Barina said, speaking a little louder and slower for him. She kept her gaze on the nobility. "Kyle, please have them arrested and taken to the cells."

"My pleasure. Mark, will you help me?"

The lords, all of them, were taken away.

Barina rubbed the bridge of her nose. "They were annoying. Onyx, could you please destroy Toler's body? I don't want to risk him being reanimated if another member of the Bask was to figure out how to do it."

Onyx smiled, sending a shockwave that shriveled Toler's remains into dust. He then snapped his fingers, and they were gone.

At last, Aria began to heal all of Barina's wounds and injuries.

The thief turned queen took a deep breath as some of the pain subsided, though not all of it. Still, enough so she could get some sleep. "Thank you, Aria."

She yawned. "Right, um, well. This fight took a lot out of me, so I need to get some sleep soon." She turned to Morgan and the others. "Ladies, you are welcome to stay here as long as you like, or we can have some of the guards escort you home to your families." She then looked to some of the guards. "We still have some daylight. Would you all be so kind as to have someone let the people know that Toler is dead. They have nothing more to fear from him, and certainly not from me."

"Of course."

"And, could you have the staff come here please. I'd like to speak with everyone."

Tyra protested. "Barina, you need to rest."

"I will, but those that live and work here need to know what's going on." Barina sat down on the throne with an audible sigh, getting off her feet. She turned to look at the fireplace, squinting her eyes. "Vic, are you going to just watch all day or join us?"

A man, who had disguised himself in the fire, stepped out of the flames. It was the man who had organized the mission. He wore his finest clothing, and upon his head he wore a simple, yet beautiful golden crown.

"How long have you noticed me?" Vic was smiling.

Barina's eyes were playful. "Since you showed up half-way through the fight. I was wondering how the fire in that fireplace didn't go out during all this mess."

Vic nodded. He took a moment to look around the room, and then saw Barina sitting on the throne surrounded by her friends.

"I think this is a good look for you," he said, studying her while she sat.

"You weren't sending us to expand your lands?" she questioned, hardly able to lift her head.

"I wasn't sure what the outcome would be. If there wasn't a suitable ruler, I would have considered it, but I think the people have already spoken." He looked around. "I love what you've done with the place."

"Seriously, who the hell are you?" Onyx asked.

Twarence was slightly annoyed too. "We just went through hell. Tell us who you are."

Barina laughed a little through a large yawn. "This is his Majesty, King Victor of Larindana."

The king gave a bow. "At your service."

They had not expected to find out that the one who sent them on this trip, the one who hired them directly, was the king of their own kingdom. They knew they should probably bow, but none of them had it in them.

Aria furrowed her brow. "Did you want the stone back? Seems like it would be better suited to be near the one who can use it."

Victor shook his head. "It's with who it belongs."

"Did you know that she could do this?" Jaras asked. "Did you know that we had all met before?"

"I knew she could use the stone, yes. That you knew each other just happened to be a bonus.

"I used to carry the stone with me often. I liked the way it looked, so I wore it. Years ago, I had her father craft a sword for me. I had set it down on a chair for a moment, and a five-year old Barina picked it up. That's when I knew. After her family passed, I met up with Berklion and I asked him what happened to her. When the stone was taken, thankfully I knew how to find Berklion, and he told me how to find her so I could hire her. If needed, she could get hold of the stone and use it. When I told him who else I had in mind for this journey, that's when Berklion let me know that you had all met."

"So, what now?" Twarence asked.

"What do you mean?"

"What's the next step for this kingdom?" Arkon clarified. "What's the next step for all of us?"

"It seems that this kingdom has a new leader," Victor said, "and Barina has to figure out what to do from here. There will need to be an official coronation ceremony and then rebuilding this kingdom."

Barina looked at her companions. "I'd like to keep any and all of you here as counsel if you'd want." She directed her attention to the group she had traveled with. "You don't have to answer me today, but I'd feel better knowing you were here."

She stood up gingerly when she saw people start to fill the room. All of the workers in the palace—maids, chefs, butlers, everyone—filed in, each one craning their necks. There were so many people.

Barina knew she would have to make a point to speak with all of the guards and soldiers in the next day or so, as well as make the rounds in the kingdom. She had no idea if this was what she should be doing, but it's what she would want from a leader.

"Is this everyone?" Barina asked the workers.

They all looked at her, unsure of who this woman was, who this group of people with her were. They could see the diadem that she wore and the star on her forehead.

Barina was so glad that Kyle was there as the point person. He stood next to her.

Unsure how to start, Barina simply said, "Hello."

Kyle put a hand on her shoulder. "Let me give you an introduction." He then stepped forward.

"Hey everyone!" He gave a wave. "You know me. And this, this is Barina Raine, our new queen. She has defeated Toler and Uraki. Along with the help of the people here with her, she can also control the Anna Stone. I've known her personally for many years, and I can vouch for the person she is." He stepped aside. "Your Majesty."

She whispered, "That's really going to take some getting used to."

"Well hurry up and get used to it." He nudged her arm.

Barina bowed her head before she spoke to the room.

"Hello again. I'm Barina Raine. I wanted to meet all of you. I know that you were here in the castle, at ground zero, not only as the battle against Toler was going on, but in all this time while his rule was holding you captive. I want you to know that you have nothing to fear from me. Your lives are your own now. Your wages will be enough to provide for you and your families and have some left over. Over the course of the next few days, I will personally make it a point to visit each and every one of you. I want all of you to know that you're safe and that I'm going to do my best to protect you and everyone else in this kingdom. If you would like to remain here and serve in the castle, please do. If you would like to find other work outside, that's fine too. There will be no repercussions. I am going to do my best to make this kingdom a home you can be proud of."

She watched, hiding her nerves, and was relieved when she started to see everyone smile. It still made her uneasy to see people in front of her, but she was glad that nobody was kneeling. She didn't want them to. They were smiling, and that was a good sign.

"Thank you. Everyone, please, get some rest. I trust you know your jobs, and I'll get to know all of you very soon. In the meantime, if there's anything you need, please know I'll do my best to help."

She felt a wave of relief wash over her even before she heard them clapping, some with tears in their eyes. If for nothing else, seeing them this happy made the whole battle worth it. And this sight made the daunting task of ruling a kingdom worth taking the mantle.

She turned to Kyle. "Who is being held in the prisons unjustly?"

"Everyone but the people you just sent there," he said with a scoff.

"Free them all. Get them to their homes and, if they don't have one, find them a place to rest here until we can get them situated."

You got it."

Kevin placed his hand around her waist as she started to sag and her speech slur.

"Barina." Aria gently touched a hand to her arm. "You need to rest."

"You've been working so hard this whole time too, Aria. You need to sleep as well. We all do." Barina looked around the room. "Where the hell are the bedrooms?"

"Getting lost in her own castle. Gotta love it," Twarence said.

Onyx was smiling. "To be fair, it's only been hers for about an hour."

"You do realize I'm right here, and I can hear you?".

"Get to bed," Tyra ordered. "We'll find you in the morning. Everyone, get some sleep."

Kevin put an arm around Barina. "Come on. We both need our rest. I'm exhausted, but I won't go without you." His gray eyes were soft looking into hers.

She nodded. Using her sword to still lean on, she limped along next to Kevin.

"I can carry you on my back," he suggested.

She shook her head. "Everything hurts like a mother fucker right now. While I would love to get off my feet, moving around is helping me stretch things out a bit."

"You also need to rest your body." Kevin sighed. She could be so stubborn, and when she was tired, she could be even worse. He grabbed both of her hands and, before she knew it, her arms were draped over his shoulders, and he was carrying her on his back.

"You win," she whispered.

He turned to Jason. "See you guys in the morning."

"Goodnight Barina!" Arkon called after her.

"How that girl can be such a mess sometimes, I just…" Twarence laughed. "I think I want to get something to eat before I go to bed."

"Food, yes," Jaras said. "Aria, you up for something to eat?"

She nodded. "I am starving."

Arkon pointed toward a random hallway. "To the kitchens."

The kitchen staff was not expecting visitors.

"Oh, hello," a young serving woman said in surprise. "You're them, aren't you? The ones who freed us from Toler?"

When the rest of the staff heard her speak, they looked over.

Twarence nodded. "Hi, yeah. Is it okay that we're here?"

"Absolutely," said a man as he walked over. "I manage the kitchen. Are you hungry?"

"We are so hungry, yes." Onyx was so hungry that he knew he had to eat before he slept.

"Have a seat, and we'll fix something right up for you." The manager led them to one of the small tables where the staff normally sat.

"Will her majesty be joining us as well?" he then asked.

"No, she is exhausted," Jaras told him, "but I'm sure that Kevin might…"

They looked over when they saw Kevin walk into the kitchen.

"Is she asleep?" Arkon asked.

He shook his head. "No. She's a damn mess. It's like she's fighting sleep. She's hungry and wants to take a bath. So, I'm grabbing us something to eat. I honestly don't know how she has the energy to do anything." He turned to the healer. "I know you treated her Aria, but she still has some wicked bruising, and she's still really red where she was burned from the dragon fire."

Aria nodded. "I'm not surprised. She'll need a few days before she's completely healed. I mean, the nerve damage to her arm alone, I don't really know how she was able to move her arm. I was able to repair the major damage, but with things this serious, there will be bruising, and she'll be sore. She'll be fine eventually, it's just gonna take some time."

Kevin sat down with the group. "I certainly have my hands full with her." He was laughing to himself. "But she's worth it."

One of the kitchen maids approached. "What would Her Majesty like to eat, and you sir?"

"I can't even think," Kevin said. "How about what's easiest for you."

"We have some cold cuts, fruits, cheese, and bread?"

"Thanks. I'll take it with me to the room."

"We'll put something together right away sir. How about the rest of you? We could make some pot pies if you don't mind waiting a bit."

"Those sound great." Arkon rested his chin on a hand. "And could I please get a good stiff drink."

The serving girl nodded. "I'll leave the bottle."

The group sat relaxing and enjoying each other's company for the first time in a long while. Soon, the server brought a covered platter and basket of breads for Kevin. He gave everyone a wave and headed back.

"I like him," Arkon said, watching him leave. "He really seems like a great guy. I'm happy for her." A wave of peace washed over him. "So, what do you all plan to do? Are you going home or staying here? I'll have to go back to the forest eventually, but I'll be here till things settle down I think."

Twarence thought it over. "I think, well, I might stick around here. I'd like to see what Barina can do and see if I can't help out. Being part of a council in rebuilding a kingdom could be pretty interesting."

Onyx nodded. "I'm gonna stay, too. I want to help, but there's also that part of me that wants to offer some protection to this kingdom in the event that another member of the Bask shows up."

Aria yawned. "I'm staying, too. You have all become my family, and I think I could do a lot of good here. Jaras?"

"I think I'd like to see if maybe I can't help Kyle. There's going to be a lot of work to rebuild and retrain. That, and well, I never thought I'd be willing to serve with anyone, but that crazy chick." Jaras lit up a cigarette and took a long drink of the beer that was now in front of him. "She took down a fucking dragon. I don't think I could take down a dragon."

"I couldn't," Arkon said looking down in disappointment while taking a pull of his mead.

"You came really close," Onyx said, "so don't you dare talk down on yourself. You almost had him. It was incredible to watch. I couldn't take down a dragon either." He nudged Arkon's arm. "We all did really well. Barina though…" Arkon was cut off.

"She ultimately took down Toler, yes," Twarence said. "But without all of us working together, keeping him busy while she fought Uraki, weakening him, who knows? All of us contributed in our way," he assured them. "Aria and Kevin taking a couple of Toler's lives, Onyx you definitely weakened him before she fought him. Arkon, don't pretend you weren't able to siphon some of Uraki's power. And Jaras fought Toler head on while B was fighting Uraki. I'm just so glad we're all together again—that she's with us again."

"Same," Aria agreed. Her eyes lit up when she saw the pot pies. "Oh that food looks amazing. Who would've thought that this is how things would turn out? But I'm really glad it did."

* * *

Kevin walked into the bed chambers and found Barina sitting on the balcony, the door to the room slightly ajar. She had washed all of the dirt, blood, and the battle from her body and hair. She wore a pair of baggy pants cut short and a shirt with the sleeves off as well. He could see the red marks on her left arm where it had been burned earlier, and the angry bruises that were forming all over. Her ankle was still sore, but not sprained, just bruised.

When he walked onto the balcony, he also saw that she had fallen asleep sitting on the bench. Her head hung down, and her breathing slowed. He set the tray on the small table next to her and touched a hand to her leg. "Hey, B."

One eye opened barely a sliver before it closed again.

"I need you to eat just a few bites of something," he whispered, "then we'll get you to bed."

Barina opened her eyes and looked at the food. She reached out a hand to the tray, not even caring what she grabbed, and started to shove food in her mouth.

Once she had managed to eat a few pieces of fruit, a little cheese, and a couple of the cold cut slices washed down with some water, Kevin was satisfied that she had eaten enough.

"Can you walk to the bed?" he asked.

Barina still hadn't spoken. Her hand grabbed hold of the arm rest, and it seemed like it took everything in her to stand up.

Kevin helped her into the bed, tucking her in once she laid down. Her eyes closed, and she was out cold. He watched her for a moment before bringing the food in from outside. He took some time to sit in front of the fireplace and eat, wanting to clear his thoughts. Finally, once his hunger was satisfied, he changed into his night clothes. Before he could climb into bed, there was a knock at the door.

Kyle stood on the other side looking apologetic.

"Hey, two of those lords that were arrested, they've escaped. We're going to place extra security outside of your room, and for the others as well, but I wanted to let you know."

Kevin met Kyle's eyes. "How dangerous are they?"

"Bad news. I have search parties out looking for them right now, and with the extra security outside, you should be fine, but still, I wanted you and Barina to know."

Kevin nodded. "Thank you. She's out cold, so I feel better knowing you have people outside."

"Get some rest."

"You too."

Kevin closed the door and went to lock the door to the balcony. There wasn't much that could wake up Barina at this point. Even if there was, he wanted her to rest. He had fought that day, yes, but compared to what she had done, it was nothing, and he wasn't injured.

These men who escaped concerned him. Kevin let out a sigh. *The things I'll do for her.*

He put a chair close to the bed on the side by the balcony. He didn't like that there was a door on either side of the bed, making it hard to decide which way someone would try to break in. If it was him, he'd go for the balcony. He sat back in the chair, sword in his hand, and slept very lightly for the rest of the night.

CHAPTER 20

Barina woke up feeling the sun warming her skin. She opened her eyes slowly and took a deep breath, but it hurt to do so. There was a soft light coming in through the window, and she saw an empty chair next to the bed. She couldn't hear anything or anyone else in the room. Kevin must have been already up.

She sat up, feeling her bandaged ribs and ankle. Aria had done a great job healing her after the battle. Now she just had to wait for the bruises and some swelling to go down. Till then, she'd still be in a lot of discomfort.

She heard Kevin's voice speak softly as one of his hands touched her arm. "Not too fast."

The feel of his touch relaxed her. "Good morning." She watched one of his eyebrows raise.

"You mean good afternoon," he said, his gray eyes matching the amused look on his face.

"I've been asleep all day?"

He sat down and started to gently rub her stiff shoulders. "Days."

"Come again?"

"You slept all of yesterday and most of today. You got up to use the toilet, but other than that, you've been out." He kissed her cheek.

"I don't even remember getting up to do that."

"I didn't think you would."

"Why didn't anyone wake me up?"

He didn't try to hide his laugh. "There was not a soul in this kingdom who wanted to wake the new queen. Not because they were afraid of the repercussions, but simply because she had earned her rest."

Barina eased her shoulders as Kevin started to work the knots out of them. "That's very sweet. What have I missed?"

"First night, right after you fell asleep, Kyle came to tell me that Baron Harl and Duke Ferwell escaped the cells. The guards have been searching for them, but no luck finding them yet.

"Twarence has been working to find out who in the kingdom would be fit to represent the various regions. He's been speaking with the people, finding out who they trust. He'll be bringing them in for your approval. It seems like Onyx is going to set up shop for himself here. He wants to make sure that you'll have protection in the event anyone from the Bask order tries to come around. Aria has been sensing people able to heal all over the place and wants to set up a school on the grounds. She wants to stay.

"Jaras is working with Kyle and teaming up with training the guards and soldiers, improving their fighting. Jaras is sticking around. He wants to stay. Arkon is going to be around until after your official coronation, but then he needs to get back to his clan. And it looks like he's going to take Morgan, her daughter, and Megan with him. He's offered them protections in his world, and they're gladly taking it. The rest of the women have gone home to their families.

"Jason has been going through the city and surrounding towns and villages, learning what people need and how we can help them. Tyra has been with him, helping as many people as she can who've been sick or hurt. They'll be going back to Estella after your coronation."

Barina glanced back over to a chair next to the bed, registering what he told her of that first night. "That first night, did, well did you sleep? Or were you sitting in that chair just in case?"

He gave her a sweet kiss. "Just in case, and I slept a little."

She felt herself blush. "Thank you. What about you?"

Kevin stopped rubbing her shoulders for a moment. "What do you mean?"

"What's your plan? I mean, things have changed a bit with me."

He wrapped his arms around her, pulling her closer, and kissed her again. "I'm wherever you are. That hasn't changed."

Barina returned the kiss. "You'll stay with me?"

He nodded as he stood up and helped her to her feet. "How about you get dressed, and we'll head to the dining room? I know you've got to be hungry."

"Famished," she said, standing up gingerly. Kevin stood close if she needed him.

"They brought some dresses for you to wear, and I grabbed your bags from the inn. Marsha says hi."

Barina beamed thinking about the innkeeper. "She is too cute." She limped over to the wardrobe and looked at the dresses. They were a bit too fancy for the moment. She grabbed a gray skirt and a white blouse from her bag, wanting to keep it simple. She put a belt around her waist and strapped on her swords and dagger while slipping into her zori sandals.

Kevin waited patiently while she changed behind the screen. He watched her walk out as she ran a brush through her hair–still a little messy cause she couldn't be bothered. He picked up the diadem and placed it on her head. He knew she wouldn't have worn it otherwise.

Once in the large dining room, the two of them had a quiet meal. Barina was still moving slowly, but she was glad to have food in her system.

"There you are," Twarence said as he walked into the room. "She lives." He was grinning ear to ear. "Glad you're finally awake."

"Hey, how are you?" Barina was happy to see him. "Kevin was saying that you're planning on sticking around."

"Yeah, I think I can help do some real good here. And you said you'd like us to, so I'd like to offer my services for your counsel." He carried a stack of papers. "I have a list of people that the citizens have said are the most trusted in their regions. They would make the best ones to represent their areas as the new noble houses. I also have all the specs on everything from how large the kingdom is to how many people. All of it."

Barina visibly relaxed. "I'm so glad you're staying. Thank you for doing all of this. We'll sit down later in my study and can go over everything together. I'll call those people here before too long so they can start their jobs in the regions."

"Your Majesty…" another woman walked into the room. "We need to take your measurements for your dresses and so the head seamstress can start working on your gown for the coronation ceremony."

Another person entered. "Your majesty, there are dignitaries coming in from surrounding kingdoms to meet with you. We will have rooms ready for them, and here is a schedule of when to expect to meet with all of them."

In the next few minutes, the room held over a dozen more people, all with things that she needed to start looking into. Barina took it all in, while Kevin was getting dizzy just listening to it all.

Barina thought about using the stone to get rid of the rest of her pain and bruising, but she didn't want to become dependent on it. Still, she needed to focus on the situations at hand. She touched the stone around her neck, and everyone saw the star appear for a moment as she finished healing herself.

"Alright," she said, standing. "I'll meet with the dignitaries tomorrow after breakfast. Twarence, I'll meet you in the study in ten minutes, and we can set up times for me to meet with those who have been selected to represent their regions. Mandy, tell the seamstresses I'll come to them at six this evening. That's all."

Everyone left the room, giving her a minute to catch her breath. Kevin was impressed. She was turning out to be a natural.

She looked at him with wide eyes. "Yikes."

He took her hand. "That was pretty good. You didn't let them see you sweat. So what do you need from me?"

Barina couldn't quite explain what it meant having him there, knowing he supported her as much as he did. "Could you see if there's anything Onyx needs help with. If he's good, check with the staff and see if they need help getting their stations set."

He nodded. "I'll see you later today. You got this."

The rest of the day, Barina took care of the new matters of the state. She had never been so thankful to have all the people around her to help. There was so much she had to learn, and quickly, that without someone like Twarence to guide her, she would've struggled.

She was a little bummed that she didn't see anyone until dinner that night. Even then, Aria and Jaras were only there briefly. Twarence and Onyx stuck around longer, while Jason and Tyra were still out in the crowd. Kevin was still busy helping the castle management get it up and running smoothly again.

When Barina got back to her room, she found herself having trouble winding down from everything that had happened in the last couple days. She closed the doors to her room and took a deep breath, looking around. She hadn't taken even a few minutes to see what her apartment looked like.

Her bedroom was huge—larger than any home she had lived in. Directly adjacent to that room was a set of double doors that led to the stone balcony. To the right of that was the bed that was big enough for a giant or two to be very comfortable. There were end tables—each with a lantern—and she saw a book on one of them. She was pretty sure that Kevin had been reading it while she slept.

On the other side of the room was a sitting area with a sofa, wing tipped chairs, a couple of bookcases, and the stone fireplace that gave enough warmth for the whole room. There was a half wall that separated the rest of the room from her bathtub, wardrobe and a vanity. Another small room held the toilet.

She was sure she'd end up remodeling down the road, but for now, this was fine.

The fire was already lit, as were some of the lamps, so that her room was comfortable. She appreciated the little touches. Barina would have to remember to tell her maids thank you. Leaning against the closed doors, she took off the diadem and rubbed her forehead. She still hadn't wrapped her head around the fact that this was happening.

The diadem was light and thin, but she realized she hadn't completely grasped how heavy this would become. She hoped she could do what everyone seemed to think she could.

Barina walked over to the bathing area, her eyes shining at the sight of the large bathtub. If there was one purely selfish thing she was okay using this stone for, it was to fill up the tub with the water at the perfect temperature. She scooped out a bucket full of the water to scrub her body and hair clean. Adding some oils to it, she sank into the tub, relishing in the soak.

On the floor next to a stool, she saw Kevin's small bag that held his razor, comb, and soap. She imagined he had cleaned himself the night before or that morning. She also found herself wishing he was with her. Barina was honestly tired enough she could fall asleep as soon as she got to bed, but she had other ideas for when Kevin returned.

After her soak in the tub, she put the Anna Stone in the wardrobe, someplace it wouldn't be seen. She didn't want to wear it all the time, especially when she was sleeping. Dressing in a simple nightgown, she headed over to the chairs and found a book to read in front of the fireplace.

Kevin returned almost an hour later. He was quiet—not wanting to wake her if she was already asleep. When he didn't see her in the bed, his eyes scanned the room quickly. She had fallen asleep in the chair by the fireplace. Her reading glasses were still on her face, and her hair had frizzed a little after drying.

He kicked off his boots and headed over to her. Gently taking the book from her hands, he touched a set of fingers to her shoulder.

Her eyes opened, her face turning up to see him standing near. "You've been busy."

"You slept for another whole day," he joked, trying to see if she'd buy it.

Barina let out a tsk, her lips twitching with laughter. "Considering my company, I'd rather be asleep."

Kevin inhaled a sharp breath, impressed with the comeback. "Damn, that was brutal."

She stood and stretched, wrapping her arms around his shoulders. Her fingers directed his head down so she could kiss him. His heart sped up, and his hands tightened on her waist to pull her closer. "I'll try to make it up to you," she promised as she pulled his shirt off.

"I'm delicate, you know?" he whispered, his hands moving lower.

"Did you want me to stop?" she teased while her fingers trailed down his chest.

Kevin let out a breathy laugh, enjoying her lips on his collar. "Not that delicate," he said, pushing her up against the nearest bookcase as his fingers started to unlace her nightgown.

She didn't stop him.

* * *

Barina woke early the next morning, turning to see Kevin asleep next to her. She felt a slight chill in the room. The chill subsided when one of his arms pulled her close as he ran his fingers along her bare shoulders and back.

"Morning," he whispered, one eye opened a sliver. "I don't think I've ever seen your hair more epic."

She was sure it was a complete mess. "I blame you," she said, using her fingers to mess up his own.

"Probably safe to assume that." He kissed her shoulder. When she started to rise, he pulled her back onto the bed. "What's the plan for today, and can we push those plans back? I'd like to repeat last night." He kissed her deeply while his hands went exploring.

She loved feeling him against her. "As much as I would love to push everything back, I..." Her words trailed off while he ran a set of fingers along her waist and down her leg, his lips protesting her absence.

"Okay," she whispered. "We have enough time for an abbreviated version of last night."

"I can work with that," Kevin said, pulling her even closer.

* * *

Much later than she had intended, Barina got out of bed. "How was that an abbreviated version, sir?"

Kevin watched her walk with a lazy and satisfied smile. "Are you mad about it? Didn't sound like you were."

She placed her hands on her hips as if she was going to say something but gave him a wink instead. "Furious." She purred as she started getting ready.

He swung his legs over the bed. "I'll make it up to you later." He ran a hand through his hair before getting ready himself.

She mused aloud to herself about what her day would bring. "I have to meet with the dignitaries from the other kingdoms, and I have no idea how this is gonna go. Then do the final fitting for my dress for the coronation. It's tomorrow. This is happening so fast."

"Yeah, but you're going to be great at this, babe." He wrapped his arms around her, giving her a small kiss on her neck.

"I'm glad you believe in me." Barina headed to the wardrobe and picked out one of the more elegant dresses. If she was meeting with other heads of state, she would need to put her best foot forward.

When he finished dressing, Kevin glanced over and watched her movements.

She slipped into a mauve dress with delicate gold lace lining the hem and the collar. It didn't completely hide her tattoos, but she obviously didn't care. She had no desire to ask for the assistance of a handmaid, so Kevin helped her with the buttons on the back.

While she brushed her hair and put it back in a braid, he finished putting on his socks and boots. He was smiling. Even now, as royalty, she kept her routine simple. She had finished hooking up her swords and dagger to her side, slipped on some shoes, and put on her diadem—all by the time he had finished getting ready.

Kevin went his own way after breakfast, while Barina went to the throne room to begin meeting those from surrounding kingdoms. She was surprised to see so many who she knew. She and King William from Treklea were old friends. Next was Devon. Even though he was very young, he was wise beyond his years, and a fair and just ruler. King Devon was someone who she had met not long ago and was glad to see him. King Victor was still there. He had been staying in the palace and would remain until after her coronation.

There were a few princes and dukes from surrounding nations who had rushed, riding day and night, to meet the new queen of Thoron. She didn't know much about them aside from what Twarence had told her. She had read over their information the night before.

There was one king who she hadn't expected to see but was very glad that he showed up.

Arkon entered the throne room first. "Barina... I mean, Your Majesty. It's my honor to present His Excellency, ruler of all elves, King Trekto."

The elf king gave a low bow.

Barina beamed from ear to ear upon hearing this.

Trekto was tall with a dark beard and hair to match. His crystal blue, almost clear eyes, were shining when he saw her. He stretched out his arms, and Barina ran from her chair to give him a big hug. He even lifted her off of her feet for a moment.

"Trekto!" she cheered. "It's so good to see you!"

He took a moment to hold her at arms' length. "Barina, my dear girl, just look at this! I never would've expected. Well, maybe I should've, but you're Queen! You've done what nobody has been able to do. Get rid of Toler. Even my own forces had been hesitant to confront him."

"Thank you. I had a lot of help, especially from Arkon and the rest of the group that came with us."

The mortals in the room stood with their jaws dropped. Humans hardly ever got to know the name of the king of all the elves, let alone meet him. And Barina was talking to him as if they had always been equals.

"Please, have a seat," Barina said, addressing King Trekto before turning to everyone in the room. "I'm sure you and everyone else have a lot of questions, and I'm gonna do my best to answer them."

"Ah but first, I have something for you." Trekto held out a hand, and one of his retainers handed him a box. He seemed excited to give this to her.

"As soon as Arkon told me what happened and that you were queen, I contacted The Circle. We decided to have a gift made for you. I don't think I've ever seen them work so fast to create something so beautiful. We all contributed to it, each one of us."

Barina opened the lid of the box and couldn't believe her eyes.

"Trekto? Are you sure? Is this made by the same smithy who…?"

"The same who made your dagger? Yes." He was smiling, "He just knew what to make for you and went right to work."

She lowered her voice. "Holy shit, I mean, but these items, shouldn't they be…?"

"We can think of no better place for them to be than with you."

Barina was speechless for a moment as she hesitated to take this gift.

Trekto reached his hand into the box and took out a beautifully crafted crown. The white gold seemed to shimmer with slivers of dark green, delicate cream feathers entwined in the gold, a tiny engraving of a wolf on either side, pearls embedded around two tiny black diamonds, and in between those was a deep purple amethyst. The tiara itself swirled to a point at the top and almost seemed to shine on its own.

She knew all of the symbolism and what it meant. "No pressure," she breathed to herself.

King Trekto bowed his head as he handed it to her. "We would be honored if you would wear this. Your Majesty, this belongs to you."

Barina bowed her head and took the crown from him. "Thank you." She carried the box with her back to the throne and sat down. It was only then that she seemed to realize how many people were in the room.

The rest of the day, going into the afternoon, was spent talking about trade deals, treaties, all of it. Barina looked over numerous scrolls and documents, but she found it interesting.

"Your Majesty," one of the princes said. "We really need to address another matter at hand."

"Prince Gerald?" Barina gave him her attention. She could tell he had been wanting to bring up a subject all day.

"It is extremely rare for a queen to rule without a prince consort by her side. That is to say, to not be married. There are cases of a widow or a woman waiting until she is old enough to wed, but this is something that you should consider, and soon. It will give you more validity."

Another man, Duke Chester, spoke up as well. "He's not wrong, Your Grace. You would need to pick someone and soon, and of noble blood. We know there is a man with you, the one you came to the palace with. While we are all sure that he is probably of fine character, he isn't noble, and he doesn't suit you."

Just as that conversation started, Kevin had quietly made his way to the throne room to see how she was doing.

Hearing that she would need to find a husband and that he wasn't worthy, it cut him deeply. He and Barina were just starting their relationship. There was no question in his mind that he wanted to be with her. But it was too soon to think about marriage. And to have it forced on her like this, and to not even let her consider him as an option when they loved each other...

Kevin left before he could hear more. If she was to agree with them, it would destroy him. If she fought with them and went against this, it could hurt her. He had a lot to think about.

Barina waited for the dignitaries and others who were nodding and agreeing to finish speaking. She closed her eyes and took a deep breath. Those that actually knew her could see she was trying to control her emotions.

When Barina's eyes opened, her stare was dark. "Like fucking hell I'm going to marry someone I don't want to marry. And like fucking hell I need to have a husband at all to be a valid ruler." Her words were firm. She didn't raise her voice, but she did not sugarcoat her tone or words. "Do all of you have to be married?"

Chester blurted out, "No, but it's different with you. You should realize that."

"Why? Because I don't have dangly bits between my legs? That is what you're saying to me." Her tone grew more forceful by the sentence. "I literally took off Uraki's head. I took down Toler—once without the stone and again using it to finish him off completely. And you're saying that people will think that I'm not valid simply because I'm an unwed woman when any one of you could be unwed and it'd be seen as okay? Fuck that noise."

"Your Majesty, it's just…"

Barina cut off the prince and pointed a finger at him. Her tone was commanding. "I'm not done." She stood, her eyes flashing a dangerous anger. "I will not be forced to marry anyone, and if I do decide to get married, it will be the person I want to be with, commoner or not. Any one of you is able to marry a commoner, and I know some of you have, and nobody questions your rule. I will expect and demand the same respect that all of you give to each other, single or married. I hope I make myself clear."

William tried not to laugh. "You tell 'em B." He turned to the room. "You guys, my late wife had been a commoner, and we cannot ask her to do what we wouldn't be willing to do ourselves if the roles were reversed. Besides, she could easily kick any of our asses."

"She could even kick my ass," Trekto said, smiling. "She's smart, powerful, and the most respected and trusted human among the magical community. She will have our support in the world of magic to be with whoever she wants or to stay single for as long as she wants."

Devon shook his head. "This is the dumbest thing I've ever heard. Even if I didn't know Barina and the person she is, trying to force this on someone who has damn well shown their worth a thousand times over is low."

The men who had been trying to convince her to marry were quiet until their faces gave way to what they were really getting at.

Barina's face showed disgust mixed with annoyance. "You were hoping that I would pick one of you! Not one of you is in line for the throne to your own kingdoms, not without a whole lot of people dying. Were you thinking I'd pick one of you, and then you'd be able to…" She started laughing and couldn't stop.

Their faces paled. Those rulers who knew Barina sat back, trying not to laugh.

"You boys are young," William said, "and very stupid if you think for one second that she'd give you what you want. She is a monarch, and we will treat her as such."

"I'm young," Devon scoffed, "younger than anyone in here, and I'm not that stupid. They knew what they were trying to do. It's called a dick move."

William, Victor, and Trekto turned to the young king. "How much time have you spent with Barina?" William asked him. "That sounds like something she'd say?"

Devon grinned. "Enough to know that *is* something she'd say. I'll take that as a compliment."

The young lords sulked quietly to themselves.

Barina exhaled a breath. "Now, if we're done with all of that nonsense, I think we're also done with this meeting. Gentlemen, please make yourselves at home. I'll see you tomorrow night."

She stood and pushed the doors open as she left. Angry and annoyed, she needed to get some air, so she headed out to the gardens. It wasn't often that something could rile her temper so close to blowing her top. She needed to center herself.

She sat down at a fountain and took a deep breath before she closed her eyes.

"Heavy for your thoughts?"

Barina smiled hearing Twarence's voice and looked over to him. "Little pissed off at some of those idiots I met with."

"Arkon just told me what happened. He was in the room while you met with the dignitaries. This is what makes you able to lead. You won't put up with anyone's bullshit."

Barina gave him a little smirk. "Fuck those guys."

Twarence laughed. "Spoken like a true queen."

"I'm a goddamn lady," she said, grinning. "Anyway, how are you?"

"I'm good. I am so glad we won and that you're here with us now. And who would've thought that, when we started, it would've ended like this." He sat down next to her and put an arm around her, giving her a hug. Twarence was happy to be with his friend. "Honestly though, I couldn't think of a better ending."

She leaned her head on his shoulder, before she looked up at him.

"Barina, you look like you're still thinking of a different ending."

She watched her breath in the cold night air. "It's just, well, there are two sides to this coin. I know that I can make a lot of great and positive changes. I can keep these people safe and, I hope, can lead them in the way they deserve. I have no idea if I'm cut out for the last part, but I'll try.

"On the other hand, I was planning on just heading back to Estella when this was all over. Living the life of a smith with my friends and Kevin, and still being able to help those I can with my blades. These walls feel so confining. I learned to fight so that I could spring into action at a moment's notice, not so that others would fight my battles. I guess this is what I get for trying to have a plan for once."

"You'll make a hell of a queen. We already know you're a hell of a warrior."

"Thank you for that."

"I've done a lot of work studying law, so, if your offer still stands, I'd like to be an official part of your counsel."

She slugged him on the arm. "We established that, silly. Of course, I need you and the others by my side. I feel a lot better knowing that you're here. Knowing that if I need someone to help me take care of things, you're here." Barina then had an idea. "In fact, thanks for the talk. I think I know what I'm going to do."

She stood up. "I need to test something, and bring Josh, Mason, Greg and Berklion here. This stone will come in handy. I'll see you later." She winked and then ran off.

Twarence smiled to himself that she was never dull. He continued his stroll through the gardens. It was a beautiful night—the autumn air was crisp and fresh—and he was happy. He hoped he could be a part of something amazing with the new rule of this kingdom.

He found Kevin sitting on his own, looking at the ground. Twarence had never seen a man look so troubled and torn.

"You okay?" Twarence took his flask out of his pocket and handed it to him.

Kevin shook his head while gladly taking a drink. "Not sure, if I'm being honest."

"So, what is it?"

"She deserves a prince, she deserves the best. What am I?"

Twarence nodded understanding. "Heard about what those guys told Barina, didn't you?"

"They're not wrong. I mean, she deserves to be with…"

"I'm gonna go ahead and stop you right there." Twarence placed a hand on Kevin's shoulder. "You're not saying this because you think it's a matter of station. You're legit worried about not being a good enough man to be with her, aren't you?"

"I love her, that's not a question. What if, I mean, what if there's someone out there who can do this for her more than I can. Then she deserves them."

"Kevin, she told all of those guys to fuck right off. She's not going to be with anyone she doesn't want to be with. After what we saw from you the other day, how much you helped her and us, you more than showed us who you are. And she loves you."

Kevin kept his eyes to the ground. "I know she does. But I don't want anyone to question her claim to the throne, especially because of me. I don't want *her* to question her claim to the throne because of me."

"They won't. Not if she has anything to say about it." Twarence patted his shoulder. "And she had a lot to say about it. Barina won't be with anyone she doesn't want to be with, and to hell with anyone who says otherwise."

"Thanks." Kevin's shoulders relaxed.

Twarence headed back inside, leaving Kevin with his thoughts.

The idea of leaving, of letting Barina go, terrified Kevin. The thought of others questioning her ability to lead this kingdom all because of her choice of partner scared him more. He wanted her to have the absolute best chance, and she needed as much support as possible. If that meant he wasn't in the picture, then he had to leave. He determined he'd spend one more evening with her, and then leave after her coronation. He didn't want to walk away, but he was sure that this was best for her.

Kevin stayed outside for a while just to collect himself and his thoughts. When he saw Barina come back into the castle, she wasn't alone. Berklion and three other men were following her. He wondered how Berklion had come so far this quickly, but then realized she must have used the stone to summon them.

Barina beamed. He loved seeing her happy. What he was about to do would hurt her, but he hoped that someday, she'd be able to forgive him. Perhaps in the next life, they would be together.

Kevin made his way inside and to their room. She was already there, excited to tell him that the most important people in her life were there. Kevin listened, soaking everything in.

"Hey, are you okay?" she asked him. She felt his face in her hand. "You're quiet."

He nodded before he pulled her close and kissed her passionately. Kevin needed her to know just how much he loved her.

Later that night, Kevin watched Barina sleep. She was curled up with her face pressed against his arm. He put his arm around her and savored his last night keeping her close.

CHAPTER 21

The day of the coronation was a busy one. There were so many things happening that it was amazing how smoothly it went.

Kevin dressed for the ceremony in the finest clothes the tailors could make for him. He went to the throne room with everyone else. Nobody was allowed to see the Queen before the ceremony, not even him.

King Trekto himself would conduct the coronation, with King Victor, and King William standing by. The room buzzed with anticipation.

Kevin stayed close to Jaras, Twarence, Onyx, Aria, and Arkon. He wanted to see Jason and Tyra, too, but they were waiting on the other side of the room with Berklion and company. He would like to have said hi to Berklion.

King Trekto and the other monarchs stood at the base of the steps and turned to look as the doors opened. Barina stepped through them and walked to the throne.

She wore an elegant, royal blue gown with dark blue embellishments of leaves adorned with pearls along the bust and the hem. Her sleeves hung low, and the collar was low enough to showcase the stone that hung around her neck. The Anna Stone had been turned so that it touched her skin and the star appeared on her brow. Around her waist was the belt she wore to carry her swords and her dagger. Her hair was curled and flowing behind her. She looked as her position suggested.

Barina bowed her head to her fellow monarchs before turning to sit on the throne.

Trekto stepped forward, along with William and Victor.

King Victor held a scepter made of rich briar that had been hand-carved, curling into a circle at the top. It had been made by the finest craftsman of the elves only days beforehand. He gave it to Barina, who took hold of it in her right hand.

King William held an orb carefully in his hands. It was made of glass that glowed with a light that would pulse between green, yellow, red, blue, and purple, representing the colors of the elements. This had been crafted by a glassblower from the giants. The king placed it in Barina's left hand.

It was these objects, and seeing that Trekto, King of all Elves was about to place the crown on her head, that drove home to those in the court just how deep her connection to the magical world ran.

"Barina Raine, do you vow to govern the people of the Kingdom Thoron? Will you, by your power, cause justice, law, and mercy, to be executed in your judgments? Will you protect the people of this land with all your might, up to and including your own life?"

"I swear, that I will govern, cause justice, law, and mercy, and protect the people of this land with all of my might, up to and including my life." Barina nodded.

Trekto placed the crown upon her head. "Now rise, Barina Raine, Queen of Thoron." He gave a low bow, which the other monarchs mimicked. "People of Thoron, your Queen."

The people in the room all bowed before her. It was still so strange, people humbling themselves before her. She made sure her friends knew to never bow. She turned to the pedestal that was next to the throne and placed the scepter and the orb on it, relieved she had not broken the orb.

Sensing her unease, Trekto leaned in. "Don't worry, Lord Nortel assured me that the orb is very sturdy."

She stifled her laugh.

A fanfare began to play, and there was great applause. Barina felt as if she wasn't herself.

When the applause died down, music played in the background as Kevin stood before her. He held out his hand to escort her to the dance floor.

"Did I do okay?" she asked him quietly while they swayed to the music.

"You were amazing. There's a party in the kingdom right now, and it's all thanks to you." He was savoring these last moments with her.

"Thanks to everyone," she reminded him. "Everyone helped make this happen. I'm so thankful that I have you and the others with me. You help give me strength and drive."

Kevin couldn't respond. He pressed his forehead to her own. "I love you. I want you to know that I love you more than anything."

She felt her face flush. "I love you, too," she said.

"May I cut in?"

Kevin was unwilling to let her go, and if it wasn't for who asked, he would've declined.

Berklion stood next to them with a smile that spoke volumes of how proud and happy he was of his student and adopted daughter. He turned to Kevin.

"I always hoped the two of you would meet someday." Berklion shook Kevin's hand before pulling him in for a hug. "It's good to see you again."

Kevin had to share his delight. "Good to see you, too. How are you?"

"I'm great. My daughter and her friends have saved a kingdom. Jason and Tyra are alive, thank the stars. I am so incredibly proud of you, of all of you." Berklion looked as if he could cry from happiness. "Thank you for helping her. I heard what you did, how you took one of Toler's lives. That's impressive."

Barina looked startled. "What? How have I not heard about this yet?"

"From what I understand," Berklion began, looking at her, "Kevin used a hunk of metal to shield Twarence, then fought him with his chains. They said Toler taunted him about harming you and, before the king knew it, the chains wrapped around his neck and snapped it. Kevin also threw him into the wall." Berklion leaned toward Kevin. "I mean, come on, that's pretty badass."

Kevin turned red, and Barina's mouth fell open a bit.

"That's freaking amazing!" She put a hand on his shoulder. "I really would like to have seen that."

"You were busy fighting a dragon," he said, kissing her cheek. "You had your hands full." Kevin stepped back a bit. "Berklion, I believe you two have a dance."

Barina gave Kevin an adoring look and then began to dance with Berklion.

Kevin knew that she would end up being so busy from this point on that he could slip out. He went back to their room to grab his things and changed out of the formal clothes.

He walked through the nearly empty hallways—an occasional maid or guard passing by—and left through the side entrance. He mixed in with the crowd of people waiting outside the palace, waiting to see their new queen for the first time as she stepped onto the balcony. He had made it all the way to the edge of the crowd when he heard the cheers. Kevin turned one more time to look at the woman he had fallen in love with as she appeared. He took a deep breath and left.

* * *

Barina stepped onto the balcony and was overwhelmed by the cheers of the people waiting to see her. She was glad to see them and to know that they finally had a reason to be genuinely happy. When the cheering died down, she spoke.

"Thank you all for now placing your trust and your faith in me to lead you into a brighter future. As your queen, I will always do my best to make sure that this kingdom will thrive. No longer will you have to live in fear. I will be just and fair and defend the people of this kingdom.

"I also feel that, for me to do my best work, not just for the people of this kingdom, but for people everywhere, that I need to be able to blend in with the people, to live with them. Therefore, I will not always contain myself to the walls of the palace. Instead, I will often travel the world, helping those I can the best I can. When I'm not here, Twarence will rule as my regent, and in my absence, his word is law.

"I will always be here when the need is at its greatest. I will always protect you and fight for you. Thank you, and may today be the beginning of a beautiful future for this kingdom."

The people cheered even though they were stunned. Their queen, this woman, wouldn't be living in the palace fulltime.

Barina headed back inside where Twarence stood still, unable to speak for a moment. He finally hissed, "What the hell lady?"

"I probably should've clued you in on that, huh?" Barina had a very sheepish grin on her face. "Sorry about that."

"The absolute hell?" He groaned again.

Aria, Arkon, Jaras, and Onyx started laughing knowing that Barina really hadn't changed at all.

"The look on your face is just priceless, Twarence," Aria said.

Onyx patted him on the back. "You're well suited for this, so don't worry."

"And we're all going to be here to help," Jaras added.

"Come on. All of you, to my study, and I'll explain. Oh, hey Berk, guys, you come with us." She looked around, excited to finally explain her idea. "Kyle, I want you there, too."

She led her friends to her study, closing the doors behind her. Her eyes searched for Kevin. She was sure he was there for her speech, but she would have to explain her plans to him later.

"Twarence, I apologize for dropping this on you, but there hadn't really been time to discuss it. Don't worry, I have it all worked out," she reassured him. "Check it out."

In the study, there was a large mirror and several pocket mirrors as well. "Each one of these is linked to the one that I'll be carrying," Barina explained. "The big mirror here will be connected to two other large mirrors that will let me get from there to here in a few steps. One at my place in Miork, and another at my home in Estella. This way, if there's an emergency, all I or any of you have to do is walk through the mirror. Just say, 'Estella, or Miork'. It'll also be an easy way for me to get here and check in."

She looked around at them. "As it stands now, anyone can use this mirror to speak with me, but only people who are allowed to use this to get from here to there are the people in this room, Kevin, and myself. This will also work for any of your kin or if you hold onto a person or have a hand on an animal like your horse." She touched the pendant. "This stone is pretty handy."

"Clever," Aria said. "Can we, well, can we test this out?"

Barina nodded. "Um, Berk, would you and the others who have been to Miork stay here for a minute? I'm gonna take Aria, Arkon, Jaras, Onyx, and Twarence through to the cave."

"We'll hold down the fort, I mean, palace." Berklion waved a hand lazily while sitting back in a chair.

Barina set her eyes on her traveling group again. "Are you guys ready?"

"Your majesty," Arkon said with a bow of his head. "Lead the way."

Barina looked at the large mirror. "Miork."

The mirror began to glow, and they could see through to a large cave-like room on the other side. Barina stepped through first and the others followed. Once through, those who had been to the cave with her before didn't recognize the room.

"What is this?" Jaras looked around the large cavern that had mats on the ground, practice dummies, and what looked like weights in the room.

"Oh, I didn't show you guys the place in my cave where I do my training. But this was the best place to put the mirror. There's not enough room in the kitchen or really in the living space, and the bathing room is out," she told them. "I'm keeping my place here as a safe house. It's a great space to lay low if needed. If you go either here or to my place in Estella, I'll know. My fingernails will light up for a couple seconds to alert me."

Barina held up her hand to show them as she turned back to the mirror. "Thoron."

They saw her fingernails glow a brilliant white, and she walked through the mirror again, the rest of them following.

"Barina," Twarence said, "this is really clever. Is this so that I can contact you?"

"All of you can contact me. There's going to be questions from all of you, and this is my kingdom. I am queen, and I will take responsibility, but I mean it when I say that I think I can do more for everyone by being with the people. The little mirrors will let us contact each other right away if we are not near the big one or if I just need to talk to you."

"But you're not even going to be living in your own kingdom," Aria said. "Well, you'll be partially here but not full time."

Barina shrugged. "Eh, technicalities. I can literally step through the mirror and be here in a second."

They looked at her as if she was crazy. "You be you, girl." Tyra sighed while shaking her head.

"Twarence, I fully expect you to contact me, and I you, on a daily basis after I go back to Estella. I plan on being here for the next month, maybe longer, to make sure I know the ins and outs of what's going on here. I also," she paused for a second, "plan on leaving the stone with you, Twarence."

That got everyone's attention.

Josh couldn't believe that decision. "Why the hell wouldn't you keep it?"

Barina held up a hand. "There are a number of reasons. I don't want to abuse the power of the stone, and I don't want to become dependent on it for every little problem. Also, do you guys remember *why* this is called the Anna Stone?" Her eyes were serious. "It was named after King Theadore's wife who died after the power in the stone took his anger and turned destructive. I don't have much of a temper, but I don't want to even remotely chance it happening. So, I'll leave it here in Twarence's care." She then looked to the scholar. "I should've asked, Twarence. Will you be my regent to rule in my place when I'm not here?"

Twarence met her gaze, he saw what she did when she looked at him. She had complete and total faith in him. "I'll do my best," he said, and gave her an uneasy smile, but he would take the challenge.

"I'll be just a mirror away if you need me." Barina gently touched her hand to his shoulder. "I'll never be far."

"Well then, your majesty," Jaras said, enjoying calling her by her new title if only for the fact that she wasn't used to it, "what would you have us do from here?"

Her face lit up. "There's a party, isn't there? We go out and enjoy it, and then tomorrow, we get to work figuring out how the hell we're going to run this place."

Jason opened the door, and they headed back out into the room.

Barina looked for Kevin, but she couldn't find him anywhere. She searched the halls and then went to her room, thinking maybe he was there to get away for some air.

"Kevin," she said quietly walking into the room. "Kevin?"

The room was quiet, and there wasn't any sign of him. It felt cold. Barina's face paled and her heart sank when she saw that his bag was gone.

Did he really leave?

Barina rushed back through the hallways. She had to find him and stop him, or at least find out why he was leaving.

"Barina? What's going on?" Twarence asked when he saw the panicked look in her eyes as she went for the doors.

"I can't find him. I think Kevin left." She sounded out of breath.

Twarence's brow wrinkled. "No, I didn't think he'd do it."

"What do you mean?"

"He overheard those guys trying to convince you to leave him for one of them. Kevin didn't want your claim to the throne to be questioned because of him. I didn't think he'd do it," Twarence said, shaking his head. "I told him that you were with who you felt was best for you and…"

"Damn it!" Barina bolted out the door. She secretly found a way around the crowd and took off down the city streets of Lavenbo.

The streets were lined with people celebrating—singing, laughing, and dancing. They never would've dared a few days ago.

Ignoring all of this, Barina focused on finding Kevin. She arrived at the inn where she and Kevin had stayed, and was glad to find Marsha was there.

"Barina, oh, I mean, your Majesty. It's so good to see you." She was beaming.

"Marsha, Kevin didn't come here, did he? Have you seen him?"

Marsha tilted her head. "He popped by about an hour ago and said goodbye to me. Said he was heading home. I thought you knew."

Barina struggled to keep her lip from quivering. "Thank you Marsha, thank you." She ran out the door, and would have run all the way to the Forest of Lithor if she had to. About fifty steps farther, and reality hit her.

There's no point in running after him if he's decided he's leaving.

She hung her head slightly, trying to hold back her tears and steady her breathing. Barina didn't want her new subjects to see her sad or crying. She didn't want them to see her as weak. She was trying to hide her humanity, and she was failing.

People nearby recognized her. It was hard not to with the crown upon her head. But when they saw her tears, many of them decided to try comforting her. None of them saw their queen—a person they couldn't approach, as a person who wanted to keep others at arm's length. They moved closer. An elderly man put a hand on her shoulder, and a young lady offered her a flower. Soon, two young children wrapped their arms around her legs, trying to hug her.

She was grateful that they didn't see her as weak. "Thank you," she muttered to those who were near.

When three horses came near, the crowd parted to reveal Berklion, Jason, and Josh riding near. The men were silent, they didn't have words for her.

"He's gone," was all Barina said to them.

Jason held out his hand—a simple gesture, but one she knew the depth behind. He would help her begin to work through the heartache.

He pulled her onto his horse, and she gave a bow of thanks to the people in the crowd before riding back to the palace with her family. Barina remained quiet as she placed her forehead against Jason's back, trying to get herself under control.

Jason recognized her pattern of breathing, and it worried him. It was the same pattern she used to quickly push her emotions aside and move forward, as when she had suffered a loss in battle, or most certainly when she thought he and Tyra had been killed. *Damn it, don't put that wall up,* he thought.

Barina didn't trust easily when it came to romantic love, yet she had done that with Kevin. She had trusted him completely, and she now felt that she shouldn't have.

When they returned to the palace, Barina slid off the horse. Jason jumped down and put a hand on her shoulder. "Don't give up, he whispered with his brow furrowed.

"I don't want to," she said and walked back inside.

Berklion and Josh stood near Jason. "She's shutting herself off," he muttered.

"Damn it," Josh groaned. "I hate it when this happens. I understand why she does it for battle, but this…"

"Give her time," Berklion said. "She's hurting. We've seen this, but we also know that her capacity to love is her driving force." He walked past them and headed inside.

The party was still happening. Barina wanted the distraction, but it only did so much good before she slipped away and went to her room. She was grateful for the solitude. She set her swords by the bed, keeping her dagger near, and locked her crown in a case in the wardrobe. She did the same with the stone after using it to fill the bathtub with hot water. She removed her clothes, added some scented oils to the water, and after putting her hair up, stepped into the tub. She watched out the large windowed doors that led to the balcony as the wind blew the leaves in the trees. The opened doors allowed the fresh night air into the room. It was cold, but she didn't mind that much. It was a nice contrast to the hot water.

After her bath, she dressed in a simple nightgown before laying down in her bed. The tears fell while she clung to a pillow, closing her eyes in a restless sleep.

CHAPTER 22

Over the next three weeks, Barina developed a routine. She woke in the morning, dressed, had breakfast, then went about figuring out what her kingdom needed and how to best care for her people. Twarence shadowed her, learning everything that she was doing and how best to serve Thoron.

Josh and Tyra had gone back to Estella, while Jason opted to stay with Berklion in Thoron until Barina left. Arkon, along with Megan, Morgan, and Morgan's baby, departed a couple days after the coronation. He was going to give them a safe home with the Spirit Elves. Morgan had finally named her baby Serenity.

Everyone saw Barina laughing during the day. She was glad for the distractions—very loving and wonderful distractions. She loved her friends and enjoyed her time with them, but smiling all day when half the time she didn't mean it was exhausting.

Going through the same motions, she entered her room, opened the doors to the balcony, and set her swords by her bed. She kept her dagger near. She breathed in the scent of the rain as it mixed with the cold air. Flashes of lightning and the thunder made the downpour even more soothing.

Barina heated the water in the bathtub, put her hair up in a bun, and sat back to relax. It wasn't long before her eyes began to water and the tears fell. She tried to clear her thoughts, tried to adapt to the fact that Kevin was gone. Even though they had only known each other for a short while, there was no denying the bond they had. Not for her anyway. She wished, at the very least, he would've said goodbye. Even left a note. If he didn't care enough to say goodbye, then it had all been one-sided, and that hurt as much as realizing she was drowning without him. It had been three weeks since he had left her, and she could hardly breathe. It made her just as angry with herself that she still hoped he would come back.

Though she knew that leaving the balcony door meant that Kevin could find his way in if he wanted to, it also meant that she was leaving herself open to danger. Just like it would tonight.

Barina sensed the men climbing onto the balcony and heard them make their way into her room. She stood up out of the tub, casually putting her robe on and tying the cord. She kept her movements simple, not even remotely worried about them.

"Stupid," she muttered while taking her dagger in her hand and resting it by her side. "You know, going for a sneak attack while it's raining is really dumb," she told them. "Especially if you don't bring a change of clothes or shoes. I can see your footprints and hear your shoes squishing on the floor. You can't hide from me." She could hear them snickering.

"Not even bothered that we've seen what the queen looks like under her gown?" one asked from the shadows. "Not worried that we're all going to have a taste of that before we kill you for humiliating us?"

"So forward." She stood still. "Is this your idea of foreplay?"

Six men started to show themselves. She placed her hand on her hip, annoyed more than anything.

"She has a nice ass, a decent body," one man said, and then grabbed his chest. "But too small here."

Barina let out a tsk. "Rude."

The man turned red and drew his sword. "It'll still be fun getting to know what a queen is like when she screams in bed."

"Screaming *Is it in yet*? I can't feel anything." Barina was toying with them. "I mean, you guys are really freaking stupid coming in here. You have noticed how I haven't called for help?"

They moved closer. "Six men versus one, barely-armed woman." And they drew their swords and closed in on her. "Are you ready to die?"

"My, what small swords you have."

* * *

Jason and Berklion had turned the corner to the hallway that led to their and Barina's rooms. Both men slowed for a split second, sensing danger, before they began to.

The two guards stationed outside her room saw the men rushing to the door.

"Sirs?" one of them asked.

"She's not alone in there." Berklion called to him.

The guards looked at each other, realizing they had failed their duties. "But we didn't hear her call. No struggle."

The doors burst open from the force of the man who had been launched against it. He hit the wall hard just as two other men crashed into him, all of them slumping to the ground, unconscious.

Jason and Berklion peeked into her room in time to see Barina pick another man clean off of his feet and pile drive him to the ground before she gave a powerful kick to one and punched another hard enough that he was knocked out cold.

Barina looked out the door and smiled at everyone. "Hi guys! Dave and Hank, sorry I didn't invite you to the party."

"We failed you," Hank said, bowing his head, his eyes filled with regret.

"Nah, we're good." She tightened the cord on her robe a little tighter. "I kind of needed this."

Dave was still worried. "But, they knew, and we should've…"

Barina's eyes were soft. "I didn't call for you. You heard no disturbance, and I wanted to fight them. It's okay guys. You're still some of the best and most highly trained people I could have guarding me."

"How did Jason and Berklion know?" Hank asked.

Jason nudged his arm. "We have a connection. It's hard to explain. We just know."

Berklion patted each guard on the back. "Don't be too hard on yourselves."

Barina touched a hand to each of the guards' chins, directing them to look at her. "It's okay, both of you."

Both Dave and Hank saw the sincerity in her face before she tilted her head ever so slightly and focused her eyes. They all heard a thud against the wall outside.

Barina turned, dagger drawn, just as a man dropped from a zip-line, rolling into the room and standing up with a sword in one hand and a mace in the other. Hank and Dave stepped in front of Barina while Berk and Jason drew their weapons.

The new cutthroat didn't get more than two steps before he was pulled back when a length of chain wrapped around his neck and yanked him back onto the balcony and against the stone railing. The would-be assassin looked up to see another man standing over him, holding the chains and grabbing him by the collar. Kevin didn't say a word as he slammed the man's face into the stone wall, knocking him out cold. He turned to Barina, his gaze fixed on her.

Barina had not been expecting this. She was beginning to give up on the hope that he would ever come back, let alone like this. She didn't know how to react.

Kevin's dark hair was plastered against his face, and the rain dripped from him as he hurried into the room. With the chains still around his hands, he kept himself between Barina and the door to the balcony. "There's more on the way," he warned as he held the chains in either hand, ready to swing them with amazing accuracy and force.

"Blow those whistles, and get more help," Berklion told the guards. "You'll need them to help lock all of these guys up."

In the next few seconds, Barina heard the whistles as five more men climbed into the room.

"Give us the queen and you'll live," one of them commanded.

"Come any closer," Kevin said, his cold gray eyes staring at the men, "and you'll be in a cell when you wake up. If you're lucky."

"Do you realize who we work for?" one of them asked with a cocky smile. "Duke Ferwell and Baron Harl have paid us a lot and have promised more if we bring them her head. I'm sure they'd give you a decent amount of gold if you helped."

His lips twitching slightly, Kevin reached into his pocket and tossed two rings to the ground, each with a sigil on them. "You mean who you *worked* for. They're not gonna be able to pay you anything else."

One of them yelled, "They were going to give us titles and land! They were going to make us lords of this land once we got rid of her!" and he launched himself at Kevin.

Kevin moved ever so slightly as he stuck out his foot, tripping the man. The man's head met Berklion's foot, and he lay unconscious with a nasty gash on his skull. "I learned that move from her," Kevin said.

He turned to look at the others. "She killed a fucking dragon, she took down Toler, and she could take all of you without breaking a sweat?" Kevin sounded more annoyed than angry. "And by the way, this is Berklion of Halk. Drop your weapons and surrender. You are seriously outnumbered."

The men still standing looked behind them and saw the guards and the other two warriors now in the room. The queen wasn't paying attention to anyone else. Her eyes were set on Kevin.

The cutthroats dropped their weapons and held their hands up as the guards arrived to take them and the unconscious men into custody.

"Kevin, you came back," Jason said and clapped him on the shoulder.

"I never left town," Kevin said, glancing from Berklion and Jason to Barina. "Those guys got in my head and made me doubt if I was good enough. I didn't want her to be questioned, and I didn't want her to question it for herself. I was halfway out of the city, but couldn't make myself leave completely. Every night I'd go to sleep thinking tomorrow I could do it, I could leave and let her have a chance to be with someone who can really make her happy. Every morning I'd wake up, and I couldn't take one step further from her."

He stepped closer to Barina as she held her breath.

"I decided that, when I woke up tomorrow, I'd come back to the palace and throw myself at the mercy of this amazing woman I'd fallen in love with. I would beg her to forgive me and give me a second chance. While I was sitting at my table at the inn, I overheard Baron Harl and Duke Ferwell speaking to each other about what they had just sent a bunch of guys to do. I followed them both when they left the inn. They tried to put up a fight when I met them in the alley, so I made quick work of them and ran here. I knew they would go for your balcony."

Berklion and Jason were smiling at him.

"It's good to have you back," Berklion told him. He was surprised to see Barina still processing what was happening, studying him.

"Kev, we'll leave you alone." Jason nodded his head before he and Berklion headed to the door.

"Good luck." Berklion bowed his head to Kevin and excused himself, closing the doors behind them.

When they were gone, Barina put her head down.

"Barina, umm, listen, I'm…" Kevin's voice trailed when she walked to the wardrobe and opened a drawer. He watched her closely.

She tossed him a pair of pants and a shirt. "You left some clothes here. You'll freeze if you don't change." She grabbed a nightgown for herself and turned to look over her shoulder, but wouldn't make eye contact. "Use the changing screen, and don't come out till after I say I'm done."

Kevin nodded and went behind the screen. He knew that Barina wasn't the type to be shy, and they had both seen each other without a stitch of clothing on. He knew her well enough to know she was playing it safe until she was certain how she would react.

The weather outside had turned cold, and the rains had chilled him to the bone. He hadn't realized it till his adrenaline had worn off. When he had heard the duke and baron's plans, his only thought was getting to Barina. There was no time to grab his cloak or jacket. He changed out of his wet clothes and felt warmer wearing nothing.

"It's safe," he heard her call quietly.

"I'll be out in a minute." Kevin put on the dry clothes, exhaling in relief to feel the warmth of the fabric. He walked out from behind the screen and saw the balcony doors were closed.

Barina was adding more wood to the fire. Illuminated by the soft glow of the flames, he watched her, taking in the view. She was wearing a short dark nightgown and had left her hair in a bun, little strands escaping. She sat down on a chair, an elbow resting on one arm, her fingers touching her lips while thinking. Her other hand clung to her nightgown. Barina was looking at the fire, and her expression was blank.

Kevin grabbed a throw from the bed and went over to her, placing the blanket around her shoulders before kneeling in front of her.

"Barina."

"Baka."

He blinked. He had figured out what that meant in their travels.

"Bar…"

Her eyes finally met his, and tears welled because of her frustration. "Bakayarou," she cracked. "Bakayarou! Aho! Baka! Omae wa sayounara mo iwazuni… Nande? Sonna koto wo suru nante. Hidoi. Nande?"

He didn't know all the words—aside from her calling him an idiot, and probably a few other choice words—but he could figure out the context.

He reached a hand up to touch her face, gently stroking her cheek with the pad of his thumb. "I know I hurt you. I'm sorry."

She finally leaned forward, and he fell to the floor from her sudden movement. Kevin knew he deserved the outburst that was about to follow.

"Bakayarou!" Her voice was stronger. "Why the hell couldn't you tell me you were leaving? The hell is wrong with you? I went looking for you. I searched the fucking city for you! You couldn't even say goodbye! Who the hell does that? Do you have any idea what this did...? I don't even know if...damn it! Fuck!" She placed her face in her hands to hide her tears and muffle her sobs. The last thing she wanted was for Kevin to see her crying because of something he did. She didn't want him to see how weak he had made her and how much of a weakness he was for her.

Kevin sat on the floor, listening to every word, tears streaming down his face. He knew that Barina was trying to mask the fact that she had been weakened in some way. Her wall had gone up, and that scared the hell out of him.

He saw, or maybe he felt, that the wall wasn't up completely, but he would have to act now. Kevin gathered himself up and again knelt in front of her, placing a hand carefully on either leg.

"Barina." He could hardly speak through his tears.

His hands were shaking as he reached for hers and lightly kissed her fingers. His warm tears touched her skin.

"I didn't say goodbye or tell you I was leaving because, if I had tried, I wouldn't have been able to go through with it. It sounds stupid, and it is, but I saw it as a way to protect you." He needed her to know that he was speaking the truth. "When those lords were talking to you about finding someone noble... What if I would somehow jeopardize your validity as a ruler? What if it made you vulnerable to a hostile takeover? I couldn't live with that guilt or that weight, and I sure as hell didn't want you to have to make that call."

"But it was my call to make, and I made it." Her tone was soft.

"I know you did. But Barina, if something happened to you because of me,...if men tried to take over your kingdom and oust you because of me, I wasn't sure if I could live with that.

"There's not a question in my mind whether we belong together or not, because we do. There's not a shred of doubt about how much I love you or if I know I could make you happy. And you me. I love you enough that I felt the best thing I could do for you was to walk away."

"Why did you come back?" Barina's question was simple, her eyes still lost on this.

Kevin leaned up and kissed her on the lips. "Because I can't breathe without you. I know that if I can't breathe, you probably can't either. I left your heart vulnerable, and that's worse than any other type of attack you could face.

"I realized that the best protection I could give you wasn't by leaving. It's standing by you, holding your hand, fighting beside you against anything that comes your way. And if need be, put myself between you and danger. I love you more than I could've ever imagined loving anyone. I will spend the rest of my life making this up to you if I must. I am at the mercy of, not the queen, but at the woman in front of me. I love you. If you'll have me, if you'll give me another chance, I'll…"

Kevin didn't get to finish. Barina placed a hand on either side of his face and kissed him. He returned the kiss and pulled her off the chair, closer to him.

"Thank the stars," he breathed, holding her as close as he could, kissing her again.

"I had been leaving the balcony doors open in case." She felt safe and warm in his arms again.

He kissed her ear before whispering, "And not only did you get me, but a whole lot of assassins."

"Worth the risk," she said, finally able to breathe.

He ran his hands along her back. "I'm worth the risk. You sure?"

"Bakayarou."

"I figured out what baka means. What's it mean when you say bakayarou?"

"Fucking idiot."

Kevin belted out a short laugh and fell back onto the ground, bringing Barina with him. "I deserve that." His arms tightened around her. "I guess I have to learn how to live in a palace."

"I mean, if you want. But I'll be heading back to Estella eventually."

That got his attention. "Wait, what?"

Barina propped herself up on his chest. "This tells me when you left and what you missed. Twarence is going to be my regent. I made a portal with the stone so I can come and go as I please between here and Estella, and mirrors for them to talk with me. I'm still queen, but I feel as if I can do more without being stuck in a palace. Plus, I still want to make swords. My forge should be ready when I get back. I'll have to hire the carpenters to start work on building me a house next."

"You could use the stone to build a house."

"I don't want to take the work from those who need it, and I don't want to depend on it for every little thing. I still might, cause I wanna live in my house. I can pay the workers what they would've made. But it's also why I'll be leaving the Anna Stone here with Twarence as well.."

Kevin propped himself up on his elbow. "Seriously, is that a good idea? After everything you went through to get it?"

She nodded. "I don't want to become dependent, and I don't want to be wearing it someday when my emotions cause it to do something I don't want it to do."

He nodded, understanding her reasons. "You hold off on temptation better than most. I don't know a lot of people who wouldn't abuse that thing."

"I use it to heat the bath water, but that's about it." She then tapped his chest, as if a sudden thought occurred to her. "Do you want me to make you a new sword once we get to Estella?"

"Are you serious? Fuck yeah I do." He then eyed her with a teasing smile. "What's the cost?"

She looked down. "Just don't leave again without saying goodbye or telling me why."

"How about I just don't ever leave again?" he said, smiling.

Barina tried to feel his reassurances, but she couldn't meet his eyes for a moment.

Kevin touched a couple of fingers to one of the little strands of hair that had escaped from her head and pushed it behind her ear. "I don't expect you to move past all of this right away," he told her. "Babe, I can't promise that we won't argue, that we won't drive each other crazy at times, but I can absolutely promise that keeping you happy and safe, and making sure that you know everyday that I love you, is what I'm going to work toward.

I don't ever plan on leaving again. But if, for some reason that does happen, I promise, I will make sure to explain myself."

Barina gazed deep into his eyes. She looked past the color of his irises, past the pupils, and into the depths of his soul. He did not flinch or waver while she studied him. Her fingers felt his energies. She could normally tell about a person and their heart right when she met them. Kevin—she knew the man he was. She knew it. Still, she had to feel his energies up close just to put her own heart at ease.

Barina didn't want that wall to go up around her heart—not for something like love, and not when it came to Kevin. In his absence, she couldn't help it. It was a defense she had developed over the years to deal with heartache in the thick of a fight. She hated that it had come to this.

Suddenly, she felt a wave of warmth go through her, and it made her inhale a deep breath. He was right, she had been suffocating without him.

Kevin watched her eyes grow brighter. He knew the two of them would be okay. He felt her place a very gentle kiss on his lips before she wrapped her arms around him, settling into his hold. He pulled her as close as he could and simply breathed her in.

They stayed next to each other, on the floor and fell asleep, knowing that their story would continue.

CHAPTER 23

The next week went by smoothly and, before too long, it was time for Barina, Kevin, and Jason to go back to Estella. Berklion would be heading to Nippon for a while after he went to Estella with them. There were warm goodbyes, everyone knowing that they would see each other frequently.

They had done it. They won. They had gone beyond what was expected of them, and the reward, as King Victor had promised, was great. They defeated a tyrant, they freed a kingdom from a life of fear and terror, and they now had the opportunity to give the people the future they had always deserved.

"I'll keep the stone safe," Twarence promised, "and let's hope that things will always be peaceful after this."

Barina stood in front of the mirror. "You know it won't always be, but we'll handle it as it comes to us."

"So optimistic." Onyx patted the queen's back while Aria messed up her hair.

"She's realistic and optimistic," Berklion said, the horses anxious on the stone floors in the palace.

"I'm a new monarch and an unmarried woman," Barina reminded them. "Despite the fact that I have proven myself capable, there's gonna be plenty who will contest my claim. They've already tried to bully me into marriage, and there will be others who will try and push me off still." She shrugged her shoulders. "But, fuck them. I do what I want."

"Yes, spoken like a true queen," Aria said, shaking her head. "Fuck them, I do what I want."

Barina's eyes were playful. "I'm diplomatic."

Kevin pulled her by the arm. "Let's go, dear."

Barina, Kevin, Berklion and Jason headed through the mirror which led into the living space of her new house.

"Used the stone to build the house and workshop?" Berklion asked, looking around.

"Thought about not doing it," Barina admitted, "and changed my mind, but I still paid the tradesmen full price who would've built it. I just wanted to get settled and start crafting again."

Josh arrived just as they took the horses out of the house. "When are you leaving for Nippon, Berk?" he asked, hugging his teacher.

"Day after tomorrow," Berklion said. "I wanted to rest a bit before I do. Can I crash at your place?"

"Well, yeah, but I have a little visitor there now. He showed up a couple days ago."

"Who?" Jason asked as they all headed to Josh's house.

Barina and Berklion threw their heads back, laughing.

"He doesn't know!" she squealed in delight.

"Second thought," Berklion said, "can I stay at your house Barina?"

Jason looked incredibly confused.

"We should go inside," Josh told him. "Your cousin's here. And there's something you need to know."

Tyra opened the door of Josh's house the second she saw her fiancé. Jason then heard a baby crying and stepped inside.

"Barina?" Kevin was completely out of the loop.

She leaned up to whisper, "Josh knocked up Jason's cousin."

Kevin's eyes widened. "That escalated quickly."

The next thing they heard was Jason's voice. "Are you fucking serious! My cousin!"

"Always an adventure around here," Barina joked.

They headed into Josh's house, meeting his son for the first time. That night, after everyone had gone home, and the town of Estella had fallen asleep, Barina woke up and smiled at Kevin who was sound asleep next to her. She felt a chill in the air and, not bothering to cover her nightshirt in a robe, headed outside to the cold night. It had started snowing a soft snow and there was a calm in the air. She sat outside and listened to the quiet.

Barina embraced the calm, the quiet, the peace that surrounded her. She knew that it wouldn't last forever, but she took these moments when she could. She didn't know when the chaos of the world would call for her again, just that it would. She didn't know where her life would take her, but she would take it in stride like she always did. All Barina did know was that the road ahead of her would be filled with both beauty and horrors and that, as long as at the end of it all she had the people she loved waiting for her, the impossible would only ever be for the weak of heart.

* * *

In the Forest of Lithor, Anna sat on a fallen tree as she watched a fox run through the brush and heard the birds sing. These small things, they brought her comfort when she knew there was always a pain in her heart. She felt a sudden warmth like she hadn't known in centuries, and a bright light shown. She looked over her shoulder, and her eyes filled with tears as she rushed toward the light.

"Teddy!"

She felt the strong arms of her husband take hold of her in an embrace she hadn't dared to dream of in all this time.

The light vanished, along with her.

Anna was at peace.

To everyone who has believed in me: I will never completely understand what I have done to have the people in my life that I do, but I am so thankful that I have you. All of you make up a piece of my heart and my soul, thank you.

Special thanks to those who helped me with the last and final leg of this journey goes to:

Diane Smith, Elizabeth Burkart and Drew Burkart, Colton Vickery, Debbie Burchett-Carden, Jennifer Whitworth, Marcus Powell, Caroline Amy Dawson, Joey Kerns, Pablo Caceres, Adam Chmelka, Larry McDonald, Greg Jakovina, Lindsey Freel, Sally Crawford, Ashley Nolan, Adam Guerich, Eric Taylor, Kristopher Huff, Augie Meier Jr. Joyce Rakestraw, Nicole Meier, Lizzy Meier, Augie Meier III, Ashley Traxler, Mary Howell, Amber Hansford, Jennifer Beam, Matthew Montgomery, Ian Penrod, Joseph Trevino, Holly Renner, Bob and Maggie Walshire, Julia Bailey, Joy Bishop, Nedi DaSilva, Benjamin Meissner, M Olivares-Escobedo, Andrew Hayworth, Augie Meier IV, Madeline Smithson, Britt Beasley, Danica Gibson, Jeremy Currant, Haley Brown and Ben Walshire, Kenneth Warren, Alan Wong, and Rebecca Glotzbach. And a big shout out to the Lawrence Public Library.

Thank you, for everything.

Keep an eye out for:
Rainstorms
Book 2
Sins and Secrets